# The

# Corpus

# Conundrum

# The
# Corpus
# Conundrum

## A Third Case from the Notebooks of Pliny the Younger

**A NOVEL BY**

# *Albert A. Bell, Jr*

INGALLS
PUBLISHING GROUP, INC

# INGALLS PUBLISHING GROUP, INC

PO Box 2500
Banner Elk, NC 28604
www.ingallspublishinggroup.com

copyright © 2011 Albert A. Bell, Jr
Text design by Luci Mott
Cover design by: Luci Mott
Cover Images from
*The Illustrated Ben Hur*, by Lew Wallace,
with illustrations by William Martin Johnson. New York: Crown Publishers,
1978, from the original edition published in 1901.

Library of Congress Cataloging-in-Publication Data

Bell, Albert A., 1945-
The corpus conundrum : a third case from the notebooks of Pliny the younger / by Albert A. Bell, Jr.
p. cm.
ISBN 978-1-932158-96-0 (trade pbk. : alk. paper)
1. Pliny, the Younger--Fiction. 2. Tacitus, Cornelius--Fiction. 3. Rome--Fiction. I. Title.
PS3552.E485C67 2011
813'.54--dc22
2011003455

# Acknowledgments

As in all my other recent books, I must begin by expressing thanks to Bob and Barb Ingalls and Judy Geary for their support and encouragement—and the occasional kick in the pants. I am also deeply indebted to members of my writers' group at the Urban Institute for Contemporary Arts in Grand Rapids, Michigan. Steve Beckwith, Dan (D. E.) Johnson, Vic Foerster, Paul Robinson, Karen Lubbers, Jane Griffioen, Nathan Ter-Molen, Patrick Cook, Roger Meyer, Norma Lewis, Carol Bennett, and Dawn Schout are the most regular members of the group. Others have come and gone during the course of the writing of this book. The group itself deserves recognition for fostering the growth of a number of writers over the past ten years. Dan, Vic, Patrick, Roger, and Norma have all had books published. Dawn is enjoying success through the publication of several dozen of her poems. I've never heard of another writers' group outside of New York or Los Angeles where so many members have enjoyed this kind of success.

This is the first novel I've written under a tight deadline. My publisher pointed out, gently but firmly, that the six years that elapsed between the first and second Pliny novels could not be allowed to go by between the second and third. And a number of readers have asked me when the next one would appear. So, nine years will have passed between the publication of the first Pliny novel and the third, and yet Pliny will have aged only one year. Fortunately I don't have to factor in technological advances, as Sue Grafton and Janet Evanovich and others do in their long-running series.

For further information about me and my books, go to www.albertbell.com. For further information about Ingalls Publishing Group, go to www.ingallspublishinggroup.com.

# Author's Note

Although it is a work of fiction, this book strives for historical accuracy (if I may be pardoned some anthropomorphizing). One of the most gratifying things any reviewer has ever said about my work was *Library Journal's* comment that the second book in this series, *The Blood of Caesar*, was "outstandingly researched." Two books which I found extremely helpful in writing this novel are Daniel Ogden's *Magic, Witchcraft, and Ghosts in the Greek and Roman Worlds: A Sourcebook* (Oxford Univ. Pr. 2002), and J. D. P. Bolton's *Aristeas of Proconnesus* (Oxford Univ. Pr. 1962). As Ogden's title indicates, his book is a collection of passages from a wide range of ancient authors. Bolton's book is the only study of Aristeas in English of which I am aware. It is fascinating how someone can write a book about a person who may have lived at any time during a two-hundred-year span and who may, or may not, have written a poem which no longer exists, except in a few fragments.

The setting of this book is Pliny's villa at Laurentum, which he describes in a long letter (*Ep.* 2.17). I have included my own translation of that letter as an appendix. Laurentum was a major town in the early days of the Roman Republic, but it seems to have shrunk to an insignificant village by the first century AD. Pliny does say, however, that it had three baths. He has a bath in his villa and, even though he has to rely on wells and springs as water sources, his bath includes two swimming pools. The frustrating thing about the description is that it is precise in some places—the two D-shaped colonnades—and imprecise in others—the rooms off the atrium used by his servants and guests. In my files I have six drawings of what the house might have looked like, all based on the letter and all different.

For further information about me and my books, go to www.albertbell.com. For further information about Ingalls Publishing Group, go to www.ingallspublishinggroup.com.

*If I sing your praises after you've extolled me, I'm afraid I'll look like I'm just returning the flattery, not offering an impartial judgment. I genuinely do believe all your writing is first-rate. I have to admit, though, that I especially like those works in which you talk about me. The reason is quite simple—you excel when you write about your friends, and I take the greatest pleasure in your work when you write about me.*

Pliny, *Ep.* 9.8

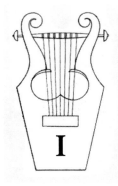

# I

WHEN THE HOUNDS BEGAN TO BAY, my scribe, Hylas, and I looked up from our work. Seated in the shade at the bottom of a ridge, we could not see the dogs, and the trees, beginning to put out leaves, muffled some of their howling.

"They sound odd," I said.

"Yes, my lord. We haven't heard anything quite like that today."

Throughout our day of hunting the dogs had barked lustily whenever they rousted game and yelped once when a boar turned on them just before they drove it into the nets, but this was the first time we had heard such a melancholy, almost mournful, sound.

"Well, Tranio will let us know if there's anything we need to be concerned about."

Hylas smiled. "Yes, my lord. I'm sure he will."

We both knew that Tranio, steward of this estate, wouldn't take a step without coming to me. He served my uncle capably for years and has served me well since my uncle's death five years ago, but his unwillingness to take responsibility on his own shoulders is the reason I will never put him in charge of one of my larger properties.

I tried to turn my attention back to the wax tablet I was writing on, but the dogs had broken my concentration. I gazed around me, hoping fervently that Tranio would not bring any news about what was upsetting the dogs. I did not want anything to disturb the tranquility of this day. It was proving to be as ideal a spring equinox as one could want. All the elements of nature seemed to be in balance—the afternoon sun bright but not too hot, the breeze cool, yet not too strong. I leaned my head back against a tree and closed my eyes for a moment.

My life seemed to be regaining some balance as well. After a tumultuous year which had thrown me into direct conflict with the most powerful man in Rome and seen me gain—and then lose—a great deal, I was enjoying a period of calm, a chance to reflect, to read and to write.

And what better place to do that than this villa, near Laurentum? It was my favorite of the houses I inherited from my uncle, who was also my adoptive father. I spent some happy days in my childhood here. My mother still prefers it to our house in Rome. This place possesses a kind of equilibrium of its own, sitting right on the shore but with a large expanse of woods behind it. It's close enough to Rome for me to get here in half a day. Yet, when I'm here, Rome and its problems might as well be on the frontiers of the empire.

Today I was hunting and writing. Odd though it might seem, in Rome writing is the more dangerous of those activities. What I had dictated to Hylas this morning was not something I ever intended to publish. I just wanted to set it all down so I would not be struggling to remember it thirty or forty years from now, should the Fates spin out the thread of my life that long, and so I would have what I knew to be a true account in case anyone else tried to twist the story.

Rousing myself, I returned to the note I had composed to my friend Tacitus and finally found the ending I'd been searching for. When I looked up from the tablet, Hylas anticipated me, something he is quite good at, and stopped his pen in mid-stroke.

"Are you ready to dictate, my lord?"

"If it doesn't interrupt your drawing."

Hylas, who's several years older than I am, never seems to relax around me. We work together only when I'm here in the country, so I can't blame him. He's a portly fellow, whose dark eyes are always on the move. He acts ill-at-ease outside the library and withdraws to it every chance he gets, like a turtle pulling its head back into its shell.

"I draw only in idle moments, my lord. I use only scrap pieces of papyrus. And I make all my inks and colors, at my own expense."

"I have no objections to your art work, Hylas. It's quite good. In fact, when I redecorate the triclinium this summer, why don't you try your hand on one of the walls?"

He beamed. "Thank you, my lord. I never thought I would have that opportunity."

"We'll start with one wall. Now, back to business." Trying to ignore the renewed howling of the dogs, I began to read what I had written as Hylas took it down:

*Gaius Pliny to his friend Cornelius Tacitus, greetings.*

*You'll be amused to hear that I have caught three boars, three very fine ones. You, you will say? Yes, I. And I didn't even have to give up my laziness or the quiet I sought out here to do it. I have been sitting by the nets. Around me are my pens and papyrus, not spears or hunting gear. I've been thinking about a certain matter and making some notes, so that even if I come home with my hands empty I'll at least have full notebooks. You shouldn't scorn this sort of mental activity. It's amazing how one's mind is stimulated by the stirring of one's body. Just being surrounded by the solitude of the woods and the quiet which hunting requires is a great incentive to thought. The next time you go hunting, I urge you to take along your notebooks as well as a supply of food and drink. You'll discover that Diana doesn't wander the hills alone. Minerva frequents them too.*

"You'll want two copies, of course, my lord?"

"Yes. And have one ready to send tomorrow morning."

Hylas and I looked up as Tranio came rushing up the slope to where we were sitting, thrashing his way through the brush. A tall, slender man, he pulled off his cap and held it in front of him with both hands, bending over and gasping from the exertion. "My lord, we've found ... something." He took a deep breath. "Something you need to ... to take a look at."

I put down my tablets in annoyance. "Don't make me play guessing games, man. What have you found?"

"It seems ... it's a body, my lord."

"A body? Do you mean a person's body?" I would sacrifice a ram to a deity I did not believe in if he could mean anything else.

"Yes, my lord, a corpse. Please, come quickly."

So much for equilibrium. Tranquility, *ave atque vale*, as Catullus put it. I grudgingly got up and followed Tranio for a hundred paces or so, down the incline and across a brook, with Hylas trailing behind me. Around a clump of bushes that were just starting to put out leaves stood several of my servants, craning their necks and elbowing one another for a better view.

"Step back, lads," Tranio said. "Let the master take a look."

As the servants stood aside, the first thing I saw was a pair of legs—a man's bare legs, I thought, with dark hair on the smooth, pasty skin.

"Who found him?" I asked.

"The dogs did, my lord," Tranio said. "But it's strange. They won't go near him. They just stand here barking and howling."

The dogs circled the body. But Tranio was right. They whined as though disturbed or frightened by something and wouldn't get within several paces of the dead man, like the dogs in the *Iliad* who wouldn't get close to Hector's body.

"Has anyone moved him or touched him?"

"No, my lord. I thought it best you see exactly what we found."

That much I was glad to hear. In a situation like this even the position of a body and anything found close to it can help explain what happened. Of course, Tranio probably had decided to leave the body alone not out of concern for any investigation I might make. Like any servant—slave or freedman—he just didn't want to be held responsible for whatever had happened or might happen.

I forced my way through the clump of bushes and stepped over the body. It had a layer of dead leaves strewn over it, as though someone had tried to keep the man warm or hide him rather than bury him or as though he had pulled them over himself. I broke a fresh branch off a shrub and brushed them away.

What lay before me was a nondescript man with dark hair still damp from last night's light rain. At first glance I would have estimated his age at about forty, but the longer I looked at him, the less certain I became about that. He looked like a statue that, in spite of being in excellent condition, has an aura of great age about it. Lying on his back, arms at his sides, he wore a ragged tunic but no sandals.

I could have believed he was sleeping, except that I could not detect any sign of breathing, even when I bent over and put my ear next to his nose. His chest was not rising and falling in the least. Nor did I feel his heart pulsating when I placed my hand on him. He did not even react when an ant crawled onto his face.

Leaning back on my haunches, I tried to get an overall impression of the man. Something about his appearance struck me as odd. The length of his hair—longer than I was accustomed to seeing on a man—and his untrimmed beard made him look like someone from an earlier time, perhaps a Cynic philosopher from several hundred years ago.

"Shall we move him out here, my lord," Tranio asked, "so you can see him better?"

"Not yet."

Before moving the man I examined as much of him as I could see. There were no blood stains on the front or sides of his tunic. Nor was there any evidence that he had lost control of his bowels or bladder, as frightened men often do in their death throes. He had not received a blow to his head. His neck showed no sign of abrasions from a rope, nor did his wrists or ankles. I could not immediately detect any discoloration or odor which a poison might produce, but against the earthy aromas rising from the wet forest floor around me I might be missing something. If the body were decaying, I couldn't miss that, yet I did not notice the odor of death, even when I put my face close to him and took a deep breath. All I could detect was a fetid smell, more like that of an unbathed man in an unlaundered tunic.

The servants drew back when I flexed one of the man's arms, then lifted one of his legs and bent it. There was no stiffness at all. That meant he had been dead either a very short time—too short a time for decay and the death-stiffness to set in—or long enough for the stiffness to pass, which usually takes almost two days. But if he had been dead that long, the odor should be quite strong and the first signs of decay would be evident. Insects and animals would have begun to devour him. Or were they—with the exception of that one bold ant—all shying away from him as my dogs were?

"We've been here since shortly after dawn," I said. "Did anyone see other people down in this area?"

The servants shook their heads, looking at one another guiltily, as servants do when they're hoping someone else will say something so they won't have to.

I stood and leaned back against a tree. Nothing I was seeing made sense. The color and general condition of the body suggested that the man wasn't even dead. The lack of any sign of breathing told me that he must be dead. But if he was dead, he had been here only a few hours at most. We were at least a quarter of a mile from the nearest road. Did someone kill him and carry him in here, or did he die on this spot?

In either case, what—or who—caused his death? If he was dead. And why was he out here, with no traveling gear, not even a pair of sandals? He seemed completely unknowable. I felt like the Cyclops hearing Odysseus say, "My name is οὖτις—nobody." The Cyclops said he would eat Nobody last. Could I say I had found Nobody lying in the woods?

With all the servants and animals trampling around in the wet woods, I could not tell anything about how Nobody got here. The position of his body was not that of a man who had fallen or been thrown down. For all I could conclude, he might have laid down for a nap or been placed there—I would even say posed—by someone else.

Getting on my knees again, I surveyed the ground around the body one more time. Once he was moved, I would not be able to reproduce the exact conditions under which he was found. I had to remember everything—his position, the imprint around the edge of his body. All of it could ultimately be important in determining what had happened to him.

Then it hit me. Even a drawing would be helpful, if it was accurate enough. "Hylas, do you have writing materials?"

"Always, my lord." The scribe patted the bag he carried over his shoulder.

"Draw me a picture of this scene. Use your largest piece of papyrus, even if it's a new one. The rest of you, stand back and let him work."

Hylas appeared self-conscious as he sketched Nobody, but in a short time he produced a very good likeness of the man and the area around him.

"All right. Move him out there in the open," I finally said. "Get the blanket I was sitting on and put it under him."

My servants dawdled, as reluctant as the dogs to have contact with the body. The cleverest one ran to get the blanket. The others, no doubt cursing themselves for their slow thinking, finally grabbed the body by the feet and under the shoulders and lifted it. Nobody sagged into a limp V. The dogs howled frantically.

"Hold him there," I said, brushing away debris clinging to his back. I expected to see a blood stain on his tunic, but there was none. The servant who had gone for the blanket returned and the others lowered the man onto it as I bunched his tunic up under his arms so I could examine the body.

He was wiry, but not in the way that soldiers are. His thin, hard body was more like that of an ascetic philosopher who had lived a life devoid of luxury. He appeared to have been healthy, with no wasting disease of any sort. He was not circumcised, and he bore no marks—such as a brand—that would identify him as a slave or former slave. The only unusual feature of his body was a birthmark, a purple splotch vaguely suggestive of a bird's head, on the left side of his chest, above the nipple.

"Make a sketch of that," I told Hylas.

While he worked all other constructive activity had come to a stop as word of this find spread, and the rest of my servants gravitated to the spot. A couple of them had the dogs on leashes, but the animals kept up their racket.

"Do any of you recognize this man?" I asked.

"He's nobody I know," Tranio said. I almost laughed as the others muttered their agreement. He was indeed Nobody.

I returned to my examination. What puzzled me most at the moment was the lack of dark splotches on any part of the body. During his extensive military service, my uncle had observed that, when a person dies, discolorations, almost like bruises, develop after a short time on whatever side of the body is lowest. Even if the person is moved later, those discolorations remain. If Nobldy had been lying here dead, in this position, for more than a couple of hours, discolorations should be evident on his back and buttocks. If he had lain dead somewhere else for a while, in another position, before being moved here, there would be dark spots somewhere on him.

"Put him on his stomach," I said.

Grumbling at having to touch him again, the servants turned Nobody over. His bare back showed no marks of a whip. That in itself did not prove he'd never been a slave. I would not have a slave of mine whipped unless he did something that threatened my life or my mother's. Fair treatment creates stronger loyalty, I find, than punishment or the threat of it. I take seriously Seneca's axiom: "Treat your inferiors as you would have your superiors treat you."

"Take him to the cart," I said. "We'll go back to the house."

"What about the nets and our gear, my lord?" Tranio asked.

"Leave someone here to guard it and then send the cart back for it." I barely managed to avoid snapping at him. He's old enough to be my father, but he seems incapable of making even the most obvious decisions.

As the servants carried out my orders, I knelt beside the spot where the man had been lying and pressed my hand into the leaves. I must have looked as troubled as I felt. Tranio asked, "Have you found something, my lord?"

"No ... no. Nothing ... Just leaves." But those leaves convinced me that I had to summon Tacitus and get his help.

"Must you take him back to the house, my lord?" Tranio asked as we walked behind the cart.

"I don't see what else we can do."

"We should turn him over to the duovirs, my lord. They're supposed to investigate whenever a crime has been committed."

"Has a crime been committed?"

"Well, I don't know, my lord. You're the one who's so good at figurin' out that sort of thing."

"But I don't know what happened to this man, and I'd like to know before anyone else gets involved." I snapped a dead twig off the tree I was passing and looked around to see if I could detect any signs of how someone got in and out of these woods without being seen. But there were no tracks, no broken limbs, no bushes trodden down, that couldn't be explained by my servants' activity.

"We could just bury him, my lord," Tranio said hopefully. "Not even bother the duovirs. They would appreciate that. He's probably just a runaway slave who fell in with bad company."

"I've not seen anything to point to such a conclusion."

"Well, whoever he is, my lord, there's nothing we can do for him now."

My exasperation with the man was near its breaking point. "Would you have me truss him up on a pole, like the boars?"

"Now, my lord, I wasn't meanin' to treat him with such disrespect. You're a kind man, but this fella has no claim on you."

"He is a human being, Tranio. And, as the playwright Terence said, 'I consider nothing human alien to me.' We can try to identify him. Tomorrow I'll send people around to the neighboring estates to see if anyone is missing. He might be a son of one of those families."

Tranio shrugged. "As I said, my lord, he's nobody I recognize, and I think I would know anyone from the families close around here. Not all the slaves maybe, but any children I certainly would know."

Tranio had a point. He had grown up on this estate, first as a slave, now as a freedman. He married a woman from an estate three miles south of here, after meeting her in the village on market day. My uncle purchased her from her former owner for him. His brother was the steward of a farm two miles east of us. If he did not recognize the body in the cart, no one was likely to.

In spite of those odds, I felt an obligation to try to discover Nobody's identity. I hadn't quoted Terence just to show off my erudition. This man was a human being, not just a pile of flesh we had stumbled upon in the woods. No human being should die this anonymously and ignominiously, carted away by total strangers.

Aside from simple human feeling, I also had a selfish motive for delaying the funeral. I wanted to learn how the man died. I had never seen anything like this—a person dead with no discernible trace of what killed him. Nor could I recall reading anything of this sort in the scrolls my uncle left behind.

Those 160 scrolls, written in a small script on the front and back, contained his unpublished observations on many scientific topics, including causes of death. Unless it comes by drowning or some internal disease, he concluded, death always leaves an external mark, however subtle, on its victims, if one knows how to look for it. Even drowning and suffocation leave indications, such as discoloration of the lips or evidence of a struggle. And a murderer, no matter how clever he thinks himself, always leaves some clue as to how he committed the crime.

"He may be a complete stranger," I admitted, "and we may end up burying him without knowing who he is, but I'm going to try to identify him first."

I wanted to have as much information as possible about this man and what happened to him before informing the duovirs in nearby Laurentum. I wasn't even sure if they had jurisdiction this far out of town, but it would probably be a good idea to notify some sort of authority if I had in fact found a dead man on my property. The office of duovir had been held by members of the Licinius clan for as long as I could remember. My uncle had never spoken kindly of them and had recommended I have as little as possible to do with them. Until now I had heeded that advice.

"It'll upset your mother no end to see him, my lord. She's such a gentle soul."

"We'll keep him out of her sight. If we can't identify him within two days, we'll turn him over to the duovirs and admit that was all we could do."

"Very well, my lord. They'll be glad you waited that long, I'm sure." Tranio's words were right, but their tone as well as the lift of his eyes showed what he thought of my decision.

The trip back to the villa was slowed by the bearers toting my boars over the slippery, wet, uneven terrain and by the uneasiness of our living animals. There was no odor that I could detect, nor did my servants notice any—at least the ones I could induce to get close enough to him—but the horse pulling the cart reared twice and almost dumped Nobody. The dogs continued to shy away from the cart and to bay at its contents, adding to the horse's nervousness. I finally had to have a servant ride the beast rather than lead him by the reins.

My servants had put the man into the cart head first, so his bare feet were hanging out the back. As we made our tedious progress toward the house I studied them. They were heavily calloused and dirty, as though the man never wore sandals. That might indicate he was from somewhere around here, though not conclusively. I certainly would not want to walk any distance barefoot, but some ascetics, such as Socrates, prided themselves on doing so.

"When you come back for the nets and gear," I told Tranio, "look around for a bag or a walking stick. If this man came from any distance, he must have been carrying something."

"Yes, my lord."

When we emerged from the woods and came in sight of the house the breeze from off the sea picked up. That still did not calm the animals.

"Put him in the stable," I told Tranio. "I think that's all we can do."

"Even with the way the horse and the dogs are acting, my lord? Don't you think he'll upset the other animals?"

"That's quite possible, but we can't bring him into the house and we can't leave him in the cart."

When we halted in front of the paddock adjoining the stable, the household servants gathered to admire the results of our hunting, but the sight of Nobody quickly turned their admiration into consternation. Tranio tried to wave them away from the cart. "Get on there. Tend to your business, and it's not this."

"Be sure the last stall is cleaned out and put him there," I said. "Use that blanket to cover him. Then we'll burn it. Post guards in four-hour shifts. No one is to bother him." I emphasized those last words for the benefit of the gang of servants who were slowly backing away from the cart.

Leaving Tranio to his tasks, I went into the house. Word of our find would spread quickly among the other servants. I wanted to talk to my mother before she heard an exaggerated version of the story. And, although evening was approaching, I dispatched two servants to Rome with Hylas' hurried copy of my letter and an oral message to Tacitus: *Please come as quickly as you can. I need your assistance in a matter of some urgency.*

Before having supper I went out to the stable to be sure Tranio had carried out all of my orders. I was reassured to find a guard on duty and the bar in place across the door. The thought occurred to me that I could be certain no one opened the door if I placed some wax over the bar and put my seal on it, so I sent the guard into the house to get Hylas. When they returned, Hylas crammed a wad of wax between the end of the bar and the door, where it would not be immediately noticed, especially in the dark. I pressed my seal into it, the ring I inherited—along with my name—when my uncle adopted me in his will. It has a dolphin on it. The creatures come into the bay below this house. My uncle and I enjoyed watching them and the local children who sometimes swam with them.

Once I had placed my seal on the door, I was satisfied that no one could open it without my knowing it.

I lay awake long into the night, with my mind jumping from problem to problem as often as my body turned over in the bed.

At first I puzzled over Nobody's body. Could there be some cause of death with which I was totally unfamiliar, either from my own experience or from my uncle's writings? A cause of death which left no external marks of any kind? Could a dead person not be subject to the patterns of stiffness and discoloration which my uncle had observed and which I had verified for myself? I thought about going out to the stable to examine the man again, but I chided myself that the uncertain light of a lamp or a torch could make me miss things I might easily spot in daylight.

Then another question came into my troubled mind, and I sat up in bed, breathing rapidly like a frightened child. What would Rome's ruler, the princeps Domitian, do if he heard that a dead man had been found on my property? And he would hear it. He had spies in the household of every important man in Rome, even mine, though I do not consider myself important. The antagonism between us runs especially deep. His hatred of my uncle was passed down to me, like a legacy, and in recent months I have built upon it. Would he seize an opportunity to bring a charge against me?

The answer to that question might depend on the identity of Nobody and what had happened to him.

But what if Domitian already knew the answers to those questions? What if this was part of some plot hatched by Domitian and Marcus Aquilius Regulus, his advisor in all things criminal? In recent months I have felt my life was becoming a gigantic game of latrunculi, with Domitian as my opponent and Regulus whispering over his shoulder to suggest moves. We made our moves in turn, but sometimes the purpose of a move was not to improve one's own position on the board so much as to box in one's opponent. A series of seemingly unconnected moves might be made merely to set up one later move. If a player watched only the most recent move and did not try to deduce his opponent's ultimate plan, he could find his piece surrounded and captured.

I needed to calm myself, so I went out on the terrace that runs around my suite of rooms—my addition to my uncle's house—and overlooks the small bay. My house sits at what might be called the head of the bay. Just to the right of it a stream with a rocky outcropping on this side separates my property from my neighbor's. The stream, unfortunately, isn't large enough to provide water for the needs of my household, but we have wells and springs that keep us amply supplied. Even as close as we are to the coast, the water from the wells isn't brackish.

The sight and sound of the sea at night is the most soothing thing I know, as long as I'm on land looking at it and not bouncing around in a boat. Tonight the moon reflected on the water, which is so clear I can see to the bottom for fifty paces or more from shore.

But the sea couldn't lull me tonight. Why did I imagine that Domitian and Regulus could possibly have anything to do with Nobody? Had I become so obsessed with them that every odd incident in my life seemed to happen at their direction? If they were involved, what move could they be setting up? If you attribute too much cleverness to your opponent in latrunculi, even his blunders look like strokes of genius. You begin to play into his hands. I must not let my dislike of them—or fear of them?—cloud my judgment. Domitian was rumored to have an actual list of people he considered enemies, but would I stand high enough on that list to merit the hatching of some convoluted plot?

I had inherited a spot among the princeps' enemies, and I might have moved up a few places because of my friendship with Tacitus, whose father-in-law, Julius Agricola, was at the top of the list. So it wasn't for mere curiosity that I had to discover who the man in the stable was and learn how he had died and whether there were any wider implications to his appearance on my land.

Still restless, I lit a lamp and walked out to the stable. The guard, awake if not alert, was standing in front of the stall where we had placed Nobody.

"Is something wrong, my lord?" he asked.

"I'll know in a moment." I held my lamp down to the bar. Seeing my seal still intact, I let out a breath. "No, everything is fine. Have you heard anything?"

"From in there? No, my lord. Would I? Isn't he dead?"

"Yes, of course." I sighed in relief. I was creating tightness in my stomach when none need exist. Tomorrow I would find whatever answers I could from Nobody's body and then turn him over to the duovirs. That would be the end of it.

Feeling resolved, if not calmer, I returned to the terrace and was about to go back to bed when I saw someone standing on the shore below me, looking out into the bay. With the moon as bright as it was, I could tell the figure was a man and he wasn't carrying anything. He was too far away for me to call out to him. Without thinking, I headed for the steps that lead from my terrace down to the beach. The steps are mostly naturally occurring, but I've had them carved out in a few difficult places.

By the time I got down to the beach the man had become aware of me. Before I could get anywhere near him, he turned away from the water and starting running toward the trees along the shore at the foot of one of my neighbors' houses. I broke into a run after him but lost sight of him as he went around the outcropping of rock beside the stream. When I got to the spot I slowed because I was afraid he might be lying in wait for me.

"Hello!" I called in Latin, then in Greek. "I mean you no harm."

Tensing, I stepped around the outcropping. There was no sign of anyone. The footprints appeared again across the stream, then ended several paces from the trees. Could someone have jumped from where the footprints stopped up to a tree limb or onto the outcropping of rock?

Fearing the waves would wash the footprints away, I picked up a small rock and marked where they stopped. When it was daylight I would come back and examine the matter further. As I started back up the steps a raven cawed and flew out of the trees and over my head.

Odd, I thought. I've never seen one flying around at night.

The next morning I came out of my room to find my mother waiting for me. She was accompanied, as she always seemed to be, by Naomi, a slave of her own age whom she regarded more as a sister than a servant. She even let the woman call her by name! And the affection was returned. At the last Saturnalia I had offered to free Naomi as a gift—to both her and my mother—but Naomi declined the offer because she said her status as a slave gave her a closer connection to my mother than she would feel as a freedwoman.

"Gaius, I'm so glad you're finally up," my mother said as Naomi gave the slightest of bows beside her.

I ran my hand through my hair and stretched. " 'Finally'? Mother the sun is barely up. What's the matter? Is something wrong?"

"That man you found in the woods yesterday ..."

Now I was fully awake. "What about him?"

"Naomi and I need to prepare his body for burial."

"Not yet. I don't want anyone to disturb the body until I've had time to make a more thorough examination. I told you that last night. And then we need to turn him over to the duovirs."

"What do you need to examine? He's dead, isn't he?"

"Well, yes, but I don't know why he's dead." I didn't want to admit that I wasn't even sure he was dead.

"Does the why really matter?"

"If someone killed him, it certainly does."

Mother put her hand to her mouth and turned to Naomi. "Killed him? Oh, my. If someone killed him, that means our land could be ritually unclean—polluted." Naomi nodded.

I held out a hand to calm them. "There's no evidence he was killed on our land. That's just where we found him. In fact, there's no evidence he was killed. As I said, I don't know what caused his death. It may have been natural."

Mother turned back to me. "Still, we shouldn't take a chance. We need to purify our land and ourselves and provide a proper burial for the poor man as soon as possible."

My mother has grown increasingly superstitious in the five years since we witnessed the destruction wrought by Vesuvius, during which her brother—my uncle—died. She thinks of herself as religious, but, as one who does not believe in gods, I would describe her fears and obsessions only as excessive, beyond even what is normal among women. Naomi, with her Jewish origins, has aggravated that tendency, I fear. She has even obtained scrolls of some of the Jews' arcane books, translated into Greek, for my mother to read.

"Mother, I do not want anyone to touch that body until I've examined it further. And then I'm going to turn him over to the duovirs."

"But, Gaius, you ought not to be anywhere near it. Preparing the dead for burial is women's work. A man will make himself unclean if he touches a dead body. You know that."

"It's too late for that. I touched him yesterday when we found him."

Mother took a step back from me. "By the gods! I thought you let the servants do that. You need to begin purifying yourself immediately."

"The only thing I need to do immediately is get to the latrine. Then we can talk about this. Wait right here."

23

When I emerged from the latrine, my mother was nowhere to be seen. I stopped the first servant I saw. "Where did my mother go?" Somehow I knew the answer before I asked the question.

"I saw the mistress and Naomi going out to the stable, my lord."

Damn them! I thought. They're as bad as a pair of disobedient children. Worse! They're old enough to make others do their bidding.

I hurried back to my room to put on my sandals. As I emerged again and reached the atrium, my mother and Naomi came running in.

"Oh, Gaius!" my mother cried, panic sweeping over her face. "You must come quickly."

"What's the matter? Has someone disturbed the body?"

"No, no. The body is gone!"

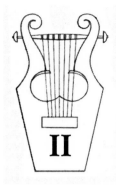

## II

"**G**ONE? **W**HAT DO YOU MEAN GONE?"

"I mean he's not there. What else could I mean?" Mother said.

"The stall is empty, my lord," Naomi added. "There's nobody there." She stood a step closer to my mother, like a soldier in a phalanx protecting a comrade.

"How do you know? Did you go inside?"

"Yes," Mother said.

I looked at her in disbelief. "Did you break my seal?"

"Your seal?"

"Yes, I placed my seal on the bar across the door."

"I didn't notice that, dear."

I threw up my hands in exasperation. "It was on the end of the bar!"

Mother looked genuinely hurt. "You don't have to shout at me, dear. If you wanted to keep people out, you should have put it where they could see it."

"I didn't want anyone but me to be able to see it, so I could tell if anyone went in against my orders."

"Sometimes you're too clever for your own good, Gaius."

"I never imagined you would barge in like that."

"We just thought we would take a look at him, to see what we needed to do, while we were waiting for you."

"We weren't going to bother anything, my lord," Naomi put in. "I made Plinia—I mean lady Plinia—promise me that before I agreed to go with her."

Excellent. Now my mother was making promises to a slave who called her by name.

Mother wrung her hands. "We weren't going to touch anything until you told us we could."

25

"Are you sure you looked in the right stall?"

Mother nodded vigorously. "The one on the far end. The only one with a guard on it. You said you wrapped him in a blanket. It was still there."

I rushed to the entrance to the servants' quarters off the atrium and called, "Tranio!" He came running.

"Yes, my lord."

"The body is gone."

"Gone, my lord? But, how—?" The steward was already counting the lashes he might receive for someone else's dereliction of duty.

"I don't know. Round up everyone on the place. We've got to find him."

As Tranio started yelling orders, I asked my mother, "Was the stall door closed and barred when you got there, even if you didn't see my seal?"

"Yes, dear, and the guard you posted was right there."

"He was wide awake, my lord," Naomi added, protecting her fellow servant.

"He wasn't supposed to let anyone in but me," I said.

"But you were on your way," my mother pointed out.

She was right, of course. Nobody didn't disappear between the time the door was opened and the time my mother stepped into the stall where the body was lying. And if the body was already gone, my seal was broken before my mother got there.

But why was I still thinking of him as a 'body'? If the guards did their duty, no one could have gotten in to remove him, so he must have not been dead. He had to have been unconscious, in a deep sleep of some sort. When he awoke during the night, he managed to find some way out of the stable. It was as simple as that. My seal was already broken before my mother and Naomi lifted the bar.

It *had* to be that simple.

"All right, let's go take a look," I said.

The stable is about thirty paces south and east of the house. Mother walked beside me with Naomi on the other side of her and just far enough behind us to keep up the pretense that she was my servant. If I had not been there, I knew, she would have walked right beside my mother, as she always did, usually arm in arm with her. In the past year they had realized a closeness through similar losses they both had suffered—a daughter dead at birth years ago and a brother taken by an untimely death in recent years.

"Hurry, dear," my mother urged, but I forced myself to walk at a steady pace.

"There's no need to hurry," I said, "if he's already gone." I would not let myself be thrown into a panic by women's chatter. The disappearance of Nobody's body, though, was unnerving me.

The stable is a rectangular building with six stalls in it, each opening into the paddock, which runs the length of the stable and is about ten paces wide. The fence enclosing the paddock is attached to the stable at each end, with an archway in each of its short ends and a larger archway on the long side to allow carts and wagons to enter. When animals are loose in the paddock, bars are inserted to block the archways.

We entered the paddock through the opening on the long side. Tranio slowed to touch the image of Epona, goddess of stables and the animals kept in them, which hangs on the fence beside the gate. My uncle, who commanded a cavalry squadron on the Rhine and wrote a book about using the javelin from horseback, brought the thing with him when he returned from one of his campaigns. The goddess is depicted sitting sideways on the back of a horse which has one of its front legs lifted as though in motion. Her cloak billows around her to add to the illusion of movement. I accord her all the respect I do any deity—which is to say, none—but Tranio is quite devoted to her.

Our arrival in the paddock seemed to disturb a large raven perched on the top of the stable. It squawked its protest and flew off.

The door to the stall on the end stood open. I could see fear on the guard's face. He knew I could have him tortured to get answers to any questions I might want to ask. That's the only way the testimony of slaves is accepted in court. I had no intention of doing so, but it wouldn't hurt to let him dangle at the end of a noose of uncertainty for a while.

"Can I trust what this man says?" I asked Tranio as we stopped in front of the stall. "Or will I have to drag it out of him?"

"He's one of our most reliable men, my lord. I can say that about all three men who stood guard here during the night."

"You're Nicias, aren't you?" I asked the man.

27

"Yes, my lord."

I remembered him from the time I had spent here in my childhood. He was a few years older than me. Even as a boy, he was big, and I had watched him bully the children of other servants. "I will have the truth out of you," I said to him, "one way or another." I might have intimidated him more if he hadn't been taller and heavier than I am.

"Tell the master what happened," Tranio demanded.

"Nothing happened," Nicias said, as though daring me to prove otherwise.

"Something obviously did happen," I said. "The body that was in the stall isn't there any more. Did you hear anything from inside the stall?"

Nicias shook his head vigorously. "No, my lord. Nothing. I swear it ... on my life."

"You certainly do," I said. "How long have you been here?"

"Since the end of the second watch, my lord. Just like Tranio told me to."

I inspected the bar, picking off a few specks of wax. "Was the stall door locked then?"

"The bar was across it, my lord."

"Did you open it to check on the ... the body?"

"No, my lord. I was told no one was to open the door under any circumstances."

"Did you look in?" The door had a small opening near the top with three solid bars in it.

"No, my lord. What could I have seen in the dark?"

So Nobody could have disappeared before this man even came on the scene. I turned to Tranio. "Who was on guard before him?"

Tranio named the men who had the first and second watches and I ordered him to send for them.

"Was the man before you alert and on duty when you got here?" I knew for myself that at least one man had been awake when I came out here.

"Yes, my lord."

"And I checked on the men during each watch, my lord," Tranio volunteered.

"Did anyone report hearing or seeing anything unusual?"

"No, my lord," Nicias and Tranio answered in unison.

My mother stepped up and tugged on my arm. "Why are you wasting so much time out here, Gaius? Go look inside."

"There's nothing to see inside," I said. "You've told me the man's body is gone. I'm trying to understand how that could have happened." And trying not to give in to the sense of fear that I could feel knotting my stomach. Something bizarre was going on. Something more bizarre than even Domitian and Regulus seemed capable of concocting.

My uncle was a rational man. He taught me that whatever I can explain, I do not need to fear. But ever since those hounds began to bay yesterday afternoon, I had been presented with one conundrum after another, each more inexplicable than the last. A seemingly lifeless body had appeared in the middle of a wilderness, leaving no evidence of how the man died—if he had died—or how the body got there. Now that seemingly dead body had disappeared from a locked building under the nose of a guard.

Did the man I saw on the shore during the night have anything to do with this business? But he couldn't. I checked the door just moments before I saw him, and the seal wasn't broken then. He couldn't have gotten from the stable to the beach before I got back to the terrace. He would've had to get past me. That was at least one question I could answer and not worry about any more. Whenever Nobody got out of the stall, it was after I saw the man on the shore.

"Get some lamps," I ordered Tranio. The door of the stall faced east, so there would be some sunlight penetrating it, enough for my mother and Naomi to have seen that Nobody was gone. But the roof extended over the front of the stalls by the length of a man's arm, putting the doors in the shade and providing more comfort for the animals. I wanted to be able to scrutinize the interior from front to back.

When several lamps and a torch had been procured, I led the way. Tranio, holding the torch, hesitated until Naomi slapped him on the shoulder. "Two women have been in there already. What are you afraid of? Go and protect your master."

"If there's nothin' to be afraid of," Tranio said as I entered the stall, "why does he need protectin'?"

"Assist him then," Naomi said, and I heard another thwack on some part of Tranio's body.

29

With Tranio standing far enough inside the door to avoid another swat from Naomi, I walked slowly from the front of the stall to the back. The windowless room was the length of a horse and half again as much and narrow enough that I could reach out and touch both walls. It was empty except for the manger by the door. There simply was no place a man could hide.

"We laid him right there, my lord," Tranio said, "on the floor. And we wrapped that blanket around him."

The blanket was the only thing on the floor now. Tranio's eyes got bigger as we stepped closer to it.

"That's exactly how it was when we left, my lord, all neat and snug around him."

The blanket was not thrown back, as I would have expected if a man had awakened and decided to rid himself of the hindrance. It still looked as if it were wrapped around something, something that had simply disappeared, like melted snow.

I took the torch from Tranio and raised it to examine the back wall. A bat, disturbed by the light, bared its teeth at me, hissed, and flew out the door. Tranio let out a squawk and threw up his hands as the creature passed over his head.

"I hate those things," he muttered.

In spite of the tension, I chuckled. "My uncle always told me they were harmless, but that didn't make me like them any better either."

"I've never seen one in our stables before, and that was a big one. And that white face—I've never seen anything like that."

I raised the torch higher. "It could have come in through the opening in the door. Or there may be some crack or opening up there. Perhaps there's even a place where a man could have squeezed through."

"No, my lord," Tranio assured me. "We keep the place in good repair, just like you've told us to, and like your uncle did before you. You've lived here, even played in this stable. You know we don't slack on that."

He was right. I had been in this stable—in this very stall—enough times to know that the structure was sound, from the stonework in the foundation to the tiles on the roof. I moved some of the straw at the back of the stall with my foot, but there was no evidence that Nobody had dug his way out.

"My lord, could we leave now?" Tranio pleaded.

I raised the torch again and scanned the roof beams once more to disguise my own uneasiness. There was no sign of other bats. Lowering the torch almost to the straw on the floor, I could not detect any of the droppings the creatures always leave. The one we saw must have been a recent arrival. I would have the opening in the door covered to make sure it did not return. Instead of keeping someone from getting out of here, now the task was to keep anyone, or anything, from getting in. "Yes, I think we've seen enough. Lock the door and post guards—different guards. Do not let *anyone* in here until I tell you to."

At midday I returned to the house, exhausted from leading my servants and the dogs on a search for our missing man on foot and on horseback. Mother—with the inevitable Naomi—was reclining in the long covered arcade which connects the main part of the house with my rooms. It was still too cool for her to sit on the terrace that overlooks the water, but the arcade, with its glass windows, allowed her to enjoy light and warmth. At this time of year it was her favorite spot in the house. The mosaic floor and some plants in large pots made it feel like an indoor garden.

The servants brought wine and food, and I gave an account of our search while I ate.

"And you've found no trace of him?" Mother asked when I concluded.

"We covered the grounds of the estate from the seashore out to the road to Laurentum. We could not find a footprint or any evidence that a companion or a horse had been waiting for him."

"Could someone have picked him up in a boat, my lord?" Naomi asked.

Her audacity made me pause. Except in an emergency, slaves should not speak unless asked to. The chair in which Naomi sat beside my mother's couch was the only thing that distinguished her from a member of the family. Yet, as often as I was tempted to rebuke the woman, I had to remind myself that her quick thinking had saved me from possible arrest last summer. Even if I wanted to forget that, my mother would not let me.

"If a boat was involved, we wouldn't likely find a trace of it." Several other villas overlook the small cove where my house sits. I enjoy a walk on the beach—the sand is particularly soft—but it's a spot where landing and launching a boat requires considerable skill, in part because of the current created by the stream that runs beside my house. Could the man I saw running on the beach last night have come out of a boat or been waiting for one? Did he have anything to do with Nobody's disappearance from my stable?

"What could have become of him then?" Mother asked.

"He might as well have vanished into the air. I simply don't know."

"Maybe he sprouted wings and flew away," a man's voice said from the doorway. Tacitus stepped into the arcade, followed by four of his servants and the two of mine who had summoned him.

I stood and embraced him. "Thank you for coming so quickly. I know this is a difficult time for you and Julia."

Without waiting for my mother to order her, Naomi sent the servants who had arrived with Tacitus off to be fed and then remained standing near the door.

My mother offered her cheek for Tacitus to kiss. "How is the dear girl?" she asked, putting her hand on his arm and pulling him down to sit on her couch.

"The doctor says she'll suffer no ill effects from the miscarriage, but her spirits have been slow to recover. She's been very withdrawn from me for the past month."

"You men have no idea what we women go through bearing your children." My mother shook her head mournfully, her hand still on Tacitus' arm. "Until you've carried a child yourself, you'll never understand what it feels like to have ... a part of you die. You expect us to get up the next morning and resume our lives as though we've recovered from a ... a toothache."

"Lady Plinia, I don't think you're giving us enough credit. Men sympathize with women and appreciate what they endure. Euripides has Medea say that she would rather stand in the front line of battle three times than give birth once."

"Did Euripides ever give birth?" Mother's eyes narrowed and her voice took on an edge that surprised me.

Tacitus drew back. "Why, no. And I doubt he ever stood in the front line of battle, for that matter. Playwrights aren't much given—"

"Well, when he, or any other man, does give birth—and loses a child—then I'll be ready to consider what you have to say. Until then, keep your opinion to yourself." She patted Tacitus' arm and gestured to Naomi. "Come, dear, let's let the men talk, hopefully about things they know something about."

Tacitus stood and watched the two women leave the arcade arm-in-arm. When he turned to me, his face registered bewilderment. "Did I say something to upset her?"

"Not at all. Yesterday was the anniversary of the day her daughter was stillborn. We come down here every year because this is where she was living at the time. The girl's grave is here."

" 'The girl'? 'Her daughter'? You talk about her as though she were someone else's child. She was your sister."

"I never saw her. I was only three at the time. They kept me in another part of the house. I understood nothing of what was going on. All I knew was that something was wrong with my mother and I couldn't see her for several days." Dredging up my earliest memory made me eager to change the subject. "I'm sorry to hear that Julia isn't bearing up well."

Tacitus motioned to a servant to fill a wine cup and cut himself a piece of bread. "She is finding comfort with her mother. They've become closer than they've ever been, I think. They're planning a trip to Sicily for some warmth and sunshine."

"That's certainly the place to find it."

"And to be charged an exorbitant fee for it." Tacitus rubbed his hands together like a man getting ready to work. "Now, what is so urgent? Your messengers were absolutely close-mouthed."

"As I told them to be." I motioned with my head toward the terrace overlooking the sea, and Tacitus followed me out there. The pounding of the waves on the rocks below would make our voices indistinct to anyone not standing beside us and, with my back to the sea, I could watch for anyone who might be spying on us. I could not see distinctly through the glass windows of the arcade, but I could discern if anyone was moving around in there. There was no other vantage point from which someone—not even the best of Regulus' spies—could get close enough to hear what we said.

Tacitus leaned on the balustrade around the terrace and looked out over the water. "You've sung the praises of this house since practically the first day I met you, but you've not done it justice."

"I'll give you a tour later." I was content to talk trivialities until I was sure we were alone.

"You must enjoy a lot of fresh fish from that bay," Tacitus said.

"Actually, no. There aren't many fish in the water. We do get some good prawns, though." When I was satisfied that no one could hear us, I said, "The reason I asked you to come down here is that, while we were hunting yesterday, my servants found a man's body."

I expected a strong reaction, but, without even taking his eyes off the water, all Tacitus said was, "I know you well enough by now that I know, when you say 'body,' you mean a dead body. And, since you sent for me, you must think he did not die without some help."

"That's part of it. The bigger problem, though, is that I'm not sure he was dead. I would call him 'lifeless,' but is that the same as 'dead'?"

Now Tacitus straightened up and looked at me in disbelief. "If anyone can determine whether a man is dead, it's you, Gaius Pliny. What makes you doubtful?"

"Several things. The second one—"

"Wait! Shouldn't you start with the first?"

"Under normal circumstances, yes, but there's nothing normal about these circumstances, as you'll see if you'll let me continue."

"By all means."

"The second thing that makes me doubtful he was dead is the fact that, as of this morning, the body has disappeared."

"Disappeared? And that's the *second* thing? Then I can't imagine what the first is going to be. Disappeared from where?"

"We brought him back here, put him in a stall, barred and sealed the door, and posted guards. But, when Mother and Naomi went out there this morning to prepare him for burial, he was gone."

"You're sure he wasn't hiding in there?"

"I'm sure. There was nothing in the stall but the manger and the blanket he had been wrapped in. Oh, and a bat."

Tacitus shuddered. "You're lucky there was only one. A whole colony of the nasty things tried to establish themselves in one of the sheds on my farm in Gaul. It took us—"

"The bat doesn't matter. It's the dead man I'm interested in. When you find a dead man on your property, you can't just shrug it off."

"But if he got up and left, then obviously he wasn't dead. He was just ... taking a nap. You don't have to worry about him any longer."

"What confounds me, though, is that he wasn't breathing when we came across him in the woods, and I couldn't feel his heart." I put my hand on my own chest. "You can feel the heart pulsating in every *living* creature, you know."

"Yes, I know. But couldn't he have been unconscious? Perhaps he was drugged."

"Even when people are unconscious, their hearts pulsate and they breathe. This man did not draw a breath the entire time I was examining him. Not a single breath. And he did not react in any way while I examined him or when we moved him."

Tacitus nodded. "That settles it. He was dead. I've seen how long it takes you, with your morbid curiosity, to examine a body."

"I'm not morbid. I'm thorough."

"However you define it, the fellow couldn't have held his breath that long." Tacitus took a deep breath and held it for a moment or two. His eyes got big, then he exhaled noisily. "See. Now, what did he look like?"

I described Nobody as accurately as I could.

"So, some wandering beggar, or perhaps a philosopher." Tacitus sipped his wine. "No great loss in either case and nothing you have to report to anybody. He could have been trying to live off berries or fruits on your land and ate something that rendered him unconscious for a while, until his body could throw it off."

"There was no sign that his body threw anything off. He didn't vomit or pass anything through any other orifice. I can't find any explanation for this."

"Does everything have to have an explanation? Remember Er in Plato's *Republic*. People were so sure he was dead that he was placed on a funeral pyre, but he came back to life after twelve days."

I waved my hand impatiently. "That's just a myth. Yesterday I was sure this man was dead. I couldn't detect any breathing, and he didn't react in any way when we lifted him or carried him back here."

"All right. You say the disappearance of the body is the second thing that makes you doubt he was dead. But you had already sent for me before he disappeared. So the first thing that made you doubt it must have been something that happened yesterday. What was it?

And if it's something more than a body disappearing—"

"It wasn't something that happened. It was something I ob-served—the leaves."

"The leaves? Well, yes, there certainly are lots of those around here to observe."

"I mean the leaves where we found him. It rained the night be-fore last. Just a light rain, but enough to wet everything. The man's hair was damp."

"What does that have to do with leaves?"

"When my servants picked him up, I felt along the ground where he had been lying, to see if there were any objects that might identify him. The leaves under him were dry."

"All right, so someone placed him there before it started to rain."

"But the leaves were also warm. I didn't mention it to anyone at the time because I was so surprised."

"Surprised by warm leaves?"

"A dead body has no heat. The leaves wouldn't have been warm if he was dead."

Tacitus turned back to look out over the bay. After a few mo-ments he said, "Well then, he wasn't dead, and now he's gone. No crime was committed. No one can accuse you of anything. You have nothing else to worry about. Why are you so perplexed about this?"

"Because—whether he was dead or alive, or something in be-tween—it's as though he vanished into the air, and we both know that's impossible."

"Agreed. It just means he got out of your stall somehow."

I shook my head. "He was in a barred and sealed, guarded room. There was no way out except through the door."

"Then he got out through the door. That's a logical necessity."

"But the door was locked from the outside and a guard was on duty all night."

"Was your seal broken this morning?"

"Yes, but I can't tell when it was broken because my mother and Naomi went out and opened the door. Come on. I'll show you."

We went back into the house by the door next to the bath. Taci-tus put his hand on the wall where the ducts were feeding heated air into the room. "Nice and warm. It feels like it's ready for us."

"I'll need it after tramping all over the woods looking for this man."

Passing the door we could hear the voices of the women who were using the bath at that time.

"So you don't follow Domitian's example?" Tacitus asked.

"Certainly not. I'll never have men and women bathing together in my house. It's bad enough that my mother invites the servant women to bathe with her."

We turned into the central courtyard of the house, with its geometric pattern of tiles in the floor, and exited through the atrium. I turned right toward the paddock. It's far enough south of the house that, even when we get a breeze from the east, the smell blows out to sea without bothering us. Tranio and his men were caring for the horses that Tacitus and his servants had ridden from Rome. The stall where Nobody had been kept was still locked and under guard. The cart we had hauled him in stood by the gate nearest that stall. I dismissed all of the servants so Tacitus and I could talk.

"This is where he was," I said in Greek, which few of the servants on this rural estate could understand. I took that precaution in case any of them were still within earshot. "A guard was at this door all night, a new man every four hours."

Tacitus surveyed the building, running his hand over the door and its frame, then stepping back to get an overall view. "Are you certain they were *here*, in front of this door, all night? And that they were awake every moment?"

"No one was seen sleeping. Tranio checked on them and they vouch for one another."

Taking a quick look into the stall, Tacitus scoffed. "As would any servants who were afraid of punishment. Even if they were awake, someone could have bribed them."

"Tranio says the men he picked are absolutely trustworthy."

Tacitus threw back his head and laughed. "Oh, Gaius Pliny, most of the time you seem wise beyond your years. It's refreshing to be reminded now and then of how naïve you can be. Everyone can be trusted up to a point, but no one is *absolutely* trustworthy. In Rome, living long enough to see your grandchildren requires finding the point at which each person can no longer be trusted. That's how Regulus works. Surely someone who's as skilled at latrunculi as you are knows that any move you make can mean something other than what it appears to."

Though I consider myself a realist, Tacitus' cynicism sometimes weighs heavily on me. I'm afraid he may pass it on to me, like a disease. "But these are my servants. I've known them all my life. I grew up among them, played with them or their children."

"And any one of them would slit your throat while you slept." He drew his finger quickly across his own throat. "*If* someone found the point at which their trust could be turned into mistrust. Everyone has such a point. That is the fundamental fact of life in Rome."

"If you're right, then I have to conclude that there is a point beyond which I can no longer trust you."

He rested a hand on my shoulder. "There probably is, my friend, but the secret we share has moved that point so far along on the continuum of trust that no one will ever be able to find it."

I rolled my eyes. "How reassuring."

"I appreciate your sarcasm, but in Rome that's the most reassurance you'll get. At least you can trust one person. Pity our poor princeps. There is absolutely no one he can trust." He slapped my shoulder and turned to examine the stall door. "Now, I think you're approaching this problem of the disappearing lifeless-but-not-dead man from the wrong direction."

"How so?"

"You're trying to understand how he could have appeared to be dead. What you need to ask yourself first is how he got out of this stall. Can we go inside?"

Nodding, I unbolted the stall and stepped back to allow Tacitus to enter. As soon as he was in, I closed the door and dropped the bolt back into place.

"Hey! What are you doing?" Tacitus' face appeared at the barred opening in the door.

"You think he could have gotten out," I said with a smile. "Show me how."

Tacitus reached through the bars and tried to grab the neck of my tunic, but I stepped back out of his reach. He gripped the bars and rattled the door.

"It doesn't look like he attacked the guard," I said. "Or pushed the door open."

Tacitus rested his head against the bars, then looked up again. "You said your guards were on duty for four hours each?"

"Yes. And each man reported that the one before him was at his post and awake when he was relieved."

"I would not expect them to say anything else," Tacitus said, giving the bars another futile tug. "But, in a four-hour watch, a nap might be tempting, especially if you've been told the man you're guarding is dead."

I did not appreciate the way he was eroding my confidence in my own household. "All three of the men swear they were awake at all times."

"A flogging might produce a different story."

I shook my head. "I couldn't do that. Tranio checked once during each man's watch. He says he found them awake and at their post."

Tacitus stuck one arm through the bars and motioned for me to come closer. "Would you let me out if I gave you fifty denarii?"

"You think Nobody might have awakened and bribed the guard?"

Tacitus nodded.

"But he had no money bag on him and not a single piece of jewelry. What could he have used for a bribe?"

"Then someone from outside provided the bribe."

"No one knew he was here. You're creating some preposterous conspiracy without any evidence."

"Is it any more preposterous than your notion that the fellow disappeared, like Athena did after she convinced Hector to stop running and fight Achilles? I've always wondered what that poor fool felt like when he looked over his shoulder for help and discovered how badly he'd been duped." He slapped his hand on the door. "But perhaps that's the solution! This man was a god who had taken on human form. You disturbed his nap, so he—"

"Now you've moved beyond merely preposterous to utterly ridiculous."

Tacitus' let his arm sag, but the window was high enough and small enough that he couldn't reach the bolt. He screwed up his face like a man thinking hard. "Four hours is a long time. A man standing watch here during the night might need to relieve himself."

"He could do that right here."

"Do you enjoy standing in your own piss, Gaius Pliny? Or smelling it for several hours?"

"No, of course not."

"Few men do. And what if he needed to empty his bowels?"

"I suppose he might have ... stepped outside the paddock for a moment." I looked at the gate, estimating how long a man might be away from the door.

"Please do that. Count to twenty, slowly."

I passed through the paddock gate and did as Tacitus asked. On the other side of the paddock wall I picked up a stick and scratched in the leaves but did not detect any evidence that a man had relieved himself recently. After allowing the time Tacitus had specified—even crouching down as though relieving myself—I stepped back into the paddock and took up my position outside the stall door.

"So what does that prove?" I asked.

There was no answer. I looked through the bars but could see nothing in the dark stall.

"Tacitus?"

When there was still no answer, I unbolted the door and flung it open.

Tacitus was gone.

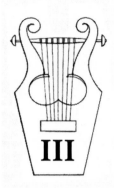

# III

**I** ENTERED THE STALL and searched frantically for a hole or any other means of escape I had overlooked.

"The manger!" I muttered. "Why didn't I look under the manger? That's the obvious place to hide a tunnel." But when I turned the manger over, the ground beneath it was solid.

Dropping to my hands and knees, I began feeling my way toward the back of the stall. I was halfway there when the door slammed shut and the bolt dropped into place. I looked back over my shoulder to see Tacitus grinning at me from the other side of the bars.

"You make a handsome horse," he said, "if on the small side. More of a pony, perhaps."

I jumped to my feet and grabbed the bars in the small window. "How did you get out? A tunnel? There must be a tunnel. Where is it?"

"There's no tunnel. As I told you, if this door is the only way out, then that fellow got out through the door."

"But how?"I felt a complete fool.

He took a step away from the door. "If you haven't figured it out by the time I finish my bath, I'll come back and tell you."

"Don't leave me in here!" I reached through the bars and made a futile grab for him.

Tacitus wagged a finger at me. "That tone might work on your servants, but it's not the way you ought to speak to a friend."

"I'm sorry. Please don't leave me in here. Tell me how you got out."

"Better than that, I'll show you. This is an excellent stall for holding a horse, but it makes a poor prison for a man. A horse can't reach through the bars and raise the bolt, but a man can."

I stretched my arm as far as I could reach, but I couldn't touch the bolt. "You couldn't even reach it, and you're taller than I am. Nobody was shorter than I am. How could he have reached the bolt?"

"My friend," Tacitus said, "you're either not thinking enough or thinking too much. Look around you."

I couldn't decide whom I was angrier at—Tacitus for outwitting me and now making sport of me or myself for being so slow-witted. But I looked around, and then I saw it. A piece of rope hanging from a nail beside the door. It already had a loop tied in it because it was used to control the horses. I could reach it easily. Then it was just a matter of letting it down and catching the end of the bolt. One tug and the bolt was raised and the door swung open.

Greatly chagrined, I stepped out of the stall. "So you think Nobody regained consciousness, opened the door like this, and absconded."

"It's the simplest, most logical explanation."

"But it depends on the guard not being here, and they all swear they were."

"A servant might step away to relieve himself and not even think it worth mentioning, especially if he thought he was keeping watch over a dead man. In his own mind, resentful of the loss of sleep, he would have been here all the time."

"But even if one of the men did step to the other side of the paddock wall, This man still had to get out of the paddock without being seen. How did you do that?"

Tacitus pointed to the cart in which we had hauled Nobody back to the house. "I hid behind that. Your servants left it right beside the gate. When you returned to the door, you looked into the stall, as anyone would, I think, on instinct. While your back was turned, I slipped out through the paddock gate."

"And the guard would have seen the blanket in place on the floor—if he saw anything in the dark—and would have thought everything was as it should be."

Tacitus nodded. "That blanket is what he was wrapped in?"

"Yes. It's what I was sitting on when we found him."

"It's still in the shape it was when it was placed around him, isn't it?"

"Yes, and that's a little unnerving. I would expect a man awakening with a blanket wrapped tightly around him to throw it off."

"That would be the natural reaction, I think, but this man would make it look like he was still in the blanket, in case anyone looked in through the bars."Tacitus opened the stall and bent over to examine the blanket. "Why hasn't anyone moved it yet?

"I didn't see any reason to move it. ... And none of my servants would touch it."

"None of them would touch it?"

I shook my head. "They're convinced there's something magical about it."

"Just because the man who was sleeping in it got up and walked away?"

"They don't believe that's what happened. They're already spreading nonsense about him coming back to life. They say the blanket is in that shape because his body vanished and reappeared somewhere else."

Tacitus' face darkened, like a man who's heard deeply troubling news. "You need to nip something like that in the bud. Tear it out by the roots, if you'll pardon the slightly mixed metaphor. That kind of story can lead to hysteria among women and slaves. Just one more reason for you to make your guards tell you which one of them was away from the door long enough for the fellow to get out."

He picked up the blanket and brought it to the door.

"It's just an old rag," I said.

"Not the one you slept with as a child?"

"Certainly not," I protested, but I could feel my face reddening.

Tacitus laid the blanket out in the light so that the side which had been touching Nobody's body was uppermost. He peered at it with great curiosity, turning his head from side to side. "It seems to have some stains on it."

I had not examined the blanket earlier, beyond noting that there were no visible urine or excrement stains. "It was clean, even if a bit worn." I knelt down to examine the stains.

Tacitus knelt beside me and ran his finger along some of the lines. "Am I seeing a man's face?"

I put my face down close to the blanket, then pulled back. "All I see are some stains, and they're blurred at that."

"You said you were sitting on it," Tacitus said. "Did you leave a stain?"He picked up the blanket, sniffed at it suspiciously, and turned it one way and another so the light fell on it from different angles. AI definitely see the outline of a face. Right there."He poked his finger at one end of the thing. "Was the blanket over the man's face?"

"Yes, we covered him decently. I thought he deserved that."

"And you really can't see a face there?"

I could see a couple of my servants at the gates of the paddock, acting like their work had brought them there. I wasn't sure which of them could speak Greek, so I said in Latin, "No. I just see ... some stains. What you're claiming to see must not be very clear if you can't tell the difference between a butt and a face."

"They both have a hole in them. Very useful orifices, too."

I lowered my voice and shifted back to Greek. "If you're worried about creating hysteria among the women and slaves, you shouldn't be talking so loudly about a face." I took the blanket from him and folded it with the stain on the inside.

"What's wrong, Gaius Pliny? You seem almost afraid of something."

"Come with me."

I led him back into the house and into the small library. It holds only a fraction of the scrolls that are contained in my library in Rome, but I have encouraged Hylas to borrow works from my neighbors and copy them.

Hylas jumped up as we entered. "Good afternoon, my lords. May I help you with something?"

"I need to see that picture you drew of Nobody," I said.

Tacitus gave me a blank stare. "Nobody? How can you draw a picture of nobody?"

"That's just how I thought of the man. Nobody, like Odysseus in the Cyclops' cave."

"So, you would be telling the truth whether you said nobody is in the stall or Nobody is in the stall."

"I thought it quite clever, my lord." Hylas shifted a few pieces of papyrus around on the table where he was working. "Ah, yes, here's the drawing."

"I've discovered that Hylas here has an artistic gift I hadn't appreciated before." I held up the drawing. "He made some copies of this face and I've sent them around to the neighboring villas and into the village up the road."

Below the face Hylas had written:

G. PLIN. CAECIL. SECUND. SEEKS INFORMATION
ABOUT THIS MAN.
100 DENARII WILL BE PAID.

Tacitus studied the portrait and pointed to the blanket. "But that's—"

I cut him off. "Of course it is. I'm not blind. Now, could we go somewhere else and talk in private?"

We were halfway across the atrium when I heard someone coming toward us and turned to see Tranio running into the house.

"My lord," Tranio said as he caught his breath, "one of our men saw someone in the woods, near the place where we found that fella."

"Was it the man we found?"

"I don't know, my lord. The man who brought this message didn't see the first fella."

"What was this man doing?"

"Just sittin' near that same clump of bushes, my lord."

"We'd better get out there," I said.

"How long will it take?" Tacitus asked.

"About half an hour."

"Then what would be the point of all that trooping around? It must have taken the man who saw him that long to get back here. This intruder will have an hour's start on us and be long gone. Then it'll take us another half hour to get back."

"Are you afraid of not finding him or of walking for an hour?"

"I'm reluctant to walk for an hour *and* not find him." Vigorous exercise is never Tacitus' choice of a way to pass the time.

"He was sitting down half an hour ago," I said. "That suggests he's not in any hurry to dash off."

"If he is gone, my lord," Tranio put in, "perhaps the hounds can track him."

"Perhaps?" Tacitus chuckled. "Do your dogs have a cold?"

I told him about their odd behavior when they found Nobody.

"Hector's body was protected by Aphrodite, as I recall," Tacitus said.

"There was no goddess hovering over this fellow, I'm sure."

"Then perhaps they smelled rotten meat," Tacitus said.

"That's what was so unusual it. There was no smell at all that I could detect."

"Dogs can smell and hear things we never notice."

"I'm aware of that. But you weren't there. I've never seen dogs act that way around a person or an animal."

"If he's up and moving around, my lord, I think they'll go after him," Tranio assured us.

"All right, then, let's go. Tranio, get me several men and a couple of dogs. Then you store this somewhere safe." I stuffed the blanket into his hands.

"You don't want me to go with you, my lord?"

"No, I want you to put this out of sight, in the most secure place you can find. Immediately."

In short order we were off into the woods at a good pace, with four servants leading the way, two of them with dogs on leashes.

"Why can't we take horses?" Tacitus asked.

"The woods are thick, as you'll see. We can move faster on foot."

"Half an hour, you say?" Tacitus was already breathing hard.

"A little less, if we keep up a good pace."

"A forced march, eh? Did you look there this morning when you were searching for Nobody?"

"No, I thought he would be trying to get away from here."

"He might have had some reason for being there in the first place. Perhaps he was planning to meet someone."

"I hadn't considered that." There were too many things about this puzzle, it seemed, that I hadn't considered. I started to chide myself for not being as observant as I've tried to train myself to be, but then I had never encountered a situation quite like this one.

The day had turned warm, but the woods grew thicker and the air cooler as we put distance between ourselves and the house. The need for wood to fire our kitchen stoves and bath furnaces compels all of us who own houses here along the shore—and there are many—to gradually strip the forests, starting at our doors and moving inland. My uncle, though, had established the practice of sending servants farther into the woods to begin with and first using any trees that had fallen from age or in storms. The practice involved more labor, but he used to tell me how bleak Judaea looked when the army had stripped it to get wood for its war machines and the ramp up to Masada. "I'm not sure that poor province will ever be green again," he said. So he had preserved some of the old trees closest to the house, and he planted more trees than our neighbors do. Those were still too small to serve for firewood, but they were large enough by now to offer some shade to the house and would eventually fuel stoves and furnaces for my heirs or whoever owned the place after me.

"I think the spot is just over this ridge, my lord," one of the servants said.

The hounds were straining at their leashes and barking, but at least they weren't baying the way they had yesterday. "They seem to sense something," I said.

"Yes, my lord. The wind is from that direction. It could be an animal, though."

When we got to the top of the ridge we did see something moving, but on two legs. A man, with his head down, was walking around the spot where we had found Nobody. He appeared to be looking for something.

"And there he is," Tacitus said. "Puzzle solved."

"No, a new puzzle," I said. "That's not the same man."

Whoever the intruder was, as soon as he saw us, he began to run as best he could over the rough terrain. The dogs strained at their leashes.

"Stop, or I'll turn the dogs loose!" I shouted.

The man looked back, stumbled, but got up and kept running.

I nodded to my servants. "Turn them loose."

As soon as the first dog was set free, the other one tore the leash out of his handler's hands. Competing against one another as much as chasing their prey, they quickly overcame the intruder's head start and narrowed the distance between them.

"We'd better try to keep up with them, my lord," the servant said. "They might hurt him."

We hurried after the dogs, hampered, as the man was, by the uneven ground and the thick trees, which proved no serious obstacle to the dogs. The man disappeared over the next ridge with the hounds on his heels. We heard a loud cry—a very human cry—and, when we topped the ridge, we saw him scrambling up a tree. One of the dogs had the hem of the rascal's tunic in his teeth and, as the man struggled to a higher branch, the garment ripped. The dogs circled the base of the tree, leaping and barking. My servants had difficulty getting them back under control.

"Come down from there," I ordered as Tacitus and I came up to the tree.

"I don't speak Latin, sir," he said in an accented Greek. "I don't speak Latin."

I was relieved to hear him say that. None of the servants I'd brought along could speak Greek. I hadn't chosen them for that reason, but now at least I could talk with this man without giving rise to any more fantastic stories than had already sprouted in the few hours since we found Nobody. I repeated my order in Greek.

"With all due respect, sir, I feel safer up here."

"Your comfort is not my concern. You're trespassing on my land and I'm ordering you to come down. The dogs won't hurt you, unless I tell them to." I motioned for my servants to pull the excited animals farther away from us.

That seemed to satisfy the man. He dropped from the tree and brushed himself off. He was about my height, thirty or so, with dark hair, high cheek bones, and smooth swarthy skin, a color which looked like he'd been born with it and not acquired it from long hours in the sun. His garment was a Greek chiton, dyed a pale green. The chunk my dog had torn out was not the only worn spot. The man wore no sandals.

"Who are you and what are you doing here?" I demanded.

"My name is Apollodoros, sir, and I'm looking for my father."

"Why do you think your father might be in my woods?"

"I've been following the signs, sir."

"Signs? What signs?"

"They're his way of letting me know where he's been and where I'm to go."

Tacitus broke in. "Show us these signs." He's taller than I am and better at intimidating people.

But this intruder didn't seem impressed. A faint smile even played on his lips. "I can't do that, sir, with all due respect."

"Are you a Roman citizen?" Tacitus asked. It was an important question. How we could treat him depended on his answer.

"No, sir. I am a citizen of Alexandria."

"Alexandria in Egypt?"

"Yes, in Egypt. One would not boast of being a citizen of any other Alexandria."

"But we have to ask," Tacitus said, "because that egotistical Macedonian named so many places after himself."

"Yes. Almost as many as your Julius Caesar," Apollodoros shot back.

Since 'Caesar' sounds the same in Latin as in Greek, my servants picked up on that last word. I stepped in before the conversation went any further. All of our rulers since the deified Julius have taken his name. I did not want my servants to think we were talking about the current resident on the Palatine Hill, whose family had taken Rome by force and treated the name 'Caesar' as part of their booty.

"I want you to come with us," I said. If the man's claim was true, we owed him a degree of civility. Alexandrians guard their citizenship jealously. It's difficult to obtain except by birth. We Romans, on the other hand, like whores, give ours to any man who will meet our price.

Apollodoros remained where he was. "Are you Roman magistrates? Are you accusing me of a crime?"

"No, but I am the owner of this land and I want to know why people have taken to traipsing over it like it was a public garden."

Apollodoros' face brightened. "There have been others? Have you seen my father then, sir?"

"I'll ask the questions," I said. "What were you looking for back there?" I nodded in the direction of the spot where I had found Nobody.

"I would not know it until I found it."

"Seize him!" I ordered my servants.

As two of them grabbed his arms he said, "This is not necessary, sir. I've done nothing."

"You haven't answered any of my questions, and I am tired of evasive responses." I was also tired of disappearing bodies—even if there had been only one—and was determined that this one wasn't going anywhere except where I wanted him to.

"But am I under arrest?"Apollodoros asked. "You said you weren't magistrates."

"No," I said. "We're simply escorting you back to my house where we can talk more comfortably. I can summon the local magistrates if I'm not satisfied by your answers. Now, you can come with us or you can take your chances with the dogs."

The animals barked like actors on their cues.

"And, as you can see, our dogs understand Greek," Tacitus said.

Apollodoros drew back, pressing himself up against the tree he had climbed. Looking from the dogs to me, he gave a mocking bow of his head. "Thank you for your hospitality, sir."

I signaled for my servants to release him. "On our way we're going to stop by the spot where you were looking for your father."

"Have you seen my father?" His voice was insistent, almost demanding. "Do you know something about him that you're not telling me?"

"I don't know who your father is, so I wouldn't know if I had seen him."

"His name is Aristeas, son of Caystrobius. He's a bit taller than I am and has a short beard."

"Many men would fit that description."

"Do many men have a birthmark here?" He touched the left side of his chest, below his shoulder, exactly where the mark was on the man we found.

"I imagine some do," I said.

"One shaped like the head of a raven?"

"I suppose it might look like that … to some people."

His annoying smile told me he had seen through me. "Is my father well?"

"Do you have any reason to think he might not be?"

"You are capable of evasive answers yourself, sir. And you have not yet told me who you are. I believe Roman law allows me to know my accusers."

"We're not accusing you of anything."

"Except trespassing," Tacitus put in. "This is Gaius Pliny, the owner of this land. I am Cornelius Tacitus."

Apollodoros seemed pleased. "Gaius Pliny? The author of the *Natural History*?"

I get so tired of people confusing us. "No, that was my uncle. He died in the eruption of Vesuvius."

"My condolences. But I am where my father wanted me to be."

"Why would your father want you to be on my land?"

"He wanted to talk to your uncle about what he wrote about him."

"My uncle wrote something about your father?"

"Yes, in the *Natural History*."

I found it difficult to believe that someone from Alexandria was aware of what my uncle had said about him. The massive *Natural History* takes up thirty-seven of the longest scrolls one can buy and it hasn't been translated into Greek. There must be thousands of people named in it, as examples of whatever condition or situation my uncle was examining. Tacitus' father and brother are mentioned because my uncle knew of the brother's physical abnormality. The boy grew almost to adult size by the time he was only a few years old. I haven't read the entire work, so I wasn't aware of the passage before I met Tacitus. The brother lives on Tacitus' farm in Gaul and is cared for by servants there.

"What did he say about your father?"

"You probably wouldn't believe me if I told you. If you have a copy in your library, I can show you the passage. It's brief and it wasn't so much what your uncle said, but the skepticism with which he said it. My father wanted to show him that his skepticism was unfounded."

"There is a copy of the work here. I'll have my scribe gather it off the shelves. Do you know in which scroll the passage appears?"

Apollodoros shrugged. "In one of the early scrolls. I'm sorry, but that's all I know."

"It will take some time to find it then. Now, what kind of sign were you looking for when we spotted you?"

"I think I've found it, sir, in my meeting with you."

On our way back to the house we stopped at the spot where Nobody—or I should now say Aristeas—had been found. Even with a careful examination, I could not discover anything that had been disturbed. Like his "father," Apollodoros was not carrying a bag so he could not be concealing anything. I wondered if he could be the man I'd seen on the beach last night. That man had not been carrying anything, but in the dark I couldn't tell what color his tunic was.

Tacitus and I kept Apollodoros between us as we walked back to the house. In Latin I instructed the servants, who were walking behind us now, to unleash the dogs if the man made the slightest movement that looked like he was going to bolt. In Greek I repeated to Apollodoros what I had told them.

"I will not run away," he promised. "I have no desire to play Actaeon for your hounds, and I think I have a better chance of finding my father if I cooperate with you."

"I told you, I don't know where he is."

"But you know where he was. That can be an important clue to where he is now. And you are Pliny. That is my most important clue."

51

As we got closer to the house Apollodoros seemed to settle down, like a horse that has accepted the bridle. He looked around, taking in everything with a faint smile—almost a smirk—as though he understood it all or was too simple-minded to understand anything. His expression reminded me of a slave my uncle once owned, the witless child of an overseer on one of his farms. The poor creature had perished when he managed to set the family's small house on fire and had no idea how to get out.

"How did you become separated from your father?" Tacitus asked. "Were you traveling?"

"We're all on a journey, aren't we?" Apollodoros replied. "A journey from birth to death and then to—"

"Did your journey begin in Alexandria?" I asked. Pseudo-philosophers prattling about the mystery of life quickly exhaust my patience.

"This stage of it, yes."

"What other stages have there been?"

"My mother's family came from India to Alexandria. That's where my father met her."

"So you are a half-Greek," Tacitus said.

"Yes, a Greekling, not a Greek. My father is a Greek and a citizen of Alexandria."

"From what town in India did your mother's family come?"

"They came from Bucephala, in the far east of India."

"That place Alexander named after his horse?" Tacitus said. "I don't think Caesar ever went that far."

Apollodoros smiled. "Caesar's modesty becomes him. Yes, the town is Alexandria Bucephala, to give it its full name. It's where the Macedonian's beloved steed died in a battle. But Alexander won, of course. That's why there's a town of Alexandria Nicaea just across the river, celebrating his victory."

One of the hounds sniffed the back of Apollodoros' leg. He jumped and the servant holding the animal tightened his grip on the leash.

I couldn't understand the dogs' reaction to this man, compared to their reaction to Aristeas. If they were father and son, wouldn't the dogs have sensed something similar about them? "The man I saw didn't look old enough to be your father."

"I'm not sure how old he is."

"People often don't know their exact age," Tacitus said. "My father didn't. All we could put on his tombstone was 'He lived about sixty years.' How old are you?"

"I would have to ask my mother."

Another evasive answer.

"Your father's name is Aristeas, you say?" Tacitus asked.

"Yes, sir."

Tacitus rubbed his chin. "There is something vaguely familiar about that name. Would I have heard or read about him somewhere other than in Pliny's work?"

"Have you read Herodotus' history?"

"Of course."Tacitus sounded like he'd been insulted.

"There is a story about my father in there, near the beginning of the fourth scroll, the one that opens with the account of the Scythians."

Tacitus stopped so abruptly in his tracks that one of the dogs ran into him. "But Herodotus wrote ... five hundred years ago."

"Yes"—that damnable smile again—"and my father was old even then."

**IV**

**O**UR ARRIVAL AT THE HOUSE brought my mother and Naomi, along with almost every female servant I owned, into the atrium. They flocked around Apollodoros the way women in Rome throng around gladiators and actors, giggling and reaching out to touch him. He accepted their attention as though he were entitled to it.

While they installed him in a room off the atrium and got him a clean tunic and something to eat, Tacitus and I headed for the library on our way to the bath.

"What makes them act that way?" I wondered. "They look like a pack of wolves going after raw meat."

"He is a handsome young man," Tacitus said with a lingering glance back at him. "One could even say exotic."

"You'll have to fight your way through that crowd of women to get at him."

"Hmm. Fighting my way through a crowd of women?" He pantomimed placing his hands here and there. "That idea has its own appeal."

I took Tacitus' arm and drew him toward the library. His penchant for partners of either gender was the one thing about him that caused me some uneasiness, although he had never made any overtures to me. He either sensed I wasn't interested or didn't find me appealing in that way. I'm content not to know which.

"You are aware that my mother disapproves of men like you who are so ... so ..."

"Versatile?"

"That's one way to put it, I suppose."

"Then she would have disapproved of Scipio Africanus and a number of other notable men in Rome's history. Even Julius Caesar was 'every woman's husband and every man's wife'."

"She's not much impressed by historical examples. I've never won an argument with her by using them."

"I need to give you some lessons in disputation." Tacitus was already gaining fame among orators in Rome. "At least she always seems happy to see me. You haven't said anything to her, I take it."

I shook my head. "I prefer to stay out of other people's bedrooms."

"Unfortunately, my wife wants me to stay out of hers since she lost the baby."

"In the time I've known you, you've never lacked for partners."

Tacitus stopped and took one more look at Apollodoros. "No. I'll respect Julia's wishes, but I'm not going to live like some celibate philosopher. And that is a beautiful young man. I wouldn't mind playing Zeus to his Ganymede."

"Even though he's a bald-faced liar?"

"I don't imagine Zeus and Ganymede did a lot of talking beyond 'bend over'. And I get the feeling Apollodoros has heard that phrase a number of times himself."

"What do you mean?"

"He looked at me in a way that ... well, in a way that I recognize. I believe he would find a partner of either gender equally appealing."

"Could you concentrate on the problem at hand?"

"And what is that?"

"Apollodoros' father—whoever he is—can't possibly be someone who was mentioned by Herodotus."

As we turned a corner and lost sight of the handsome Greekling Tacitus seemed to awaken. "No, of course he can't."

"Then why would he say such a ridiculous thing?" I pulled open the door of the library harder than I intended, slamming it against the wall.

"Don't get yourself so agitated, Gaius Pliny. I'm sure we'll uncover ... I mean unmask him."

Hylas wasn't in the library. I would have to find him and set him to looking through the *Natural History* for whatever my uncle had said about Aristeas. It wasn't a task I would want to undertake. While I searched for the scrolls of Herodotus, Tacitus examined the work on my scribe's table.

"This is a lovely scroll of Catullus. And rather old, I believe."

"Hylas found that in a neighbor's library recently." Catullus' poems, more than a hundred years old, had fallen out of favor soon after his death. I had become aware of them a few years ago and had introduced Tacitus to them.

"He's making a fine copy, even adding some pictures."

I interrupted my search to look over the new scroll. Beside the poem in which Catullus expresses his envy of the pet bird his mistress, Lesbia, is playing with, Hylas had sketched a woman with a bird perched on her finger. Her gown was flimsy enough that the outline of her delicate body could be seen.

"He obviously grasps the poet's underlying meaning," Tacitus said, tracing the contours of Lesbia's breasts. "If you're inclined to give me a present for the Saturnalia this year, you could have him make me a copy. And I can think of some of the poems I'd especially like to have illustrated. *Mellitos oculos tuos, Iuventi.*' In fact, why wait? Could I purchase this copy?"

Judging from what Catullus wrote, he had been as flexible in his tastes as Tacitus. Several of his other poems praising the beauty of young men would fit with the one Tacitus had quoted, but many others expressed his passionate love for Lesbia and his despair when she broke off the affair. "I'll consider it. Right now, help me look for Herodotus. The Greek writers are over here."

With his incredible memory, my uncle never had to be fastidious about sorting his scrolls. He could recall where any particular item was, no matter how disorganized the library. I've told the scribes in each of my houses to work on establishing some order in my collections. Hylas, beyond grouping the Greek and Latin texts on opposite sides of the room, hadn't made much progress on that task, but I finally found the nine scrolls containing Herodotus' history. Tacitus and I rolled up the two copies of Catullus and laid Herodotus out on the work table.

"He said the fourth scroll, didn't he?"

"Yes, about the Scythians." Tacitus glanced at the opening of one scroll and set it aside. "That's not it."

"Here it is," I said, unrolling the second scroll I picked up. "He said it was near the beginning."

I ran my finger over the lines, not really reading, just looking for a name. It took only a moment before I found it and began to read:

*There is additional information about this part of the world in a poem by Aristeas, son of Caystrobius, a native of Proconnesus. He says he was inspired by Phoebus Apollo to travel to the land of the Issedones, beyond whom live the one-eyed Arimaspians, and beyond them the griffins—guardians of gold—and beyond the griffins the Hyperboreans, whose land reaches all the way to the outer sea.*

Tacitus snorted. "Mythological monsters and one-eyed people—that's just so much nonsense."

"Where is Proconnesus?" I asked. Tacitus has a voracious appetite for information about places. He reads maps the way some people read poetry.

"It's an island, in the Propontis, south of Byzantium but closer to the coast of Asia. All those other places are figments of poets' imagination, supposedly in the far north and east. I doubt there's a word of truth to any of it."

I nodded. "Poets are allowed to lie. But there's more about Aristeas." I continued to read: "Since I've mentioned Aristeas, the author of this poem, let me record a story I heard about him in Proconnesus, and in Cyzicus as well."

"Another digression!" Tacitus said with a groan. "Herodotus never met a story he didn't like. The more improbable, the better. I doubt he visited half the places he claims to have seen."

"Nonetheless, stop interrupting me." I unrolled a bit more of the scroll so I could resume reading:

*Aristeas belonged to one of the noblest families in Proconnesus. One day he went into a fuller's shop and, while he was there, fell down dead. The owner closed the shop and rushed to tell Aristeas' family what had happened. But, as news of his death was spreading, a man from Cyzicus, who had just arrived from the nearby town of Artaca, contradicted the rumor. He claimed to have met Aristeas going toward Cyzicus and to have talked with him. He swore this was true and would not change his story, no matter how many people contradicted him. Meanwhile, Aristeas' family were going to the shop to prepare him for his funeral. When they unlocked the door, the room was empty. There was no sign whatsoever of Aristeas, dead or alive.*

"By the gods, I know just how they felt," I said. The similarities in that story and what I experienced since yesterday were startling. A man apparently dead for no discernible reason, the body in a locked room, people coming to prepare for his funeral, but he's gone. Then I read on: "Seven years later he reappeared in Proconnesus, wrote the poem the Greeks call 'The Tale of the Arimaspians,' then disappeared again."

I must add something that I have learned happened to the people of Metapontum in Italy two hundred and forty years after Aristeas' second disappearance. (I computed the time from records in Metapontum and Proconnesus.) The Metapontines say Aristeas came into their city and told them to build an altar to Apollo, and next to it a statue dedicated to Aristeas of Proconnesus, surrounded by laurel. He explained that they, of all the people in Italy, were the only ones whom Apollo had visited and that Aristeas himself had been with the god in the form of a raven. Then he vanished.

"He's a hard fellow to keep track of," Tacitus said with a laugh. "Now you see him, now you don't. Three times!"

I sat down in Hylas' chair, my breathing labored. Tacitus noticed and put a hand on my shoulder. "Gaius Pliny, what's wrong?"

"Didn't you hear what Apollodoros said about the mark on Aristeas' chest? It was a raven's head."

"Did you see the mark? Is that what it looked like to you?"

"Yes, I saw it, and it looked more like a raven than I want to admit. Hylas drew a picture of it. I'll have him find it when he returns."

Tacitus suddenly became somber. "Does that prove anything?"

"Perhaps not, but this morning, when we went out to the stable, there was a raven perched on top of the building. It flew off just as we got to the door."

"The raven is associated with Apollo," Tacitus said, "just as Herodotus says. And the fellow we just found claims his name is Apollodoros."

"This is like a bad dream where nothing makes any sense." I looked over what I had just read. "A man who's mentioned by Herodotus can't be alive today."

"Unless he's ... not a man," Tacitus said quietly.

"But then what would he be?" I could hardly bring myself to ask that question when the answer might undermine the very principles of rational thought on which I based my life.

"I hate to say it." Tacitus ran his hand over the scroll of Herodotus. "But ..."

"But what?"

"Stories about ... gods taking on human form have been around for as long as people have been telling stories. And I know you don't want to hear that."

"No, I don't. Because they're just that—stories. Plato was right. If we ever want people to become educated, we need to keep those stories out of their minds. Next you'll tell me that you believe Julius Caesar's soul actually ascended to the sky and became a star."

"A member of the Roman senate swore he saw it happen."

I laughed in derision. "You mean some incompetent fool in the senate who was paid by Caesar's family." The instant I finished saying that, I looked at the door, hoping no one was lurking outside it. No one took such things seriously—Domitian's father, Vespasian, had joked with his dying breath that he was becoming a god—but someone who was looking for a chance to attack me could pounce on what I'd said and turn it into an expression of disrespect that amounted to treason.

Tacitus stepped to the door and looked both ways. Returning to the table, he shook his head. "But who would be paying Apollodoros to claim that his father is so old?"

"No one, I'm sure. What would be the point? What would anyone gain by it? Perhaps he's just an incompetent fool. Did his smile unsettle you as much as it did me?"

"Yes, he has a wise but child-like air about him. Somehow not quite normal for a human being. It reminds me of the half-smile on a very old Greek statue. I wonder if he posed for one of those statues. Could he be that old?"

"For that to be true, we would have to admit the enormous improbability—no, it's an impossibility—that his father is over five hundred years old."

"Over seven hundred, actually." Tacitus pointed to the scroll. "Herodotus wrote five hundred years ago and he says this incident in Metapontum happened over two hundred years before his time."

I looked up at him. "You're not making me feel any better."

"The Jews tell of people living to be hundreds of years old in some of their books, don't they?"

"I'll have to ask Naomi, but you're still not making me feel any better."

"Maybe Apollodoros is just too simple-minded to understand what that amount of time means. My brother has no concept of time. It doesn't matter to him whether I visit once a month or once a year. He always thinks he saw me yesterday. He may remember something that happened several visits before, but it was always yesterday."

I was sorry to draw encouragement from Tacitus' misfortune, but I couldn't help it. There had to be a rational solution to this conundrum and the example of his brother offered one. It even led me to another conclusion. "If his father is actually named Aristeas, he could have read the name in Herodotus and thought he was reading about his father, if he doesn't understand time."

Tacitus nodded. "Perhaps his father went along with him, as a sort of joke, thinking it wouldn't make any difference. I never tell my brother it wasn't yesterday when he saw me. I do it out of kindness because I've seen the distress on his face when I try to explain the truth to him."

"We'll have to question Apollodoros more closely to see how clear his mind is."

"And to see if he can tell us how his 'father' could appear to be, as you said, lifeless but not dead. Are you sure it wasn't just a very deep sleep?"

"It could have been, but I doubt it. My uncle was one of the deepest sleepers you can imagine. But words fail to describe the racket he made with his snoring." I gave a cacophonous imitation of my uncle, drawing a laugh from Tacitus. "People breathe when they're asleep, and the man I found was not breathing. I'm not sure of much right now, but of that I am sure."

"I didn't see him, so I can't dispute what you say, but the fact is, he was gone this morning. We'll have to see if Apollodoros is still here tomorrow, or if he disappears like his 'father'."

I jumped up. "By the gods, my mother is with him."

"Calm down," Tacitus said, pushing me back into my chair. "There's no indication in these stories that Aristeas ever harmed anybody. And Apollodoros doesn't seem dangerous. My brother may be simple-minded, but he wouldn't hurt anybody."

"I have to be sure my mother's safe." Brushing his hand away and hurrying out of the library, I turned toward the atrium but stopped when I saw my mother coming from the direction of the bath. Naomi was pulling her as Mother kept looking back.

"Are you all right, Mother?" I asked.

"There you are, Gaius." She sounded as light-hearted as I had ever heard her this close to the anniversary of the loss of her daughter, almost giddy. "I thought you and Tacitus were going to take a bath."

"We wanted to check something in the library first. We'll bathe in a moment."

"Well, I don't think you'll want to use the bath right now, dear."

"Why not?"

"Apollodoros is bathing, and some of our girls are in there with him."

"You know how I feel about that."

She patted my arm. "Oh, I think it's all right in this case, dear. The girls insisted on it. If I were younger, I might be in there with them."

"Mother! Why are you women acting like this over him?"

"Acting like what, my lord?" Naomi asked.

"Like ... like ..."

"Like mares in heat around a stallion," Tacitus put in.

Mother's laugh rang around the atrium, something I hadn't heard since Vesuvius erupted, and she didn't even blush. "Oh, I wouldn't go that far. But he's quite charming. One might even say alluring."

"I'm afraid his charm—or his allure—is lost on me." But not on Tacitus, I wanted to add, and in a way that would shock you.

My mother didn't even seem to hear me. "And when he sings—oh, when he sings!" Her face seemed to glow.

"Sings?"

"Yes, songs his mother taught him, from India. They have the most amazing effect on you. You're drawn to them—and to him—almost in spite of yourself."

"He sounds like one of the Sirens in the *Odyssey*," Tacitus said.

"Very much like that." Mother sighed deeply. The faint sound of singing—a man's voice with women accompanying him—floated toward us. Mother glanced over her shoulder in the direction of the bath, a longing, far-away gaze in her eyes.

I took her by the shoulders and turned her to face me. "Are you all right?"

"Yes, dear. Never better." She took my cheeks in her hands. "Now, why don't you and Tacitus ride into the village and use the public bath? I think ours is going to be occupied for a while. By the time you get back, dinner will be ready. That is, if I can coax a few of the girls out of there."

Wonderful! I thought. I have to ride two miles round trip to bathe while my own bath is turned into a ... a brothel for some stranger. And my mother approves! Naomi, her servant, seemed to have better sense at this point.

While Tacitus and two of our servants prepared for the ride I showed Hylas the passage about Aristeas in Herodotus and told him to look in the *Natural History* for any mention of the man, and of Apollodoros while he was at it.

"And Tacitus wants to purchase that copy of Catullus you're making. Whatever price you settle on, the money will be yours."

"Thank you, my lord." He barely suppressed his delight.

"Tacitus will give you instructions about additional drawings."

"Yes, my lord."

"Then make a copy for me," I concluded, "but without pictures."

While the servants were preparing horses for our ride to Laurentum I asked Tacitus to accompany me down to the beach. "As long as we're considering things out of the ordinary," I said, "I want to see what you think of this."

The rock was still where I had put it to mark the end of the footprints. I explained to Tacitus how I had followed a man up to that point. "He must have jumped from here."

Tacitus stood by the rock and gauged the distance to the edge of the woods. "That would be a long jump indeed. You say you saw the fellow until he went behind that outcropping of rock?"

"Yes. I lost sight of him for a moment or two. By the time I got around the rock, he was gone, and the footprints ended just where I put that stone."

"Well, let's give it a try. The fellow was running? How fast?"

"It was dark. I just know he was running."

Tacitus backed up, got a running start, and leaped when he got to the stone marker. He landed at least a full pace short of the grass at the edge of the woods. "Why don't you try it?"

I started farther back than Tacitus had but my jump still left me well short.

Tacitus paced a long stride, beyond where I landed, to the grass, "Either one of us would have left footprints. But I don't claim to be the most athletic sort. A man in better condition than me might have made it to the grass. You came closer."

"But it took all the effort I could muster." I looked at the trees hanging over the sand. "Could he have jumped up and grabbed a branch?"

Tacitus, the taller of us, reached up and shook his head. "He'd have to grow wings."

When we got back to the terrace Tranio was waiting for us. "My lord, the duovirs are here."

"What do they want?"

"They won't say, my lord. Just that they want to talk to you. They're in the atrium."

"I hope this doesn't take long," Tacitus said. "I'd really like to get to that bath."

"The ride doesn't take very long." But I had a bad feeling about why the duovirs were making this call.

The older of the two men was examining the frescos in the atrium when we entered. He was a sturdy man, handsome except for the pock-marks from some childhood disease on his complexion. He wore his authority as unobtrusively as he wore his toga. I estimated him to be in his late fifties, with a full head of dark hair that did not show much gray yet. His son, a tall, slender man in his mid-thirties, stood by the door, with his hands behind his back, like a servant awaiting his master's order. His thick hair was light brown. Even as he looked at me, his right eye seemed to be looking at something to one side of me. The strongest hint of a familial resemblance between them was that they both looked singularly unhappy.

"Good day, gentlemen," I said. "What brings you to my door?"

"Good day to you, Gaius Pliny," the older man replied. "We've not met formally. I am Publius Licinius Scaevola, duovir of Laurentum. This is my son and fellow duovir, Lucius Licinius Strabo."

So the son's cognomen was not randomly chosen. Many cognomina, whatever their original meaning, have come to be traditional in some families. Scaevola might not be left-handed, as his name implied, but his son definitely was cross-eyed.

"Good morning, duovir. I am Gaius Plinius Caecilius Secundus." I didn't have any legal authority, but at least I could outnumber him with my names.

I know your uncle never liked to waste time, so I'll come right to the point. We have heard that you found a dead man on your estate yesterday."

"Where did you hear that?"

"The source of our information doesn't matter. As magistrates it is our duty to know what's happening around here."

"This isn't Laurentum, Publius Scaevola. I'm not even sure my estate falls within your jurisdiction. And, in any case, you're mistaken. There's nobody dead on my property."

Scaevola motioned for his son to step forward. As he did so, Strabo brought his hands from behind his back and held up a rolled-up piece of papyrus. Scaevola took it and unrolled it so I could see it. It was one of the posters I had had Hylas make and put up in Laurentum.

"Who is this man?" Scaevola asked. "And why are you offering a reward for him? You put this up in my town. That is what makes this my business."

"I don't know who he is."

"Where is he?"

"I don't know that either. He was trespassing on my land yesterday, but now he's gone."

"That's not what we heard," Strabo said. "We were told he was lying dead in your stable."

"Who told you that?" I am very nervous about spies in my household, apparently with good reason.

"It doesn't matter," Scaevola said. "If there is a dead man on your property, we need to make an investigation."

"As I told you, nobody is dead here. If he was dead, I would know, wouldn't I? I found him trespassing yesterday, but now he's gone. You may search the place, if you like."

"Did he steal anything? Is that why you're offering this reward?"

"No, I just wanted to know who he was and what he was doing on my land." And now I wanted to know why the duovirs were so interested in Nobody.

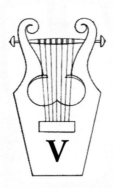

# V

LAURENTUM IS AN EASY RIDE from my house. The road isn't paved, but it is hard-packed and drains well. On any other day this pleasant little jaunt would have dispelled my anxiety about anything that might be worrying me.

Not today, however. Since we found Aristeas in the woods yesterday, nothing that had happened made any sense. I needed to puzzle things out in my head, and I often do that while I'm riding. Tacitus kept up a stream of light conversation. I let him chatter without really listening to him, any more than I would listen to a brook babbling over the rocks on its way.

Even if we had arrived at the right conclusion about Apollodoros' lack of understanding of time, we hadn't explained Aristeas' disappearance. Tacitus had shown me how a man could have gotten out of the stable, but it depended on so many factors converging at just the right moment, like intersecting roads. Aristeas had to awaken from whatever lifeless-but-not-dead state he was in as the guard left his post for even the briefest time. He had to be aware of the rope hanging outside the door of the stall. Could he have seen it when he was being carried in? The guard had to look in the door when he returned, just long enough for Aristeas to sneak out of the paddock from his hiding place behind the cart. Just because Tacitus had done it that way, I couldn't be sure he had duplicated Aristeas' method of escape.

Even if he had, that didn't explain how the blanket Aristeas had been wrapped in was left lying undisturbed.

Or how the man's image had gotten onto the blanket.

Or that damn raven on the roof.

Now the passage in Herodotus made all of this even more difficult to understand. Seven hundred years ago a man named Aristeas appeared to be dead, yet vanished from a locked room. Then he disappeared and reappeared, seemingly at will, at different times and places. Above all, the reference to a raven unnerved me. They're common enough birds, but the one on the roof of my stable this morning, and the timing of its departure, was uncanny.

For once I wished I could believe in coincidence. Then I could dismiss the raven, even if I couldn't explain much of the rest of this puzzle. Not yet, anyway.

We emerged from the woods just before reaching the town of Laurentum, if 'town' isn't too grandiose a word for the place. It's really just a market village for the surrounding farms and estates, not a port town like Ostia. According to some of our historians, it was once a grand enough place to be called the capital of Latium. Today it's a run-down village, with remains of old buildings on its edges covered by shrubbery and trees. Even the aqueduct that runs down here from Ostia is so decrepit that it leaks like a woman crying over a lost love.

The village's primary amenities are the bakery, the three baths and the three taverns surrounding the baths. It boasts three baths because a number of the neighboring villas do not have a steady enough water supply to maintain their own baths. In the early afternoon the village is a busy place as people come in to bathe. To save on wood, my own household members use these public baths when I'm not at the villa.

One bath and two of the taverns are owned by the Licinius clan. The crown of the village is its cheese shop, one of the best in all of Italy. As a child, it was always a consolation to me, when we left the villa to return to Rome, that we would stop there and stock up on cheese. The shopkeeper was generous to me with small bits of his wares. Mother still makes sure we take a supply back to Rome with us.

Like a bath in any small town, this one was reserved for the women in the morning. The men took it over shortly after midday. The dressing room was combined with the frigidarium, and there were no separate warm and hot rooms, but the place was bright and well-maintained and the crowd small. When I come down here for just a day or two, I often bathe in the village to save firing up my furnace for that short time. But then it is my choice. Today bathing in Laurentum was not my choice, and I resented that. At least most of the crowd was gone.

"There's your notice," Tacitus said as we walked up to the building. The papyrus with Aristeas' picture was nailed up just outside the door.

"I told Hylas to have it put up in a place where everyone was sure to see it."

"And the duovirs did." Tacitus stood before the notice, studying it from several angles. "Your scribe is quite the artist, whether he's using his imagination or drawing a real face."

"I know. I'm going to have him do a fresco on one of the walls when I redecorate the triclinium this summer."

"He'll do an excellent job, I suspect. And you won't have to hire someone from outside your household. That will save you some money."

"Oh, I'll pay him. Not as much as if were hiring someone else, but I'll pay him. It's only fair."

"What does fairness have to do with slaves?" Tacitus asked.

I couldn't answer that question without starting a symposium on the subject. If life were fair, would there be any slaves? Pour the wine and let the conversation begin.

We paid our fee and went into the combined dressing room and cold room, which was decorated with blue tile on the floor and frescoes of sea creatures that made me feel like I was already in the water. There were only a few sets of clothes in the row of niches around the wall.

"Hardly any more company than if we were bathing at your house," Tacitus said as we undressed and handed our tunics to our servants.

"Good. I'm in no mood to dally." I washed off at the large bowl of water on its pedestal in the center of the room. "I want to get back before Apollodoros casts his spell over every woman in my household."

"He's off to a good start, to judge from your mother's reaction. She had a look in her eyes that I've seen on Julia's face after she watches one of her favorite actors—as though she's waking from a dream."

Tacitus has told me many times how much he admires my mother's solid, old-fashioned character. To him, she embodies the virtues of a matron of the old Republic, and she deserves that sort of praise. I suppose someday I'll have to put on her tombstone the time-worn phrase, "She worked wool." In her case it will be true. She does domestic work right along with the servant women.

"Since my uncle's death," I said, lowering my voice, "I've grown concerned about how her moods change. She's usually melancholy, but now and then she becomes euphoric. I'm afraid she's susceptible to unwholesome influences."

"Unwholesome? How so?"

"Bizarre religious cults that prey on the emotions of women and slaves. She seems to think they can give her some purpose in life again. The death of my uncle made her mood even darker, but I realize now that she has never recovered from the loss of her daughter all those years ago."

Tacitus arched his eyebrows. "That's a long time to grieve and brood. Do you think Julia will be affected that way?"

"For women some wounds never heal."

"And on top of that they bleed every month."

"Just another reminder of the weakness of the sex. I think my mother might have let herself die years ago, if she had not had me to raise. Have I ever told you that, when we were fleeing from Vesuvius, she told me to leave her and save myself?"

"You've never told me much about those days."

"I'm only now getting to the point that I can bear to think about it."

We got our vials of perfumed olive oil and strigls from our servants and went into the room that combined the tepidarium and caldarium. Since the furnace had been heating the place all day, it was as warm as one could wish. We had the place to ourselves, except for one man in the pool and one being massaged by a slave in the far corner.

Tacitus lowered himself into the pool and sat on the underwater bench running around the edge so that the water, which was unusually deep, came up to his chin. Considering how badly the aqueduct leaked, I was surprised the bath had this much water in it. He cupped his hands and scooped up water to throw over his head.

Leaning back, he said, "Do you think Julia will spend the rest of her life brooding about the child she lost? You didn't really answer my question, and I am greatly concerned about her."

Since I'm shorter than Tacitus I would have drowned if I had sat on the bench with the water this deep, so I stood near him and slowly bobbed up and down, luxuriating in the warmth of the water. "It seems to make a difference if a woman has someone she can talk to about her sadness, especially if the other woman has had the same experience. Did Julia's mother ever lose a child?"

"No one has mentioned it."

"Naomi has been a great comfort to my mother. She's been the friend I cannot be to her, and they share that tragedy of losing a child."

Tacitus took a deep breath, stuck his head under the water, and came up shaking himself like a dog. "When did they learn this about one another?"

"Only recently, I gather. Naomi and her son have been in our household since they were taken captive at the end of the Jewish rebellion, but Naomi did laundry and other tasks in our house in Rome that didn't bring her into much contact with my mother. She didn't travel with us when we went to any of our other houses, and Mother has always preferred to spend as much time here in Laurentum as possible. Then, about two years ago, Mother says, she found Naomi sitting in the garden one night, crying. It was the anniversary of the loss of her daughter at birth some years earlier. Mother sat and held her and cried with her. They've been inseparable since."

"Well, it's good that they can console one another."

"I guess so. It worries me, though, that Naomi has imparted some of her Jewish superstitions to Mother. During the last Saturnalia Mother gave Naomi a nine-branched candlestick and allowed her to celebrate some barbaric festival associated with the thing. I do worry about the woman's increasing sway over Mother."

"I wouldn't worry. A lot of people are drawn to the fringes of Judaism, but when they get closer they see the intrinsic absurdity of it—all those rules about what you can and cannot eat. At least Naomi's not a Christian. Take comfort in that."

I couldn't, not entirely. Within the past year I had discovered a nest of Christians in my own house. All those I could identify as such, I had moved to my least favorite property, the villa at Misenum, to try to keep the contagion from spreading. With all the memories of Vesuvius associated with that place, I don't like spending time there anymore and Mother absolutely refuses to set foot in the place.

We got out of the pool and were anointing ourselves with the oil when the man who was being massaged in the corner sat up. "Is that young master Pliny?" he asked.

I recognized the voice of the owner of the village's cheese shop and turned toward him. "Good day, Saturninus." I remembered thinking of him as old when I was a child. Now he had only a fringe of gray hair and his cheeks had sunk in as his teeth fell out. Plato once said that old men and women should not exercise naked with the young. Saturninus' wrinkled skin and flabby muscles were testimony to the ancient philosopher's wisdom.

"This is good fortune," Saturninus said as he dismissed the masseur and, much to my relief, wrapped a towel around himself. "Been meanin' to get in touch with you."

"What can I do for you?"

"It's what I can do for you, sir. I seen that fella you're lookin' for."

Tacitus and I exchanged a glance. "Where did you see him?" I asked.

"He come into my shop about three day ago."

"He didn't suddenly drop dead, did he?" Tacitus asked.

The old man drew himself up with as much dignity as his age and his near nudity would allow. "Is that a slur agin the quality of my cheese, sir?"

"No. Sorry, it was a poor attempt at a joke."

"Poor indeed," I said. "I apologize for my friend. I'll make sure we buy some cheese before we head home. After he tastes what you have to offer, he'll make no more jokes."

Saturninus nodded as though placated.

"Now, about this man ..." I wanted to get him back to the important topic.

"Yes, sir. He come into the shop with two women."

"Did you know the women?"

Saturninus snorted. "Everybody knows them and their kind. These two are the sisters what rent the rooms behind my shop."

"Oh, yes. I remember them. They were always friendly to me, but my mother didn't want me to speak to them."

"And right she was about that, sir." The venom in his voice surprised me. "Them two don't deserve to breathe the same air as a fine lady like your mother."

"Few women do," Tacitus said. "If you disapprove of these two so strongly, why do you rent the rooms to them?"

Saturninus hesitated, as though searching for an answer, then rubbed his thumb and two fingers together. "As long as men have the urge to eat and to fornicate, cheese-makers and whores will survive."

"Blessed are the cheese-makers," I heard Tacitus mutter. "And thank the gods for whores."

"How was the man acting when he came into your shop?" I asked.

"Very quiet. Almost ... dignified, like he was some kind of royalty, or a god in human form, and it was his right to be waited on by them women. I don't remember him sayin' a word. Even odder, it was the women what paid for the cheese. And them two ain't in the habit of givin' money to men."

"Was the man carrying anything—a bag, a staff?"

"No, sir. He warn't even wearin' shoes. A ratty tunic looked to be all he had in the world."

"I'd like to talk to those two women," I said.

"So would I," Tacitus chimed in. "So would I."

"Where are we likely to find them?" I asked Saturninus.

"They'll be in their rooms or in the tavern across the way from my shop."

"I hope we don't disturb them," I said. When I was twelve I barged in on my uncle and his mistress, an image that still haunted me and made me leery of opening any door behind which a couple might be ... engaged.

"You'll know if they got customers," Saturninus said with venom. "The older one's a bit of a screamer."

We thanked Saturninus, dressed quickly, and walked a block north. When we didn't find the two women in the tavern—where I had earnestly hoped we would—we left our servants there with a bit of money and crossed over to the cheese shop. The small building consisted of two stories. Saturninus, whose wife was dead, lived in the rooms above the shop. Between it and the building next to it ran an alley so narrow that hardly any sunlight penetrated it. I could barely walk in the alley without turning sideways. In addition to allowing access to the back of the building, the alley seemed to serve as a latrine for anyone who was too lazy to walk down to the latrine attached to the bath house.

Tacitus nodded at a phallus drawn on the wall, pointing toward the back of the dreary passageway. "At least they're not hard to find."

Before we started down the alley, three men turned the corner from the rear of the building and walked toward us, single-file, adjusting their tunics and belts.

"Don't worry, gents," the one in front said with a smirk. "Plenty left for you."

"Especially the redhead," the other said over his companion's shoulder. "She's always got somethin' for the next fella."

We stood aside to let them cross the street to the tavern, then picked our way over and around the stinking puddles to the back of the building, emerging into a courtyard formed by Saturninus' building and the ones around it. Much of the courtyard was taken up by the arches of the aqueduct bringing water to the bath. Even more than most aqueducts, it leaked so that the ground in the courtyard resembled a marsh. Someone had put stones down at the back of Saturninus' building to create a patio that stayed dry.

Stepping out of the alley we turned to our right and immediately stopped, transfixed by the sight of a young redheaded woman, outside the rear door in the sunshine, bathing herself at a basin on a low stand. She was nude and stood facing us. Tacitus gasped audibly. I stopped breathing.

The woman, who was a few years older than me, seemed indifferent to our presence. "Good day, gentlemen," she said as she scrubbed her thighs vigorously, as though trying to get out a difficult stain. "I'll be with you in a moment."

"No hurry," Tacitus managed to mutter.

The woman picked up a brush and applied it to the insides of her thighs, leaving them glowing pink. "Do you like what you see?" she said, her voice hovering between teasing and sarcasm.

Tacitus and I could only nod. This had to be the younger sister, whom I remembered from my childhood as a quiet girl of about fifteen. At the moment I couldn't remember her name. All I could think of was the statue of Venus by Praxiteles, in a temple on the island of Cnidus. My uncle, in his *Natural History*, called it "superior to anything in the whole world." He admired the statue so much he had a copy of it in his villa at Misenum. I could imagine I was looking at the woman on whom Praxiteles based it, if the statue weren't four hundred years old.

But, if a man from the pages of Herodotus could appear in Laurentum, what was there to prevent a statue of a goddess from coming to life? Or perhaps she offered proof of Ovid's story of Pygmalion. As my eyes followed her hands up her body, I wondered if a woman so beautiful wasn't, in herself, a violation of rationality. No creature should be so perfect.

The young woman kept her eyes down as she washed her stomach and her breasts, which I could only describe as perfect in their size and shape, with the nipples turning slightly upward. She cupped water in her hands and let it run down from her throat over her chest. With one hand she piled her copper-colored hair on top of her head while she washed her neck with the other hand.

As she picked up a towel, she called to someone inside, "Myrrha, come on out. We've got company. Two of them."

When the young woman wrapped the towel around her, Tacitus' heavy breathing began to subside and I became aware that I had hardly drawn a breath since I came around the corner and saw her.

Another woman, with dark hair and dark eyes, emerged from the back door of Saturninus' building. She was clearly older than the redhead. "My, we're busy today," she said, "and two gentlemen wearing a stripe. We don't often get such quality."

She had been touching up the layers of powder and paint with which she tried to hide her age. From ten years ago I remembered her as somewhat louder and brasher than her sister. Now time—and her occupation, I suppose—had taken their toll on her. More than just tired, she looked worn out, used up.

"What's your pleasure, sirs?" she asked with a smile that revealed a missing tooth on the upper left side of her mouth. "With two of you and two of us, there's lots of possibilities, aren't there? And we're open to all of 'em."

"We'd just like to ask you a couple of questions," I said. Beside me, Tacitus groaned as if in pain.

"Questions? What sort of questions?" Myrrha's air of forced conviviality was replaced by suspicion. "If you're looking for an oracle, you've come to the wrong place."

"You don't have to be an oracle to answer these questions. They're about a man who was with you several days ago."

Myrrha laughed derisively. "You'll need an oracle unless you can be more specific than that, sir."

"You bought him some cheese in Saturninus' shop," I said.

Myrrha and her sister exchanged a glance which I couldn't read beyond sensing that they were now both on alert, like sentries in a legionary camp. I wasn't going to be able to sneak past them to get any information. I would have to see if I could get them to open the gate.

"How did you meet the man?" I asked.

"Sir, pardon me for being so blunt, but we're whores. *That's* how we meet any man. Many of them don't even tell us their names, as you haven't."

The sight of the redhead had rattled me. "This is Cornelius Tacitus, and I'm Gaius Pliny. I own a house a mile down the road."

Myrrha nodded knowingly. "I'm sorry for the death of your uncle, sir, even at this late date. He was a kind man."

"You knew him?"

"After his woman died he ... bought a lot of cheese. He said, when the time was right, he would bring you here to make a man of you."

I looked at the red-haired Venus. This could have been the woman with whom I had my first coupling?

She smiled at me. "Even if I'm not your first, sir, I promise you I'll be your best."

Tacitus elbowed me, but I shook my head. I was surprised, to say the least, to learn that my uncle had taken the time to visit these women. He was so fanatical about not wasting time that he had a servant read to him while he was bathing, and he rode in a carriage or had himself carried everywhere in a litter so he could have a servant read to him while he was traveling. Whenever he heard an interesting passage, he would have the servant mark it to be copied later. For a number of years he lived with a slave woman, Monica, as though she were his wife. I wondered why he took the trouble to come up to Laurentum when he could have found female companionship among his servants, as many Roman men do.

The redheaded woman dropped her towel and took a few steps to where her gown was hanging on a hook beside the door. She did not hurry, and I realized I was looking at the best reason why my uncle might not have considered this trip a waste of time at all.

In the silence I had created Tacitus said, "You know our names, and we know you're Myrrha. What's your sister's name?"

"She's Chloris."

The redhead looked straight at us as she slipped on her gown. Once her body was covered, I met her eyes for the first time. They were a clear blue and icy, like a frozen lake high in the Apennines. Whatever screaming she might do, those eyes told me, was a cover for her dislike of men and anything they did to her. I wondered if she knew Ovid's advice that, if nature denies a woman the final pleasure in coupling, she should cry out and do her best to pretend. Or had she learned that technique on her own?

"You put up the notice about Aristeas, didn't you?" Chloris asked.

"Yes, I did."

"The one you read to me?" Myrrha said.

Chloris nodded to her sister and, with a slight lift of her chin, said to me, "My sister cannot read, but I can."

"There was a reward offered, wasn't there?" Myrrha asked, apparently realizing that I was a possible source of more income than her usual customers provided. And she could keep her clothes on while earning it.

"Yes, there is. Do you know where the man is?"

Chloris grew wary and held up her hand before her sister could speak. "Why do you want to find him?"

"He was on my land yesterday and he left ... without saying goodbye."

"But he made a lasting impression," Tacitus said.

"As he did on us," Chloris said.

"How did you meet him?" I asked.

"We were in the tavern across the way. He came in and asked if he could sit with us."

"The men around here are happy to lie with us," Myrrha said, "but they won't stoop so low as to share a table with us in public. Their wives'll never let them hear the end of it. But Aristeas, he treated us real nice. He didn't just slap his money on the table and tell us what he wanted."

"That's because he didn't have any money," Chloris said.

"Did he tell you where he was from? Where he was going?"

"He said he was from Alexandria and was on his way to Metapontum."

"Metapontum?" Tacitus said in disbelief. "Why would anyone be going there? That place is little more than a fever-ridden swamp. It's been dying since Hannibal's day."

"When was that?" Myrrha asked.

"About three hundred years ago," Tacitus said.

"That's a long, slow death indeed."

The passage about Aristeas in Herodotus had mentioned Meta-pontum, but I couldn't understand why this Aristeas would be going there. And Metapontum, or what's left of it, is on the Gulf of Tarentum, at the southern end of Italy. Why would someone from Alexandria go so much farther north, where we were, to get there?

"Your announcement said you'd give a hundred denarii for information about Aristeas," Chloris said. "We've given you information."

"But I'm no closer to finding him."

"Your announcement just said you wanted information about him. It didn't say anything about finding him."

I couldn't argue with her logic, but I wanted a bit more for my money. "Did Aristeas tell you why he was in this part of Italy? If he's going to Metapontum, this is a couple of hundred miles out of his way."

"He said he had been to Rome, trying to find you."

Now I was completely confused. "Why did he want to find me?"

"He didn't say. He just said people in your house in Rome told him you were here. We showed him the direction to your villa." Chloris waved her arm toward the south. Her pale skin glistened in the sun.

"That's the last we seen of him," Myrrha added.

"Did he mention his son?" I asked.

"Son? No sir, he didn't say anything about a son."

"Saturninus said you bought him something to eat," Tacitus said. "Why did you do that?"

Myrrha bristled. "You think we can't be kind to a man, just because we're whores?"

"Why, no, I wasn't suggesting—"

"He told us he'd been set on and robbed," Chloris said. "Said he'd pay us back after he saw you. Since we knew your uncle, we figured you might be as kind as he was."

"And he was such a nice man," Myrrha added. "He just made you feel good and want to be nice right back."

"Did he sing for you?" Tacitus asked.

"Why, yes," Chloris said in surprise. "Lovely, haunting songs, like nothing I've ever heard. How did you know?"

"Just a guess."

We heard men coming down the alley, their voices loud and slurred with drink. Rolling her eyes, Myrrha gave a heavy sigh.

"That'll be the Long and the Short of It." She looked over her shoulder at Tacitus and me. "That's our nicknames for them."

"Do you have nicknames for all your customers?" Tacitus asked.

"Do you honestly want to know?" Chloris cut in. She held out her hand. "The hundred denarii?"

I reached under my tunic for my money bag and counted out four aurei, the equivalent in gold of one hundred denarii. Before Chloris could close her hand I added a fifth aureus. It alone would more than cover what they would make from the drunks in the alley. She looked at me with a question in her eyes.

"For what would have been my first time," I said.

Tacitus and I met the two men—one skinny, the other fat, but both the same height—emerging from the alley and turned them around. To judge from the smell and the stains on his tunic, the fat one had fallen in the filth. "Sorry, gents," I said. "The ladies are occupied for the rest of the day."

"Ladies? What ladies?" the skinny one protested as we pushed him back up the alley.

"Come back tomorrow, boys," Myrrha called behind us.

## VI

**W**E POINTED THE DRUNKS in the direction of the bath and I gave them a bit of money to encourage them to stay there for a while. They mumbled thanks and, with the women already forgotten, staggered off.

"Perhaps the fat one can steal a clean tunic," Tacitus said, rubbing his hands on the wall of Saturninus' building to clean them a bit. "I don't think the one he's wearing can be salvaged. I wonder which one was the Long and which one the Short of it."

As I watched the fat man sink to his knees and require his companion's assistance to stand again, I shook my head. "While I am curious about most natural phenomena, there are some things I'm content not to know."

We crossed the street to the taberna, actually an inn with a few rooms for rent upstairs. The timbers of its ceiling were as smoke-stained as the one described by Horace. The paintings on the walls were no longer discernible. The room boasted six tables, four of them occupied. Our servants got up to give us the table where they had been sitting and moved to a bench at the side of the room. We ordered water to wash our hands, drinks and bread, all of which were brought quickly.

The heads of every man in the room turned when a man and a woman came down the stairs. The woman I didn't know, but the man was Licinius Strabo, the younger of the duovirs, dressed in a dark green dinner gown with a gold border. He patted the woman's bottom, gave her a kiss and sent her on her way. Then, walking unsteadily and adjusting his garment, he approached our table.

"Gaius Pliny, welcome to our humble establishment. You never did introduce us to your friend this morning." His right eye seemed to have a mind of its own, wandering from me to Tacitus as though it was as drunk as Strabo himself.

"This is Cornelius Tacitus. We just came up here to bathe and get a bite to eat."

"Tacitus? Julius Agricola's son-in-law? No wonder Pliny didn't want to introduce you." He clearly didn't know how loud his voice was, as is often true of men when they're drunk.

Tacitus stood and Strabo stepped back, steadying himself on a chair at the next table. Tacitus can be imposing when he draws himself up to his full height. "Sir," he said, "my father-in-law has retired after long and honorable service to Rome. I am proud to have my name linked to his."

"Better you than me," Strabo muttered. "Pliny, my friend, have you found that man you were looking for yet?"

"We've been given some helpful information."

Strabo waited for me to say more. When I didn't, he lurched toward the door. We heard him vomiting out in the street.

Tacitus resumed his seat.

"As soon as we get home," I said, "I'll send someone to Rome to find out about Aristeas' visit to my house there. He must have spoken with Demetrius." The steward of my house in Rome was the most trustworthy servant in any of my households. "I'm sure we can get a good report."

"Why wait?" Tacitus asked. "Send a couple of the men we brought along with us. They could be there by nightfall and back here by tomorrow afternoon.

I summoned one of my servants and Tacitus called one of his over to our table. After I had given them instructions and the copy of my announcement which had been posted in the taberna, we bought food and wine for them to carry along.

As they turned to leave, I reiterated, "Tell Demetrius I want to know every word that man said, what he looked like, what he was wearing, who was with him—everything, no matter how seemingly insignificant. And don't spare the horses. Demetrius can get you fresh ones."

"Yes, my lord," they both said. I waved them on their way.

"Why would he have gone to my house in Rome?" I muttered as I turned back to the table.

"He was looking for you."

"But why? What does he want from me?"

"He's the only one who can answer that question." Tacitus signaled the serving girl for more wine. She leaned against him more than she needed to as she poured it.

"There's a crime—or the possibility of one—involved," I said in Greek. "I'll wager that."

Tacitus rolled his eyes. "You and your paranoia. Do you think Regulus is behind it, like you always do?"

"Isn't he usually?"

"But how could Aristeas have any connection to Regulus?"

"Regulus' web spreads everywhere, even into my own house. You know that. If Aristeas came to the door of my house in Rome, Regulus knows about it, if he didn't send him in the first place."

"You sound like a latrunculi player who's making his opponent's moves seem more important than they are. I thought you were a better player than that. You're going to box yourself in if you're not careful."

Tacitus has never beaten me at the game, but his warning gave me something to think about. "I grant you, it seems a bit far-fetched to imagine he has a connection with Aristeas. I won't dismiss the possibility, though."

Tacitus shook his head. "If Aristeas is acting on his own, and I think he is, what could he be trying to accomplish by lying down in your woods? What does he want?"

"If you think about it—and I have been lately—most crimes are committed for a very limited number of reasons. Someone wants to gain money, to attain power or to keep it, to exact vengeance, or because of sex—either attraction to another person or jealousy because one cannot have that person."

Tacitus thought for a moment, then nodded. "I can't argue with what you're saying. In fact, I can provide examples. Achilles killed Hector to avenge Patroclus' death. The Ides of March was motivated by desire for power. The list of men who've been killed for their wealth would stretch from here to Rome."

I sipped my wine and nodded. "Whether they were murdered by some thug in an alley or by a thug like Sulla. So what does Aristeas want?"

"Not meaning to offend, but I doubt that he wants sex from you."

I drew back in revulsion. "Oh, that's certain."

"And power comes from only one man in Rome."

I nodded. "So that means he's out for revenge or money. I don't know what I could have done to him that he would be seeking revenge. I've never heard of the man."

"Could your uncle have done something to him or his family?"

"I'll have to ask some of the older servants if they know of anything. With his military and government service, my uncle must have hurt people along the way."

Tacitus raised his cup in a toast. "Perhaps we should hope he's just after money."

"That's the most likely motive in my view. He and Apollodoros have gone to a great deal of trouble to concoct some sort of plot. It was no coincidence that they both appeared on my land."

"Does a plot necessarily mean a crime?"

"I suppose, if you plot to persuade someone to give you money—or buy you some cheese—it's not a crime if they fall for it."

"And you're afraid your mother will?"

"Yes. Before that can happen I'm going to find out what Aristeas and Apollodoros are up to. At least there's no murder involved in this mystery."

Tacitus held a piece of bread at his mouth and looked at me over it. "At times, Gaius Pliny, I find you a mystery I cannot fathom."

"Why do you say that? I think I'm very much like other men."

"No, my friend, you're not. For example, why would you pay a woman for not lying with you?"

"Maybe because she was kind to my uncle."

"And got paid well for it, I'm sure."

I tore off a piece of bread and shoved it in my mouth so I wouldn't have to reply to him. My uncle had certainly been generous to his mistress, Monica, much to my mother's dismay, so I imagine he rewarded Myrrha and Chloris well, too, for their services. I didn't think I could explain to a man like Tacitus—and I've observed that most men are like Tacitus—why I could not abide the thought of those drunken louts pawing Chloris. Even if I knew they would come back tomorrow, I didn't want them thrusting themselves into her when I was so close and knew what was going on. By this time tomorrow I might be busy enough, and far enough away, not to think about it, but right now the very idea sickened me.

The first woman I ever lay with, while nowhere as beautiful as Chloris, left me with an abiding sense of how precious a woman should be to a man and a yearning to experience that closeness again—not just a quick, furious coupling. I don't claim to be a moral exemplar, and I don't condemn other men for regarding women the way they do. I don't fully understand my own attitude, or theirs.

I was fifteen, spending a month that summer on the estate of Verginius Rufus, a friend of my uncle's and an estimable man who had almost as much influence on me as my uncle did. His niece, Terentia, who had just turned sixteen, came to visit while I was there. We had met on two occasions before that, but not for almost two years. I knew Verginius and my uncle had discussed the possibility of a marriage between Terentia and me. By her age, most girls would have been married, but both families were waiting for me to shave my first beard and put on my *toga virilis*. Our betrothal was announced just before her visit. Since we had met only twice before, we were supposed to spend that month getting acquainted.

Terentia proved to be a lively girl, with a quick laugh. I felt comfortable with her from the very beginning. The top of her head came up to my nose, and she was slender with ink-black hair and eyes almost as dark. She did not have a particularly robust constitution and seemed to be always thirsty, a trait I did not recall from our earlier meetings. We spent most of our time talking and reading in Verginius' garden. She introduced me to poets such as Catullus and Cornelius Gallus, whose work I had never read. Her favorite, though, was Tibullus, because included in his books were poems by a sixteen-year-old girl named Sulpicia. After a few days Terentia grew brave enough to show me some poetry she had written. That emboldened me to sing her a song I had composed, accompanying myself on the lyre.

One hot afternoon I was lying in my room after lunch. The shutters were closed, so the light was subdued, more like that of dawn or evening than midday. I heard one soft tap on my door, then it eased open just wide enough for Terentia to slip in. She crossed the small room in two steps. I sat up on the edge of the bed and she stood in front of me. Without a word being spoken, she unpinned her silky hair and shook it out. Then she unfastened the brooches on each shoulder of her gown. I realized she was acting out the poem of Ovid's that we had read that morning, when his lover Corinna comes to his room, so I tugged at the gown. As Ovid says, she put up a *pro forma* resistance.

She put her arms at her sides and shivered, but she couldn't have been cold. I took her in my arms and we lay down. I realize now that I was inept and bumbling. At the time all I knew was how much I wanted her and how aware I was of her beauty and her fragility.

We managed to find several other occasions to be alone during that month. My experience with her left me feeling that any woman should be treated as more of a goddess than a whore. It's not their nature to be whores; it's our disregard for them that reduces them to that level.

Even now I wonder how different my life would have been if Terentia had not died of some undetermined illness early in the next year. The doctors stood by, helpless, as she wasted away.

"Can I do anything else for you gents?" The serving girl's voice got my attention, like a whip cracked over a mule's head. She giggled as Tacitus slipped his hand up under her gown. "Now, sir, that's not on the menu." Leaning over, she whispered, "But we can make arrangements, for special customers. In back, in the room next to the latrine."

As Tacitus got up to follow her, he said, "She's no Chloris, but ..."

The ride back to my villa seemed longer than the ride up to Laurentum, probably because Tacitus wouldn't stop talking about his time with the serving girl. It seems she was especially limber. I tried not to listen, but the two servants riding with us were greatly amused, and Tacitus loves an appreciative audience.

The sun had slipped below the horizon when we turned off the main road onto the lane that led to my house.

"I hope Apollodoros isn't lord and master of the place by now," I said as the roof of one of my outbuildings came into view.

"He was well on his way when we left," Tacitus said.

Before I could respond, a bat swooped over our heads, coming from behind us. "That cursed thing is back," I muttered.

"At least it's still just one," Tacitus said.

"If it's the same one. Where did it go?"

"It stopped in that tree, my lord, on the left," one of the servants said, pointing ahead of us. "Biggest one I've ever seen."

In the twilight the new leaves seemed more gray than green. My eyes are very sensitive to bright sunlight, but in this softer light I could make out a form hanging, head down, from a branch high in one of the trees. The creature stretched its wings and then folded them, as though embracing itself. It did not stir as we passed under the tree where it had come to roost, if that's the proper term for what a bat does.

A few moments later we came within sight of the house. "Everything seems in order," Tacitus said as we drew our horses to a stop at the paddock and dismounted. "There's no bacchanal going on out here—no satyrs chasing nymphs through your garden."

Tranio emerged from one of the stalls, wiping his hands on his tunic. "Welcome home, my lord." He spotted the sacks draped over one of the servants' horses. "You stopped at Saturninus' shop, I see."

"Yes. There'll be no shortage of cheese in our house any time soon. Is everything all right here?"

He seemed surprised by my question. "Certainly, my lord."

"Do you know where my mother is?"

"She's in the triclinium, my lord, entertainin' that fella you found in the woods today. Or at least feedin' him. I think he's providin' the entertainment."

Something about the way Tranio said that made me uneasy. Leaving the servants to care for the horses and take the cheese to the kitchen, Tacitus and I hurried into the house. In the atrium Naomi got up from the bench where she was sitting and took a step toward us, with her hands clasped in front of her.

"My lord, may I speak with you?"

I could hear the voices of a few women and one man, joined in a song, coming from the triclinium. "Can't this wait?"

"I'm worried about your mother, my lord." Her face was more somber and gray than usual.

That, of course, brought me to a halt. "Worried? Why?"

"It's this man, Apollodoros, my lord. I think he's having an ... an unwholesome effect on her. And on many of the other women in the house, for that matter."

"But not on you?"

"He frightens me, my lord. I don't understand what he wants, or why he's here."

At least I had one ally, the last person I would have expected to be on my side, a woman whose influence on my mother struck me as baleful. "Has Mother offered to give him anything?"

"Not that I've heard, my lord."

"Thank you, Naomi. I have the same concerns. You can be with my mother at times and places where I can't be. Please let me know about anything else that worries you."

Instead of being stuck off to one side of the house, as a triclinium usually is, the one in this house overlooks the bay. It has folding doors and windows which can be opened to admit a breeze off the water on fine days. When they are open, diners have a view of the sea on three sides and, on the other side, a view through the inner court of the house all the way out into the woods and the hills.

Tacitus and I went into the triclinium together, causing the singing to break off as soon as we entered the room. My mother was reclining on the high couch, in the host's position. She signaled for Naomi to recline next to her. Apollodoros occupied the guest of honor's spot on the middle couch. He was sitting up so he could play the lyre—*my lyre*. Some of the freedwomen in our household occupied the other places on the couches, while servant women stood behind them or sat on the floor.

"Gaius, dear!" my mother said. "Don't spoil the party. Come, join us." She waved the freedwomen off the low couch across the table from her. "There's plenty of food. We've been so enthralled by Apollodoros' songs, we haven't eaten much."

We took our places on the couch and two of the servant women unfastened our sandals and washed our feet. After our excursion through the alley beside Saturninus' shop, that was more than just a courtesy.

"What sort of songs?" I asked.

"Songs his mother taught him," my mother said. "He's teaching us one about the moon over the Ganges."

"That's a river in India," Naomi informed me.

Mother beamed at Apollodoros. "Why don't you give my son a sample?"

Apollodoros bowed his head to acknowledge her request. "My mother brought many songs with her when she came from India with her family. I've heard her sing them since I was a babe at her breast. I did have to retune your lyre a bit, sir. Indian music uses a different scale than you Greeks and Romans."

That lyre had been a gift to me from Verginius Rufus. "I can correct that when you're done with it." I didn't try to conceal my annoyance.

Adjusting one of the strings, he began to sing in what must have been his mother's native language. Even as determined as I was not to like it, I could sense its inherent charm. The melody rose and fell like nothing I'd ever heard in Greek or Roman music. And Apollodoros' voice—which seemed to be the gift of Apollo that his name implied—matched the beatific expression on his face. When he finished the song, every woman in the room sighed.

Apollodoros reached across the table, offering the lyre to me. "I understand you sing and play yourself, Gaius Pliny. Will you favor us with a song?"

I pushed the instrument away. "I'd rather not play Marsyas to your divine namesake. It was the Muses." I gestured to the women around me. "Who decided the contest between Marsyas and Apollo."

He laughed as though he was utterly at peace. "I doubt these ladies would condemn you."

"From what I've seen, I doubt that my own mother would prefer my songs to yours."

"The noble Plinia would never render an unfair judgment, I'm sure. Please, play us a song. Even if the ladies prefer my music, I'm not going to skin you alive."

The women dared to laugh at the reference to Marsyas' fate, but his smile, with just a flicker of something sinister in it, frightened me. I stood up from the couch. "Now you're baiting me. I won't be treated that way in my own house. Because it's so late, you may stay the night. At dawn we'll give you supplies and send you on your way to ... wherever you're going." I didn't mention Metapontum because I didn't want to alert him that we knew anything about what he might be up to.

As I left the room with Tacitus trailing behind me I could hear the women talking in consternation. The last thing I heard was my mother saying, "I'll talk to him. Now, let's work on that second verse."

"You're not rid of him yet, you know," Tacitus said.

"She can talk all she wants. He leaves tomorrow morning."

"Shall we make a wager on whether he eats dinner here tomorrow evening?"

"I wouldn't take your money. It's my house and I will make him leave." What I really feared was that I would lose the bet.

I noticed a light coming from the library. Grateful for the distraction, I said, "Let's see if Hylas has found anything about Aristeas in my uncle's work."

"He's working long hours at it." Tacitus' voice brightened. "Or perhaps he's finishing my copy of Catullus."

It's highly unusual for a scribe to light a lamp or a candle in a library. The scrolls and the wooden boxes in which they're kept pose a serious fire hazard, so most work on them is done during the daylight hours. I require the scribes in all of my libraries to keep buckets of water in each corner of the room.

Hylas stood when Tacitus and I entered the library. I quickly waved him back down on his bench and looked over his shoulder. "Have you found anything about Aristeas in my uncle's work?"

"Yes, my lord. And I didn't have to look far, only into the seventh scroll of the *Natural History*."

"What does he say?"

Hylas pointed to a spot on the scroll that was open before him. "He tells about a man named Hermotimus of Clazomenae, who could leave his body and see things some distance away that only those present at that spot could know. His enemies burned his body, though, depriving his soul of its resting place. At the end of that passage he mentions that 'the soul of Aristeas of Proconnesus was seen flying out of his mouth in the shape of a raven.'"

"A raven? By the gods!"

Tacitus looked over Hylas' other shoulder, then up at me. "You said you saw a raven on the roof of the stable where you stashed Aristeas' body, didn't you?"

"Yes, and he had a mark on his chest that looked like a raven's head."

"But, my lord," Hylas said, "your uncle dismisses these stories. He says that in the account he read 'a great deal of fable-telling nonsense follows.'"

"That describes Herodotus perfectly," Tacitus said, "especially that bit about Aristeas appearing in Metapontum two hundred years after the last time anyone saw him."

Hylas nodded. "Probably so, my lord. And he thinks the story no more believable than that of a man who slept in a cave for 57 years without growing any older."

I followed Hylas' ink-stained finger as he drew it along a line on the scroll. My uncle did seem to discredit the stories, even as he reported them. The man who slept for 57 years supposedly became an old man in only 57 days, although he lived to be 157 years old.

"That's ridiculous," Tacitus said. "About as believable as the adventures of ... Odysseus."

I wanted to agree with him, but I hadn't seen a man who claimed to be Odysseus and had some sort of mark on his chest. What I *had* seen was a man who appeared to be dead but wasn't, or who was dead and then was alive again.

As the sun at last dipped below the sea, Tacitus and I stood on the terrace, sipping wine, watching the sky darken, and trying to make sense of all that had happened today. Apollodoros' song-fest in the triclinium had finally broken up and Mother had set the servant women to a few neglected tasks. Then, with Naomi in tow, she sought me out.

"Gaius, I need to talk to you," she said as she came across the terrace, wrapping a cloak around her against the evening breeze.

"He will have to leave tomorrow, Mother. There's nothing more to talk about."

"But why, dear?"

"He's disrupting the household, and he claims that his father—the man we found in the woods—is over seven hundred years old."

"What harm is that little delusion doing to you, Gaius?"

"That man, Aristeas—if that is really his name—came to our house in Rome, looking for me. He was not on our land by accident, Mother. He and Apollodoros want something."

She shivered as the wind picked up and waves began breaking on the rocks below. "Why don't you ask them what they want, dear?"

"Do you think Apollodoros would tell me?"

"I believe he would. He's a sweet young man."

"I think he wants to skin me alive, if not literally, then in some symbolic way. To take something that I value away from me."

"Why on earth would he want to do that?"

"I don't know, and that's why I want him out of my house."

Mother jutted her chin up at me, a sure sign of her determination. "But I want him to stay, and I'm your mother."

"My lord," Naomi said, "pardon me, but it might be wiser to keep him here, where you can watch his every move."

Tacitus drained his cup and spoke up. "She has a point, you know."

"And we did not have a bet."

Mother looked from one to another of us in puzzlement. I wasn't going to explain what we meant, but Tranio saved me from the necessity.

"My lord," he said in an apologetic tone, "there's someone to see you."

"At this hour? Who is it?"

"A young woman, my lord."

"Do you know her?"

"No, my lord."

"Wonderful! Yet another stranger at my door. Well, bring her in, and give her servants something to eat, I suppose."

"There's no one with her, my lord."

Tacitus, Mother, and I exchanged glances.

"She's traveling alone?" I said.

"At this hour?" Mother chimed in. "She must be lost, or separated from her party. Bring her in right away."

"Yes, my lady."

"Could we move inside?" Mother asked. "It gets so chilly out here in the evening."

"Certainly," I said. "We'll talk to her in the arcade. Bring her in there, Tranio."

"Right away, my lord."

"I'll have the women bring some lights," Mother said as she and Naomi followed Tranio off the terrace.

"This has been a most interesting day," Tacitus said.

"And this will be the perfect ending to it. A body disappears into thin air in the morning and a woman appears out of nowhere in the evening."

"Do you suspect a connection?"

"You know I don't believe in coincidences."

The woman whom Tranio escorted into the arcade had black hair, which she wore loose and unkempt. Her eyes were dark, glistening in the light of the torches which the servants had lit along the length of the arcade. She wore a gray linen gown and a mantle—not quite as long as her gown—of the same color and material, which she kept wrapped around her, with her arms crossed in a X-shape, as though she was trying to keep herself warm. Something about the gesture was oddly familiar. I couldn't tell her age, in part because of the thick layer of white make-up on her face. She wore no shoes. That seemed to be the fashion for people who were dropping in on me these days.

"Thank you for seeing me so late, sir," she said in Greek. Her voice was weak, as though she was tired from a long journey.

"May I ask your name and why you're here?"

"Oh, Gaius," Mother said, "don't be so rude. Please, dear, sit down. May we get you something to eat or drink?"

The woman remained standing but began to sway. "Thank you, my lady, but no. I won't trouble you for long." She put a hand on the arm of a chair to steady herself.

"Are you ill?" my mother asked.

"No, my lady—" She sank to her knees.

"Help her!" Mother told her servants.

Two of the women got to the woman and helped her lie down on the floor. Tacitus and I stood over her. I noticed a dark stain beginning to appear on her cloak, just below her shoulder.

"I think she's bleeding," I said.

"We ought to take a look at it," Tacitus said.

When I tried to move her hands to see if she had been injured, she cringed.

"Please don't touch me, sir."

"You're hurt. I just want to help you."

"It's nothing. I scraped myself on a sharp branch as I was walking through your woods."

"It looks serious. Let us help you."

"Please don't—" Before she could say any more, she passed out.

"See if you can tell what's wrong," I told the servants. I turned my head to avoid embarrassing anyone and elbowed Tacitus to make him turn away. My mother knelt down with them and began pulling at the woman's cloak and gown.

"Oh, my," Naomi muttered. "Her skin—it's got scaly patches all over it. It looks awful. And look here, my lady."

"Gaius, I think she's been cut," Mother said. "Here on her shoulder."

"Can I look?"

"Yes, dear," Mother said. She's decent."

"Too bad," Tacitus muttered.

The gash was just below the girl's shoulder. "I don't think it's that bad," Tacitus said.

"I agree. If we wrap it up tightly now, we can see how it is in the morning." I sent a servant to get some pieces of cloth to wrap around the wound.

"Make sure it's linen," my mother said.

"What difference does it make."

"All of her clothing is made of linen. Some religious cults won't eat or wear anything that comes off of an animal. She's not wearing shoes—no leather. I don't want to put wool on her and violate some principle of hers."

I shook my head in disgust at another example of my mother's devotion to bizarre ideas.

As we dressed the wound the woman began to stir. "Please don't touch—"

"You're all right," I said. "We've stopped the bleeding."

"And we used linen," Mother said.

"Thank you."

"Get her some wine and something to eat," I ordered. "Would cheese and some bread suit you?"

"Thank you. I would be grateful."

We helped her sit up and lean against the wall of the arcade while she ate and drank a bit.

"You can rest here tonight and we'll try to help you tomorrow."

"That's not necessary, sir. I just need to know where my father is."

"I can't tell you that," I said, "because I don't know who your father is. Or who you are."

"My name is Daphne. My father is the man you call Aris—"

She broke off and all of us turned our heads as a commotion

arose in the hallway leading to the arcade. Suddenly Apollodoros burst in on us.

"You!" he shouted. "What are you doing here?"

The woman seemed to gain strength from somewhere as she jumped up. She seemed to grow larger and she stretched out an arm, her finger pointing right at Apollodoros, who stopped in his tracks.

"You!" she snarled. "What have *you* done with my father?"

## VII

**I** STEPPED BETWEEN Daphne and Apollodoros before they could get any closer to one another. "What's going on here? What are you two talking about?"

They both began yelling at once.

"Stop it!" I said. "I won't listen to this. You'll speak one at a time, in a reasonable tone, or I'll throw you both out. I don't care how dark it is."

"Oh, the dark suits *her* just fine," Apollodoros snapped.

Daphne crossed her arms over her chest again, drawing her cloak around her. "Don't start spreading your pack of lies about me."

Tacitus stepped in between them and pointed to one, then the other. "I take it you two know one another."

"She has been my Nemesis—and my father's—for years," Apollodoros said. "Wherever we go, she pursues us, like the Furies hounding Orestes."

"Because he's not your father," Daphne said. "He's my—"

"Enough!" I shouted. "Enough. Apollodoros, I've heard your story. Tranio, take him to the room where he's staying, and make sure he doesn't leave. I'll listen to what Daphne has to say, then I'll talk to Apollodoros again."

Over the last couple of years I've learned that, when there is contention between two people, it's wiser to question them separately, out of one another's hearing. It helps me spot the lies each one is telling and keeps them unaware of any contradictions in their stories. Even if two people are in agreement about what lie they're going to tell, they will eventually slip up when questioned separately.

"We could just turn the two of them loose on one another," Tacitus suggested in Latin. "It would make for an interesting fight. Let the winner have Aristeas and we'd be done with him." He looked from Apollodoros to Daphne and back. "Frankly, I'm not sure where I'd put my money."

"You're not helping me," I said. In fact, his suggestion had a certain appeal, and I was equally ambivalent about who might win. In spite of her injury, Daphne exuded confidence and strength, a good match for Apollodoros' passion. "We can't let the winner have Aristeas—if that is his name—because we don't know where the man is, and I don't want to admit that at the moment." I studied Apollodoros' and Daphne's faces to see if either of them understood what we were saying.

"Naomi," my mother said, shifting us back to Greek, "would you go with Apollodoros? Please see that he's comfortable and has whatever he needs."

Twisting her mouth, Naomi nodded to my mother and gave me a glance as she followed Tranio and Apollodoros out of the arcade. Before I could say anything to Daphne, Mother took charge.

"Now, dear, please, sit down and let's talk." She gestured to a chair and sat down, but the young woman remained standing, as did Tacitus and I.

"Thank you, my lady. I know this is an odd time of day for a visitor, but it was the time that suited me best."

"Because of your travels?" Mother asked.

"No, my lady, because I'm more comfortable in the subdued light of evening."

"Oh, my son has trouble with his eyes, too. Bright light can give him a headache. Is that true for you?"

"Something like that."

I lost my patience. "Why are you here?"

"I'm looking for my father. I had followed him to this area, and I saw your announcement in Laurentum. Two women in a tavern told me where to find your house, so I came here."

"Two women? Was one red-haired?"

The woman nodded. "Like a daughter of Menelaus."

"But if Aristeas is your father and Apollodoros' father, then aren't the two of you brother and sister, or half-brother and half-sister?"

"I am no kin of that lying bastard who calls himself 'Apollo's Gift'."

My mother stood again. "You have no reason to impugn him.

And I'll thank you to watch your language in my house."

"I see he's already begun to cast his spell over you, my lady."

"Young woman, you are abusing our hospitality," my mother said.

"Not as much as Apollodoros did my family's."

"This sounds like a complicated story," I said. "Why don't you stay the night and we'll talk in the morning?"

Daphne looked alarmed. "No, I can't stay here. Apollodoros will kill me if he gets the chance."

"Apollodoros isn't going to kill anyone," Mother said. Her attitude toward the woman had shifted to obvious hostility. No one could accuse her new favorite of anything. "If it would make you feel any better, though, we can post guards on your room and his."

*Just like we did on the stable,* I thought.

"No," Daphne said, shaking her head vigorously. "No, I can't stay here tonight. I just want to know if you can tell me where my father is."

"Why do you think I would know anything about him?"

"Because this is the last place I can trace him to. He was on his way here the day before yesterday."

"Being on his way here isn't the same as being here," Tacitus observed.

"But there was no trace of him between Laurentum and here," Daphne said.

"No trace?" Tacitus almost mocked her. There are so many places to hide between Laurentum and here, a legion would have a hard time finding him."

"A legion could not search for him the way I did."

"What do you mean by that? How could a lone woman, on foot—?"

"You're making assumptions, sir."

"Stop it," I said. "We need to get the whole story, and we will get it before you leave."

Daphne turned to face me, dropping her hands in front of her like someone about to be shackled. "Am I your prisoner then?"

"What?" my mother said. "How dare you talk to my son that way? You came here willingly, and you may leave any time you like—"

"Be assured that I will." She drew her arms across her chest again.

I ignored her impertinence and her arrogance. "But if you want me to help you find ... this man, you need to tell me whatever you know about him."

"Please, sit down," my mother said, making one more gesture of hospitality. "We'll just have a nice talk." She put her hand on Daphne's elbow to guide her to a seat, but the young woman grimaced and jerked away from her.

"Don't touch me!"

"She means you no harm," I said. "None of us means to hurt you."

Daphne turned to my mother and bowed her head. "Forgive me, my lady. It's just that I have ... a strong aversion to being touched."

Naomi came back into the arcade and resumed her position at my mother's side. She was followed by two servant women carrying wine, bread, and cheese.

"Is our guest settled comfortably?" Mother asked.

Naomi made a harrumphing noise. "I don't believe he has anything to complain about, although that doesn't stop him from complaining."

"That hasn't changed," Daphne said disgustedly. She sat down in a chair that was set apart from the couch my mother and Naomi occupied. Tacitus and I pulled up chairs directly opposite her.

"When you say, 'that hasn't changed'," I began, "it suggests to me that you have known Apollodoros for some time. I would like to hear your story."

"I feel like someone from Homer," Daphne said. " 'With words on wings—'"

"I hope you'll give us the truth, not some Homeric fable."

"Yes, sir. The truth. You may count on it."

Considering everything that had happened in the last two days, I wasn't sure I could believe anything she said, but I was ready to listen. I just hoped she got to the heart of the matter directly, not in a round-about fashion, like Odysseus telling his fanciful tales in the palace of Alcinous.

She took a deep breath and began. "As I told you, my name is Daphne. My mother was Xanthippe and my father is Aristeas of Alexandria. Well, I say 'of Alexandria,' but he was born on the island of Proconnesus. His father was a merchant from Alexandria who lived on Proconnesus for much of his life. He came back to Alexandria when my father was ten."

"Gaius, you look odd," my mother said. "Your face is white. Is something wrong?"

"No ... No. I ... I read something about Proconnesus the other day. I was just struck by hearing the name again."

Tacitus got me off the hook. "You say your mother is dead?"

"Yes. She died fifteen years ago, when I was ten, while giving birth to a child, who also died."

Tacitus and I looked at my mother and Naomi, as if to apologize to them and to all women.

"Is Apollodoros actually the name of the man who is in my house now?"

"It's what he calls himself now, sir. He also has an Indian name."

"So he is not the son of a Greek man and an Indian mother?"

"He is, sir. His mother is Indian. Her family has lived in Alexandria for years. Her husband is now dead. Apollodoros claims to be the son of her first husband, who was Greek."

I looked at my mother but before I could say anything, she said, "You're living under a name you weren't born with, Gaius."

I could see there was going to be no dissuading her from her affection for this scoundrel. "How did you meet Apollodoros?" I asked Daphne.

"Five years ago he met my father in a bath and heard him playing the lyre."

"Is your father an entertainer?" I asked.

"No, sir. He and a circle of friends fancied themselves poets and musicians. They gathered regularly in one of the baths to work on their compositions."

"If they were in a bath," Tacitus said, "Apollodoros must have seen the mark on his chest that you mentioned."

I tried to quiet him, but it was too late.

"The raven's head?" Daphne asked. "You saw it? Then you *have* seen my father." She sat forward in her chair. "Why won't you tell me where he is?"

"He's not here. That's all I can tell you. I and others in my household saw him yesterday."

"Was he well?"

I had to think about my response. "That's a hard question to answer. All I can say is that he was well enough that he's not here any longer. Do you know where he got the mark?"

"He was born with it. He made it his symbol. The *plectron* of his lyre was shaped like a raven's head. Please, tell me what you know of him." Her distress seemed genuine.

My mother started to say something, but I held up my hand to quiet her. "In time. You're telling your story now, and I want to hear all of it."

Daphne took a cup of wine from a servant and leaned back in her chair. "Apollodoros came to our home and wanted my father to become his partner, the accompanist to his singing. I was worried because my father isn't a smart man, and he's easily influenced by flattery. Since my mother's death I've worried about him being duped."

"Duped?" Tacitus said. "Duped out of what?"

Daphne raised her chin, and I thought I detected pride. Or perhaps arrogance. "My family has enough wealth to make us comfortable, sir. Not nearly this comfortable." She gestured at her surroundings. "But comfortable. Most of it comes from an inheritance from my mother's family. She had no brothers or sisters, so she inherited all that her family had. We're fortunate to have a capable and trustworthy steward who managed our affairs until I was grown."

"That does make you one of the fortunate few," Tacitus snorted. "In that situation, most stewards would have siphoned off the money before you were grown, like Demosthenes' guardians robbed him."

"But our steward, Ictinus, was an honest man in his own right," Daphne insisted. "And I believe he was ... my mother's lover."

"You say 'was'—"

"Ictinus died three years ago."

"But he was resolved to manage your mother's affairs well," I said, "to protect her wealth from a man he must have resented."

"Yes, and I am not his daughter, in case that's your next question. When you see my father and me side-by-side, you'll know whose child I am."

It would be difficult to spot a resemblance with all the make-up she wore. "But you're old enough now to manage your own affairs, aren't you?" I said.

Daphne nodded. "For the last several years I've been overseeing where our money goes. Ictinus taught me well. I am usually able to rein in my father's love of schemes."

"Schemes?" I glanced at Tacitus. That was what I expected, but I hadn't expected to hear the word blurted out like that. "What kind of schemes?"

"Anything he thinks will make him money. I think he resents living on my mother's money."

"He might have been aware of his wife's affair with your steward as well," Tacitus suggested.

"He's never mentioned it, but he could have been. He wants to make himself important. He wanted to buy a chariot-racing team, or import Nubian slaves—it always turned out to be just a way for someone else to get his money."

"So you were suspicious of Apollodoros."

"From the first moment I met him, but my father was eager to make a name for himself as a musician. It would be something he did himself, not something he got from my mother and her family."

Tacitus put his hand over his mouth and muttered to me in Latin, "Every gelding's wish—he'd get his balls back."

"How much money did Apollodoros want?" I asked.

Daphne took a sip of wine and ran her tongue around her lips. "That's the odd thing. He didn't want any money. My father tried to give him some, but he wouldn't take it. He said he would bear the expense of training my father because he was so confident they would win prizes in the big musical festivals and become some sort of popular idols. Then they would be able to give performances in all the big cities around the empire."

That wasn't an unreasonable aspiration. Musicians and actors are treated as demigods. They make large sums of money—as much in a single day as a teacher might make in a year—and they're invited to entertain in the wealthiest homes in Rome. But, like Daphne, I felt a vague uneasiness about Apollodoros' ultimate objective. Performers of that sort, no matter how popular and how wealthy they become, always remain social outcasts. Why would anyone aspire to that status? Most people fall into it when they have no other options. Was the money all that mattered to Apollodoros?

"I can see why Apollodoros might expect to win," my mother said. "His singing is absolutely divine."

The servant woman standing behind her giggled and Mother

turned to smile at her. "You know what I mean, don't you, Blandina?"

Blandina nodded energetically. "I hope we'll get to hear him again, my lady."

"Perhaps he'll favor you with a song on his way out tomorrow morning," Naomi said, drawing a glare from the other two women.

I raised a hand to silence them. "Blandina, make yourself useful. Get us some more bread and cheese."

"Yes, my lord." With a smile still playing on the corners of her mouth, Blandina hurried out.

I turned to Daphne. "Please continue."

The mysterious young woman drew her cloak almost up to her chin, as though she were cold or wanted to conceal something. "Apollodoros and my father spent a month practicing, then they left Alexandria. Apollodoros said they were going to spend a year in Greece, competing in musical festivals. I had two letters in the first two months, just saying they were in Corinth or Athens and doing well. After that, nothing."

"And this was five years ago?" I asked.

"Yes, sir."

"Did you try to get information about them?"

"Yes, sir. I met ships coming from Greece and asked people if they knew anything about the contests there, but no one had heard of my father or Apollodoros. When Ictinus died, I sold my family's business and some property we owned and began trying to find my father. At first I hired others to do the job, but they took my money and found nothing, so I decided to search for him myself. I've devoted my life to that goal for the last two years."

"You're a brave young woman," my mother said with a slightly softer tone, "to strike out alone like that."

"I've always had to take care of myself, my lady, because my mother died when I was so young."

"It sounds like you've had to take care of your father, too," Mother said. "If our parents live long enough, we do sometimes change roles and become their guardians, as they were for us when we were children. You've taken on that role, I think, at a younger age than most."

"He's my father," Daphne said. "What else can I do?"

"What have you learned about your father and Apollodoros?" I asked.

"They've not been singing. That was what made it so hard to find them. I was looking for two musicians, but no one had ever heard of them. Last year I was in Antioch two days after they left, but I didn't know that because I was looking for them at musical contests."

"Where did you finally find them?" Tacitus asked.

"I picked up their trail in Padua. Apollodoros has made some connection between the mark on my father's chest and a man named Aristeas, so he's pretending that my father is this Aristeas and that he's hundreds of years old."

"For what purpose?" Tacitus asked.

"They've been selling small vials of blood, supposedly my father's blood. Apollodoros claims that anyone who drinks his blood will live for hundreds of years."

"Who would ever believe such a ridiculous thing?" I said.

"Do you want to die, sir?" Daphne said.

"We're all going to die. There's nothing we can do about that." I got up and began to pace.

"Some people claim there is. Have you ever heard of Aristeas?"

"We've read about him in Herodotus and in my uncle's own work." I hated to admit it.

"Herodotus claimed that he was hundreds of years old in his day," Tacitus added, "and that he appeared to be dead a couple of times but came back to life."

"That's the story Apollodoros uses to convince people to buy his little vials."

"Why would anyone believe such nonsense?"

"People have been reluctant to tell me much, I think because they're embarrassed. I've been told that they go into a town and stage some sort of argument. A fight results and my father appears to fall dead, but he comes back to life by the next morning."

I nodded. "And then Apollodoros touts the vials filled with his blood."

"I don't know what they're filled with."

"Animal blood, no doubt," Tacitus said.

"That's what I suspect, sir."

"But he can't have many vials with him at any given time," I said. "How can they make any money off of this scheme?"

"I've been told that people will pay a hundred aurei for a single vial."

"Apollodoros had no money with him when we found him in my woods. He wasn't carrying anything. Neither was the man with the raven's head mark we found the day before yesterday. I thought he was dead."

Daphne gave a contemptuous laugh. "Apparently the only thing Apollodoros has taught my father is how to put himself into a death-like trance. Not even a doctor can tell if he is alive or not. Is that how you found him?"

I nodded, feeling better about my inability to determine whether Aristeas was alive. If a doctor couldn't tell, how could I expect to?

"Where is he?" She got out of her chair and knelt before me, like a client or a suppliant throwing herself on my mercy. "Please tell me, sir."

"He's gone."

"Gone?" Daphne sat back on her heels, putting her hands on her face. "Why should I expect anything else? I'm always one or two days behind him. Do you have any idea where he could be?"

"We thought he was dead, so we put him in my stable and posted a guard, but the next morning the stall was empty. Do you know how your father brings himself out of this trance?"

"No, I don't. He must be able to at will, though, from the reports I've heard."

"That's an amazing story," I said.

"I don't believe a word of it," my mother said. "Apollodoros couldn't possibly be doing something so underhanded."

"I'm sorry to disillusion you, my lady," Daphne said, returning to her chair. "He is a charming man who can weave a kind of spell with his songs, like Homer's Sirens."

"Does that mean he's out to destroy those who cross his path, like the Sirens?" I asked.

"I haven't heard of him harming anyone, and I've been following him for two years now. A few people have ruined themselves financially trying to buy one of his vials."

"I'm surprised," Tacitus said, "that no one has tried to capture Aristeas and keep him prisoner to have a supply of the blood for his own use, as ghoulish as that sounds."

"Apollodoros always stresses that a second drink from a vial will not add more years. Quite the opposite. It will kill a person on the spot. And then he and my father leave town as quickly as they can."

"Before someone dies from drinking whatever is in those vials," I said.

"Do you think he was coming here to try to dupe us?" Mother asked.

"I've never been able to tell in advance what he was doing," Daphne said. "I always seem to be a few days behind him."

"Well, you're both here now," I said, "and I'd like for you both to stay until we can find your father—or Aristeas, or whoever he is—and clear up this whole business."

"Thank you for your help, sir. It will be a great relief for me to have someone on my side."

"I didn't say I was on your side. I just said I want to get this cleared up. My mother will show you to a room. Mother, tell Tranio I want two guards on her room and two on Apollodoros' at all times." I stood and started out of the arcade, with Tacitus following me.

"What are you going to do now?" Mother asked.

"Now we're going to talk to Apollodoros again."

The guards were alert when Tacitus and I arrived at the door of Apollodoros' room. Tranio had rigged a bolt across it to guarantee the man stayed there.

"Have you heard anything unusual?" I asked.

"No, my lord. He asked for a bit to eat, but nothing else. He's been singing."

"Perhaps you should put wax in their ears," Tacitus said, "like Odysseus did for his crew when they sailed past the Sirens."

"Don't worry, my lord," one of the guards said. "This one seems to appeal to women only."

The other man snickered. "We could let him sing to Melanthos."

"That's enough of that," I said. "Let's talk to him."

One of the guards unbolted the door and I was relieved to see Apollodoros sitting on the bed.

"I hope you've come to tell me I may leave." He looked up at me but not did stir.

"No one's going anywhere until I have some answers that satisfy me."

"What did that lying bitch tell you?"

"What she said is not your concern. All I want from you is the truth."

He rested his head against the wall. "The truth is so bizarre you would never believe it."

"You don't know what I'll believe until you tell me."

"I'm sure she told you her pathetic story of her mother dying when she was young and how she has spent years trying to find her father whom I lured away under false pretenses."

Neither Tacitus nor I acknowledged what he said.

"It's all lies. The truth is … that she's some sort of ghoulish creature of the night—an empusa."

Tacitus and I laughed. "An empusa?" I said. "That's ridiculous."

"They're just legendary monsters," Tacitus said. "They supposedly drink the blood of anyone they find roaming around at night. My nurse used to tell me stories about them—and about the Lamia—so I would stay in bed at night when she put me there. I still wake up in a sweat sometimes."

Apollodoros shook his head. "This one is very real. And she wants the blood of Aristeas. She has convinced herself it will make her immortal."

"But you've been telling people that more than one drink would be fatal."

"She wants to drink it all at one time. We've been trying to escape her for years. We keep on the move, changing our names, but she's always on our trail."

"This makes no sense at all," I said. "According to the stories I've heard, doesn't the empusa have feet of bronze?"

"That's one version," Tacitus said.

"But Daphne's feet are perfectly normal. I didn't see anything about her that wasn't normal."

"She did keep her cloak wrapped closely around her," Tacitus said.

"The evening is chilly." I didn't mean to defend her, just point out the obvious.

"I've heard an empusa can take on any shape, even the shape of a pretty young woman in order to seduce a man and drink his blood."

Apollodoros fell on his knees and grabbed the hem of Tacitus' tunic. His eyes grew wide as he looked from one of us to the other. "That's it exactly. I know you'll think me insane, sirs, but she drinks blood to keep herself young. I don't know how many people she has killed or how old she is."

"If she has drunk other people's blood," Tacitus said, "why is she so interested in Aristeas'? Won't anyone's blood do?"

"She believes that, if she can drink Aristeas' blood, she won't have to keep hunting down victims and risk being caught."

"Oh, right." Tacitus' voice dripped with sarcasm. "Because he is practically immortal himself."

"Stop it," I said. "This is preposterous. First a seven-hundred-year-old man, now a blood-drinking ghoul—I won't believe any of it."

Tacitus chuckled. "Maybe Regulus is behind it."

"Regulus has recruited all sorts of scoundrels and cut-throats to do his dirty work, but I can't believe this nonsense even of him."

Apollodoros' ears perked up and he got to his feet. "Regulus? Do you mean Marcus Aquilius Regulus?"

My stomach knotted as I felt the movement of another latrunculus piece. "What do you know of Regulus?"

"I? Nothing, but when I was following Aristeas, someone told me they had seen him near Regulus' house in Rome."

"Does he know Regulus?"

"He never mentioned him. I don't even know if what I was told was true."

I wanted to get my mind off of Regulus for the moment. When I had time and quiet, I would puzzle over his involvement in this ... scheme. "I want you to tell me the truth." I pushed Apollodoros back onto his bed. "How can Aristeas appear to be dead?"

"He doesn't appear to be, sir. He is. And he comes back to life."

"How can you prove that?"

"His heart stops throbbing. If a man's heart isn't throbbing, he's dead, isn't he?"

That was the question I still couldn't answer. Yesterday I would have been sure I knew the answer. "Did you teach him how to do that, how to make his heart stop throbbing?"

"Is that what the empusa told you?"

"If an empusa can take on any shape, how do I know you're not one?" I hoped my servants guarding the door couldn't hear this conversation. If the rumor of some blood-drinking monster got started in my household, I would never be able to quell the panic.

"What we need," Tacitus said, "is to talk to Aristeas—if that is his name. He's the only one who can tell us which story is the truth."

"We should be out looking for him," Apollodoros said, standing up and grabbing his cloak.

I pushed him back down on the bed. "No one is going anywhere tonight. You're going to stay here, under guard, and Daphne is going to stay in another room, under guard."

"I doubt you can keep her where she doesn't want to be, sir. The empusa has powers you haven't even dreamed of. Do you know how she got here? Have you seen a horse? A carriage?"

"No, but I don't know how you got here either. Where is your horse? Your carriage? Now, enough of this nonsense. I'll talk to you again in the morning."

Tacitus and I left the room and I gave strict orders to the guards not to unbolt it or the room next door, where Daphne would be, for any reason. "No matter what they say to you or what you may hear in there, do not open these doors without my orders. Not my mother's orders, mind you, *my* orders. You will be whipped if you do anything else."

As we took seats in the arcade and helped ourselves to some wine, I sighed. "I hope that keeps the situation under control until tomorrow. I don't think I could deal with any more weirdness tonight. Is there a full moon?"

"Not for several more nights."

Blandina came into the arcade, reluctance written across her face. "My lord," she began and stopped.

"What is it?"

"Excuse me, my lord, but there's someone asking to see you."

I sighed. "No. It's dark, and I'm tired. Tell them to come back in the morning."

"She says it's urgent, my lord."

"She?"

"It's that woman from Laurentum, my lord, Chloris." She said the name with all the disdain that a servant in an aristocratic household could muster for someone who, being free, was actually of higher legal status than the servant herself.

Tacitus gave me an unmistakable pleading look. "We should see her, Gaius Pliny. She has come all this way."

I couldn't deny that I would welcome the sight of Chloris, even with her clothes on. "All right. Bring her in and have someone take care of her horse."

"There's no horse, my lord. She walked. Or ran mostly, from the look of her."

When Chloris came into the arcade she did look like she'd run a considerable distance, but she remained standing before us. She didn't have her breath back yet. "Thank you ... for seeing me, sir, at ... this late hour."

"Please, sit." I gestured to a chair. She didn't sit down so much as collapse into it.

"Blandina, get her something to drink." I hoped the stern look I gave my servant warned her not to spit in the cup. "Now, what brings you here so late?"

"It's murder, sir."

"Someone's been murdered? Who? Oh, by the gods, not your sister?"

"No, sir. It's that man who was looking for you yesterday."

"Aristeas?"

"Yes, sir. They found him in my sister's room, dead."

I sat back and dismissed her fears with a wave of my hand. "Then you don't have anything to worry about."

She looked at me in disbelief. "What do you mean? They've accused my sister of killing him."

"He only appears to be dead." I shook my head and smiled. "It's just an act. Wait until morning. He'll be awake again and everyone will see that your sister did nothing to him."

"Not meaning to offend, sir, but that can't be."

"I know it's hard to believe, but, trust me, he'll be all right in the morning."

She gave me a look of complete disbelief. "Sir, I've never seen a man wake up in the morning when his throat's been slashed the night before."

# VIII

**I** JUMPED UP FROM MY SEAT. "You ... you can't be serious," I said.

"I've never been more serious, sir."

"His throat was cut?"

Chloris drew a finger across her own throat.

"And the body was found in your sister's room?"

"Yes, sir."

Tacitus put a hand on my arm. "Slow down, Gaius Pliny." He turned to the redhead. "Why don't you tell us exactly what happened, Chloris, instead of us trying to pull the story out of you piece by piece?"

Tacitus and I moved our seats closer to her.

She took a long drink of the wine Blandina brought her and let out a deep breath. "Well, sir, I got back home less than an hour ago and there was a crowd around the door and all sorts of noise."

Tacitus snorted. "A crowd? In Laurentum? What is that, three people?"

"I didn't have time to count them, sir. Saturninus told me they had found this man in my sister's room. He said they were accusing Myrrha of murdering him and told me to get out of sight before they turned on me, too."

"So you didn't see the body?"

"No, sir."

"Then how do you know who he was or what happened to him?" Tacitus asked.

"Saturninus saw him. When my sister found him, she screamed and Saturninus came running to her. He recognized the man because he was the one who was in the cheese shop with us a few days ago. I had to get some help and you are the person I can depend on."

"Why me?" I asked.

"Because of this." She held out her right hand and pointed to the ring on her index finger. "Your uncle gave it to me."

I took her hand and bent over to examine the ring. It was silver, large and thick. Engraved around it I read *AMICA G PLIN SEC*— Friend of Gaius Plinius Secundus.

Chloris' red hair fell around her face as she leaned close to me. "He told me that, if I ever needed help, all I had to do was show this to someone in his household."

I let go of her hand and sat back to clear my head. This felt too much like the recognition scene in a Greek comedy. There's always some improbable token left with the abandoned child or the parted lovers—two halves of something that fit together. "He never said anything about it—or you—to me."

Tacitus leaned over to examine the ring. "This could have been made by anyone."

"But could this have been made by anyone?" She turned the ring on her finger so I could see the other side of it. There was a small imprint of a dolphin incised into the ring. "You wear your uncle's signet ring, don't you? I noticed it when you visited us."

I held up the ring on my right index finger. It has a dolphin embossed in the center and my uncle's name—now my name—around it. "Yes. I've worn it since he died."

"I believe you'll find that the dolphin on your ring fits into this one. Your uncle told me this one was made with his ring as the mold."

She took off the ring and handed it to me. I studied it for a moment, knowing that, if the two rings did fit together, my relationship with this woman would change forever.

"Aren't you going to try it?" Tacitus asked.

I put Chloris' ring on top of mine. The dolphin on my signet ring fit perfectly into the impression on her ring. I pulled them apart and tried it a second time, just to be sure. The dolphin fit as snugly as it had the first time.

"Well, there it is," Tacitus said.

There was no denying it. I leaned back in my chair and looked at the two rings. If my uncle had indeed accepted this woman into his *amicitia*—the status of a special friend—he had given her a claim on our family and imposed on our family an obligation to her.

"All right, friend of Gaius Plinius Secundus," I said as I handed the ring back to her and slipped my signet ring back on my finger, "what can I do to help you?"

"Please help me prove that my sister didn't kill that man."

"How do you know she didn't?"

She leaned forward, her face betraying a mixture of earnestness and fear. "Myrrha would never do anything like that. She *couldn't* do such a thing. She's a kind, loving person. She won't even kill the mice that infest our rooms—because of all that stinking cheese. I have to do it."

"It's impossible to say what any person would or would not do, given the provocation." My stomach tightened as I recalled what it felt like to plunge a knife into a man in order to save my own life. It wasn't something I ever wanted to do again, but I would if necessary. "Haven't you or your sister ever felt a threat from a man who was with you?"

"Once in a while a man gets a little rough. But they know, if they go too far, we won't let them in again."

"Do you keep a knife in your room?"

"Well, yes. Any woman who has men she doesn't know in her room would be a fool not to. But neither of us has ever had to resort to it."

"Besides," Tacitus said, "I think in those circumstances, she would stab the man, not slit his throat."

"But Myrrha wouldn't do either," Chloris insisted.

"Since you didn't see the body, how do you know how the man was killed?"

"Saturninus told me. He ran his finger across his throat, like this." She drew a long, elegant finger across her throat again, from one ear to the other. "He said it was a deep cut, the kind you make when you're sacrificing an animal. And there was blood on her gown."

"On the front or the back?"

"I don't know, sir. I didn't see her. I was just told."

"Could Myrrha have done this—?" Tacitus started to ask.

"She didn't do *anything*," Chloris said, jumping up from her chair. "She's the kindest person you'll ever know. She raised me. She's as much a mother to me as a sister."

"Please, calm down," I said. "Let's rephrase it. Could anyone have slit the man's throat while facing him?"

"I don't think so," Tacitus said. He got up from his chair and picked up the knife we'd been using to slice cheese. "To slit a man's throat deeply, you need to be behind him, to apply enough pressure." He stood behind Chloris, very close behind her. "And you have to hold his head, like this." He put his hand on her chin, drew her head back. Chloris grabbed his arm but didn't resist. "Then you plunge the knife in on one side and make the cut."

"You speak like one with experience at this," Chloris said as she pulled away from him.

Tacitus put the knife back on the tray. "Anyone who's sacrificed a sheep knows how to do it."

"But I could have pulled your arm away. Or bitten you."

"Not if I caught you completely off-guard."

"So we should assume," I said, "that whoever killed this man wasn't defending himself, or herself."

Tacitus nodded as he sat back down. "If the wound is as bad as Chloris has told us, it had to be murder."

I turned back to Chloris. "You say you learned about the murder when you got back home. Where had you been?"

"Why are you asking me that?"

"If your sister is already under suspicion, you soon will be."

"But I wasn't there. I wasn't even in Laurentum."

"Where were you?"

"Out for a while." She looked down at her hands.

"Chloris, if you want me to help you, you're going to have to be completely honest with me. That's your obligation if you're in my family's *amicitia*." I paused to let that admonition sink in. "Where were you?"

"I was keeping company with a gentleman in one of the villas around here."

"You were at his villa?"

"Yes, sir. We met in the tavern yesterday and he arranged to take me out to his house in a carriage. He picked me up about the second hour this morning. He brought me back the same way just before sunset."

"Who was he?"

"His name was Marcus, sir."

Tacitus snorted. "You can't turn around in Italy without hitting a man named Marcus."

*Including Marcus Aquilius Regulus,* I thought. "What did he look like?" There were so many villas along this stretch of the shore I couldn't know the owners of all of them—and some of them were rented out—but I might get lucky.

"He was older, probably fifty, with dark hair, thin on top. A little on the heavy side."

A description that fit Regulus ... and half the members of the Senate. "And Marcus is the only name he gave you?"

"Yes, sir. I knew he didn't want me to know who he was—many of my customers don't—and I didn't really care. Marcus, Publius, Gaius—what difference does it make to me? If you'll pardon me for saying so, I think of them all as just Mentula."

She spat out the derisive word for a man's private parts, but her voice carried a tone of acceptance rather than bitterness. I suspected she had gone past bitterness a long time ago.

"Where was his villa?" I asked.

"I'm not sure."

"How can you not be sure if you were there?"

"He said he wanted to play a little game, like he was kidnapping me. So he came into my room, tied me up and blindfolded me and took me to his carriage. He said he didn't want anyone to see us. It was part of the game."

"Did he blindfold you on the way back to Laurentum?" Tacitus asked.

"Yes, sir."

"And you didn't mind?"

"He paid very well." She pulled out a bulging coin pouch tied around her neck. "When a Mentula pays that well, I don't mind ... anything."

Tacitus' eyebrows arched. "Exactly what sort of 'anything'—?"

I cut him off with a wave of my hand. "That's not relevant right now." I reached out to Chloris but didn't touch her. "So you can't name the man. Was there anything about the villa that would allow you to identify it?"

She shook her head. "It was big, and very pretty. Mostly what I saw was one bedroom and the bath. All I know is, it wasn't this villa."

"And your sister wasn't with you?"

"No, sir."

"Do you know where she was during that time?"

"She was with a man. He took her out to his villa, too."

Tacitus and I exchanged a glance. "Were you both gone all day?" I asked.

"Yes, sir."

"Did the man who took your sister arrange that in advance?"

"Yes, sir. Yesterday. He told her he would come to our rooms. She was waiting for him when I left. We thought we were lucky to both have such well-paying ... offers. My sister is, as you saw, somewhat older than me. We're not sure how much longer men will want her. She wants to make all she can while she can."

"Do you know who she was with or where they went, or when she got back?"

Chloris wiped a tear. "I haven't had a chance to talk to her. They had already locked her up when I got home. I couldn't even get into my own rooms because of the crowd."

I looked over at Tacitus, who shrugged. "I guess we have to go," he said.

"Go where?" Chloris asked.

"To Laurentum," I said. "At once."

"But, sir, it's already dark. I was scared half to death coming out here. There's who knows what sort of creatures out there."

"I think most of the ones you need to be afraid of are locked up in my house right now."

She scrunched up her face in confusion.

"Never mind. If we're going to make any sense of this, we need to see your sister's room and, if at all possible, see the murdered man's body where it was found."

"He's dead, sir," Chloris said. "And he'll still be dead tomorrow morning."

"I'd like to think so, but—"

"Be reasonable, Gaius Pliny," Tacitus said. "It's a dangerous journey in the dark. And we wouldn't be able to see anything when we got there."

"I'm concerned about them moving the body before I can see it. You know how important that is to me."

"They've no place else to put it, sir," Chloris said. "I think they plan to leave him in Myrrha's room tonight and send to Rome to-morrow for someone to take charge. That's what Saturninus said. He was unhappy about it. Nobody'll want to buy cheese in his shop, he said, when there's a corpse in the back room."

"I imagine a dead man on the premises would dampen sales," Tacitus said. "Perhaps Saturninus could charge admission to see the fellow. That might offset his losses. Oh, and an extra fee to touch him. A bit more, even, to put your finger in his throat."

Chloris looked at him in dismay. "Sir, you can't be serious."

"You need not ever take Tacitus seriously," I said. "For him the world is a funny place."

"Not funny, my friend. Bizarre." He turned to Chloris. "Gaius Pliny, on the other hand, is never anything but serious. Since the day I met him, I've been trying to loosen him up. To no avail. I can't even get him drunk."

Ignoring him, I sent Blandina to get Hylas with his writing gear. When he arrived and was set up, I dictated a note to the duovirs, offering my services in determining what had happened to the man found in Myrrha's room and asking them to leave him there until I arrived. I also dictated a letter to Saturninus, asking him to do whatever he could to keep anyone from moving the body until I got there.

"I'll send these first thing in the morning, my lord," Hylas said.

"No. Find a couple of men and send them tonight. It's impera-tive that no one move that body."

"Isn't it risky, my lord, to have them on the road at night?"

"Give them money to stay overnight in Laurentum. I'll get there as soon as there's enough light to travel and try to get to the bottom of this."

I sealed the notes, looking at my signet ring in a new light, and Hylas went off to find messengers.

"But you're not a magistrate, sir," Chloris said.

"That's never stopped him before," Tacitus said.

"We've got the duovirs in Laurentum. Shouldn't they be the ones investigating?"

I snorted in disdain. "The Licinius family are still treating that office like it's their birthright, aren't they?

"Yes, sir. At least one of them holds it every year."

"They seem to have an endless supply of cousins and nephews."

"This year it's Scaevola and his son Strabo."

"Oh yes, those two. My uncle had some choice things to say about them. And they've not made any better impression on me in the past couple of days. They have no more idea of how to determine what happened in this case than they would of how to command a legion in battle."

"And you do, sir?"

"I have learned how to observe."

"Doesn't everyone do that, sir?"

"Everyone sees, few observe." That was one of my uncle's favorite aphorisms.

"Now, see," Tacitus said. "That's exactly what I mean. Have you ever heard anything so pompous?" He drew himself up and put his hand on his chest like an orator stressing his main point. " 'Everyone sees ... few observe.' "

I looked him right in the eye. "And fewer still know what to make of what they observe."

I slept very little. Three strangers were housed under my roof, and I wasn't sure if I could trust any of them, not even the one who wore a ring my uncle had given her. I locked my door, though I wasn't sure what good that would do against some sort of mythical monster, if that was in fact what I had confined in one—or more— of my bedrooms.

I felt I had gleaned one bit of useful information from talking with Chloris. It could not be coincidence that she and her sister had both been hired to be away from their home for the entire day. And whoever hired both women had tried to insure that no one saw them or the women leaving.

During one of my waking spells I decided to see whether the guards at Daphne's and Apollodoros' rooms were on duty. My suite of rooms is separated from the rest of the house by the long arcade where Tacitus and I had talked with Daphne and then Chloris. I built it that way, with its own latrine, furnace, and a small library, to assure me of privacy. Tonight, though, the walk over to the main part of the house seemed unusually long. I realized an empusa could devour everyone else in the house and I would have no knowledge of what was happening, just as I could not hear the merry-making when the servants were celebrating the Saturnalia.

Or something could kill me and no one else in the house would hear anything.

I stepped through one of the doors in the arcade onto the terrace overlooking the shore. The breeze extinguished my lamp, but my eyes quickly adjusted to the dark and the moonlight. Listening to the sea lapping against the rocks below me, I chided myself. The sea and the rocks were real. The moon that was trying to shine through the thin clouds was real. I would not let myself believe for even an instant that an empusa was real. As Tacitus said, it was just a story told by ignorant nurses trying to frighten their charges into behaving themselves.

When I got to the rooms where Daphne and Apollodoros were confined, next door to one another, I was relieved to see the guards safe and alert.

"Have you heard anything from inside?" I asked.

"No, my lord," one said and the others shook their heads.

I almost wished they had heard a complaint or a song. Without opening the doors, I couldn't guarantee there was anyone in either room. And I couldn't bring myself to open the doors, because I wasn't sure exactly who, or what, was in either room. A conundrum indeed.

"Do you want us to roust 'em out, my lord?" one of the guards asked. His face showed his lack of enthusiasm for the prospect.

"No. As long as everything is quiet here, I'll assume we have no problem. If we have to deal with something in the morning, then so be it."

"Yes, my lord," another one said. "At least it'll be morning. The empusa loses its powers when the sun comes up."

I let out a groan. "Who's been spreading that ridiculous story?"

"I've heard about the empusa all my life, my lord. My father swears he saw one when he was a boy."

"There is no empusa in there," I said, pointing to Daphne's room. "There's a *woman* named Daphne in there. And a *man* named Apollodoros in the other room."

"Whatever you say, my lord."

The only way I could win this argument would be to open the

door. I stepped up to Daphne's door and moved the heavy post which Tranio had set up as a brace to hold the door closed. My servants stepped back, hands on their swords.

"Everyone, be absolutely quiet," I said.

I pulled the door open just enough for us to peek in. The bed was at the far end of this room. The lamps outside the door cast barely enough light for us to see Daphne's sleeping form, with her face turned toward us, her garish white make-up clearly visible.

"Now, are you satisfied?" I whispered, closing the door and replacing the brace, jamming it in solidly. "There is no empusa. Just remember my orders: do not open these doors under any circumstances until I tell you to. And I mean *I*, in person, not my mother or anyone else who claims to be acting on my authority."

"Yes, my lord," they chorused.

The walk back to my room, even without a lamp, did not seem as long as the trip over here. The moon had broken through the clouds, giving me enough light, and my uncertainty was quieted by finding Daphne sleeping soundly in her room. And yet I was angry at myself for letting the fear of some monster creep into my mind. That was not how my uncle and my tutors had taught me to think. What's real is what you can see and touch and hear. If you have a report of something, even from someone you trust, you have to reserve judgment about it until you can verify it for yourself.

Chloris said she spent the day with some Mentula named Marcus. How would I ever prove that? Daphne said she was the daughter of the man I knew as Aristeas. Apollodoros said he was the son of that same man. The only way I might have verified either claim was to ask Aristeas, who was now lying on a prostitute's bed with his throat slit. If that was, in fact, what was real.

As I neared my room, I stopped. The door was open. I was sure I had left it closed. Straining to listen for any suspicious sound, I took a few steps toward the door. Something bumped.

Someone was in my room!

# IX

**I COULDN'T DECIDE** whether to call for some of my servants or risk going into the room alone. If I went to get help, the intruder could be gone by the time I got back. I wasn't afraid that there was a monster in my room. I don't believe in such things. And, besides, I had just seen Daphne asleep in her room.

Something bumped and a woman's voice said, "Ow!"

I stuck my head in the door and saw a form standing near the door to the latrine—the back of a very human form. Whoever it was had bumped into a small three-legged table and was rubbing the spot. That wouldn't have bothered an empusa. They supposedly have bronze legs.

Regaining some confidence, I called out, "Who's there?"

"Oh, good evening, sir." Chloris turned around toward me, straightening her gown. "I know this is forward of me, but I hope you don't mind if I make a claim on your friendship." She held up the hand on which she wore the ring my uncle had given her. In the moonlight coming through the windows the pale skin of her face and arms took on an alabaster sheen. Her red hair gleamed like a highly polished copper bowl. Her pale green gown seemed to shimmer. "I was frightened, being on that side of the house with some monster." Her voice had a convincing—or well-rehearsed—quaver to it.

"You've heard my servants jabbering, I take it."

"They say you have an empusa locked up over there."

"No. I have two people—admittedly two unusual people—locked up because they've told me very different, and very bizarre, stories about the man who's lying dead in your sister's room."

"What are you going to do with them?"

"Keep them locked up until this is all sorted out."

"You don't think they killed him, do you?"

"It seems unlikely, but I can't say until I know how the man died and how long he's been dead."

"How can you tell that?"

"There are signs I've learned to recognize."

She stepped close enough to me to put her hand on my arm. "I really am frightened, sir. Would you mind if I stayed the night here?"

"Not at all. There's a second bed in that alcove, behind the curtain." I pointed to a corner of the room. I liked to sleep there on the hottest summer nights. "You're welcome to use it."

From the slumping of her shoulders I could tell that wasn't what she had in mind when she came into my room. "Thank you, sir."

She drew back the curtain and left it open. Standing in front of the window she slipped off her gown and stood looking out at the bay for a moment.

In one respect Tacitus is right about me. I think about things too much, analyzing them from every possible angle, looking for analogies from things I've read to help me understand. This was one of those times. A beautiful woman was standing nude a few feet away from me, waiting for me to let her know that I wanted to get in bed with her. What was going through my head, though, was a Socratic argument about absolute beauty. One always seems to be able to find another woman more beautiful than the last woman one saw. If there is such a thing as absolute, perfect beauty, shouldn't one be able to find the absolutely perfect beautiful woman? Plato, of course, would argue that she could exist only on the level of the forms, to be known only—

Chloris turned away from the window and got into the bed. "Good night, sir."

"Good night, Chloris. I ... I hope you sleep well."

"Thank you, sir. And you too."

But I did not. I hardly slept at all. What kept me awake was Chloris' question: 'You don't think they killed him, do you?' She said they. It was just a slip of the tongue, I was sure, but it caused me to reconsider everything. I had been thinking of Daphne and Apollodoros as adversaries. What if *they* were in collusion?

I was thinking about getting up and walking on the veranda when Chloris slipped into my bed. I was lying on my side, facing away from her. Her breasts pressed against my back.

"Is this all right, sir? I could tell from your tossing that you weren't asleep."

Her sultry voice made Daphne, Apollodoros and the whole business vanish from my mind. She reached one hand around me and began to stroke me, turning me into an instant Priapus.

"Did Tacitus pay you to loosen me up, to make me less stiff?"

"If he did, I'm not doing such a good job, am I?" Her voice was low and throaty, as warm as a fire on a January night. "You seem to be getting even stiffer."

"You don't have to do this," I said. As good as it felt, I really didn't want to be just one more Mentula to her, or to any woman.

"You don't have to talk so much, sir." She kissed me on the shoulders and gently turned me onto my back.

Before I could tell her again that she didn't have to do anything, she took me in her mouth. *Oh, well,* I thought as my mind went blank. There's no sense making her give the money back. I'd never hear the end of it from Tacitus.

When we were finished, Chloris started to get out of the bed, her usual practice with most Mentulas, I presumed. There was always another one waiting outside the door.

"Please, stay," I said, patting the spot beside me where she had just been lying. Unable to hide her surprise and pleasure, she slipped back into the bed and I drew her close to me. Once she was settled, with her head on my chest, I realized I didn't know quite what to say. Not sending her away had felt like the right thing to do, but what now? Finally I came up with, "Thank you."

"Thank your friend Tacitus. He's very generous. I hope *you* got *his* money's worth."

I stared at the ceiling. It saddened me to think that such a moment of pleasure and intimacy as we had just shared was, in her mind, reduced to a commercial transaction. Was value received for money paid? The same question could be asked when I bought cheese in Saturninus' shop. I recently read a treatise by Musonius Rufus, a man whom I admire immensely, on why women should study philosophy. He says that, "above all a woman must be chaste and self-controlled ... pure in respect of unlawful love, not a slave to desire."

But in Rome how could a woman ever live such a life? If she was a slave, she could be bought and sold, used and abused, on a man's whim. If she was free, we men made certain that she went from her father's house to her husband's. If, like my mother, she found herself a widow, she had to depend on a male relative, unless she managed to outlive them all. The only women who weren't constantly under a man's direct control were those who sold their bodies to us, one Mentula at a time. Even they could be obligated to a man if they fell into the clutches of a procurer. I wondered how Myrrha and Chloris had avoided that fate.

The itch that I get to know things compelled me to ask. "How old were you the first time you were ... with a man?"

Chloris' voice got very soft and I felt her whole body tense. "I was ten."

"By the gods! That young?" I held her closer and looked at her. Marriages are often arranged for girls of twelve or thirteen, if they have started their monthlies by then, but ten?

"A Mentula came to see Myrrha one day." Chloris pulled the blanket up over her. Her voice took on a child-like quality. "She had gone out on an errand. He was angry because she wasn't there when he expected her to be. He said I would have to do."

"Who was the monster?"

"It doesn't matter. He turned up dead a few days later."

"Dead?" I was surprised, but I thought it was exactly what he deserved. "What happened to him?"

She pulled me closer beside her and patted my chest. "Please, sir. I don't ... want to talk about it."

"All right. I'm sorry to dredge up such an awful memory."

"We all have them, sir. They spring up of their own accord at times, it seems."

I could feel her relaxing as she leaned into me. I ran my hand over hers as it rested on my chest, tracing the lettering on her ring. "Did my uncle give a ring like this to Myrrha?" I asked.

"No, sir. He said mine was the only one he'd ever had made."

"Did he tell you why he gave it to you?" The reason seemed obvious—after tonight I would gladly give her a lot more than a ring—but I still had to ask the question.

"No, sir." She rested her chin on my shoulder. "And it's not what you're thinking. I never coupled with him."

"You never—?"

"No, sir. Never."

"Then why did he come to see you?"

"He said he liked to talk to me. I think he was lonely after his woman Monica died. He talked a lot about her."

"And you didn't mind? You weren't jealous?"

"Jealous of what? He paid me for my time, just like any other man, but he wasn't just like any other man."

"He wasn't a Mentula?"

I could feel her cheek warming as she blushed. "No, sir. He was very kind, and very generous. He hired a tutor for me to teach me how to read and write, and he gave me books to read. You should be proud to carry his name."

By the time the sun was fully up the next morning we were on the road to Laurentum. Because the road is unpaved, riding horses is faster, but, with rain threatening, I thought we would welcome the cover of a raeda. Mine carries four comfortably. It had been delivered just a month ago, so the paint and decorations were still fresh. The scent of the wood permeated the interior and the cushions on the seats were plump. Chloris sat in the rear-facing seat, with Tacitus and me opposite her, facing forward.

On the floor between us sat a basket. My mother insisted on sending food with us, as though we were on some sort of pleasure outing. She assured me that she would not release Apollodoros from his room before I returned. I doubted that, but I knew she wouldn't let Daphne out, so the two of them shouldn't have a chance to come to blows.

"It'll be interesting to see if a seven-hundred-year-old man has finally met his match," Tacitus said as we set off.

I was sorry he had brought that whole business up because we had to explain to Chloris what we had read about Aristeas and what Apollodoros claimed about him. She took it all in and asked several questions. She seemed as agile with her mind as she was with her hands and mouth. I could see why my uncle would enjoy talking to her. That would make the trip to Laurentum worth it.

But I wanted to change the subject. "I used to hear my uncle talk about the Licinius family. What do you know about them?" Small-town magistrates, especially those living close to Rome, can be either ambitious men who want to advance their careers to the capital or men whose ambitions and abilities will never carry them more than a few miles from where they were born. My uncle had had nothing but contempt for this clan.

"I know that Licinius Strabo likes to take me from behind," Chloris said. "And he'd sooner part with one of his balls than an extra denarius."

Over Tacitus' laughter I said, "I was thinking in ... larger terms. What sort of men are they?"

Tacitus elbowed me. "I think she just told you a lot about this Strabo."

Chloris touched the ring my uncle had given her, as if to reassure herself of something. "The Licinius family think the post of duovir is their personal property, and I guess it is. Nobody has challenged them in years. This year Quintus Licinius Strabo and his father, Lucius Scaevola, have it. Strabo runs the show. His father is just there because there have to be two."

That certainly wasn't the impression they'd given when they came to my house, but Chloris saw them in different situations than I did. "They must have some wealth."

"They own two of the baths and two of the taverns."

The raeda drew quite a bit of attention as we pulled up in front of Saturninus' shop. Jaws dropped when Chloris stepped down. Like a lady accustomed to traveling in such style, she ignored the gawkers and led us into the shop.

"Good morning, sirs," Saturninus said. "I'm glad you come so early."

I stopped to inhale the glorious aroma of his cheeses before I returned his greeting. "Did you deliver my note to the duovirs?"

"Yes, sir. That I did. And they was none too happy about it, especially Strabo. He told me to let him know the moment you arrived."

"Let's pretend that moment isn't here yet. I would like some time to examine the body before I have to deal with an annoyed local official."

Saturninus shook his bald head woefully. "It's a terrible sight, sir. Terrible. Don't know why you want to get yourself involved in this business." He gave Chloris a disapproving glance but otherwise did not acknowledge her. I had to ask myself again why he rented rooms to women whom he so obviously despised.

"I have more reason to be involved than you know. I hope you won't be in too much of a hurry to notify Strabo."

"I'm an old man, sir. I can't hurry, but news of your raeda will get to him before I do. We don't see contraptions that fancy around here every day."

"Let's get to work then," I said to Tacitus and Chloris. She pulled out her key to the room and we followed her out of the cheese shop.

Chloris and Myrrha lived in three windowless rooms on the back of Saturninus' building. Given the stench from the alley leading to the back of the building, the lack of windows was probably a blessing.

"Just a moment," Chloris said as she unlocked the outer door, which faced west. It led into a common room, with a bedroom off to each side. The whole place, in spite of colorful frescos with old-fashioned geometric shapes, was as dim as a cave, but I could make out a table and two chairs in the center of the room.

Moving as comfortably as a blind man in his own surroundings, Chloris found and lit a small oil lamp for each of us. With even that little light, I could see a pair of feet at the end of Myrrha's bed.

"He's still here, thank the gods," I said.

Tacitus pinched his nose. "The smell and the flies testify to that."

The aroma of the women's perfume and cosmetics could not mask the stench of death emanating from Myrrha's room. Instead of making it bearable, the sweetness made the reek even more nauseating.

I led the way into Myrrha's room, which held only a bed, a small table beside it, and a chest. Except for the unsightly naked corpse, it appeared as neat as it did modest. Tacitus and I took up positions on opposite sides of the bed, while Chloris hung back in the doorway.

"I thought there would be a lot of blood," Tacitus said, raising his lamp and running it over the bed and the wall.

"Yes, that is curious," I said. I turned to Chloris. "Has anything been disturbed?"

She raised her lamp and glanced around. "No, sir."

"You said your sister keeps a knife near her bed. Where is it?"

With her back touching the wall, Chloris edged her way around the bed to the table beside the head of the bed. Reaching under it, she pulled out a knife. "There's a bracket under the table."

"Out of sight, but very handy," Tacitus said with admiration.

"Myrrha designed it herself. She's as good as most men when it comes to things like that."

I held the knife up to my lamp. It was extremely sharp. "There's no blood on it."

"I told you, sir, she didn't do this. She couldn't have. You've got to help me prove that."

"The first thing I have to do is see if I can figure out how this man was killed. Then we'll worry about who did it."

Replacing the knife, I took Chloris' lamp and set it on the table. I cast only a cursory glance at Aristeas' head, enough to see his thin beard and satisfy myself that this was the man I'd found on my property and locked up in my stable. The only difference I could see was that he was no longer 'lifeless but not dead.'

He was definitely dead.

Tacitus held his lamp over Aristeas' torso. "I thought you said he had a mark like a raven's head on his chest."

I jerked my lamp over the man so quickly that I spilled some hot oil on him. If his gaping throat and the smell weren't enough to convince me that he was dead, his lack of any reaction to the burning oil provided all the proof I needed.

"It was above his left nipple." But there was no raven's head, no mark of any kind, on either side of his chest. Leaning over and holding my lamp close enough to singe a few hairs, I still could not make out any trace of a raven's head.

"You're sure this is the same man?" Tacitus asked.

I straightened up, hoping the gloom concealed the consternation on my face. "Yes, I'm sure of it." I waved my lamp over his face again. There was no mistaking him.

"It is, sir," Chloris said. "That's the man Myrrha and I met in the tavern and directed to your house. I didn't see any mark on his chest, but I'd know him anywhere."

"The mark must have been drawn on," I said, "and he erased it before he died. Or whoever killed him erased it."

Tacitus pursed his mouth and shook his head. "I don't see any indication that anything was erased. There's no redness." Like a woman teasing a lover, he ran one finger across Aristeas' chest. "One side feels the same as the other." He wiped his finger on the bedding.

125

"Well, I saw it, and a number of my servants did, too. That's all I know."

"There's no mark here," Tacitus said. "That's all I know."

"Maybe it was his soul," Chloris said from behind us.

"His soul?" I turned to face her. My lamp made her shadow flicker against the wall. "What are you babbling about?"

"Remember what your uncle wrote," Tacitus said. "The soul of Aristeas was seen flying out of his mouth in the shape of a raven."

"I remember that. Do you remember that my uncle dismissed the story as nonsense? And so do I."

Chloris held out her hands, as though pleading with me. "But, sir, you should examine—"

"What I'm going to examine right now is the body of a dead man." With my hand on her shoulder I guided her toward the door. "This space is too small for three of us, so please wait outside."

"I want to know what you know, sir, if my sister is charged with killing him. And I might be able to answer questions for you."

She had a point, and a good grip on the doorpost. I wasn't going to be able to move her and I didn't have time to persuade her to leave. The duovirs might arrive at any moment. "All right. Stand in that corner and keep out of our way."

I turned to the business of examining Aristeas' body from the feet up, with Tacitus holding the other lamp and leaning over from his side of the bed. Grasping one of the dead man's ankles, I tried to raise his leg, but it wouldn't bend.

"The full death stiffness has set in. He's been dead at least twelve hours." In his unpublished notes, my uncle had commented on how bodies gradually stiffen after death, remain stiff for a couple of days, then relax again. He had no explanation for the phenomenon, nor did I yet.

"What's that mark on his ankle?" Tacitus asked. "Wait, on both ankles."

We bent over and brought our lamps close to Aristeas' feet. Bands of discolored skin ran around his ankles. "I think he was tied up."

"What about his hands?" Tacitus asked.

We moved up to examine Aristeas' hands and found similar, but lighter, marks around his wrists. His arms, straight down by his sides, were as stiff as his legs.

"Why do the marks around his ankles look so much darker?"

"Equally puzzling, why are there no dark splotches on the lower side of his body?"

"Are you sure your uncle was right about that? Whichever side of the body a person lies on after death, dark splotches develop there?"

"He noticed it a number of times, and I have yet to see otherwise."

"So, if there are no dark splotches on any part of this man's body, does that mean he died standing up?"

I looked at Aristeas' ankles again. "No, he died hanging upside down."

Behind us Chloris gasped.

Tacitus looked at me in disbelief. "Hanging ... by his feet?"

"Yes, like an animal being slaughtered. That's why the marks around his ankles are darker, from his struggle and from his weight."

I moved up to Aristeas' head and focused on his throat for the first time. The gash across it was every bit as gruesome as the descriptions I'd heard. The flies buzzed in and out of it like bees going in and out of their hive. His head was barely still attached to his shoulders.

"He was hung by his feet and the blood drained out of his throat," I concluded.

"Who would do such a thing?" Tacitus asked, shaking his head.

"The woman we have locked up," a man's voice said behind us.

We turned to see Licinius Strabo standing in the door of Myrrha's room. Scaevola and several attendants lingered behind him.

"Good morning, duovirs."

"What are you doing here?" Strabo demanded, omitting any pleasantries.

"I'm here to assist Chloris. She is—"

"I know who she is," Strabo sneered.

*And I know you like to take her from behind*, I thought. "What you probably don't know is that I count Chloris among my friends."

Strabo understood what that meant, even if he couldn't fathom why a man wearing the equestrian stripe would elevate a prostitute to that status. I had no doubt he would sacrifice one of his testicles to gain it. Probably cut the thing off himself. He looked from me to Chloris and back again.

"What are you doing here?" His tone still wasn't friendly, but he had softened it, the way men do when they speak to someone from whom they might someday need to ask a favor. "And why did you send me that imperious note last night?"

"I'm sorry the note offended you, duovir. Chloris asked me to look into this matter. Since she is a friend, I am obliged to do so and—more importantly—happy to do so. I needed for this room to be undisturbed until I could get here."

"And so it is," Strabo said.

"Yes, it is. Thank you for acceding to my request."

"What choice did I have?" he groused. "That old fool Saturninus locked the door and wouldn't let anyone near it." He surveyed the room. "Have you seen what you need to see?"

"We're making progress."

Scaevola still hadn't spoken, but from behind he gave Strabo a barely perceptible nudge. "Well, I want to finish this business to-day," Strabo said.

"Are you that far along in your inquiry? The body was just found yesterday evening."

Strabo waved an arm in exasperation. "It's a simple case. A man was found in Myrrha's room with his throat slit. This time she won't get away with it."

" 'This time'? What do you mean by that?"

"Fifteen years ago a man was murdered in this same fashion. He was found in the old well behind this very building."

I looked at Chloris, who seemed to be trying to make herself smaller in her corner. That was an important detail to fail to tell a friend.

"Now she's murdered a man in her own bed," Strabo went on. "This time she'll meet the fate she deserves in the arena."

"Before you pack her off to Rome, duovir, may I ask you one question?"

Strabo nodded smugly.

"Where's the blood?"

"What do you mean?"

"When a man's—or an animal's—throat is cut in this fashion, blood spurts everywhere. We've all seen an animal being sacrificed."

Strabo rubbed his chin, still red from that morning's shave, while

128

he searched for an answer. Scaevola finally spoke. "Most of it is on the whore's gown."

"Are you suggesting," Tacitus put in, "that a woman could cut this man's throat without splattering blood on the walls and bed linens?"

"If she were sitting or standing right over him, I think she could," Scaevola said. He stepped around Strabo and into the room.

"Why would she kill him?"

"Why do women do anything?" Scaevola shot Chloris a menacing glance. "In any case—blood or no blood—she killed him. Why else would the body be here?"

I pointed to Aristeas' ankles. "Do you think she tied him up, too?"

"She's a whore. I'm sure he wouldn't be the first man she's tied up."

Once Scaevola began talking, Strabo fell silent and moved to the side of the room, deferring to his father just as he had at my home the previous night. I wondered if Chloris had been right in her perception of who was running things.

"With all respect, duovir, I don't see any reason for Myrrha to have done this to a man who was a stranger. He'd been in Laurentum only a day or two. Myrrha and Chloris bought him some cheese. There's no evidence of enmity between them, no reason for her to kill him."

"She had no reason for enmity fifteen years ago either. The man she killed then frequented this ... place."

"Why wasn't she arrested then?"

"Because your uncle found witnesses—I won't say he paid them—to testify to her innocence."

I was only seven when all of that happened and had heard nothing about it. "No one was ever arrested for that crime?"

"No, no one."

"Who was the man who was killed?"

"A nephew of mine, Marcus Licinius Macer."

With each word out of his mouth I felt like Myrrha had taken another step toward the arena.

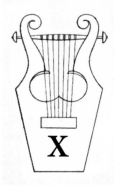

# X

"**H**AVE YOU SEEN ENOUGH, Gaius Pliny?" Licinius Scaevola said, leaving me in no doubt that I had indeed seen all I was going to be allowed to see.

"I guess I have. What do you intend to do with the body?"

"What does one do with any unwanted corpse? We'll burn it as soon as possible and dispose of the remains."

I couldn't let that happen yet. "Let me offer to save you the trouble."

"What do you mean?"

"Two people who claim to be this man's son and daughter are presently at my house." Tacitus coughed, but I ignored him. "They should have an opportunity to perform the appropriate rites for their father. I'd like to take his body with me."

To judge just from the number of attendants, like a pack of hounds, that I could see over Scaevola's shoulder, I knew I would not be able to force the issue, but I did not want this body reduced to ashes so quickly. I had seen enough to conclude that Aristeas had died in a bizarre manner. The missing raven's head mark was one question I had not yet answered. I wanted to examine his chest in full daylight and at my own leisure—or at least as much leisure as a decaying corpse afforded me.

The two duovirs looked at one another for an instant, then Scaevola nodded. "We have sufficient witnesses to the condition of the body. I see no reason to deny your request. We always try to be respectful of family obligations." His tone was as oily as his hair. "I didn't know this man had children."

"I met them only yesterday," I said.

"Where is my sister?" Chloris asked from the dimness of her corner. "May I see her?"

"That was to be my next request," I said.

"She's locked up," Scaevola said. "I suppose we can make arrangements for you to talk with her before we send her to Rome. She's a strong one, and a fighter. She'll give them quite a show in the arena."

Like any ambitious magistrate across the empire, Scaevola knew how to curry favor with Rome. Domitian has a voracious appetite for victims for the spectacles in his father's amphitheatre. Punishment of criminals is not the only purpose of the games. The audience must be amused, and they have become so jaded that the quest for new types of entertainment has strayed into the realm of the bizarre. Women are now being forced to fight as gladiators or act out mythical scenes such as Minos' wife Pasiphae mating with a bull. I couldn't let an innocent woman be subjected to something as humiliating as that.

"You're going to send her to Rome?" Chloris cried. "Please, sir, why are you—?"

I raised a hand to silence her. There was no need to heighten Scaevola's animosity toward the two women. He clearly held a grudge against them, and against my family, and it went back to the murder of his nephew.

"Chloris, you asked me as your friend to look into this matter. Please, let me do that." I turned to Scaevola. "I would like to talk to Myrrha and I'll need to hire a cart to take Aristeas' body out to my house."

Scaevola nodded. "You certainly don't want to be hauling him in that fancy rig of yours. It will take a bit to arrange that. That's how long you'll have to talk to Myrrha. I'll take you to her. Strabo, find a cart and a driver to take the body."

I left one of my servants to stand watch over the raeda. The rest of us followed Scaevola and his pack of hounds along the main street of the village, two blocks east to his house. It was the last house in town and had a wall around it like some country estates. He led us through the gate and around to the back. The grounds were meticulously kept. Walkways paved with travertine wound among fruit trees that were beginning to put out leaves and flowers. Several four-legged dogs greeted him and inspected us. Behind the house was an exhedra decorated with a fresco of the gods banqueting on Olympus. Zeus looked suspiciously like the master of this house. Beyond the exhedra was a well and storage areas for tools and animals' tack. Farther on I could see stables.

Scaevola stopped and pointed to an ergastulum, the small shed used to confine unruly slaves. This one had no windows. "She's in there." He turned and walked away, scratching the head of one of the four-legged dogs.

The door of the shed had a bar across it. Chloris ran ahead of me, lifted the bar and opened the door. Even though the weather was mild, the inside of the shed was oppressively warm and airless. Myrrha sat slumped against the back wall, her chin down on her chest, her gown and her hair soaked in sweat. She looked ten years older than the last time I saw her.

"Myrrha! It's me." Chloris took her sister in her arms.

Myrrha slowly opened her eyes. "Help me," she whispered.

"She needs water," I said, kneeling beside Chloris.

Tacitus went to the well and drew a bucketful. "Give it to her slowly," he told Chloris. "Too much too fast will make her sick."

"Can we get these things off of her?" Chloris grabbed the manacles on Myrrha's wrists.

"I don't have a key," I said, "and I think we've asked all the favors Scaevola's likely to grant us. Let's move her out here." With Tacitus taking one arm and I the other, we helped Myrrha stand up. That's when we noticed the brownish-red stains.

"That must be the blood he was talking about," Tacitus said.

I peered closely and sniffed the large dark splotch on the lower part of the woman's gown. "Yes, it is."

We moved Myrrha to the shade of a tree and helped her sit on a bench. Chloris pushed in close and put her arm around her sister, who began to revive with the water and the fresh air. I sent a servant to get the basket of food my mother had sent with us. It appeared it would be useful after all.

Before I could ask a question, Myrrha said, "I didn't kill nobody, sir. I'll swear it by any god you like. I didn't kill nobody."

I put a hand on her shoulder. "If we're going to find out what happened, you need to tell me everything you can about where you were and what you did yesterday. And you'll have to tell us how that blood got on your gown."

"Somebody threw it on me, sir."

"Who? When?"

"I don't know who, sir, but it happened yesterday." Her words still came with effort.

"How could you not know who threw blood on you?"Tacitus asked.

"I was blindfolded, sir."

"Wait," I said. "Start at the beginning and tell us what happened to you yesterday."

"Yes, sir. 'Twas a most unusual day, even in my line of work. Just when a whore gets to a point where she thinks she's seen or done anything a man is willing to pay her to do, somethin' stranger always comes along. Day before yesterday a man came in the tavern and gave me fifty aurei. He told me to be sitting alone at the table in my rooms yesterday mornin' at dawn, with my back to the door, and not to be surprised at anything. There would be another fifty aurei when we was done, he said."

"How long does it usually take you to earn that much?" Tacitus asked.

"Three months, sir. Four months if things is slow."

"Did you know the man?" I asked.

Myrrha shook her head. "He were a servant, though, I'm sure."

"Do you often get ... invitations to men's homes around here?"

"Oh, yes, sir. Especially when they come down from Rome without their wives. They'll sometimes take us on for several days. It's a bit of a vacation for us."

"So what happened this time?"

"I did just like he said."

"Chloris wasn't there?"

"No, sir," Chloris said. "Like I told you, I had been ... engaged for the day. When I left Myrrha was sitting at the table."

"Go ahead, Myrrha. What happened?"

"A man jumped me from behind and threw a sack over my head. I started to fight back until he said, 'Fifty aurei.' Then I let him do what he wanted."

"And what was that?"

"He tied and gagged me."

"With the sack still over your head?"

"Yes, sir. I could hardly breathe. He carried me just a short piece and threw me into a carriage and we rode for a while. When we stopped he tossed me over his shoulder like sack of wheat and took me inside a house."

"Can you describe the man or the house?"

"No, sir. I was blindfolded and tied up the whole time. He coupled with me a few times during the day. Or it might have been different men, I suppose. No one ever said anything."

The servant who had gone after the food basket returned and Chloris helped Myrrha eat. When she was finished I asked, "Can you tell us anything more about where you were? Did you hear any sounds you could identify? Waves on the shore? Servants talking? Animals?"

"No, sir. I'm sorry. I want to help. I just know I was in a room with my hands tied behind my back and a tight blindfold on. And I was tied to a bed."

"And someone threw blood on you?"

Myrrha nodded. "A couple of times somebody brought in a chamberpot for me to piss in. After I did that the second time, I felt them throw something wet on me. I thought it was my own piss. You know, to humiliate me."

"When did you realize it was blood?"

"My gown started to feel clammy and sticky, and blood has a smell all its own."

"Do you know how long you were there?"

"No, sir. There wasn't no window in the room, so I couldn't get a sense of where the sun was. After what felt like a long time somebody come and untied me from the bed but left my hands tied and the blindfold on. They put me in a wagon and drove me back here. They dropped me just inside my door."

I had to wait while Chloris helped her eat a little more and drink some water. "How were you able to get loose?"

"They loosened the ropes before they put me out of the wagon. I managed to get 'em off me soon enough."

"But not soon enough to see who did all of this to you."

"No, sir. They was long gone by then."

"So they didn't pay you the other fifty aurei?"

"Oh, but they did, sir. It was in a bag around my neck, with a note in it."

"What did the note say?"

"I wish I knew, sir. I could recognize my name on it. That was all. Chloris is the one that can read. But it must have been somethin' bad."

"Why do you say that?"

"I wondered why they had thrown blood on me and ruined one of my gowns. I thought maybe the note was an apology for that. As soon as I got my bearings I went into my room to get a clean gown. That's when I found him—that man, on my bed, with his throat ripped open."

"What did you do?"

"I screamed. I screamed so loud Saturninus heard me and come running."

"And there you stood," Tacitus said, "with a dead man in your bed and blood all over your gown."

Myrrha started to cry and Chloris embraced her. "I tried to tell him I didn't do it," the older woman said, "but he wouldn't listen. He hates me anyway. He grabbed me and sent a servant to get the duovirs."

"You said the note said something bad. How do you know?"

"Well, the duovirs read the note and looked at one another like they knew something. Then they put these on me." She raised her shackled hands. "And took the bag of coins."

"But they didn't read the note to you?"

"No, sir. They just nodded and Licinius Strabo tucked it into the sinus of his toga. They said the money was all the proof they needed."

Tacitus applauded. "Amazing. I've never heard such a preposterous concoction. It's worthy of a Milesian tale."

"But, sir, it's true. I didn't kill that man. That was the money for what I'd been through that day. And it warn't nearly enough."

"What makes you think she's not telling the truth?" I asked Tacitus. "It looks like someone wanted her away from her rooms for the day and didn't want her to be able to identify anyone or any place she saw."

"But what if she did kill him and wanted to come up with a story that puts her away from here but doesn't make her actually account for where she was?"

"Then where was she today?"

Tacitus picked a few leaves off the tree he was standing under and crushed them between his fingers. "Possibly right here killing Aristeas.

She's got blood all over her, and her knife was certainly handy. That's the argument Scaevola's going to make."

I turned back to Myrrha. "Are you sure you can't tell anything about where you were or who you were with?"

"No, sir. Not a thing."

Pulling Tacitus away from the women, I lowered my voice and said, "Do you think a simple woman like her could make up such an improbable story?"

"It would fit right in with a seven-hundred-year-old man and an empusa, wouldn't it?"

"Do you really think she could have killed Aristeas?"

"No, but I wanted you to see how easily Scaevola could make his case."

"Do you have any idea what's going on?"

"None, and it scares me."

I was glad to hear I wasn't the only one who was unnerved by all that had happened over the last couple of days. "Someone clearly wanted these women away from their home for the entire day, but in a way that left them unable to establish where they were."

We sat down with the women and I questioned Chloris. "You weren't treated like your sister, were you?"

"No, sir. I was blindfolded in the wagon going to and from the place, but not once I arrived at whatever house I was taken to."

"But she's not the one who's being made to look guilty," Tacitus said.

I nodded. "For some reason they want to shift all the blame onto Myrrha. And there have to be several people involved to carry out such an elaborate scheme."

"Two houses," Tacitus said.

"Not necessarily. Both women could have been at the same house, each unaware of the other."

"Agreed. But why would someone go to such lengths to make it look like some stranger was killed by a couple of whores?"

I flinched when Tacitus used the term. After all, Chloris was one of my friends. "And why would someone take so much trouble to kill an iterant shyster like Aristeas? Why not just ambush him in an alley or on the road out in the country?"

Licinius Scaevola walked around the corner of the house, with

Strabo by his side and followed by his dogs—both two-legged and four-legged. "The body is ready for you to take back to your house," he announced, "so your interview with the prisoner is over."

As the younger man I should have stood to show my respect to Scaevola, but my equestrian stripe outranked his plain toga. "I still have a number of other questions to ask her."

"What other questions could there be? We have a murdered man, found in this whore's room. We have the whore herself standing over him in a blood-soaked garment. We have a money bag she must have taken from the dead man—"

"How do you know that?"

"Where else would she have gotten it?"

"You know her profession."

Scaevola shook his head. "No whore makes the kind of money that was in that bag."

Tacitus gave a quick laugh. "I've known a couple—"

"What if someone paid her to kill the man?" Strabo asked over his father's shoulder.

Chloris gasped and Myrrha wailed, "Oh, sir! I didn't kill him!"

In his effort to indict Myrrha, Strabo had given me another argument in my case. "Isn't the person who pays someone to commit a crime just as guilty as the person who does the deed?"

Scaevola folded his arms over his chest. "You're wasting my time, young man." I wasn't sure if he meant me or his son. "This woman is going to be sent to Rome and, I'm sure, will be in the arena within a few days."

"But she hasn't been found guilty in a court. There's been no testimony against her."

"She provided all the testimony anyone needs. She was found standing over a man who had been savagely murdered." He signaled two of his brutes. "Lock her back up."

With Chloris clinging to her, Myrrha was dragged back to the ergastulum. One man pulled Chloris away while the other one, with scratches on his face from his earlier encounter with Myrrha, crammed her, still protesting her innocence, into the shed and closed and barred the door. I moved to Chloris' side and guided her away from the shed before Scaevola's man could hurt her.

"You must leave," Scaevola said. "*Now.* You can't do anything here but upset the prisoner."

"I am going to look into this matter further," I said. "I want you to keep Myrrha here, under kinder conditions, for at least ... two days." My words were drowned out by Myrrha's cries and her pounding on the door.

"Gaius Pliny, you have no authority here. And no interest in this case. Even if that creature is." —He sneered at Chloris.— "for some unfathomable reason, a 'friend' of yours, this other one isn't. I must demand that you stay out of the way and let me do my duty. All you have to take care of is a rotting corpse."

This time there was no mistaking that Aristeas was dead. Although the cart Scaevola had provided to transport the body stayed behind my raeda on the way home, the breeze was from that direction, and the day was growing quite warm. If it had not been for the aroma of new cedar wood in the raeda, I think we all would have gotten sick from Aristeas' stench. As it was, the bouncing of the carriage combined with the odor brought me dangerously close to nausea.

"Is my sister going to die in the arena, sir?" Chloris asked, wiping her nose and sniffling. She was sitting next to me, with Tacitus across from us. The warmth of her leg, pressed against mine, gave me something more pleasant to concentrate on.

"I will do everything within my power to prevent it. I have to warn you, though, that Scaevola has what looks like enough 'evidence' to convince most people of her guilt. He'll have to bring a charge against her and call for a hearing. I'll speak in her defense, but I don't know who the jury will be."

"The cream of Scaevola's *clientela*, no doubt," Tacitus said.

"The dregs, more likely. And no matter how many of them have coupled with Myrrha, they'll vote the way he wants them to." I put my hand on Chloris' knee, causing Tacitus' eyebrows to rise. "I'll present her case as I see it, but I don't know what I can do beyond that."

"Thank you, sir. I'm sure you can save her."

"I'll have a better chance if you don't conceal information from me in the future."

Chloris looked down and shook her head. "I didn't mean to hide anything, sir. I just didn't see how something that happened fifteen years ago had any connection to this."

"When a close relative of the duovirs was murdered and your sister and my uncle were suspected of having something to do with it, there is a strong connection. Scaevola has been waiting all this time to get back at Myrrha. Now that I've walked onto the stage, he sees a chance to settle another old score at the same time."

Chloris took my hand and placed it over hers so that the dolphin on my ring fit into the place it had made on hers. I knew she was staking her claim on my friendship and I could not back away from this fight.

"I'm sure you can beat him, sir."

I wasn't at all sure. I looked out the window at the budding trees and wondered if I had really been sitting under one only two days ago congratulating myself on how tranquil my life was. Scaevola was determined to exact his vengeance on Myrrha, for his own reasons and to curry favor with Rome. Holding no official position here, it would be difficult for me to stop him. The cases in which I had appeared in court thus far had been civil, not criminal. It's one thing to win a jury to your side when only money is at stake. With a life hanging in the balance, I might have to ask Tacitus to teach me a few of his oratorical tricks.

"What do you make of that mark disappearing," Tacitus asked, "and that business of Aristeas' soul leaving his body like a raven flying off."

"I'm sure when we can examine the body in full daylight we'll see where the mark was erased, just as you can always see the erasure on a piece of papyrus if you look closely enough."

"You don't think his soul could have darted off?"

I snorted in derision and shook my head.

"You shouldn't be so quick to dismiss something because you don't understand it, sir," Chloris said, leaning into me more than she needed to as the raeda took a curve.

"You presume a great deal on my friendship," I reminded her. "I understand that when we die, that's the end of our existence. Birds don't come flying out of our mouths, or out of any other orifice. I've stood over a man as he died, so I can bear witness to that."

"That may be true, sir, for most of us—the ordinary ones. But what about those who are ... extraordinary?"

"Are you saying this man was some sort of god or demigod?"

"He either was or he wasn't. Aren't those the only two choices?"

"Yes." I suddenly felt like one of Socrates' students being led to a conclusion he didn't want to agree with. The money my uncle spent on Chloris' tutor had not been wasted.

"And if he was a demigod, then he was something between a mortal and a god—more than a mortal and less than a god—wasn't he?"

"Yes," I said with a grunt as the raeda hit a hole in the road.

"And the lives of demigods are either the same as ours or different from ours, are they not?"

"Yes," I said, to Tacitus' great amusement.

"Then it seems reasonable that Aristeas, if he was a demigod, would have different limits on his life than we do."

"But I don't grant that he was a demigod, or anything other than a mortal man."

"You've come down on one side of the question, sir," Chloris said. "I'm just suggesting that you wait until you've examined the matter in greater depth before you decide."

Tacitus laughed. "Gaius Pliny, the girl is playing Diotima to your Socrates."

"I believe Diotima taught Socrates about the nature of love."

"She could do that, too, I'm sure," Tacitus said. "But her point is valid. Isn't it at least possible that Aristeas might be something more than mortal? You said he was lifeless but not dead when you found him."

"But that stinking hulk in the cart behind us is very dead."

The men who drove Scaevola's cart refused to unload Aristeas' body. Members of the guild of mule drivers, they insisted they'd been paid and instructed to drive the body to my villa. Nothing had been said about unloading it. Even when I offered them extra money, they refused the job.

I called out some of my servants and they deposited Aristeas in the same stable he'd been in before, this time laying him on a couple of boards so they could move him out into the sunlight without having to touch him when I was ready to examine him. Which would have to be very soon.

After the servants had sprinkled the place generously with spices and perfume, I sent them to start constructing the funeral pyre and put my seal on the bar across the door.

"You don't think he's going to get up and walk out again, do you?" Tacitus said, with his hand over his nose.

"At this point I don't know what might happen." I removed the piece of rope Tacitus had used to get out of the stable earlier. "But I'm not going to take any chances. I would put something over the opening in the door, but the stench would become unbearable if the place were completely closed up."

"I don't think you have to worry, sir," Chloris said, waving her hand in front of her face. "I believe he's finished with this body."

"Is a body something we just use for a while and then discard?"

"Plato says our souls have been in other bodies before this one and will be in other bodies after they leave this one. Perhaps an animal, or another human."

I was amazed at the breadth of her reading. I had decided, by the time I was fifteen, that Epicurus was right. There is no such thing as a soul which survives the death of the body. What we think of as the 'soul' is made up of atoms that are lighter and more loosely joined than the atoms which make up our bodies. What, then, is the body? Is it a container we just use for a time? Can a human 'soul' move from one body to another, human or otherwise? What are we doing when we use another person's body, as I had used Chloris' last night—or was she using mine? Cicero says the gods must have physical bodies in order to feel what we feel. Then what makes them different from us?

I looked at the stable door, half expecting to see something other than an odor seeping out through it. "Are you suggesting that he'll be looking for another body?"

"I would not dare to suggest that I know what a god might do, sir."

As we left the paddock, trying to get a deep breath of fresh air, Tranio approached us. "My lord, the men you sent to Rome yesterday are here. I told them to wait in the garden, to keep them away from your mother. Will you see them now?"

The man had actually made a decision on his own, and a good one. "By all means."

I sent Chloris into the house. Turning toward the garden, we passed the spot where the first layer of the funeral pyre was taking shape. In the open space between the paddock and the garden we would be assured of the best breeze, to fan the flames. "Make sure it's at least as tall as you are," I told Tranio. "And drive some posts into the ground around the edges to hold it all together."

Tacitus nodded. "We don't want a half-burned body tumbling off a collapsing pyre. That happened at my poor mother's funeral." He fell silent for a moment. "It's a ghastly sight."

"If we had time, I would send to Ostia for a skilled pyre-builder."

When we entered the garden I was surprised to see not only the two men Tacitus and I had sent to Rome, but a third man with them—Narcissus, the recently appointed chief doorkeeper and assistant to my steward Demetrius. A few months ago he had replaced his father Moschus, who had held that post since before I was born but had become too feeble-minded to recognize people any more. Some days he even seemed unsure of who I was. I could have turned him out, as some masters do when their slaves are too old to be of further use, but in return for a lifetime of service to my family I was quite willing to continue to feed and house him.

"Is there something wrong?" I asked his son.

"No, my lord," Narcissus said. "These men said you wanted to know everything we knew about that odd little man who came to our door. I was the one who spoke to him, so I thought I would come and tell you directly."

I would have preferred to see almost any other servant from my house in Rome. Narcissus is not untrustworthy—to the best of my knowledge—but he makes no secret of his desire to be free and rich. He moves toward the second goal by taking small bribes to admit people to my house, even when he knows I do not want to see them. Then he tells me he thought they had something important to tell me. I could rid myself of the nuisance, I suppose, by manumitting him, but that would only reward his arrogance. Having him flogged would probably just make him more difficult to deal with. Since he had inherited his position as rightfully as I did mine, I could do little beyond enduring him.

"What do you have to tell me?"

"Not much, my lord." But I could see from his face that he was still expecting a reward for his 'trouble.' "The man came to the door three days ago, about the third hour. At first I thought he was one of your clients coming late, but I'd never seen him before."

"Was anyone with him?"

"No, my lord."

"Was he carrying anything?"

"No, my lord. He wasn't even wearing sandals."

"What did he want?"

"To see you, my lord, of course."

"Did he say why he wanted to see me?"

"That's what I couldn't make much sense of, my lord. I think he really wanted to talk to your uncle, about something the old gentleman wrote."

"Can you be more specific? I need to know exactly what he said."

"Well, my lord, I didn't pay close attention. He seemed a bit daft, and I just wanted to get him on his way."

In other words, I thought, he had no money to grease your palm.

"As best I can recall, my lord, he said, 'I need to talk to Pliny. In his book he didn't get it quite right about the raven.' I figured he must be looking for your uncle, and I told him he was dead. He looked so disappointed I told him he could find you down here, just to get rid of him. I didn't think he would actually find you. He thanked me and set off right then."

Tacitus had been quiet up to this point. "Did anyone else in the house hear your conversation with him?"

"Yes, my lord. There's always a few who hang around to listen whenever a stranger comes to the door. It brings a bit of excitement to the house."

I knew what Tacitus was thinking. Someone in my house could have let someone in Regulus' house know about the visitor. And not even maliciously. They could have mentioned it as a curiosity, a tale told over a cup of wine in a taberna or while watching someone's clothes in the bath.

"Did he seem to be afraid?"

"No, my lord. Just disappointed that he couldn't talk to Pliny. What did he mean about the raven?"

"If I could answer that question, a lot of other things might make sense too."

143

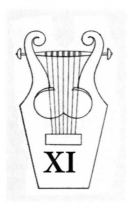

**XI**

**I TOLD NARCISSUS** he could stay the night and return to Rome the next day.

"If you can spare a horse, my lord, I'd better get back this afternoon. My father is not doing well. He seems to be losing more and more of his mind each day. I'm the only person he still recognizes, and he has moments when he doesn't even know me, so I don't like to be gone for too long."

Narcissus' words made him sound like a sympathetic son, but the tone of his voice revealed him as more like the self-absorbed character from mythology for whom he was named. He clearly saw his father as a burden. I recalled the words of the poet Caecilius, "The saddest thing about growing old is knowing that other men find you tiresome." I could only hope that Moschus, as his awareness of people and things around him dimmed, didn't sense how his son felt about him now.

"By all means then," I said, "get on back. Tranio will give you a fresh horse. Be sure your father is comfortable. I told Demetrius before we left to give him whatever he needs."

"Thank you, my lord." He started toward the stable, then turned back. "I almost forgot, my lord. Aurora asked me to give you this."

He removed a cord from around his neck and under his tunic with a leather tube attached to it. The tube contained a single piece of papyrus, rolled up and sealed with wax. In place of a carved seal, Aurora had pressed her thumb into the wax, a signet she had used since childhood.

"How is she doing?" I asked.

"Well, my lord."

"I'm glad to hear it. Give her my greetings when you get home."

Aurora was the daughter of my uncle's mistress, a slave named Monica, but she wasn't my uncle's daughter. She'd been born before he purchased Monica. Being the same age, we had spent a lot of time together as we grew up. My mother resented Monica and, since my uncle's death, had not been particularly kind in her treatment of the woman's daughter. I had considered moving Aurora to another of my estates but—

"Aren't you going to open it?" Tacitus asked.

"Later." I slipped the cord over my own neck. Tacitus was already too interested in my relationship with Aurora. I didn't need him reading her note over my shoulder.

"I still don't understand why you don't bring her with you when you come down here," Tacitus persisted. "In Rome she does things for you like a wife. She even shaves you. How do you get along without her?"

I did sometimes ask myself that question. "You know how my mother felt about Monica, and she harbors the same animosity against Aurora. It's better for them to be apart for a while."

"Is it better for you?"

I tugged on the cord to make sure the letter was secure. "My friend, that's enough about Aurora. Right now we need to let Apollodoros and Daphne out of their rooms and tell them what happened to Aristeas."

"Do you want to bet on whether either one of them is still there?"

As soon as we entered the atrium my mother descended on us.

"Gaius, why haven't you released Apollodoros?"

"You haven't done that already?"

"No, dear. You gave very explicit instructions." She waved her arms in exasperation. "The servants are too terrified to do anything I tell them."

Perhaps, I thought, this whole business will have at least one positive outcome.

"And what about Daphne?"

"Do what you will about that hideous creature," Mother said with a shrug. "Just let Apollodoros out."

I told one of the servants to go tell the guards to unbar the doors and free Apollodoros and Daphne.

"That won't do any good," Mother said, hands on her hips. "All they'll say is that they're under orders to open the doors for no one but you."

"Then I'll be back in a moment."

Tacitus accompanied me, mostly, I think, to see if anyone was actually in the two rooms. I wasn't sure what I would do if either room proved to be empty. As we turned a corner we heard a rattling noise and a human voice making a barking sound.

"I think one of your servants just made the dog throw," Tacitus said.

When we came within sight of the rooms we found the four guards on their knees over a small pile of coins. One of them spotted me and alerted the others. As they all jumped to their feet one scooped up the dice and the money they were playing for.

"Sorry, my lord," the senior man said. "We was just—"

"It's all right. At least you were in front of the doors where you were supposed to be."

"Oh, yes, my lord. Haven't left all day." He stood as rigid as a legionary.

"Have you had any trouble back here today?" I asked.

They looked at one another before one said, "Only from your mother, my lord."

"My mother?"

"Yes, my lord," another man said. "She's been back here three times trying to get us to let this Apollodoros character out."

"But we haven't, my lord," the first man said. "We just told her politely that we had orders to open the door for no one but you."

"Well, here I am and I'm telling you to let them out and bring them to the atrium."

"Yes, my lord. Of course. Right away."

"And keep them separated, like wine and vinegar. Bring them out one at a time."

"Then I think we'd better bring Apollodoros first, my lord, or your mother will—"

"You're right. She'll have a fit."

"Not my words, my lord."

Tacitus and I returned to the atrium and waited a few moments until Apollodoros was escorted in. Mother embraced him as she does me. With their backs to me, they talked so softly I couldn't hear what they were saying. Naomi stepped back, the farthest I had seen her from my mother in a long time.

When Daphne was brought into the atrium she stopped just inside the entrance, glowering at us. She had not had a chance to repaint her face—that's the only way I could think of the heavy make-up she used—so the cracks on her cheeks and forehead made her appear even more gaunt and frightening than she had last night. She drew her cloak close around herself. I remembered what my servant had said about an empusa losing her powers during the day, then chided myself for even thinking about such drivel.

"Both of you listen to me carefully," I said. "You will have the freedom of the house, only as long as you stay away from one another. If *either* of you causes any further problems, I'll lock you *both* up again. Is that understood?"

They both nodded without taking their eyes off one another.

"Are we still your prisoners then?" Daphne asked.

"You may leave any time you like," Mother said before I could open my mouth.

"I would prefer that you stay," I said, "until I can get answers to some questions."

Apollodoros pulled away from my mother and took a step toward Daphne. "How can you get answers when you can't believe anything she tells you?"

I stepped between them, forcing Apollodoros to retreat. "We had that argument last night and I don't intend to have it again. I do have some unfortunate news, and I know of no gentle way to tell you ... Aristeas is dead."

Apollodoros started to laugh. "Sir, you *still* don't understand—"

I turned on him. "No, *you* don't understand. He won't wake up tomorrow morning. This time he is really dead."

Tacitus ran his finger over his throat. "As dead as it is possible for a person to be. Even deader, perhaps."

I was glad he didn't say anything about the blood. I wanted to keep some of what we knew to ourselves, in order to test the answers we might get from these two.

Mother put her arm around Apollodoros to comfort him, and he rested his head on her shoulder. When Tacitus glanced at me, I wouldn't meet his eye. I wanted to rip the Greekling's head off and play *trigon* with it, but I knew the only way I could wean my mother away from him would be to make him show himself for a scoundrel.

"I feared this was going to happen,"Apollodoros said. "No, I knew it."

"Are you ready to tell him the truth now?" Daphne asked, without showing any reaction to the news of Aristeas' death.

"As ready as you are, bitch."

"I never told him a lie."

"But did you tell him *all* of the truth?"

Mother insisted that Apollodoros have lunch before I asked him any more questions. "You're so rough on him, Gaius. He needs food and a bath before he has to face you." With her arm around his shoulder they headed for the kitchen.

"Sir," Daphne said, "may I see my father's body?"

"Soon. I'm not ready to let anyone see it yet. Before you tell me 'all of the truth,' why you don't eat something?"

She looked toward the door my mother and Apollodoros had used but didn't move.

"I'll have a servant bring you something here."

"Thank you, sir."

Tacitus and I decided to wait on lunch until after we had examined Aristeas further. I'm not bothered by sights that some might consider gruesome—perhaps Tacitus is right about my morbid curiosity—but he tends toward squeamishness.

I asked Macrinus, the butcher on this estate, to accompany us. In addition to slaughtering animals, he acts as a doctor when any of my servants and animals gets hurt. He has an assortment of needles for sewing up wounds. He always wants to investigate and poke around in a wound before he closes it up. My uncle encouraged him to do so.

We wrapped thin cloths saturated with perfume around our mouths and noses and concentrated on the dead man's throat. I did not want to call attention to the missing raven's head mark. Tacitus and I would examine that portion of the body later by ourselves.

"He's spoiling fast, my lord," the butcher said.

"What do you expect from seven-hundred-year-old meat?" Tacitus muttered, drawing a startled look from Marcrinus and a cautionary glare from me.

"That's why there's a funeral pyre being prepared for him," I said.

"I'm not sure when he was killed."

"It must have been a day ago, my lord. Two, more likely. And this warm weather don't help none."

"Can you tell me anything about how he was killed?"

"Well, my lord, his throat was slit."

"Really?" Tacitus said. "We thought perhaps he'd been drowned."

"Sorry, my lord. I didn't mean to insult you by being so obvious."

"Never mind," I said. "Cornelius Tacitus has an odd sense of humor, which he seems to be indulging today. Can you tell anything about what sort of weapon was used?"

"I would say a knife, my lord, but not a very sharp one."

"Why do you say that?"

"Well, the edges of the cut are ragged, my lord. If a knife blade isn't sharp or has a rough spot or a nick on it, it tears more than cuts."

I knew how uncomfortable it was to be shaved with a razor that wasn't sharp or had a nick. This poor man had not only been slaughtered like an animal and the blood drained from his body. His killer had hurt him all the more by using a blade with a rough edge. Was it done intentionally?

"All the blood was drained out of the body," I said. "Have you ever seen anything like that?"

"Well, my lord, I watched a Jewish butcher cut up a sheep once. They've got all sorts of rules about slaughtering animals. One of the main ones is draining the blood. I've heard stories that they use it in some secret ritual."

"Is there a Jewish butcher anywhere around here?"

"The closest one would be in Ostia, my lord."

"It would take too long to get a message there and get him back here."

"If he would even come, my lord. They don't like to mix with us that ain't Jews. But you could ask Naomi."

The suggestion surprised me. "Yes, I know she's Jewish, but what would she know about something like this?"

"Her husband was a butcher, my lord. She's told me a few things about how I might do my job."

In all I had learned in recent months about Naomi and her family, who were taken captive after the destruction of Jerusalem, I had heard nothing about her husband. I could only assume he had died some years ago.

"Thank you for your help," I told Macrinus.

Tacitus and I went into the house to find Naomi. We managed to pry her loose from my mother and took her out onto the terrace. The fresh breeze off the bay was a welcome change from the stench of the stable. I drew in a deep breath before I turned to face her.

"I need to know something about how your people slaughter animals. I understand your husband was a butcher."

"Not just a butcher, my lord, but a *shochet*."

She sounded like she was clearing her throat. "How is that different from a butcher like Macrinus?"

"A *shochet* has been specially trained, my lord, to slaughter animals following our laws about the preparation of meat."

"Would those laws require an animal to be strung up by its hind legs?"

"Not require, my lord. The animal can be strung up, or it can be laid on its back. The important thing is that the knife be extremely sharp and the throat be cut quickly and without pressing into the flesh."

"You drain the blood, don't you?" Tacitus asked.

"Yes, my lord."

"How is it collected and what's done with it?" I didn't really believe it was used in bizarre rituals. I don't understand the Jews, but I've seen nothing sinister about them. I certainly am not afraid of the ones in my household.

"It isn't collected, my lord. That's forbidden. The blood must be drained onto the ground and covered. We're taught that the life of a creature is in its blood. We will not eat the blood."

"Are the animals stunned first?" Tacitus asked.

"No, my lord. Our law requires that the animal be conscious when it's slaughtered."

In Roman sacrifices the animals are hit on the head with a large hammer before their throats are cut. I had not seen any sign of a blow on Aristeas' head. That could mean nothing more than that the person who killed him wanted him to suffer right to the last moment. I didn't think Naomi had anything further to tell us about how Aristeas might have been killed, but my curiosity was piqued now. "Naomi, do you eat meat in my house?"

Naomi shook her head. "I eat fish, bread, cheese, fruits and vegetables, my lord. My lady Plinia has offered to buy meat from a *shochet* for me, but, even if the animal is slaughtered properly, we have other rules about the preparation of the meat that would make it impossible for me to eat any cooked in your kitchen."

I drew myself up. "Our kitchen seems to be good enough for everyone else in the household."

"Forgive me if I offend you, my lord. I know Gentiles find our food restrictions puzzling. Some do come to understand them and see the wisdom in them. My lady Plinia has begun purchasing garum that is prepared according to our laws."

In spite of my surprise at hearing that, I wondered if it might explain the difference in taste I had noticed lately. I thought she'd just been going to a better shop. "How is it different from regular garum?"

"No shellfish are used to make it, my lord, only fish with scales." She must have read my change of expression. "My lord, I don't mean to suggest there's anything wrong with—"

"I understand. My mother has charge of the household and can purchase what she deems best. I just want to be sure you're eating enough to keep up your strength so you can carry out your duties."

"Thank you, my lord. I would not fail you or my lady Plinia. You've been very kind to me and my son." She lowered her head and then looked back up at me. "Do you require anything else?"

Why did I feel like *she* was dismissing *me*? "No. You may go."

Tacitus waited until she was out of sight. "So, do you think the butcher did it?"

"No. But I don't think Myrrha killed him either. The knife beside her bed was sharp, with no nicks or rough spots on the blade. It wouldn't have torn the flesh the way his was torn. And it would have taken a strong woman to tie him up and hoist him by his feet."

"Myrrha could do it with a pulley or two," Tacitus said. "You saw that bracket she made to hold her knife. Chloris said she was clever with things like that, things you wouldn't expect a woman to be able to do."

"But where could she—or whoever did it—have strung the man up? You'd need a barn or a workshop, wouldn't you? It's not something you'd do out in the open or in *your* bedroom."

"Maybe not your bedroom. We'll have to see if there's any likely place near Saturninus' building that would be suitable. Maybe he's involved."

I shook my head. "He's too old and frail. He couldn't have done it."

"But he could have assisted in some way."

"Assisted Myrrha? Why?" I shook my head. "He hates her, and Chloris too. You heard how he talked about them. And he practically spit in Chloris' face when we went into his shop with her."

"True. But I also saw how he looked at them. There's something between them that we're not privy to. Perhaps a murder that took place fifteen years ago."

I hated to admit it, even to myself, but Tacitus might be right. "We can't do anything about that now. We have to find out what happened to Aristeas' blood."

"But if whoever killed him let it drain on the ground, how can we find it?"

"If what Daphne said about people buying his blood as an elixir is true, don't you think they would have collected it? And what did Naomi say? 'The life of a creature is in its blood.'"

Tacitus turned and looked out over the bay. "If it made you immortal, priceless. Speaking of drinking an elixir ..."

I was about to go inside and call for some wine when Blandina appeared with a tray holding a large cup of wine, two smaller drinking cups and some bread. I wondered if she'd been listening to our conversation.

As we drank, a dolphin surfaced in the bay below us, spouting water from the hole on the top of its head. The creatures fascinate me, as they did my uncle. He used to go out in a boat and try to study them more closely. They would swim up to the boat, make a high-pitched noise and let him touch them. He said he felt like they were trying to talk to him. That's the sort of thing I find in his unpublished scrolls—much of it helpful, but some of it nonsense.

I had no time for distractions. I needed to concentrate on Aristeas' murder, and a key element in the puzzle was what happened to his blood. "How big a container do you think you'd need to hold all the blood from a man's body?" I said.

Tacitus drained his cup and shook his head. "I doubt you'll find a volunteer to help you answer that question."

"A large hog weighs about as much as a man, doesn't it?"

"A small man like Aristeas? I suppose so."

"Then let's have Macrinus string up my largest hog and cut its throat. We'll rig up something to catch the blood."

Tacitus refilled his cup and laughed. "For some reason a line from Aristophanes just popped into my head. From the *Thesmophoriazusae*, I believe."

"By the gods, yes!" I couldn't help but be amused, even in such grisly circumstances. "Mnesilochos—wasn't that his name? —uncovers the wine skin that a woman is passing off as a baby. 'But first the sacrifice!' he says. 'I must cut its throat.'"

"That's it. And the woman says, 'Bring me a bowl. At least I can catch my lovely's blood.' " Tacitus gazed into his wine cup. "Wine and blood. What an amazing equation."

"I wonder how large a container we'll need."

Tacitus drained his cup. "Your largest amphora, I should think, just in case."

"Yes. And while the servants are building Aristeas' funeral pyre, they can construct another one to roast the pig."

When the door onto the terrace opened again I thought it would be Blandina bringing more wine, but my mother emerged from the house.

"Gaius, I want to speak to you about this man's funeral."

"We're about to take care of it," I said. "Tranio is constructing the pyre."

"But why go to all that trouble?"

I knew what was coming. Last summer she attended a Jewish funeral and was deeply impressed with their practice of placing the body in a cave and letting it decompose for a year, then collecting the bones and placing them in a box carved from stone.

"You could put him in that cave on the side of the cliff below the house, dear, the one where you used to play. It would be easy and convenient."

Easy and convenient for anyone to get to him, I thought. "Mother, if it were anyone else, I would indulge you, but this man is going on the pyre."

"Why? Are you afraid of him?"

While Tacitus and I got something to eat, Macrinus selected the largest hog on the estate and, with the help of several other servants, roped the thing and dragged it to the stable. The hog protested vehemently and fought back as though he knew what was in store for him. The rest of my servants laughed like an audience enjoying a farce in the theater.

"Do you suppose Aristeas put up that much of a fight?" Tacitus said as we watched the uproar.

I sipped some wine to wash down a bite of bread. "I wonder if someone attacked him when he was in that sleep-like state. Out there in the woods, he didn't respond at all when my servants picked him up and put him in the cart. It was as though his ... his life force had left the body."

"Why can't you call it his soul?"

"Because that's not how I think of it."

"Whatever you call it, perhaps his body was ... vacant. Some people explain dreams that way. Our souls leave for a time and see things we can't know about. If Aristeas' body was vacant, even a woman might have been able to overcome him. Myrrha's as big as he is."

"You don't have to say everything you think, my friend. There's a strong enough case against her without you adding to it."

Macrinus decided to string the hog up using the beam over the far gate of the paddock. He had reinforced it with a second beam on top of it because of his concern about the animal's weight. Using that gate would keep the whole business out of sight of the house and leave whatever mess needed to be cleaned up afterwards on the edge of the woods. My mother, Naomi, and Apollodoros stayed inside and refused to watch. Daphne, however, showed a keen interest, making sure she was in the front row. I thought I saw a trace of a smile on her face.

"We'd better pay closer attention," I said as the servants finally got the hog suspended by its back legs. Tacitus and I moved through the ring of onlookers and stood by the sweating Macrinus.

"It would've been easier if I could've bashed 'im on the head, my lord." The butcher wiped his brow with his forearm.

"Aristeas wasn't hit," I said, "and I want to duplicate what I think happened as closely as possible. The way this thing is thrashing around, though, you won't be able to collect any blood, will you?"

154

"No, my lord. It'll be spurtin' all over the place. To collect any we'll have to tie his head down somehow. But the only way to do that would be with a rope around his neck."

I had not noticed any mark of a rope on the back of Aristeas' neck, but I am nothing if not pragmatic. "All right, we'll have to compromise. Stun him and then cut his throat as quickly as you can. And remember, it has to be a deep cut, just short of taking his head off, with a blade that's not particularly sharp."

"Yes, my lord."

The hog squealed louder and jerked so violently that even the reinforced archway creaked.

"And you'd better be quick about it."

"Yes, my lord." Macrinus fetched a large hammer. He had already assembled a copper bowl with a hole drilled in the bottom and the largest amphora he could find. When everything was in place he hit the hog on the head. I heard a crunch and the huge beast went limp. Macrinus stepped in front of the animal, plunged in the knife, and slashed its throat with one practiced motion.

The initial spurt of blood was so strong that the servant holding the copper bowl had trouble keeping his grip on it. The bowl filled almost as fast as blood ran out of the hole into the amphora below it.

"That's a lot more than I expected," Tacitus said.

"There'll be a lot at first, my lord," Macrinus said, wiping the bloody knife on his apron. "Then it'll slow down and trickle out for a while."

"How long do you think it will take for all the blood to drain out?" I was wondering how long someone would have needed to leave Aristeas hanging upside down. Most murders can be committed quickly, with a thrust or two of a knife or a blow from a stone. A person can be strangled quickly. A moment of passion or anger followed by a lifetime of remorse. To kill Aristeas in the way we were slaughtering this hog would require forethought and a place where he could be concealed for ... how long?

"How long? Not sure, my lord. I've never done this before, I mean, tryin' to drain all the blood out of an animal."

"How much blood do you think there will be in all?" I asked.

"At this rate, my lord, more than a *congius*, I suspect."

"Do you think there's more blood than that in a man?"

"If you mean that scrawny little fella you had in the stable, my

155

lord, I suppose he'd have a bit more, but not more than two *congii*."

"So one amphora of that size would be large enough to hold it all?"

Macrinus nodded and patted the hog.

I had almost forgotten about Daphne until she stepped around us and put the tip of a finger into the bowl of blood. "It's surprisingly warm," she said and put her finger into her mouth.

With the hog slaughtered, I wanted to get back to examining Aristeas' body, but I didn't want a large crowd of my servants satisfying their gruesome curiosity while I worked.

"The spectacle is over," I announced. "Everyone back in the house and back to work." I turned to Daphne. "You should go back in the house as well. I thought you would want to clean up after lunch."

"That fop Apollodoros got into the bath first. Are you going to roast the pig for dinner?" She looked with interest at the blood continuing to drain from the animal's throat.

In a moment Aristeas would be brought out of the stable for me to examine him one last time. There was no gentle way to tell Daphne what had happened to him.

She spared me the effort. "He was brutally murdered, wasn't he? Like this. That's why you staged this ... spectacle."

"We think this is what happened." I turned toward the interior of the paddock. Two of my servants, with the promise of five denarii each, brought the fetid corpse out to where a platform had been hastily constructed so I wouldn't have to get down on the ground to examine him.

Tacitus and I tried to put ourselves between Daphne and the grisly sight, but she pushed past us with a strength I would not have suspected from her appearance.

"So, someone did cut his throat." She was standing over the body now. Her breathing seemed strained, but I did not see any evidence of the sort of grief I was accustomed to seeing women express. At my uncle's funeral my mother had wept copiously and beat her breasts. "But I don't see any blood on him."

"We believe whoever killed him drained the blood from his body." I stood beside her but, remembering how she reacted last night, I did not touch her.

She nodded. "Took it to sell it, no doubt. All because that fool

Apollodoros convinced people it could make them live forever. Is that really the blessing people think it is?"

Having no answer to that question, I said, "We're building his pyre. I would like to examine the body one last time to see if I can learn anything else."

" 'The body.' You can't bring yourself to call him my father, can you?"

"I don't know whose father—if anyone's—he was. And that's only one among many questions I can't answer yet."

"If you saw my face next to his, you'd know who was his child."

That gave me the opening I needed to ask about something. "Forgive my bluntness, but, with the make-up you wear, how could I tell?"

She ran her hand over her face. "It's not my choice, sir. Since I was a child the sun has made my skin feel like it was burning. I can barely endure wearing clothes. And I can't stand to have anyone touch me."

"That's what you kept saying the first night you came here," Tacitus said. "How is your shoulder, by the way?"

"Much better. Thank you." She touched the spot. "So that's why I wear this clothing and heavy make-up. When I was younger I had to stay inside most of the day if the sun was shining, and it shines most of the time in Alexandria. Other children made fun of me. They began to tell stories about me being a monster that could only come out at night. I guess I even began to believe them and act like a monster. That way they would be too frightened to bother me."

"That's absurd," I said.

"We would never give credence to such nonsense," Tacitus added.

"Thank you," Daphne said, drawing her cloak tightly around herself. "Then I'll assume I was locked up under guard last night for my own protection."

"Yes ... Exactly," I said. "I wasn't sure what to make of Apollodoros."

She smiled sadly. "And your men, of course, weren't frightened of me, even though I did hear them tell one another not to turn their backs toward the empusa's door."

"They're ignorant," Tacitus said, "given to superstition."

"No matter." Daphne shook her head, as though ridding herself of a bad memory. "I've heard it all before, and worse. All I want now is to prepare my father's body for burial."

"I'll be happy for you to do so in a little while, but now I want you to stand aside. I need to get as much information as I can that might help me understand who did this."

Finally releasing some tears, Daphne moved away from the body. "Then I'll get what I need to prepare him."

"One of my servant women will help you. She'll get you a clean tunic for him."

I told Daphne which of the servant women to ask for in the house. Once she was out of sight I hovered over Aristeas' body.

"What else do you hope to learn?" Tacitus asked. "His throat was slashed and he bled to death. Do you need to know any more?"

"What about the raven's head? Don't you want to explain what happened to it?"

"I didn't see it," Tacitus reminded me, "but perhaps it was formed by blood collecting into a swelling on his skin. Haven't you ever pinched your finger—in a door, for instance—and seen a spot like a blister turn purple. If you prick it, blood comes out."

Could it be as uncomplicated as that? I felt relief and gratitude for even the beginning of a reasonable explanation of the damn mark, but I was wary of something so simple. "I suppose that could be the case here. But there's no evidence of the skin on his chest being pricked." I looked as closely as my nose would let me.

"When the rest of the blood was drained from his body, the blood that was making this mark must have drained out too."

I nodded slowly. "That would explain why there's no sign of an erasure or a prick."

"But if the mark really did disappear when his soul left his body, that could also explain it." Tacitus didn't raise his head, but I could see his smile.

Even if I was beginning to I understand what might have happened to the raven's head, I still couldn't laugh at Tacitus' suggestion. "Let's not make any more jokes about this. Please."

"Sorry. Here comes Daphne. Are you ready to put him on the pyre?"

I nodded and stepped back. There really was nothing more I could deduce from the body, and the smell was beginning to affect my stomach.

"Since we're getting to it rather late in the day," Tacitus said, "it will probably be well into the night before the body is completely burned."

"It took from dawn to dusk on an August day to burn my uncle's body."

"He was a much larger man than Aristeas, wasn't he? That's what I remember from the time or two I saw him."

"Yes, so I hope this won't take as long. However long it does take, though, I'm going to post guards. I'm determined that this body will be completely consumed."

"What are you going to do with the ashes?"

So many strange things had happened since I found Aristeas lying in my woods that I thought the best way to put a complete stop to them was to destroy the body that so many people seemed interested in, to make it disappear forever. Under no circumstances would I bury the urn or leave it sitting where someone could find it. Every last bit of the body had to be eradicated. "I think I'll scatter the ashes out on the bay. I'll even go out on a boat, just to get away from shore."

Tacitus laughed. He knew my aversion to being on any kind of boat. "Nobody'll be able to find any trace of him then."

"Except that we don't know what happened to his blood. Is there an amphora full of it hidden out there somewhere? That feels like the latrunculus piece that's lurking somewhere on the board, just waiting to complete the trap around me."

"Why do you assume somebody collected it?"

"You heard Daphne say people were willing to pay a lot of money for even a small amount of it. Imagine what you might get for an amphora full."

**XII**

**D**APHNE INSISTED ON WASHING Aristeas' body. I wished she hadn't because I didn't want anything to make him more difficult to burn. Her grief was now evident, though, so I couldn't deny her whatever comfort she might derive from this last service to her father.

If anything could make me believe she was his daughter, it was her obvious devotion to him in this difficult task. In spite of the decay and stench, she cleaned him up as best she could and wrapped him in a white blanket as a shroud, with a separate cloth tied around his throat as though to guard against a chill. Bending over him and smoothing his hair, she looked more like a mother tending to a child than a grieving daughter.

When everything was ready we took places beside the pyre. Apollodoros stood between Tacitus and me, with Daphne on Tacitus' left and my mother to my right. Chloris and Naomi stood slightly behind us. I had dismissed everyone else. They were more interested in roasting the pig anyway. From the paddock two of my servants carried Aristeas' body, now tied to the boards on which he lay.

"I know it's difficult to lose someone like this," Naomi said, leaning over to speak to Daphne as the servants lifted Aristeas onto the pyre. "I didn't eat for three days after my husband's funeral. I seriously considered never eating again."

Daphne, now dry-eyed, said, "I lost him five years ago."

Apollodoros had agreed to tell us his story while the pyre was lit, so we could observe the proper rites for the poor man and, hopefully, finish before dark.

"Let's begin with names," I said as the torches were applied to the bottom layer of the pyre, where some of the wood had been smeared with pitch. I was glad to see the flames take hold. I didn't want to find myself, like Achilles beside Patroclus' pyre, having to invoke the North and East winds to fan the blaze. "I'm never comfortable talking to someone whose name I'm not sure of."

"My name is Apollodoros." His shoulders slumped and he appeared as somber as a man who knows that what he is about to say will change his life forever.

"Liar!" Daphne muttered. She mumbled several gibberish syllables, like some bombastic, ridiculous name out of a play by Plautus. "That's your name."

"That is my Indian name, but I was born in Alexandria. As I told you, sir, my mother's family came from the eastern part of India to Alexandria when she was a girl. She married a citizen of the city. I was born to them after some years of barrenness. My father, I'm told, vowed a ram to Apollo if he would have a son, a son who had some attribute of Apollo."

"Why Apollo?" Chloris asked. "He's not a god of births."

"But my father played the lyre," Apollodoros said. "I have some talent with that instrument as well, though I sing and compose better than I play."

"So you really are Apollo's Gift," Chloris said.

"That was what my father thought. But he died when I was quite young. My mother married an Indian man, who called me by the name Daphne just spoke. And your pronunciation, by the way, was the best I've heard from a Greek."

"I've had lots of practice," Daphne snapped. "For five years I've been using it as a curse."

Apollodoros bowed his head. "I guess I deserve that. Anyway, my mother kept me mindful of my birth name and, when my stepfather died, I began to use it."

"We can send to Alexandria and inquire about this," I said. "You know the penalties for claiming citizenship falsely are severe."

"If you wish to go to the trouble, sir, please do. You'll find my name, Apollodoros, son of Leukomenes, on the citizenship rolls."

"If Aristeas wasn't your father," Tacitus asked, "how did you become connected with him?"

" 'Connected'? That's an interesting choice of words, sir." He grimaced and a look of understanding passed between them. "We met in the stoa at the baths. He ... took a fancy to me and I invited him to come to my rooms."

"That's how he earns his living," Daphne said with a sneer.

With a sideways glance I saw my mother gasp and put her hand to her mouth in dismay. I hoped the smile I felt wasn't showing.

The smoke from the pyre was getting thick enough to make us step back. Apollodoros coughed before he continued. "I hadn't thought much about his name—it's not unheard of among Greek men. But when he removed his tunic I recognized the raven's head mark on his chest."

"You knew the story from Herodotus?" I asked.

Apollodoros nodded. "I read Herodotus because he talked about India—mostly nonsense, as it turns out. Trust me, Indians do not have black semen. Ethiopians either. But I was especially taken with the story of Aristeas because there are wise men in India, my mother and stepfather told me, who can put themselves into a state like death and then recover from it. They learn how to do it and can teach others."

"Do you think that's what Aristeas—the one in Herodotus—was doing?"

"I believe so. Herodotus says Aristeas, inspired by Apollo, traveled to places north and east of the Euxine Sea. Even if he didn't get to India, he might have encountered someone from there who taught him how to do it."

"Did you teach our Aristeas ..." —I gestured at the pyre with my head. —"to do it?"

"I don't know how, and I didn't have to. The first time we were together I thought he had died. I know I have some great skills in what your Ovid calls 'the art of love.' Literature of that sort has been written for hundreds of years in India and my stepfather had copies, which I read. But I'd never killed anyone—man or woman. I've left a few exhausted, but none dead."

My mother turned and headed for the house. Naomi followed her, but from the way she looked back at me I could see she would have stayed with us if given the choice. Apollodoros' standing in my mother's eyes was going up in flames right along with Aristeas' body. I hoped both were utterly destroyed by nightfall.

"How would you describe him at that moment?" I asked.

"I couldn't feel any breath. His limbs were completely limp. He didn't respond when I patted his face, but he wasn't cold."

"Lifeless but not dead?"

"Yes. That describes him quite well."

"What did you do when you thought you had a dead man in your bed?" Tacitus asked.

"I panicked. My first thought was to get out of there before I was accused of murdering him. I was packing a bag when a voice behind me said, 'Are you going somewhere?' I turned and saw Aristeas sitting up in the bed, smiling at me. I thought I must be dreaming."

"I've had that feeling myself the last few days." I wished I could be sure that burning the body would put an end to it.

"I asked him what had happened to him," Apollodoros continued. "He said he had been able to put himself into a death-like sleep since he was a child. He had never done it in front of anyone else before."

"Not even his family?" I turned to Daphne.

She shook her head. "I remember one morning when he didn't wake up until quite late. My mother shook him, but she said he must have had too much to drink the night before and we left him alone."

"There's one problem here," Tacitus said. "The Aristeas in Herodotus didn't just lie down and appear to be dead. He disappeared from one place and appeared somewhere else. Did this Aristeas ever do that?"

"I think he was getting ready to do it," Apollodoros said.

"What do you mean 'getting ready to'?" I looked up at the top of the pyre, just to be sure the body was still there. He might have gotten out of my stable in the way Tacitus had devised—and I wasn't entirely convinced he did—but he could not get off the pyre except by some supernatural method.

"He seemed to be growing more confident that he had some kind of ... power. As I said, no one taught him to enter this death-like state. He knew how to do it. I'm afraid I made him more aware of what else he might be able to do. He was believing in himself. Hearing him talk about it was beginning to worry me."

"You've jumped ahead in your story," Daphne said. "Tell them about luring my father away from me."

"Yes, let's keep things in good order," I said. "A beginning, a middle, and an end, as Aristotle recommends."

"All right. As Aristeas and I talked after our ... first encounter, I saw a chance to make some money. I have no skills outside the bedchamber—I'm not *that* good at the lyre—and I won't be able to

count on my beauty or my voice forever, will I?" He glanced long-
ingly at Tacitus. "It was clear to me that Aristeas had a trick of some
sort with which we might make money. The question was just how
to take advantage of it. I knew we needed to get away from Alexandria. We couldn't put anything over on people who knew us. And we
couldn't do it more than once in any one place."

The wood was crackling loudly now as the flames reached the top
layer of the pyre and licked around Aristeas' body.

"Daphne said you concocted a story about traveling to music
festivals and competing for prizes."

Apollodoros glared at her. "Yes, I presented myself as Aristeas'
musical trainer. And it wasn't entirely a joke. He was quite adept at
the lyre. With my songs and his lyre playing, we could have made a
name for ourselves as musicians."

"But you weren't competing in any festivals," Daphne said.

"Of course not." Apollodoros looked back toward the house.
"That's too much work. If my lady Plinia hadn't already left in disgust, I'm sure she would now. You see, in any town in Italy or Gaul
or Spain we could always find some man who fancied someone like
me but didn't want his wife to know. You Romans can't seem to decide how you feel about love between men."

"It exists," Tacitus said, "but we're not blatant about it, like you
Greeks."

"Precisely. Since we were just passing through, I would assure
any man who was interested that he could safely indulge himself and
I would be gone the next morning. Aristeas would burst in on us at
an opportune moment, playing the outraged lover. A fight would
ensue and Aristeas would fall after a punch or two, apparently dead."

"What if the fellow you were with had a weapon?" Tacitus asked.

"It was my job to see that he didn't, or that he couldn't get to it.
Then I would rush to Aristeas, pronounce him dead, and call out,
'By the gods! You've killed him!'"

"Setting the fellow up for extortion." The way Tacitus said it, I
wondered if he had ever experienced anything like that. My mother
wasn't the only Roman who looked with disfavor on his sexual in-
clinations. I doubted that Julius Agricola would have allowed his
daughter to marry Tacitus if he knew as much about him as I did.

Apollodoros hung his head. "The scene always played out the

same way, just as surely as if we were actors following a script. The man wouldn't believe me. He would try to awaken Aristeas. But, of course, he couldn't, and there was no breath or any other sign of life. I would tell him that, if he would bring money the next morning, I would disappear and say nothing to anyone. When he returned the next morning I would take the money, then Aristeas would appear. I would explain that he was immortal and that drinking a small vial of his blood could make someone else immortal."

"And the cost of the vial was far more than the extortion, I suppose," I said.

"It's amazing what people will pay for the possibility of remaining on this wretched earth forever."

"That seems a clumsy sort of ruse," Tacitus said. "If you tried it on me, I would come back in the night and kill you."

"I sometimes feared that, sir. And I feared that someone might come after us for Aristeas' blood. I was always careful to stress that drinking one vial would make a person immortal, but a second vial would kill him."

"So why would someone want *all* of the blood?" Tacitus asked.

"In order to sell it himself," I said, "or because he wants to make a large number of people immortal."

"A large number? As in an army?"

"Or at least a bodyguard." *Such as the Praetorians*, I thought, but did not say it. "If you and Aristeas were traveling together," I asked Apollodoros, "why did he show up at my house in Rome and then here by himself?"

"We got separated. We had come to a disagreement over keeping our scheme going. Aristeas had grown tired of it. The money never mattered to him as much as it did to me. As I said, he was starting to believe he actually had some divine gift and should learn how to use it. Five days ago I woke up and he was gone. I can't understand how he got so far away so quickly."

"Like a bird flying the nest?" Tacitus asked.

"Exactly, sir. After a couple of days I gave up trying to track him and tried to anticipate where he might be going. I suspected he would go to Pliny's house because we had looked at the passage in the *Natural History* where Aristeas is mentioned."

The flames reached the top of the pyre and Aristeas' shroud and tunic caught fire. The flesh began to sizzle.

"Back in the atrium," I said, "when I told you he was dead, you said you knew this would happen. Why did you think someone wanted to harm him?"

"I'm afraid we were too convincing in some of our performances. Aristeas appeared to be as dead as any man could be. In their panic, not wanting to believe they had killed him, men would prod him, shake him, pinch him—nothing would rouse him. But the next morning, when they came to pay me, Aristeas was on his feet, walking around, asking for something to eat."

"How did they react?" Tacitus asked.

"Some felt they had been tricked."

"Well, hadn't they?"

"Sir, I honestly don't know. I was coming to see things about him that I didn't understand."

"Did you ever see him at the moment he came back to life?" I asked.

"Yes, sir, a number of times."

"What happened?"

"Nothing. He just opened his eyes as though he had been taking a nap."

"You never saw anything ... flying back to him?"

"No, sir. And nothing flying out of him either, in spite of what your uncle wrote."

"My uncle was merely reporting what others said, and about another Aristeas. He never saw that Aristeas or this one, or vouched for the accuracy of the report." I felt like I was losing the distinction between Herodotus' Aristeas and the man on the pyre. Who was Aristeas of Proconnesus? Could they both be?

"Of course not, sir."

We could smell the burning flesh now. I turned to Daphne but did not touch her. "I know this is difficult for you, to see and hear your father's body being consumed. When my uncle died, I could hardly watch. I had to stay, though, because in Rome family members are required to. You need not feel such an obligation."

Daphne lifted her head and fixed her gaze somewhere above the pyre. "The body is just a vessel for holding the soul for a time, and the soul is the person. When the vessel is damaged—just as when a jar is cracked—it cannot hold anything anymore and is no longer useful.

We abandon the jar without a backward glance. So with the body."

"But don't you want to know who ... broke the jar?"

Daphne shrugged. "I suppose that matters to some."

"What if someone drained the jar before it was broken," Tacitus said, "and poured out a precious vintage of wine?"

I could see from the change in her expression, even under her make-up, that Daphne knew what he meant.

The body was completely engulfed in flames now. I had told Tranio to apply pitch generously to the top layer of the pyre. It seemed to be having the effect I intended.

"I've seen enough," I said. Aristeas was no kin of mine, so I wasn't obligated to stay until the body was completely consumed. "I've assigned some men to tend the fire. I'm going inside."

"I'd like to stay, sir," Daphne said.

"You're welcome to do so. We'll be on the terrace when you care to join us."

We were almost through the house when I noticed Hylas standing at the door of the library, obviously wanting to speak with me. Tacitus and I walked over to him.

"My lord, there's something I think you should see."

Those are some of the direst words in any language.

"Chloris," I said, "will you accompany Apollodoros? We'll join you as soon as we can."

"I doubt my presence would be welcome," Apollodoros said. "I'll just return to my room. Will you be locking me in again?"

"We can dispense with that. Chloris, I'll find a room for you in a few moments. Why don't you wait on the terrace?"

Tacitus and I followed Hylas into the library. He had several scrolls out on the main work table.

"I don't mean to add to your distress, my lord," Hylas said, "but I have pulled together several passages which mention Aristeas, and there are some ... unsettling similarities." He pulled out two sheets of papyrus. "I've made a copy of what I've noticed. First, the passage from Herodotus which you've already seen. Notice the references to Apollo and the raven. Aristeas was 'inspired by Phoebus Apollo' to travel to various places."

"The raven appears in a story about Apollo, doesn't it?" Tacitus asked. "He sent it to keep watch on some pregnant lover of his. When the bird reported the girl's infidelity, Apollo killed her and changed the raven's feathers from white to black."

"Yes, my lord. The girl's name was Coronis. Apollo also killed her lover, Ischys, but he saved the child, who became Asclepius."

"This is all nonsense," I said.

"But, my lord, I remembered the work of an obscure writer, Apollonius, from about three centuries ago. We have a copy of his *Historiae Mirabiles* because your uncle was interested in what you might deem fantastic tales. I copied the pertinent passage. As you can see, Apollonius reports that Aristeas' soul would leave his body, which remained 'in a state between life and death.'"

"Just as we found him."

" 'Lifeless but not dead' was how you first described him to me."

I nodded. "There were no signs of life—no breath, no pulsing of the heart—and yet none of the signs of death either—no stiffness, no odor, no decay."

"I'm not familiar with this Apollonius," Tacitus said. "He specifically mentions Aristeas?"

"Yes, my lord. He says his soul, like a bird, would travel about until it was ready to return to the body. It would sometimes be gone for long periods."

"And your uncle did record that Aristeas' soul left his body in the form of a raven," Tacitus said. "The evidence is piling up."

"Evidence of what? That we're reacting like frightened children to our nursemaids' stories?"

Tacitus sat down beside me. "Consider that you have two strangers in your house. One is named Apollodoros, Apollo's Gift, and the other is named Daphne, the girl Apollo pursued until she was changed into the laurel tree. And look here, in Herodotus. Next to the statue of Apollo, the people of Metapontum put up a statue of Aristeas, surrounded by laurel." He tapped the word ΔΑΦΝΑΙ in the text.

"There has to be some other explanation," I said, shaking my head.

"Does there? Can everything be explained?"

"Are you saying that Aristeas' murder has something to do with all of this nonsense about gods and souls?"

Tacitus sighed. "I'm saying I don't know what is nonsense and what isn't. I wasn't the one who saw a mark that isn't there any more."

Hylas put a scroll down in front of me. "My lord, Apollonius tells another story about a man's soul leaving his body. This man was named Hermotimus. His enemies burned his body while it lay defenseless so his soul would have nothing to re-enter."

"Does it say his body had a huge gash across the throat?"

"No, my lord, it doesn't."

"Then what relevance does that have right now?"

"My lord, aren't you burning Aristeas' body?"

I jumped up from the table. "I'm going back to check the pyre."

Tacitus kept pace with me. "Surely you don't think—"

"I think I'm going mad, or dreaming. I'll feel safer when I see that body reduced to ashes and scatter them myself, but I'm not sure even that will restore things to normal."

"Whatever happened to that piece of cloth with his face on it?"

I hadn't thought about the cloth since I handed it to Tranio. "I'll have Tranio get it out when we go back in the house. He stashed it somewhere safe."

We could see Daphne still keeping vigil by the pyre, with Chloris and my watchmen as her only companions. The heat had forced them all to move back.

"Your men did a good job of it," Tacitus said as we watched from a distance. "It's holding together well."

I nodded, reluctant to disturb Daphne. Flames as high as the roof of the stable engulfed the pyre now. The lower levels had turned to glowing coals and the top level was sinking, as should happen. The distorted figure of Aristeas could still be seen, drawn up like a man who was cold or in pain. "It does look like everything is under control," I said with a sigh of relief.

Tacitus slapped me on the back. "And not a raven in sight."

I ordered food to be brought to the bath. Since it was almost dark we used the indoor bath and ate while we cleansed ourselves of the stench of death. Afterward we sat on the terrace while Hylas read to us from Cicero's *Laelius*, a dialogue on friendship. When he came to the line, "Friendship is possible only between good men," he stopped.

I turned to find him looking at Tacitus and me. "Is something wrong, Hylas?"

"No, my lord. It's just that sometimes the words one reads take on a new meaning. I'm sorry for the interruption." He went on with the next line.

As the sun went below the horizon Tacitus said, "It smells like the pig's done, even if Aristeas isn't."

Before we could get up Blandina came out to the terrace. "My lord, Saturninus, the cheese man, would like to see you. Shall I bring him in?"

But Saturninus was right behind her. "Sirs, I'm sorry to barge in like this, but it's life or death."

"Whose?" I asked, standing in surprise.

"It's Myrrha, sir. Scaevola is on his way to Rome with her."

"Why is he leaving at night?"

"I think he wants to get her away before you can do anything about it. Please help her, sir."

I saw the lift of Tacitus' eyebrows. Something wasn't right, and he felt it too. Saturninus hated Myrrha and Chloris. "Why didn't you send a servant with a message?"

"Sirs, there's no time to tell the whole story."

"It will take Scaevola half the night to get to Rome and there won't be anyone around for him to turn Myrrha over to until morning. I feel like I'm stumbling around in the dark already. People keep revealing little surprises as it suits them. I need to know why you consider it so important for me to help Myrrha."

"Could we be alone, sir?"

Blandina didn't wait for me to send her off the terrace. She picked up a tray, bowed, and left.

Saturninus watched her until she closed the door. Then he turned to us, wringing his hands. "Sirs, the whole truth is ... I haven't said these words in twenty-five years. The truth is ... Myrrha is my daughter."

"Your daughter? But I've seen you practically spit in her face."

"Please, sir, I'll tell you the rest of it while we go after her."

"Saturninus, I have no authority here. I can't just grab a prisoner from the elected magistrate of the town."

"Sir, I am a Roman citizen. My father served in the legions—the Second Augusta—and got his citizenship when he retired. I have his diploma." He waited while I sorted through the implications of what he'd just said.

"And the daughter of a citizen cannot be sentenced to the arena without some sort of trial." It was a principle of law known to everyone in Rome. We don't refer to women as citizens in the same sense as men, but they enjoy the protection afforded to their male relatives.

"Does Scaevola know you're a citizen?" Tacitus asked.

"I've lived in that town all my life, sir, and so has he. We know all of one another's secrets."

"So that's why he's rushing her to Rome before we can stop him." I said. "He can claim he didn't know she was your daughter or didn't know you were a citizen, and it'll be too late to correct his 'mistake'."

"There you go, sir," Saturninus said as proudly as my tutors used to when I correctly parsed a line of poetry. "Will you help her?"

"By all means, but you will owe me an explanation of Homeric proportions afterwards."

"That you shall have, sir. That you shall have."

I told Tranio to round up a half dozen of the biggest servants on the place and arm them. I would have taken more, but that was all the horses we had on hand and there was no time to borrow any from the neighboring estates.

There was only one mounting stone in the paddock. As I waited my turn I could see that the funeral pyre was burning low. The servants tending it were still stoking it and stirring up the embers, but the flames had died down until they were no higher than a man's waist. Aristeas' body was no longer recognizable. Tomorrow, when the pyre cooled, we would sift through it and pull out whatever was recognizable as parts of his body. Having him tied to the boards should help keep his remains together. The intense heat would char the bones enough that they would crumble and could be put in an urn for me to carry out to scatter on the bay.

Or I might just throw the whole thing overboard so it would sink to the bottom. Ashes and bits of bone would float, no doubt, and I didn't want that to happen. Stories are already circulating of Christians snatching bits of the bodies of their executed fellow-believers to venerate. I don't want anyone to be able to form a cult of Aristeas.

Chloris entered the paddock by herself, with a gown draped over her arm. When Saturninus groaned at the sight of her, Tacitus and I exchanged a glance. The expression on his face revealed the truth. She was Myrrha's daughter, not her sister, and thus his granddaughter whom he had never been able to hold or kiss. But who was her father? The first answer that came into my head was one I had to reject immediately.

"Sir," Chloris said deliberately looking away from Saturninus, "one of your women let me have this. Would you let Myrrha wear it? You know what a mess she was the last time we saw her. I'm sure she's worse now."

I took the gown from her, draping it over the horse I was going to ride. "I'm glad you're so confident that we're going to get her back."

"Yes, sir. I do trust that you will."

"Where's Daphne?" I asked, glancing over her head.

"She wanted to be alone, so she walked into the woods."

The anxiety I was feeling made me snap at her. "Why did you let her do that? I have more I want to ask her about."

"I'm sorry, sir. She needed to be by herself."

I stepped onto the mounting stone and boosted myself onto the horse. I was getting control of the animal when Apollodoros came into the paddock.

"May I ride with you, sir?" he asked.

The request surprised me, but no more than anything else that had happened the past few days.

"This could be dangerous."

"I know, but I'm no longer welcome here. Your mother would be happier with me out of her sight. This is a way to repay your hospitality."

I looked down on him from my horse, glad that he was realistic about the situation, but suspicious of his motives. He didn't strike me as the heroic type. "Keeping you locked up all night is hardly what I'd call hospitality."

"I've known worse."

"All right. You can come with us. But you're not going anywhere else until I've gotten some answers." I motioned for one of my servants to give up his horse and give Apollodoros his sword. I could see relief all over my man's face.

We were all mounted and about to ride out when Tranio ran into the paddock. "My lord, I can't find that Daphne creature."

"I don't have time to sort this out. She was headed into the woods." I pointed in the direction Chloris had indicated. "Find her. Do not rest until you do."

XIII

**W**E GALLOPED THROUGH LAURENTUM in the last rays of day-light, scattering a few stray dogs and two drunkards on their way home—the Long and the Short of it, I thought.

According to Saturninus, Scaevola was encumbered by the wag-on carrying Myrrha. That worked to our advantage, but Scaevola had a good head start and several former legionaries in his entou-rage. He was one of those men of modest means who, in an effort to emulate men of my class, take on the most disreputable sort of men as clients, just to increase the size of the crowd at his door in the morning.

We'd been riding about half an hour when I saw a wagon and several horsemen ahead of us. I signaled for my small force to stop. Tacitus brought his horse up beside mine.

"I don't see any choice but a direct attack, do you?" he asked. "Do you think we could get them off their horses? It's so damnably difficult to fight from horseback, even if you have the training, and we don't."

"I'd like to see if we can negotiate first. We know he's just trying to get around the law. He thinks we don't know Myrrha is a citizen's daughter. Once we confront him, perhaps we can make him hand her over."

"He doesn't strike me as the negotiating type," Tacitus said, "but I guess it's worth a try. I'd rather not have any blood shed, especially my own."

We caught up with Scaevola's group and I hailed them. There were five men in addition to Scaevola, four on horseback—includ-ing Licinius Strabo—and one driving the wagon, the same open wagon in which Aristeas' body had been transported earlier. Torches had been attached to each side. Myrrha sat in it, still in manacles and now with a chain from one ankle attached to one of the slats in the side of the wagon. Scaevola gave the order to stop and turned his horse.

"What do you want, Gaius Pliny?"

"I want Myrrha, who is the daughter of a Roman citizen, to have the rights to which she is entitled. You know that what you're doing is against the law."

Scaevola smirked. "Everything has been done by the letter of the law. The whore had a trial this afternoon, after you left my house."

"Who tried her?"

"The duovirs of Laurentum presided, as the law requires." He pointed to himself and Strabo. "We considered the evidence and found her guilty."

"Who spoke for her?"

"The only man who was willing, Publius Gabinus."

I didn't know the name, so I looked at Saturninus. "He runs the tavern across the street from my shop," the cheese-maker said.

Of course. The tavern which the Licinius family owned.

"Scaevola, I don't want to interfere with the proper execution of the law." I regretted my choice of words immediately. "There are questions about what happened to the man Myrrha is accused of killing, questions which I don't believe we've had time to answer. All I'm asking for is a day or two's delay while I look into it. If her innocence cannot be established, I won't stand in your way."

"You're standing in my way right now, Gaius Pliny. Since you're obstructing a magistrate who is trying to carry out his duty, I have the right to remove you."

He drew his sword and his men turned on us. Saturninus tried to take the lead on our side, but he was the first to be knocked off his horse. I heard him moan as he hit the ground.

Fighting in the dark, with only the flickering torches for illumination, swords clanking, and horses neighing, made the whole scene feel like something out of Plato's description of the damned souls in Tartarus. Scaevola's men were shouting encouragement to one another, striking even more fear into my men.

Tacitus did manage to take down one of Scaevola's men, but their skill at warfare was more than we could stand against.

As soon as the first blows were struck, Apollodoros pulled his horse to the side of the road and around Scaevola's group. For an instant I thought he might be trying for a rear assault, but he lashed the horse with the ends of the reins and bolted away up the road.

Of course, I thought, as I parried a blow from Strabo and squeezed my knees tightly to stay on my horse. What other reason would he have for volunteering?

Scaevola himself led the attack, and he was ferocious. I was holding my own against Strabo, but my other men were being pushed back so rapidly I was about to give the order to withdraw in order to save their lives when a large bat swooped down right into Strabo's face. His horse reared in fright and Strabo fell off.

As soon as Strabo went down, the bat flew off. I would have sworn the creature had singled him out to attack. I seized the advantage I had been given. Dismounting, I stood over Strabo with my sword at his throat.

"Drop your weapons," I barked, "or I'll kill him."

"You heard him," Scaevola said without any sense of urgency. "Stop!" He guided his horse over to where his son lay. "It's tempting, though, to let you go ahead and kill him. Can't even stay on his horse." His lip curled in a sneer. "I have a cross-eyed fool for a colleague this year, just as I've had a cross-eyed fool for a son all these years."

"Father, please don't let him—"

"Stop sniveling. He's not going to hurt you. You're the one who pushed me into this and now you can't stay on your horse." He turned to the driver of the cart. "Unchain the whore. Isn't that what you're going to demand next, Gaius Pliny?"

I nodded, taken completely by surprise by his attitude. "You men, pick up their weapons," I ordered. "Take any others they have. I'll send them back tomorrow." I looked up at Scaevola. "And we're taking Strabo as a hostage. If you pursue us, I'll kill him."

Scaevola laughed and said in Greek, "You're a scholar, a man of books. You could no more kill my son than you could throw your own mother off a cliff. I could do it; you couldn't. But I'll pretend to be concerned so we can play this out."

"I'll send him back tomorrow with your weapons."

"Keep them—and him—as long as you like. I have little use for either."

"Myrrha does have some use for the bag with the fifty aurei in it which you took from her. That must be returned."

"Fifty aurei? In a bag? Why, Gaius Pliny, I don't know what you're talking about."

Myrrha scrambled out of the wagon, rubbing her wrists and shivering. With the sun down now, the air was growing chill and her gown was soaked in blood, sweat, and other excretions. The man Tacitus had wounded took her place and lay down. I handed her the clean gown, expecting her to step behind a tree at the side of the road to change, but she slipped off her old gown where she stood and put on the clean one. In the dim light of the torches I thought I could detect a mark of a whip on her back. She'd never been a slave. When would she have been whipped?

Seeing my startled expression, she said, "They've all seen me naked, every last man of 'em. And I mean all of yours, too."

Chloris had been right about Myrrha growing old. The glimpse I had in the unsteady light didn't arouse any erotic feelings in me.

Scaevola's horse reared as he guided the animal closer to me. "You do realize that you're interfering with a magistrate trying to carry out his duty, don't you, Gaius Pliny?"

"Is it a magistrate's duty to rush a defenseless woman into the arena to settle an old grudge?" I tightened my grip on my sword, even though he was now unarmed. "She will be as secure in my custody as in yours until we get to the bottom of this."

"Are you sure there is a bottom?"

"I'm afraid Saturninus is badly injured," Tacitus whispered to me as we watched Scaevola's party start back to Laurentum.

"There's no doctor in Laurentum. What's wrong with him?"

"He has a sword wound—a big gash across his stomach. He's bleeding badly, and he hit his head pretty hard when he fell off his horse. I don't think he can survive a trip back to your villa."

"I doubt we could do anything for him there anyway."

"At his age, I wish we could have persuaded him not to come."

Myrrha was standing on the edge of the road, fighting back tears as she looked at Saturninus. I stepped over to her and said, "It's all right. We know."

She ran to her father, dropped to her knees and cradled his head against her bosom. "Papa, please forgive me."

"For what, darlin'? I'm the one who ... needs forgiveness. I turned my own daughter out. Made her and my granddaughter ... into whores. What sort of man am I?"

I knelt beside them and took Saturninus' hand. "I know this is hard, my friend, but what can you tell me about the man who was murdered fifteen years ago? I think this whole business is as much about him as it is about Aristeas."

Saturninus took a breath and moaned. I knew he wasn't going to live long. He kept his eyes on Myrrha's face as he talked in such a low voice I could barely hear him.

"Myrrha and me, we was always ... more like cats and dogs than father and daughter. I had arranged a ... a marriage for her, but she refused. She was in love with somebody ... wanted to marry him. I threw her out and she went to him. She got pregnant."

As Saturninus paused, Myrrha said, "And then he told me he never would marry me. I wasn't good enough to be his wife, just his whore. He would never admit my child was his. He said I was never to tell nobody. If anybody came to him and told him about this child, he would know that I told 'em, and he would have me killed."

"Who was he?"

"It doesn't matter," Myrrha said. "He left here long ago."

I wanted to know more than that, but she obviously wasn't going to tell me now. "So you went back home?"

Myrrha nodded.

"I didn't want to take her back,"Saturninus said. "But my wife ... wouldn't let me send her completely away. Most of my money ... comes from my wife's dowry. She said if I drove Myrrha out, she would ... divorce me and take the dowry with her."

So their marriage had not been the most formal type possible under Roman law.

"She insisted we give Myrrha ... and her child a place to live. On her death bed she made me ... promise I wouldn't cast them out."

I turned to Myrrha. "Chloris is your daughter, isn't she?"

"Yes, sir."

"And she doesn't know that Saturninus is her grandfather?"

"No, sir. But please don't say nothin'. Let me tell her."

Saturninus grabbed Myrrha's arm as a wave of pain washed over him. "And I wouldn't let my wife give them any money," he wailed. "I locked up my strongbox ... just like I locked up my heart, and I ... turned my daughter and my granddaughter into whores. Can you imagine what that ... feels like, Gaius Pliny?"

"You did what you thought was right, Saturninus. That's all any man can do."

Saturninus coughed up blood. "The only right thing ... I ever did in my life was getting rid of that dead man in Myrrha's room ... so they couldn't accuse her of killing him. I wrapped him up and ... stuffed him down that old well."

"I didn't kill him, Papa. And I didn't kill this man Aristeas either."

"I know, darlin'. But I had to ... protect you."

"It's all right, Papa. Chloris and me can take care of ourselves."

"You'll get everything. My will ... in the strongbox ... the key." He touched a thin piece of leather around his neck. Myrrha pulled it out from under his tunic and fingered two keys hanging on the end of it. "Big one ... for the shop door," Saturninus said. "Little one ... strongbox."

"Thank you, Papa."

"I'm afraid for you," Saturninus gasped. "Scaevola wants the building ... Don't ... don't let him ..."

I patted the old man's arm. "I'll see that everything is carried out according to your wishes, my friend."

Myrrha looked at me in surprise. "Sir?"

"That's what I do for my friends." Raising my voice, I said, "With Cornelius Tacitus and Licinius Strabo as witnesses, I hereby acknowledge Saturninus and his entire family as my friends."

Saturninus shuddered and went limp. I stepped away and let Myrrha hold her father and weep over him.

"I told you," Tacitus said as I stood beside him, "there was something between them that we weren't privy too. I'm surprised your mother doesn't know all about this."

"It happened twenty-five years ago. My father was still alive. We didn't spend much time down here then."

"But you said you were here when your sister was still-born."

I nodded. "The birth was posthumous. My father died before my mother even knew she was pregnant."

"So even before your mother started buying cheese at Saturninus' shop, Chloris had already been born and the town was keeping the secret."

"Yes, small towns are good at that."

We had no choice but to hoist Saturninus' body over the back of the horse he'd been riding and tie him on. I hated to treat the old gentleman with such little dignity. Tacitus and I led the funeral procession, with Licinius Strabo behind us and my servants bringing up the rear with Saturninus' body. We kept a slow pace to avoid jostling him too much.

"Were you surprised by Apollodoros' desertion?" Tacitus asked.

"A bit, although I guess I shouldn't have been."

"Where do you think he went?"

"To wherever he stashed the money he and Aristeas made on this scheme of theirs. They must have hidden it somewhere, since neither of them was carrying anything."

"And there must be some vials of blood—or something that passes for blood—hidden along with it. Are you going to try to find him?"

I shook my head. "That wasn't even one of my best horses he stole. I doubt we'll ever see him or the horse again."

Myrrha rode behind me, clutching me tightly and with her head pressed against me. There was nothing erotic in the gesture. If there could have been, the memory of coupling with her daughter squelched it. I could tell that, by the time we reached my house, the back of my tunic would be as wet from her tears as if I'd been caught in the rain.

"That bat certainly did you a favor," Tacitus said.

"Yes. I've never seen or heard of anything quite like that. It singled out Strabo, knocked him off his horse, and then flew off, as though it had done what it came to do."

Tacitus looked over his shoulder at Strabo. "Do you have any bats among your enemies?"

"Are you sure it was a bat?" Strabo asked. "Did you see the white face on the thing?"

Riding in the dark, with Saturninus' body only a few paces behind me, I couldn't get my mind off the story he'd told of his life. How could a man live with himself when he had rejected his own daughter but had to see her every day? How could he watch his beautiful granddaughter grow up under his own roof and not want to play with her and hold her? How could he bear the thought that every man who made his way down that narrow alley was going to couple with his daughter or granddaughter?

Perhaps he couldn't.

Could the anger and pain that he felt for so long have led him to kill a man who raped his ten-year-old granddaughter? He said he knew Myrrha didn't kill the man. Did he say that with such confidence because he knew who did? Had that secret died with him? I had no way to solve a murder from years ago, but I couldn't shake the feeling that it had more to do with Aristeas' murder than I could fathom at the moment.

As we rode through Laurentum, we passed Saturninus' building. The sight reminded me that, while Myrrha's knife was too sharp to have inflicted the wound I saw on Aristeas' throat, a cheese shop must have at least a few knives in it. The presence of a rough-bladed knife wouldn't convict Saturninus of murder, but the absence of one would make me feel better about his innocence.

"Let's stop here." I reined in my horse in front of the shop.

"What are we doing?" Tacitus asked.

"We ought to get that strongbox," I said. "Once people find out Saturninus is dead, they won't hesitate to loot the place."

"I'll be surprised if my father hasn't already been in here," Licinius Strabo said from behind me. He'd been so quiet during the ride that I'd forgotten he was there.

Myrrha and I dismounted and stepped up on the sidewalk in front of the shop.

"It doesn't look like the door's been tampered with," I said. "Try your key."

Myrrha slipped the larger key into the lock and, after some jiggling, it turned. The door, on its leather hinges, sagged as I opened it. It wouldn't stand up to a determined assault. Myrrha found two lamps and a flint to light them.

"Do you have any idea where your father kept his strongbox?"

"When I was a child he kept it upstairs. He would keep a few coins down here in a bowl, to do business with durin' the day, but everything went in the strongbox at night."

"Let's hope he didn't change his habits," I said as I cupped my hand around the tiny flame and looked for the stairs. Shelves along one wall held the dozen or so types of cheeses that Saturninus made or bought from local farms. Along a side wall sat a rack containing wooden kitchen utensils.

"Your mother used to carve those, didn't she?"

Myrrha nodded. "There aren't many left. I guess Papa never found nobody else to make more ... I could have." She wiped away tears. "Mama started teaching me when I was seven."

Even in the meager light, it was painful to see her realizing what sort of life she might have had. I wanted to know so much. Whom had Saturninus chosen for her to marry? Why did she refuse? Who was the father of her child?

"This way," Myrrha said, leading me into a room behind the main room and up a narrow stone stairway. "Careful, sir. The footin's none too good."

The upper story of the building consisted of one large, dingy room, which had not known a woman's touch for several years. Myrrha lit candles in several sconces. An unmade bed, with clothing strewn around it, occupied one of the short walls. The opposite short wall was where Myrrha's mother had plied her trade. None of her tools or unfinished utensils appeared to have been touched. Another bed at that end testified to the painful separation between husband and wife. Just over their daughter?

The back wall of the room had two windows, with shutters, overlooking the courtyard and the aqueduct behind the building. A table, still littered with wood shavings, and a chair sat under one of the windows.

"Did you realize that your mother sat here working and watching you and Chloris?"

"No, sir, I didn't. I talked to her a few times over the years, whenever Papa wasn't around. She never told me she was watchin' us." Myrrha ran her hand over the table and looked out the window. "Chloris loved to play outside when she was little, and, of course, I had to send her out, if the weather was good, whenever I had ... company. She could hear too much in her room, and I knew the men would go after her soon enough. I wanted to keep her away from all that as long as I could."

"Of course. The mentulas."

Myrrha chuckled. "Chloris told you what she calls 'em, I see."

I didn't want to say any more about my connection with her daughter. "What was your mother's name?"

"She was called Livilla, and she had hair as red as Chloris'."

I scanned the room, looking for a hiding place. "Do you know where your father kept his strongbox?"

"Yes. My room is right under this one. Every night I could hear him raise a floorboard and drop money into the box. I figured he could hear me, too, so I always made some noise whenever a man was with me, just to torment him." She suppressed a sob. "By the gods, I was so stupid."

Under Saturninus' bed we found a gap between two floorboards. Using one of the knives from Livilla's tools, Myrrha pried the board up. "It's here, sir."

"That's a relief. Now, is there anything in it?"

When Myrrha shook the metal box it rattled quite convincingly. It must contain a considerable sum of money. But I also heard some papyrus crackling, so I put my hand on the box.

"Be careful. It sounds like you might be damaging whatever documents are in there. Let's take it back to my house and open it there. I'd like to get out of here before Scaevola gets any ideas about visiting the place. I don't think we could beat him in another fight."

Myrrha nodded. "We might not be so lucky as to have a bat on our side. I've never seen nothin' like that."

I didn't want to be reminded that we would have lost without another eerie incident.

Before Myrrha extinguished the candles I looked over her mother's wood-working tools. None of them had extremely sharp edges, but most of them were curved or shaped in some way that made them particularly useful for this task but not for slashing a man's throat. I held one lightly on my own throat.

Myrrha gasped when she saw what I was doing. "Sir, you don't think my mother—"

"She obviously didn't kill Aristeas, but what about Licinius Macer, fifteen years ago? If she was accustomed to sit here by the window, she could have seen him leave after he attacked Chloris."

"Did Chloris tell you about that?"

I nodded.

"That girl! I told her never to tell no one. Sir, I swear to you that no one in this family killed that man."

My face must have told her I doubted her words.

"My mother said she knew who did it."

"Who was it?"

"She wouldn't tell me. She was afraid, if I knew, I might say somethin'. 'A secret can't be kept,' she used to say, 'by more than one person.'"

"Why didn't she tell the duovirs?"

"She said they would never believe her. They might even prosecute her for bringin' a false charge. Nothin' would be gained by accusin' someone. Macer had been punished for what he done. That was all that mattered."

"But what if the person who killed Macer also killed Aristeas?"

"Do you think that's possible, sir?"

"I didn't see Macer's body, but Scaevola said he was killed the same way Aristeas was."

When we returned to the ground floor and the cheese shop, I asked Myrrha where Saturninus kept his knives.

"He only had a handful of them," she said. "When he cut cheese he used that." She pointed to a device lying on the counter. "My mother made the handle."

The device she indicated was something I'd seen many times. It consisted of a U-shaped handle, about half a cubit from end to end, with a very thin piece of metal, more like a string, attached to the ends. Saturninus simply pressed down and slid the piece of metal through any chunk of cheese he wanted to cut.

"Some cheeses crumble," Myrrha said, "when you try to slice 'em with a knife."

"I wonder what effect this would have on a man's throat."

"Oh, sir, you can't really think—"

Gripping the cheese-cutter with both hands, I stood behind her and slipped the device over her head, so the wire rested on her throat. "All I would have to do," I said, "is pull back."

"That's true, sir, but it doesn't mean that's what happened to Aristeas."

"All the same, I want to take this with me. And I want to look at Saturninus' knives."

"They're under the counter, to the right."

As Myrrha had said, there were only five knives, all extremely sharp.

"He kept his equipment in excellent condition," she said.

"Is that where you learned to do that?"

"Sir?"

"The knife under the table by your bed."

I could see her blush, even in the dim light. "A woman has to protect herself, sir."

Getting the strongbox home proved awkward. It was too large and heavy for Myrrha to hold while she was clinging to me. While Tacitus and I were considering possibilities, Myrrha solved the problem by bringing two baskets out of the shop, tying their handles together with a short piece of rope and throwing them over the horse carrying Saturninus. She put the strongbox in one basket and enough rocks in the other basket to balance the load. I put the cheese-cutter in as well, so I could examine it in daylight for traces of blood. I thought it appropriate that Saturninus got to make his final journey with his worldly goods and his most important tool so close to him.

As we mounted our horses again, Myrrha gave me the piece of leather with the two keys on it. "Can I ask you, sir, as one of your friends, if you would keep these?"

"But you won't be able to open the box."

"I want to open it in your presence. I don't want nobody to say I had a chance to tamper with whatever's in there. I couldn't, of course, since I can't read, but somebody'll come up with the idea that I might have, or that Chloris might."

Licinius Strabo, riding between Tacitus and me now, said hardly a word on the rest of the trip, and then only in response to one of us. I pitied the man. His father had humiliated him in front of other men whom he would have to face for the rest of his life. And I suspected this wasn't the first time it had happened.

Scaevola seemed to have no respect—not to mention affection—for his son. He had even given him a cognomen which drew attention to an unfortunate accident of his birth. Most men dote on the son who will carry on the family name and inherit their property.

As much as I hated Regulus, I had to concede that he could play the proud father as well as anyone. As in everything else, though, he carried it beyond all moderation, showering extravagant gifts on his infant son and expecting his clients and anyone who wanted a favor from him to treat the boy as though he was the first child ever born, some miracle that only Regulus could work.

Although my uncle's official duties had sometimes taken him away for long periods, I knew he loved me, and I always looked forward to his homecoming. I wondered if Strabo even looked forward to his father walking into the same room with him.

"I'm afraid I'll have to keep you as a hostage for a few days," I told him, "just until I can sort out some things. Please, consider yourself my guest."

"You heard my father. He doesn't care if I ever come back. And right now it doesn't matter to me either."

Even though it was quite dark when we got home, everyone was up and eager to hear what had happened. Myrrha slid off the horse and I followed her. My mother grieved genuinely when she saw Saturninus.

"He was such a fine man, modest and decent."

"Yes, he was," I said. She didn't need to know he had driven his only child out and blamed himself for making her and her daughter prostitutes. "That's why I was glad to receive him among my friends just before he died."

"Well, that was a lovely gesture, dear."

"It was more than a gesture, Mother. This is his daughter." I put my hand on Myrrha's arm and pulled her closer to me.

Mother drew back in shock. "The whore?"

I pointed my finger at my mother and spoke in the sharpest tone I had ever used with her. "You will never again say that word to her or about her—or Chloris. They are the owners of a cheese shop, and they are among our friends."

"But ... but I thought she killed a man."

"No, she didn't. And I'm going to prove it."

"Well, this is ... a lot to take in at one time," Mother said, glancing at Naomi.

"Where is Apollodoros?" Naomi asked. "Did something happen to him?" She was trying to keep the expectation out of her voice.

"He ran off," Tacitus said, "just as the fighting started, like a man who was late for dinner. Stole a horse and a sword in the process."

"Humph," Mother said. "His sort would do that, I suppose."

Tacitus lowered his head and sighed. "I suppose so, my lady. It has been an exhausting day. I'd like to go to bed."

"Of course," Mother said. "Take the room with the fresco of Chiron and Achilles. It's the second one off the courtyard, on your left."

"And Myrrha needs to see Chloris," I said. "In private. Where is she?"

"She was on the terrace the last time I saw her," Naomi said, "about half an hour ago."

I pointed to my left and Myrrha started off with a much lighter step than I would have expected from a woman who had endured all that she had in the last two days. She even forgot the strongbox.

My mother, Naomi, and the rest of the onlookers began to douse their lamps and return to the house. I supervised as Tranio and a couple of other servants moved Saturninus into the stall where we had kept Aristeas.

"I don't think he's going anywhere," I told Tranio, "but post a guard anyway."

He nodded his approval. "It's good to have someone with him, my lord. If you don't keep 'em company, the dead gets lonely and angry."

Would I always be surrounded by such fools? "Find out which room Myrrha will be staying in," I told him, "and take the strongbox there."

"Certainly, my lord. The funeral pyre is just about burned down. We should be able to gather the ashes in the morning."

"Post a couple of guards on the pyre throughout the night. And put the ashes in something that won't break."

"Not an amphora, then, my lord?"

"No. Use that brass urn in the library, and seal the top as tightly as you can."

"Yes, my lord."

"And put something heavy in the bottom, to make sure it will sink."

"Sink, my lord?"

"Just do it."

"Yes, my lord. And I guess we'd better start building another pyre tomorrow."

"Do we have enough dry wood?"

"That could be a problem, my lord. I'll send around to the neighbors and see what we can gather up."

"Before you do that, why don't you talk to my mother and Naomi. There might be an alternative."

"My lord?"

"Just ask them. I'm too tired to explain. Was there any of the roast pig left?"

"Yes, my lord. And it was quite good."

"Fine, I'll get some on my way to bed. Good night, Tranio."

I stood in the dark, watching the last embers of Aristeas' pyre glow like a sunset against a cloud-streaked sky.

"Thank you for taking such good care of my father," Daphne suddenly said from behind me. I had no warning of her approach.

I jerked around, my hand on my chest. "How do you sneak up on people like that?"

"I'm sorry to have frightened you. I learned how as a child. When people don't want you around, you learn to move quietly and quickly, so they don't notice you."

My breathing slowed down. "You didn't frighten me. You ... surprised me. I'm not one of those people you need to hide from. Just make a little noise when you approach me—a cough, anything. As for taking care of your father, I'm glad to do it."

"Even though you don't believe that the soul exists after death?"

This struck me as a strange turn to the conversation, but everything about Daphne seemed strange.

"Yes," I said, "even though. I allow Naomi to practice her rituals, although I see no point in them. People should be able to find comfort in dark moments of their lives, I suppose." I certainly wished I could have found some in the darkest moment of my life, when Vesuvius was erupting and I thought the world was ending.

"Where do you find comfort, sir?"

I didn't hesitate. "In knowing the truth."

Daphne nodded, as though weighing my answer. "Can you always know the truth?"

"Perhaps not always, but if I know I've tried as hard as I can to find it, I'm satisfied."

"Have you found the truth about Aristeas yet?"

"No, nor have I found the truth about Apollodoros, or about you." Scaevola's question—whether there actually was a bottom to whatever was going on—kept nagging at me, but I didn't want to expose any more of my uncertainty to Daphne. "I'm glad to see that you got a chance to bathe and change clothes."

She looked down at herself. "Your woman Naomi found a linen gown for me. It's the only type of material I can stand to have touching my skin. I was also given some make-up."

She had applied the make-up more heavily than any woman I'd ever known. "How is your shoulder?"

"The wound is healing." She touched the spot. "It needs no further attention."

I was still curious about one thing. "How were you traveling without any supplies? A woman traveling is usually as heavily laden as a soldier."

She laughed, but it wasn't a happy sound. "I travel lighter than most, more like a scout than a legionary. My things are in a room in an inn in Laurentum. I hope to get back there and pay my bill before the innkeeper sells it all."

"I'll send someone in the morning to settle up and get your belongings."

"Thank you. Will there be a guard on my door tonight?"

"No. Come and go as you please."

She drew her cloak around her in a way that made me shudder. "Thank you, sir. I will."

Once I was in my quarters, with the door securely fastened behind me, I pulled out the leather tube with Aurora's note in it, still hanging around my neck along with the keys Myrrha had given me for safekeeping. Contrary to all of Tacitus' lurid speculation, the note was not a love letter. Aurora and I had grown up together since she arrived in our house, fifteen years ago. When children are seven, the distinction between slave and free doesn't much matter. As children, we played together, with the children of our other servants. Being the daughter of my uncle's mistress, Aurora always enjoyed a privileged status in our *familia*.

But Aurora and I discovered that we both had an interest in observing people around us. And we weren't the only ones. Rome has always been rife with spies, *delatores*, hoping to profit from catching someone in a misstep and reporting them to the authorities for a large reward. Under Nero, Regulus made a fortune by ruining people in that way. When Vespasian came to power, Regulus made a show of defending people in court. Now he was back to his role as the bloated spider whose web extended into every noble house in Rome. He sat at the center, waiting for the slightest jiggling of that web.

Perhaps we Romans have a natural bent for spying on one another. From the time Aurora and I were twelve we made a game of sitting on street corners, trying to remain inconspicuous, and learning as much as we could about what people were talking about and what they were up to. It's amazing what people will reveal about themselves when they're not aware they're being observed, and children are the last to be suspected as spies. The only drawback to our game was Aurora's beauty. Even at that age, she had to learn to disguise herself, like Odysseus covering his heroic demeanor and making himself look like a beggar. At least he had Athena's help.

I held the letter to my nose. It bore the scent of Aurora's favorite perfume, a fragrance subtle yet unmistakable, like the woman who wears it. I think she deliberately puts a drop or two on her letters to me when I'm away. I'm grateful for the reminder of her.

I suspect Aurora has feelings for me that go well beyond friendship or the respect a servant should have for a master. But I cannot let myself feel anything of the sort for her. I don't believe a master should take advantage of his power over a servant in that way. As far as I know, my uncle didn't force himself on Monica, Aurora's mother, but that sort of relationship is frowned upon in our circles, in spite of how common it is. With no fear of hypocrisy, even emperors have had slave women as mistresses.

Aurora tends to my personal needs, almost as a wife would, and seems to relish doing so. It would be easier to have a relationship with her if I freed her, but what if I'm mistaken? If she doesn't love me—and she has never said she does—she might go off with another man once she was freed. And if she did that ...

Before I broke the seal I made sure it bore the print of her thumb.

In her letters Aurora uses one of two circular codes. In one she substitutes B for A, C for B, and so on, what we call the primary code. In the other she substitutes A for B, B for C and so on, or the secondary code. We learned the simple trick when we were reading Julius Caesar. My uncle recognized Aurora's keen mind early on and wanted her to be schooled. He felt she could provide me with a rival to make me work harder. When she seals her notes to me, if she is using the primary code, she puts her thumb print in the wax. If the letter is written in the secondary code, she puts the print of her little finger.

One of the first things I did when I assumed my role as master of the house after my uncle's death was to give Aurora permission to be out of the house any time she wanted, without answering to my steward or my doorkeeper—or to me. I did so because she has continued our spying game from childhood, but she takes it more seriously these days. Every household, she says, needs a pair of eyes and ears in places where the master cannot go. She disguises herself as a workman's wife and goes into parts of town where she can listen to people talk unguardedly. When she shaves me each morning—which she has done since we were sixteen—it gives us a private time to discuss what she has learned.

Earlier this year she struck up a friendship with a freedwoman, Callista, from Regulus' house and has gained her trust enough to find out some things that go on there. Apparently it doesn't take much wine at all to loosen the woman's tongue. I want to know who Regulus' mole in my house is, or at least have a way to get information about what Regulus is up to. Aurora may give me my best chance of doing so.

I sat down at my table in the alcove that gives me a view of the bay. As the moon broke through the clouds I could tell that the trees at the top of the cliffs around the bay were growing leafier. Their rustling could even be heard mingled with the lapping of the waves on the shore.

I opened the letter and began to decode it. After a few moments I could read:

*Aurora to her beloved lord Gaius Pliny, greetings.*

*I hope you are enjoying your time at Laurentum. I know it gives you the quiet you need to study and write. I remember the place fondly from the times we were there as children, especially that cave overlooking the bay. Everyone here misses you and looks forward to your return.*

*I'm afraid the news I have will disturb your quiet, and yet I don't see how I can delay in sending it. It's ironic that Narcissus will deliver the message, like Bellerophon carrying the letter to the king of Lycia telling the king to kill the bearer of the letter. Let me say at once that I'm not suggesting you kill Narcissus, but he's not going to tell you the truth about the man who came to our door several days ago, the one you sent to ask about. I think he would if he knew the truth—he's a decent, if unbearably pompous, man—but in this case he simply doesn't know the truth.*

*Callista told me about an 'odd little man' who came to their door a few days ago, looking for Pliny. Someone had directed him to our street but, with Regulus' house being close to ours and bigger, he went to the wrong one first. Callista said that, as soon as Regulus heard someone was looking for you, he had him brought in and talked with him in private for half an hour, then sent him down to our house. She doesn't know what they talked about, but Regulus seemed elated afterwards.*

*She was surprised that someone who was looking for you got such a gracious reception from Regulus. His hatred of you is so deep, she tells me, she has heard him say many times that he would give half his fortune to see you ruined.*

*I don't know what this man wants, or if he made some kind of arrangement with Regulus. I just wanted to warn you to be careful in dealing with him. We wouldn't know what to do if something happened to you.*

*Given on the tenth day before the Kalends of April.*

# XIV

**THE NEXT MORNING** I was up just before sunrise, eager to dispose of Aristeas' ashes. If he was in collusion with Regulus, then I had more reason than just a mark on his chest to want to be rid of him, absolutely and without any further doubt.

We had let the ashes cool overnight, with guards posted around the site of the pyre. While I was getting dressed, Tranio had collected the remains in an urn and sealed it with wax. Bones don't really burn, but they become dry and brittle enough that they can be crushed into a powder, with only pieces from some of the largest bones—the ones in the legs—still recognizable.

Tacitus doesn't get up early, so I assumed I would have to go alone. Tranio brought the urn to me on the terrace overlooking the bay. The urn is a non-descript piece, lacking decoration of any kind, that my uncle brought back from one of his campaigns, nothing like the gold urn in which Achilles placed Patroclus' ashes in the *Iliad*. About a cubit in height, it has two handles and a wide mouth with a flat lid. What attracted him to it, he told me, were the hooks at the top of each handle that allowed the urn to be hung over a fire. "Makes it very useful for warming a stew on a cold night," he said. "Or a bit of wine."

What does a body mean, I thought, if it can be reduced to a pile of ashes that will fit into something no larger than this?

"Do you think we'll have enough wood to build a pyre for Saturninus?" I asked Tranio as I hefted the urn.

"About that, my lord ... Macrinus took a look at the fella last night."

I wasn't surprised to hear that. Macrinus has a doctor's interest in the insides of the human body, which he can see only when someone has been gashed or pierced.

"Did he learn anything we didn't already know? I did see the man receive the wound."

"I know, my lord. But you probably didn't see that he's circumcised."

"He was a Jew?"

"'Pears so, my lord. Born to 'em, at least. In all the years I've known him, though, I never heard he was livin' like one of 'em."

That would explain why he had been so careful to wrap a towel around himself before he spoke to Tacitus and me in the bath, and why he was bathing at a time when the place was all but deserted. Some Jewish men who want to fit into public life find themselves embarrassed in the baths. My uncle had read somewhere that Jewish men who wanted to look non-Jewish even underwent a painful procedure to reverse the circumcision inflicted on them as babies.

I waited for Tranio to say more. "What does his being Jewish ... Oh, wait, they don't burn their dead, do they?"

"No, my lord. I was thinking we could save ourselves a lot of work—and wood—if we asked Naomi how we ought to proceed."

The man was making another decision, almost on his own. Perhaps there was hope for him. "I'll do that as soon as I get back from disposing of this thing. It's heavier than I would have thought."

"I weighted it down good, my lord. I know you don't want it bobbing around in the water."

"No, I want it on the bottom of the bay, out of sight and out of mind forever."

As I was descending the steps down the cliff I decided to look in the cave where Aurora and I had played as children. Would it be a suitable place to lay Saturninus? We could cover the mouth of it to keep animals out. Naomi said the Jews let the body decay for a year, then collected the bones and placed them in a stone coffin. Even if he had abandoned Judaism, Saturninus couldn't know or care if we treated his remains that way, and it would be a lot easier on my servants. I should also ask Myrrha. Did she know her father was Jewish?

The mouth of the cave was small. Aurora and I used to lie down there, side by side, and watch fishermen on the bay and the dolphins that seemed to enjoy the place. It was high enough above the water that it stayed dry. I did not see any evidence that anyone was visiting it, not even an infernal bat. My servants had reported stories about a bear in the neighborhood recently, but I saw no indications the creature was using this cave as a lair. With a few large rocks to cover the mouth, it should make a safe burial site for a year, if Myrrha approved.

With the urn under my arm I got down the cliff to where my uncle kept a small boat in a shed. I set the urn down in the sand and went into the shed to drag the boat out. When I got the nose of it into the water and turned around to get the urn, I was startled to see Daphne standing over it. I hadn't heard a sound.

"Are those my father's ashes?"

"Yes. How ... how did you get here? I didn't see you or hear you when I came down. I did ask you to give me some warning."

"Sorry. Force of habit. I like to be by the water early in the morning, before the sun gets too bright for me to endure it. Being down in this cove, at the bottom of the cliff, lets me enjoy the light without actually being directly in it."

I looked around at the sand along the cove. "Where did you come from? I don't see any footprints." This was the second time in as many days that she had sneaked up on me like this.

"They've been washed away by now, I guess. I was walking right on the edge of the water." She drew her cloak around her. "I like to get my feet in the water. You're about to dispose of my father's ashes, I take it."

"Yes, if I can get this boat launched."

"Let me help you."

Together we pushed the boat farther into the water. I was fumbling with the oars when Daphne picked up the urn. "It's heavier than I thought it would be."

"Tranio added weight so it would sink."

Daphne brought it to me. "Would you like for me to come with you? This boat looks like it could be hard for just one person to handle."

A voice in my head said, *The empusa wants to get you alone in a boat out on the water. Don't be a fool!*

"I would appreciate the help," I said. The empusa loses her powers in daylight, I reminded the voice.

Daphne placed the urn in the boat. I helped her step in, pushed the boat a few paces farther into the water, and jumped in myself. Picking up the oars, I rowed us out into the middle of the bay. It's a narrow inlet, with steep cliffs on each side, lined with houses.

"Do you know how deep it is?" Daphne asked, peering over the side.

"No, I don't. I've seen some fairly large fishing boats come in close to shore." I looked into the water, which was clear and calm. "I can still see the bottom. I want to get far enough out so someone won't notice the urn and think they've found a treasure. People do dive here for pearls. My neighbor, Lucius Volconius, spends a lot of time on this bay." I pointed to Volconius' villa, two houses to the north of mine.

Daphne cradled the urn. "Why are you so obsessed with destroying every last remnant of my father's body?"

"I haven't destroyed every last remnant. There's still the question of what happened to his blood."

"Do you really think someone has an amphora full of Aristeas' blood stashed away somewhere?"

I didn't have to answer just then because a dolphin broke the surface of the water. As my uncle had described, the creature swam beside the boat, making a noise like the chattering of a bird. Daphne reached over and ran her hand over its head, as though she were petting a dog. The dolphin bobbed its head up and down excitedly. After a few moments it sprayed water out of the hole on its head, making Daphne squeal, then dove beneath us.

"They're amazing creatures," Daphne said, brushing water off her cloak.

"I can show you what my uncle wrote about them, if you're interested. He never published his observations."

"I would like to see that." She winced and pulled her cloak up over her head as the sun came over the top of the cliff. "Sir, if we could get finished and get back to shore, I would appreciate it. It doesn't take much sunlight at all to cause my skin to burn."

"All right. I guess the water is deep enough here. Let me get my bearings, in case I ever need to find the spot again." I glanced at the shore on the north side of the narrow bay, trying to locate a feature that I would remember.

"Sir, do you see that man?" Daphne pointed to the shore opposite from where I was looking. "I think he's watching us."

My gaze followed her arm to a point at the top of the cliff. A man stood in the trees, obviously interested in what we were doing. I couldn't recognize him from this distance, but I didn't want to drop the urn overboard as long as he was watching. "Let's wait a moment and see if he goes away."

But, instead of turning away, the man stepped to the edge of the cliff, picked up a large rock, hoisted it over his head, and hurled it in our direction, like the Cyclops pitching a boulder at Odysseus' boat.

"Sir, watch out!" Daphne cried.

I was fumbling to get a good grip on the oars when the rock struck the rear of the boat, barely a hand's breadth from where I was sitting. That end of the boat sank and Daphne and I were thrown out. As the boat flipped on top of us, my head struck something.

I went underwater, dazed but conscious enough to know I had to get myself back up. But which way was up? Forcing my eyes open, I sensed light and tried to move in that direction, thankful once again that my uncle had insisted I learn how to swim. My face broke through the surface of the water and I gulped air greedily. Kicking to keep myself afloat, I turned in several directions. Which way was shore? Could I make it? My aching head wasn't sure.

I was struggling to stay afloat when I felt something pushing me up. I grabbed for it, expecting to feel Daphne's cloak. Instead I felt the slick skin of a dolphin. Putting an arm over its back, I let myself be pulled toward shore. It even seemed to know which part of the beach I needed to get to. Stroking with my free arm, I tried to look up at the cliff where the rock had come from. Would the man throw another one?

Something warm in my eyes—blood, I suspected—blurred my vision. Where was Daphne? Looking around as best I could, I saw no sign of her. No cloak floating on the surface of the water. Nothing. Had she drowned? I was too dizzy to go back and search for her.

The boat was gone. That must mean the urn had sunk, too, thanks to the rocks Tranio had added to it. At least that much had been accomplished. I just wish I had actually seen it go down, so I would know for certain.

The dolphin stopped swimming and I found I could stand in the water, though it was still up to my chest. Letting go of my rescuer, I staggered onto the beach. He chattered at me. I fancied he was wishing me well, so I thanked him, and then he turned back into the bay. I almost expected to see Daphne dismounting from her own dolphin, but there was still no sign of her. When I was far enough on the shore to be sure I was out of the water, I collapsed onto the sand.

I have no idea how long I had been lying there when I heard voices around me. I opened my eyes to see Tacitus, Daphne, my mother, and several others standing over me. Some of them I could not identify.

"Take it easy," Tacitus said. "You've got a pretty bad gash on your head."

Another job for Macrinus and his needles. "Daphne, you're all right?"

"Yes, sir. I'm fine."

"She got us and told us what happened," Tacitus said.

"But I didn't see you—"

"I got to shore ahead of you, sir. I saw the dolphin and figured he could help you more than I could, with my cloak on. And now I must get out of this sunlight." She turned and ran toward the cliff.

Mother knelt beside me. "Gaius, dear, your head looks awful. We have to get you up to the house right away."

I sat up for a moment. Once I was sure I could do that, I stood up with help from Tacitus.

I shook my head and immediately regretted it. I had to lean heavily on Tacitus. "We saw a man on the top of the cliff, over there." I pointed in what I thought was the right direction. "But I couldn't see who it was."

"Could it have been Apollodoros?"

"It could have been anybody. Why do you mention Apollodoros?"

"Because the horse he stole was back in the paddock this morning."

Macrinus decided, with obvious disappointment, that my scalp would need only minor stitching. I think he wanted the chance to poke around inside my head. He had to settle for shaving the spot and sewing it up with some pieces from inside an animal.

"I clean and save such things, cut 'em into strips no thicker than a piece of thread, just for cases like this," he said, picking out a small needle.

We dismissed the women from the arcade, and I drank a large quantity of unmixed wine. Not enough, it turned out, to deaden all the pain.

"Sorry we don't have any poppy syrup," Macrinus poured wine into the cut, which caused more pain, not less. "That's the best thing there is for gettin' rid of pain. Or at least makin' you not care that you're hurtin'."

Tacitus patted me on the shoulder and took a seat across the way from me. I kept a tight grip on the arms of the chair I was sitting in. At least Macrinus worked fast.

"The scar will hardly show at all, my lord, once the hair grows back," he said as he patted the rest of my hair into place.

With a salve on the cut and a large bandage wrapped around my head, the ordeal was finished. I slumped back in the chair, more exhausted than I had been when I washed up on shore. Mother and Naomi—I thought of that as one name, I realized—rushed back in as soon as they were allowed. Myrrha and Chloris followed them, keeping a respectful distance. Daphne, once again, was nowhere to be seen. I didn't feel the need to lock her up, but I wanted to know where she was.

"I'm fine," I announced with a slight slur. "Just a scratch. Really, just a scratch."

Standing in front of me, my mother raised her voice at me, something she rarely did. And this was the worst time she could have chosen to do it. My head still hurt, although it had been several hours since Macrinus had stitched up the gash in my head and I had slept off the effects of the wine. Even worse, I felt dizzy, uncertain about exactly where I was. I was sitting in the alcove in my suite of rooms, looking out over the bay, trying to reconstruct the events of the morning.

"Do you really intend to let those ... those women stay in this house?" She had come to my quarters when she heard Blandina relaying my orders for rooms to Tranio.

"Mother, I'm sure you've heard by now that Myrrha has lost her father and Chloris her grandfather. They need time to mourn and they need someone to protect them from ... something I don't quite understand yet. You'd better be civil to them, if you expect to keep buying cheese from them."

She drew herself up. "Humph! As if I'd put anything in my mouth that came from their hands."

"I told you—"

"I didn't call them whores. You told me not to call them whores."

I got up and held on to my chair to steady myself. "Mother, I know you're a kinder person than this. Myrrha's father died in her arms. I'm only asking that you show her some compassion for a day or two. Licinius Strabo is also going to be here. Perhaps you can ask him if he sings or plays the lyre."

She folded her arms and scowled at me. "You're not going to let me forget how badly I misjudged Apollodoros, are you?"

I patted her shoulder. "That's the last time I'll mention it, provided this is the last time you say anything unkind about our friends Myrrha and Chloris."

"Are they going to eat lunch with us today?"

"That wouldn't be appropriate. They're in mourning. Now, I need to talk to Naomi. I know she's waiting for you outside the door, so please send her in as you leave." I turned her toward the door.

"What do you want to talk to her about?"

"I'd like to pretend that I have at least some privacy in my dealings with my servants. Please send her in."

I could hear a brief exchange of words between the two women before Naomi came into my room. Naomi would tell Mother everything I told her. I knew that, but I still wanted to keep the pretense of some privacy in my conversation with a servant.

"What can I do for you, my lord?"

"I think we have two Jewish women under our roof, but they don't know it yet." I explained to her what I had learned about Saturninus. "Isn't it circumcision that makes a man a Jew? And wouldn't his daughters then be Jews?"

Naomi shook her head. "There are people other than Jews who circumcise their males, my lord. Not many, but some. We Jews reckon descent through the mother. If Saturninus had stopped living as a Jew and married a Gentile woman, his daughters would not be considered Jews."

I had to think about that. Saturninus had not looked like a Jew, but Jews had been living outside of Judaea for hundreds of years. I wasn't even sure what a Jew looked like. And there was no way to know whether Livilla had been Jewish. The name was Roman, but that didn't necessarily mean anything. She could have been a freed slave who took the name of her master's family. "Should I tell Myrrha what I know?"

"What purpose would that serve, my lord?"

"I always want to know as much as I can about ... anything."

"Those women have suffered a lot, my lord. Chloris is just now learning who her mother is, and who her grandparents were. They must feel like soldiers with someone hurling things at them from a catapult. Would it help to heave another stone on them?"

I dislike tension during a meal. It disturbs the digestion. To shorten the time we would have available to talk, Tacitus and I went to the library on our way to the triclinium and asked Hylas to read something.

"What would you like, my lord?"

I was too dizzy to come up with a title, so Tacitus spoke up first. "May I claim the right of a guest and suggest a reading?"

Something made me leery about saying yes, but he was my friend and my guest, so I concurred with a very slight nod.

"How about the werewolf story from Petronius' *Satyricon*? Do you have a copy of that down here? I know you do in Rome."

"As a matter of fact, we do, my lord. The old gentleman"—everyone's way of referring to my uncle down here—"enjoyed it a great deal. You know, that fellow Trimalchio really is a satire of the princeps—"

I held up my hand to stop him. By now everyone knew the tasteless buffoon Trimalchio in the story was intended to be Nero, but no one needed to say it aloud, even though Nero was long dead. An insult to one princeps can be taken as an insult to every princeps, especially by the current one.

I turned to Tacitus in disbelief, waving my hand at the room full of scrolls. "Out of the hundreds of things you could have chosen, why in the world do you want to have *that* read?"

"It seems appropriate, doesn't it, given everything that's happened the last few days?" he said with an impish grin.

"But a werewolf?"

"Granted, it's not an empusa. If you don't like the idea, suggest something yourself."

"I can't seem to think of anything right now, and I won't take back my word to a guest."

"And friend?"

"About that I'm less certain right now."

When we entered the triclinium the windows were open. If the wind stirs up the sea, the very slightest flecks of spray can come in the windows, but everything was calm today. I took my place as host on the high couch. My mother reclined below me. Tacitus took the honored guest's position on the middle couch with Licinius Strabo above him. The low couch was unoccupied. Behind Mother sat Naomi and some other favored servants. Tacitus had two of his servants to wait on him. I had supplied a few to tend to Strabo's needs.

It was already midday, so for this *prandium* Mother kept the menu light. We had boiled eggs, cheese from Saturninus' shop, apples from last year's store, beans, fish with garum—which I noticed Naomi ate—and bread. A plate of honeyed dates would be the final course.

As we settled ourselves on the couches Hylas came in, carrying a scroll. He took his place at the foot of the high couch, to be out of the way of servants bringing food to the table.

"What are we going to hear?" Mother asked.

"Something which Tacitus requested," I said in order to deflect any blame from me right from the start. Mother looked at me suspiciously over her shoulder.

Hylas looked at me with uncertainty and I nodded. He got to the point in the story where the soldier, who is the werewolf, stopped among the tombstones outside of town, took off his clothes, laid them in a circle, and urinated around them. Having done that, he turned into a wolf and ran off.

At that point Mother said, "Hylas, please stop." She shifted to her right elbow and turned to me, disappointment on her face. "Gaius, I don't see how this is appropriate for a reading at a meal, although I can see some are enjoying it." She shot a baleful glance at Tacitus and Strabo, who had been unable to suppress their amusement.

"Your son thought my choice ill-advised, lady Plinia," Tacitus said, working to keep a straight face. "It appears he was right. I'm sorry to have given offense. I only meant to offer some light entertainment after the difficult days this house has experienced recently."

"I accept your apology, Cornelius Tacitus. But I don't wish to hear any more of this piece. Ever." She waved Hylas away. "It has entirely spoiled my appetite."

She was getting off the couch when Myrrha and Chloris appeared at the door of the triclinium. They were dressed in white gowns, as a sign of mourning, but their faces could hardly contain their happiness. Myrrha looked as though she had shed years along with the secrets she'd been harboring. Chloris kept looking at her mother as though she had never seen her before. And she hadn't, of course, not as her mother. Between them they carried Saturninus' strongbox.

"May we come in, sir?" Myrrha asked.

"By all means." I motioned for the serving women to clear the table in front of our couches.

Myrrha and Chloris placed the strongbox on the table with a thud. "This may seem an odd time," Myrrha said, "but we would like to open this now."

"Here? Wouldn't you rather do it in private?"

"No, sir," Chloris said. "My ... mother and I"—she had to pause to let the gasps of the servant women die down—"my mother and I are afraid that people who hold us in low regard will think we tampered with the contents of the box. We think it best that it be opened in front of a number of witnesses. All sorts of witnesses."

I was relieved to have something to divert attention from the fiasco of the werewolf story, so I said, "All right, if that's what you want. Go ahead and open it."

"You've got the key, sir," Chloris said.

"Oh, yes." I touched the leather strap with the keys around my neck. I had put them on before I came to lunch, even though I wasn't sure what they were for. They were something important, I felt, but I couldn't remember what.

I got off my couch, steadied myself for a moment until the room stopped spinning, and walked around to stand next to the table. "Let me make it clear to everyone in this room that Myrrha and I removed this box from its hiding place in Saturninus' shop last night. She gave me the key then, but we did not open it. The key has been in my possession until this moment, so she has not opened the box. I know stories are going to fly out of this room this afternoon. Please try to keep them close to the facts."

The women turned the box so everyone on both couches would be able to see the contents. The servants behind the couches stood and craned to look over us. I gave Myrrha the keys and she inserted the smaller one into the lock, which opened smoothly. Saturninus kept it in as good condition as the rest of his equipment.

As the lid went up, Myrrha, Chloris and I blocked the view of others in the room. I saw coins—mostly silver and gold—and two leather pouches that were sure to contain written documents.

"We should count these later," I cautioned as the women ran their hands over and through the coins. "Let's look at the documents right now."

The larger document was, in fact, Saturninus' will. "It says it was dictated to Livilla," I read.

"Papa couldn't read nor write," Myrrha said. "He could carry numbers and things in his head and memorize what was read to him, but he couldn't read. He said the letters always looked jumbled up to him. My mother tried to teach me, but I never could make sense of it. I would look at the letters one time, and I could make some sense of 'em, but when I looked at the same page a bit later, the letters looked different, like somebody'd switched 'em around, jumbled 'em up. I guess I'm just too dumb to read. Chloris isn't, though. She's a very smart girl."

"This will bears Saturninus' mark and his seal," I announced. I let Tacitus examine it. "It leaves all of Saturninus' property to his daughter Myrrha and his granddaughter Chloris. I vouch for its authenticity."

"So do I," Tacitus added, handing the will back to me.

I rolled the papyrus up, tucked it back in its cover, and returned it to Myrrha. "You should let Hylas make a copy of that for me to keep here, just in case anything happens to that one," I said. "I can add a note attesting that it's a true copy."

Chloris had removed the second document from its cover. "It's a letter from Livilla to her daughter and granddaughter." She seemed to take a moment to figure out who was meant. "Oh, that's us."

"Would you read it to us, sir?" Myrrha said, taking the letter from Chloris and handing it to me.

"It might be better to wait on that," I said. "It could contain something personal."

"Don't matter," Myrrha said. "I don't want people to think I'm keepin' any secrets."

I could take her point. She was trying to establish herself in a new position among people who had known her for twenty-five years as "the whore." The oldest people in the area might remember that she was Saturninus' daughter, but for most it would be a secret unless someone got garrulous. From Licinius Strabo down to my servants, she had an audience of people of various ranks in Laurentum whom she now had to convince to accept her as the owner of a cheese shop.

"I did talk to my mother a few times over the years," Myrrha said, "when Papa wasn't around. She was a dear woman. She wouldn't write nothin' bad."

"As you wish." I opened the letter and was about to read when Chloris held out her hand to me.

"Will you let me read it, sir? It is to my mother and me."

As dizzy as I felt, I was actually glad to accede to her request. I touched the bandage on my head and handed the letter back to her. She began to read:

*Livilla to her daughter Myrrha and granddaughter Chloris, greetings.*

*I don't know when, or if, you will read this letter. My heart has ached for all these years to call you mine. I've lost my children and my husband, even though we're all still living in the same place. How many times I longed to hold you both and kiss you. I spent so many hours watching you, my beautiful granddaughter, playing and growing up. I wanted to laugh with you, but I couldn't. And I couldn't comfort you after that awful day.*

Chloris stopped reading and put the piece of papyrus down.

"It might be better if you read the rest in private," I cautioned.

"No, sir," Myrrha said. "We've been nursin' that wound for fifteen years, keepin' it covered. It's time to let it air so it'll heal. Go on, Chloris."

"But, Mama—"

"Go on, I said."

Picking up the letter again, Chloris read:

*I know what that awful man Licinius Macer did to you. I also know who killed him, my darling children, but I am afraid to put it down in writing. Even after my death that knowledge could cause my family untold grief. Saturninus refused to press a charge against Macer and, once justice had been dealt to him, I guess there was no reason to pursue his killer. We should just be thankful the whole business was settled, Saturninus said. I have left a clue to the secret in our family's quarters, if anyone wants to look, but there doesn't seem to be any point in bothering with the matter now. I only wish I could have eased your pain, Chloris, if I couldn't save you from it.*

Chloris stopped reading again and wiped tears from her eyes. As she handed the letter to me, everyone turned to look at Licinius Strabo.

Strabo sat up on his couch and took a sip of his wine. His eyes met mine and he did not drop his gaze. "The woman was right. Macer was an awful man, even if he was my cousin. Whoever killed him did us all a favor." He turned to face Myrrha and Chloris. "On behalf of my family, I apologize to you for whatever he may have done."

Strabo must have felt very strange apologizing to women he had coupled with numerous times. I wasn't sure the apology was entirely sincere, but at least he offered it.

"Does the letter say anything more, Gaius Pliny?" he asked.

I ran my eye over the last paragraph. "Only a few words about how much she regrets the way their lives have turned out and how much she loves Myrrha and Chloris." I handed the document back to Myrrha. "I would treasure that and keep it in a very safe place."

I wished I had something of the sort from my father. The only thing I have to remember him by is the bust that stands in a corner of the garden of our house in Rome.

As Myrrha put the letter back in the strongbox she picked up something else and held it up for everyone to see—a little box with a strap on it. "What's this?" she asked.

"It's called a phylactery," Naomi said, stepping around the couches and standing beside Myrrha. "Jewish men wear them."

"Jewish men?" Myrrha turned the thing over, clearly uncertain how to feel about what she had found. "How do they wear a box?"

"They fasten it on their arm or on their head," Naomi said, taking the box and showing how it would be tied onto a man's arm. "The strap on this one would fit around an arm. It contains words from our Law." She opened the box and drew out a small piece of parchment with Jewish writing on it. She mumbled something that sounded like "Shema Israel"and then a few more words I couldn't decipher.

"Why would my father have one of these?" Myrrha took the object back and let Chloris examine it with her.

I felt it was my turn to step in. "Your father was circumcised. We believe he was Jewish. This seems to confirm our suspicion."

Myrrha shook her head. "Papa never said nothin' about bein' Jewish. Mama neither. Don't other people trim off the ends of their mentulas?" She ignored the gasp that went around the room as she used the crude term.

"Not among Greeks and Romans," I said. "Some around the eastern end of the Mediterranean do."

"But Papa's father was a Roman legionary. How could they be Jewish?"

Naomi patted Myrrha's shoulder. "He's not the first, or the only one. Some Jews live among Gentiles so long that they become like them and don't want to admit to being Jews. It looks like your father chose to give up his Jewish identity. He even married a woman who was most likely a Gentile."

"So we're not Jews?" Chloris asked.

Naomi shook her head.

"Meanin' no offense," Myrrha said, "but I'm just as glad. We've got so many new things to get used to right now."

I could understand what she meant. In this small town, to be recognized as a Jew would mean merely to become an outcast for a different reason.

Myrrha was locking the strongbox when Tranio came into the triclinium and whispered close to my ear, "My lord, there's something that needs your attention."

I took him to a corner of the room. "What's the matter now?"

"There's a body floatin' in the bay, my lord."

## XV

As WE MADE OUR WAY down the stairs in the cliff to the beach I had to stop at one point and sit down.

"Are you all right?" Tacitus asked as my mother looked on, wringing her hands with worry.

"I'm dizzy. The wine doesn't seem to be wearing off as fast as I thought it would. I'll be all right in a moment." I touched the bandage on my head.

But I was still feeling strange when we got to the bottom of the stairs. The body was a man's, floating face-down, with his arms spread out, like Icarus must have looked after the wax melted and he was stripped of his wings. That much I could tell from the beach, but with my boat at the bottom of the bay, I had no way to retrieve him.

"Do you think it might be Apollodoros?" Tacitus asked.

"I'd prefer it be someone who has no connection to me."

"The way you've been drawing dead bodies the last couple of days, I wouldn't bet on that."

"Sadly, neither would I." I hadn't told Tacitus what Aurora had reported about Regulus' meeting with Aristeas. I didn't want him to know about her role as my spy. Nor did I want him making jokes about my suspicions of Regulus. If Regulus knew Aristeas was coming down here, he would have sent someone to follow him, I was sure. What if this was one of Regulus' people?

"Could he be the man who threw the rock at your boat this morning?" Tacitus asked.

"I didn't get a good enough look at that man to be able to identify him."

A voice called out from behind us. "Do you need some help, neighbor?"

207

I turned to see Lucius Volconius, owner of one of the other villas on the shore, coming down to the beach. He was older than me, but not of my father's or uncle's age. The way his hair was thinning and his jowls sagging, though, he soon would look like that generation. His skin was leathery from the time he spent outdoors on the water.

"It looks like someone has drowned," I said as he walked up to us.

"Yes, I saw that. Are you going to fish him out?" Volconius asked.

"My boat sank while I was out this morning."

He pointed to my bandage. "Is that what happened to your head?"

"I hit my head on the boat when it overturned."

Volconius chuckled. "You never have been much good on the water, have you, Gaius Pliny? I remember watching you and that slave girl floundering around in a boat. Thought I was going to have to go get you then. Let me get a couple of my men."

Volconius owns several large fishing boats that supply markets in Ostia. He and his men also fish and dive in our bay. Their presence was the primary reason I wanted to dump Aristeas' urn in the deepest water I could find. When he gave an ear-piercing whistle and waved his arms, two of his servants came down to the beach and, from a cave, pulled out a boat quite a bit larger than mine.

"Do you and your friend want to come with us?" he asked.

After introductions, Tacitus declined the offer. I decided to accompany them so I would know what, or whom, I was dealing with before the body was brought ashore. I quickly regretted my decision. The waves were higher than they had been that morning, and my head was bobbing even more than the boat. I leaned over the side and vomited. Neither Volconius nor his servants said anything as I wiped my mouth and curled up in the bottom of the boat.

The two servants rowed swiftly and powerfully, bringing us alongside the dead man in no time. A quick glance at the shore made me nervous. We were too close to the spot where my boat had gone down and the urn had—I presumed—gone to the bottom. The water was clear. I had not gotten as far out as I had hoped to.

"Let's see what we have here," Volconius said, grabbing the man's hair and raising his head. "By the gods! That's a bit of a mess."

We all recoiled, but I was the only one who vomited. The man's face had been clawed so badly I didn't think his own mother would recognize him. There were deep slashes on his chest as well.

"Do you know him?" Volconius asked as I finished emptying my stomach.

I shook my head before I could think better of it. All I could tell was that this wasn't Apollodoros. His skin was too white. "How long do you think he's been in the water?"

"Since early morning, wouldn't you say, fellas?" He turned to his servants, who nodded.

"Could some sort of sea creature have done that to his face?" I asked.

"Nothing that I know of. There are some that'll nibble on a man, but whatever did this had claws, more like a bird."

Or an empusa, I thought.

We hauled the poor man into the boat and started back to shore. When we were close enough that I was sure I could be heard, I yelled to Tacitus, "Get the women back into the house!"

Once the women were out of the way, Volconius' men beached the boat gracefully. The dead man was lying face down in the bottom of the craft. Tacitus and Tranio approached us, but I held up a hand.

"If you want to see him, prepare yourselves for a shock. His face isn't really a face any more."

"My association with you, Gaius Pliny, has prepared me for just about anything," Tacitus said, resting his hands on the edge of the boat.

Volconius grabbed the dead man's hair and raised his head. Some sort of small sea creatures were crawling out of the bloody mass that had been his face.

Tranio turned, took a few steps, and began to retch. Tacitus gagged, grabbed at his stomach and stepped back. "Just about anything, but not that."

"What'll we do with him?" Volconius asked me, letting the man's head drop with a thump. "Turn him over to the duovirs? It's pretty clear he didn't do this to himself."

I didn't want another body to dispose of, and yet I knew this corpse was one more latrunculus piece that was being maneuvered into position to trap me. But by whom? And why?

"I'll have some of my men take him up to my place," I said. "I need to see Licinius Scaevola about something else, so I'll take care of this as well."

"Good," Volconius said. "No disrespect to the dead, but I don't need to be taking care of a mangled body. There's enough strange things going on around here lately."

" 'Strange things'? What do you mean?"

"Haven't you seen that huge bat?"

I stopped myself from nodding. "Yes, we noticed it."

"Thing showed up a couple of days ago. One of my men caught it trying to kill one of our lambs. He threw a knife at it and wounded it, but it got away."

"When was this?"

"Let's see. Two nights ago, it was."

The night Daphne appeared at my door, with a gash in her shoulder.

Tacitus looked at me, and I knew what he was thinking—the werewolf story from Petronius, the part after where my mother had made Hylas stop reading. After seeing the werewolf, the narrator runs to his lover's house. She tells him that a wolf attacked their sheep. He killed several, but one of the servants wounded him in the neck with a spear. When the narrator returns to the inn where the story began, he finds the soldier who had turned into a wolf lying in bed with a wound in his neck.

Volconius and his men bid us good day. "I think we'll take another run out there. We'll see if we can retrieve your boat."

"I would appreciate that very much."

"Glad to do a favor for a neighbor." He turned to his men. "Did you boys see what I saw on the bottom?"

Both men nodded and looked eager to get back out on the water.

"What if they saw Aristeas' urn?" I asked Tacitus as we watched them row out to the spot.

"Well, the worst that can happen is that they'll open it and dump his ashes back into the bay. They'll probably keep the urn for their trouble."

I nodded. "Yes, I guess so." I wanted that body to stay disposed of.

"Meanwhile, we've got another corpse to take care of."

We wrapped a cloth around the dead man's face and I told two of my servants to carry him up to the stable.

"More like an inn for the dead," Tacitus said. "Are you going to have enough room for your horses?"

"Please don't make jokes right now."

"I have to make jokes so I won't think about what we're both thinking about."

"The wounded bat?"

Tacitus nodded. "And the wounded Daphne."

"It's not possible, is it? People don't turn into wolves and bats and then back into people. Bodies remain what they are. Something that's born a cow doesn't turn into a fox or a horse."

"I've never seen it happen. But your uncle wrote about even stranger things in his *Natural History*."

"Things he never saw. He just repeated stories that people have been telling since Herodotus' day. And probably longer. Herodotus was just the first to write some of them down."

"And writing them down doesn't make them true, does it?"

I looked around at the cliff from where a rock had come crashing into my boat and sent Aristeas' ashes to the bottom of the bay, at Volconius' estate where a large bat had attacked a lamb. "No, of course not. Papyrus doesn't know the difference between the truth and a lie. As Socrates said, the written word doesn't know to whom to speak and to whom not to speak. Right now I don't think I do either."

"Do you think some wine would help us sort it out?"

"Could it make things any worse?"

Tacitus shook his head. "I've never known wine to make things worse."

When we came to the top of the stairs and onto the terrace we found Licinius Strabo pacing like a man anticipating the verdict in his trial.

"Good morning. Are you waiting for me?" I asked.

"Yes. You said I could return home today. I'd like to ask your permission to do so."

"By all means. You've been an admirable hostage. You're free to go."

"Thank you." He turned to leave.

"Would you like to have a drink with us?" Tacitus asked.

"No, thank you. I just want to go home."

"Odd," Tacitus said as we watched Strabo hurry through the door. "Yesterday he acted like he didn't care if he ever saw home again."

A shout from the water brought us back to the edge of the terrace. Volconius and one of his men were in the boat. The other was in the water, holding onto the edge of the boat and guiding a rope which the first servant was pulling. Just as I had feared, Aristeas' urn bobbed to the surface. Volconius must have thought the urn, because of its weight, contained some treasure. He pulled it into the boat and he and his men made for shore.

"He's back," Tacitus said.

I didn't have much time to worry about the recovery of the urn. Saturninus' funeral proved to be more complicated than I had anticipated. Even though he had not lived as a Jew, Naomi insisted it would be appropriate to bury him as one. I consented because, pragmatically, it would save us building another funeral pyre, which we would have to do for the man we fished out of the bay. Myrrha and Chloris gave their approval, and Naomi provided the instructions.

Because the steps down the cliff were precipitous we used ropes to lower Saturninus' body to the cave. Naomi led a group of women—Myrrha, Chloris, my mother, and several servants—with ointments and a linen cloth to wrap the body in.

Tacitus and I watched the proceedings from the terrace. "It really is like watching some descent into the underworld," he said. "I can't understand how this is better than a cremation."

"Be thankful he wasn't an Egyptian. Then we'd have to make a mummy out of him, and that takes a couple of months."

"But now somebody will have to remember, a year from now, to go in there and pick up his bones. Who's going to do that?"

I shook my head very slowly. Would I ever feel normal again? "It won't be me. That's all I know."

We turned away from the cliff and went back inside the arcade as a cool breeze picked up.

"I hope you have better luck keeping Saturninus buried than you did with Aristeas," Tacitus said. "What if he gets up and walks out of that cave?"

"Then I will have to reconsider what I believe about life and death. But not until then."

"In the meantime, what do you propose to do about the faceless man?"

"I'd like to know who he is, but, without a face, I don't see how

anybody can identify him." The man without a face reminded me of the image of the face on the blanket that had been wrapped around Aristeas. I called Tranio and told him to retrieve it.

"You do have an odd assortment of bodies and faces lying around, Gaius Pliny," Tacitus said. "Are you going to try to match them up, so you don't have any left over?"

Some of Tacitus' questions don't deserve a serious answer, and I don't have a quick enough wit to give him any other kind, even when my head isn't spinning. All I can do is shrug or roll my eyes.

Tranio returned to the arcade with a puzzled look on his face.

"What's the matter?" I asked.

"My lord, I don't know what to say. The cloth you gave me is gone."

"Gone? Didn't you hide it?"

"Yes, my lord. In the safest place I could think of—behind the chest in my bedroom. But it's not there now."

That sounded like the most obvious place to me. "Who could have found it?"

"My wife and I are the only ones who should be in there, my lord."

"Bring her in here at once."

Tranio ran out of the arcade. He and his wife have the largest room in the section of the house where my servants live. Tacitus and I barely had time to take our seats before he returned with his wife, Lutatia, in tow. She's a tall, blonde woman who may bear some ancient Sabine blood, older than Rome itself, if one wanted to talk about blood bestowing immortality.

"You wanted to see me, my lord?" she asked.

"Yes. Tranio tells me he stored a blanket behind a chest in your bedroom, but now it's gone. Do you know anything about it?"

"Yes, my lord. I noticed a corner of it sticking out from behind the chest, so I pulled it out to see what my husband was hiding from me this time."

I wondered what Tranio was in the habit of hiding from his wife—and if he was hiding things from her, he could be hiding them from me—but the blanket was my only concern at the moment. "What did you do with the blanket?"

"Nothing, my lord. It was just a blanket. I couldn't understand why he was hiding it, so I folded it and put it in the chest."

"You didn't notice anything unusual about it?"

"No, my lord. Should I have?"

"I need to see it. Bring it here."

"Certainly, my lord." Lutatia turned, gave Tranio a curious look, and hurried out of the arcade. When she returned she was carrying a folded blanket.

I took the blanket from her and dismissed the two servants. When I shook the blanket out, Tacitus and I looked at one another in surprise. There was not even the faintest image anywhere on the piece of cloth.

"I told you it wasn't a face," I said.

"Oh, you did not! You ran straight into the library and compared it to the face that Hylas had drawn. You saw it as clearly as I did ... Are you sure that's the right blanket?"

I nodded. "I recognize a couple of places where it's been repaired."

"I guess, whatever kind of image we saw, it wasn't permanent. It faded away."

"I just wish we knew *when* it disappeared."

"What difference would that make?"

"What if it disappeared at the moment Aristeas died?"

"By the gods, Gaius Pliny. Are you suggesting it might have something to do with Aristeas' soul leaving his body?"

I ran my hand over the blanket. "I can't use those words. All I know is that the image was there two days ago and now it's gone."

"And that frightens you."

"No. What frightens is that I have no explanation, and I don't even know where to begin to look for one."

After placing Saturninus' body in the cave and sealing it, Naomi wanted Myrrha and Chloris to observe a period of mourning. But Myrrha would have none of it.

"You said I'm not Jewish, since we don't know if my mother was. My father never told me he was Jewish. Why should I sit for days mournin' a man who disowned me? I've given him a decent burial. I want to go back to Laurentum. I have business there."

I agreed with her and told Naomi she could not expect these women to observe rituals they knew nothing about. "We'll go back to Laurentum in the morning."

After lunch Tacitus and I went out to the stable to exam the face-

214

less man. It was a hopeless task. There were no marks on his clothing that would tell me anything about him.

As I lifted one of his arms, Tacitus said, "I wonder why we can't get to examine a young woman's body once in a while. It would liven up this whole gruesome business."

"I thought you had examined quite a few young women's bodies. There was that serving woman in the tavern the other day."

"Yes, but there's always a 'Don't do that,' or a 'Not there.' " He slapped one of his hands with the other.

"Perhaps you just aren't paying them enough."

Tacitus arched his eyebrows. "I'll remember that next time. Now, can you learn anything about this fellow?"

"His hands are calloused, so I think he was a workman."

"Slave? Freedman?"

"There's no way to tell. It might be best just to turn him over to Licinius Scaevola."

"That'll be easier to do than you might expect." Tacitus was facing the house, looking over my head. "Here comes Scaevola now."

Placing a cloth over the dead man's face, I turned to see the senior duovir striding across my paddock. His son was not among the men accompanying him. One of them was driving the wagon I had seen several times in recent days.

"Gaius Pliny, greetings." His tone told me this was an official visit, not a social one. "I've heard that you and Volconius fished a man out of the bay this morning. Don't you think you should have notified me?"

"News travels fast."

"It does when it's reported by a responsible citizen like Volconius. Now, may I see the man?"

I wondered why Volconius had not left it to me to decide what to do with the body. Then I remembered: he was married to Scaevola's cousin. "If you insist."

I stood aside and let Scaevola lift the cloth from what should have been the man's face. He must have been told what to expect, but he still stepped back in shock and quickly covered the head again.

"It's my duty as duovir to take this man back to Laurentum. Are we going to fight over this body?"

"This one's dead," I said. "Myrrha was very much alive." I did not want Scaevola to remove the body until I had time to consider what might have happened to the man, but I had no valid reason to interfere this time.

"And is she still in your custody?"

"She is here in my house."

"Does she intend to take over her father's business?"

"You would have to ask Myrrha about that. If she does, I'm ready to assist her as one of my friends."

Scaevola waved for his men to come take up the body.

I removed the cloth from the man's head and took one last look at what remained of his face, trying to imprint the image in my mind so I could try to understand what had happened to him, even after I was no longer able to see him.

As Macrinus finished shaving Tacitus and packed up his razors, we seemed to have a few moments of calm ahead of us.

"I'm ready to bathe," I said. "Let's use the swimming bath." I led the way to the warm pool next to the bath. While swimming there, one has a superb view of the bay.

"I don't think I've ever seen anything lovelier," Tacitus said. "Any more bodies floating around down there?"

"No. But one of Volconius' servants just emptied Aristeas' urn down on the beach. He's mixing the ashes into the sand right at the edge of the water."

"The waves will wash them away then, and you're rid of the man—again." Tacitus ran his hand over his face. "Your butcher did a good job shaving me. I do wonder, though, what else he's used that razor on."

"I make sure he keeps a set just for shaving."

"Why don't you bring Aurora when you come down here? She shaves you when you're in Rome, doesn't she?"

"Yes. And she does an excellent job. But my mother isn't always kind to her—"

"Because of Aurora's mother and your uncle. So you've said. That's too bad. She must miss you, though."

"No more than any of my servants, I assume."

"Oh, Gaius Pliny! You pride yourself on noticing things other people miss—and rightly so—but in this case you don't see what's right in front of you. What did she say in that note she wrote you?"

216

It was time that I put a stop to Tacitus' obsession about Aurora and me, even if it meant telling him more than I really wanted to. Since she had sent me the message about Aristeas and Regulus, I had some reason for doing so now.

"You're the one who's missing something," I said. "Aurora stays in Rome because ... she is my best spy. That's what the note was—a report from my spy."

"A spy? That beautiful creature? A spy is supposed to be someone you don't notice. If she's in the room, you don't notice anyone else."

"Aurora has an uncanny ability to disguise herself. Since we were twelve she and I have been practicing the art of spying. In a couple of instances we were able to gain information that proved valuable for my uncle. I've given her freedom to come and go as she pleases. Over the past few months, while in disguise, she has struck up a friendship with a freedwoman in Regulus' household. I'm hoping she'll learn the identity of Regulus' spy in my house."

"What if Aurora is Regulus' spy?" Tacitus asked softly.

For a moment I couldn't form words to reply. "Aurora? Regulus' spy? You might as well ask me to believe the sun rises in the west."

"Think about it, Gaius Pliny. You trust her so implicitly you let her hold a razor to your throat. She has permission to come and go at any time. She tells you she's talking with someone from Regulus' house, but how do you know she isn't giving information instead of getting it?"

I shook my head in disbelief. "Aurora and I have been closer than brother and sister for fifteen years. I do trust her more than any other person I've ever known—including you, if you'll forgive me for saying so. If you're going to impugn her, you and I will have difficulty remaining friends."

Tacitus chuckled. "Sorry. I thought you meant it when you said you didn't love her."

"Love her? What are you talking about? I don't love her."

"No, of course not. Obviously I misunderstood. Sorry, I won't say any more about it."

"Please see that you don't."

After dinner I promised Myrrha that we would go into Laurentum the next morning and let her take possession of the cheese shop.

Chloris asked if we could take the raeda. "It's beautiful, Mother. And everybody knows you're a lady when you come riding into town in it."

It seemed like a good idea to get these two women established in their new position in town and to let people know that they had the support of a wealthy family in the area.

At least they had my support. My mother had informed me that she would not buy anything that came from the hands of 'those women.' I made it clear to her that we would continue to buy cheese from that shop and that I was going to look into the cost of the special garum sauce she had been purchasing, along with any other food purchases that favored one particular servant.

With that argument settled—or at least silenced—I retired to my quarters, looking forward to the prospect of an uninterrupted night's sleep. Two questions, though, continued to plague me.

First, where was Daphne? No one had seen her since late morning. I had sent a servant into town to pay her bill and collect the small bags of her belongings, with my strict instructions not to pry into them. Daphne had been pleased to get them and had gone to her room. She had requested a room on the second floor of the section of the house that overlooks the central courtyard. The request struck me as odd because those rooms have windows, although windows with shutters. That was the last anyone saw of her, and she was not in her room when a servant went to call her for dinner.

The other question nagging at me was the one Tacitus raised. What if I was utterly wrong about Aurora? For most of my life I had watched her develop what seemed to be an inborn skill. She could convince anyone that she was whatever character she was pretending to be. If she could deceive others so deftly, couldn't she also deceive me?

No, it simply could not be. In spite of all the challenges of the last few days, I knew—absolutely *knew*—two things: first, Aurora was loyal to me, and, second, people's souls do not fly out of them like birds. If I could not count on those statements as true, then I could not depend on anything I had always regarded as certain.

Can one build a life on uncertainty? The Skeptics teach that we can never know anything to be absolutely true. They reached that conclusion after studying all the differing views of Plato, Aristotle, and a host of other philosophers. They couldn't all be right, the Skeptics decided, so none of them are right. Trying to hold that position makes me feel like I did this morning when I was flopping around in the water, unable to tell which direction I should go. I thought I had found that direction through my studies, but if Aristeas could leave his body and Daphne could change into different animals, what happened to the foundation on which I had built my life? For all I knew now, Daphne could have changed into the dolphin and guided me to shore.

I stood on the terrace outside my quarters, watching the moon reflect off the water below. In my somewhat addled state of mind, a more mundane question occurred to me: would I ever be able to eat fish out that bay again? Would I be consuming bits of Aristeas' ashes? But what about all the people who had died in shipwrecks? Weren't their remains somehow absorbed into ocean, consumed by underwater creatures?

I sensed more than felt someone moving along the terrace. Chloris came around the curve of the building. In the moonlight her red hair looked like burnished gold.

"Good evening, sir. Can you not sleep?"

"I do have ... a lot on my mind."

Standing beside me, with her shoulder touching mine, Chloris looked out over the bay. She was too close for me to turn my head and look directly at her, but I couldn't stop studying her out of the corner of my eye. Aurora was a beautiful woman, but I could admit her face was a trifle long and narrow. Try as I might, I could not find a flaw in Chloris. Who was her father? I wondered. Children sometimes look more like one parent than the other. Chloris certainly did not resemble Myrrha. The red hair may have come from her grandmother, but what did the man look like whose seed had blossomed into such beauty?

"You must have a lot to think about as well," I said. "Tomorrow you start a new phase of your life—owning your own shop. You'll have a new status in Laurentum now."

"Those people will never think of me as anything but a whore," she said softly. "Myrrha—I mean, Mother—and I are thinking about selling the place and moving to Ostia so we can start over."

I felt disappointment mingled with my arousal at being so close to her. "If that's what you think is best, I'll give you whatever help you need."

"Yes, sir, I know. You've been incredibly kind." She leaned over and kissed me, first on the cheek, then on the mouth.

In spite of the urgings from some parts of my body, I pulled away from her. "You don't have to do this. You don't owe me anything."

"This doesn't have anything to do with owing somebody." She put a hand on my shoulder and kneaded it. Her voice dropped to a pitch that melted any resistance I might have tried to muster. "For the first time I can couple with a man because I want to, without being paid for it. All my life people have called me a whore. I started believing them, and I became one. But not any more. This won't be my first time, but I want you to be the first man I've gone to bed with because I wanted to."

# XVI

CHLORIS AND I WERE AWAKENED out of a deep sleep by a pounding on the main door of my quarters. Because I often don't sleep well, I've given my servants strict orders not to disturb me unless the house is on fire.

"My lord!" Tranio shouted. "Forgive me, my lord, but you're needed!"

I slipped on my tunic and answered the door while Chloris fumbled for her gown.

"Where's the fire?" I asked. "You know what my orders are."

"But there is a fire, my lord."

"What—?"

"Not here, my lord. Fella's come from Laurentum. He says Saturninus' shop is on fire."

"Oh, by the gods, no!" Chloris cried as she came up to stand behind me. A quick glance told me that she had not put on her gown. She had just grabbed it and was holding it in front of her, more or less.

"Where is the man?" I asked.

"In the atrium, my lord." Tranio was craning to see over me.

"Who is he?" Chloris asked over my shoulder.

"I don't know ... lady." Tranio clearly didn't know what to make of a naked whore turned business-owner sharing my bed. "Tall fella, goin' bald in front. Kinda beady eyes."

"That's The Long of It," Chloris said, pulling her gown on over her head, much to Tranio's delight. "His name is Naevius. He's actually a decent sort."

We hurried into the atrium and found Tacitus, my mother, and a small throng of servants surrounding Naevius. My mother was clearly unhappy to see me come in with Chloris on my heels, still

221

fastening one of the brooches that held her gown at the shoulder. Tacitus just smiled.

"Oh, sir," Myrrha said. "It's terrible. The shop is on fire." She and Chloris embraced.

"Is this true?" I asked Naevius.

"Yes, sir."

"Who's taking charge?"

"Well, I guess you'd say Scaevola is, but all he's doing is keeping people away."

"He's not trying to put the fire out?"

"No, sir. He won't let anybody near the place. Says it's too dangerous. The building's old and might collapse any instant."

"Oh, sir," Myrrha wailed, "can't you do somethin'?"

The role of miracle worker was beginning to wear on me, but I had to try. If Myrrha and Chloris lost the shop, they'd have no choice but to go back to prostitution, and the burden would fall on Chloris.

"We have six horses," I said. "We'll ride two on a horse, carrying as many buckets as we can find."

In just a few moments we were mounted and making a dash for Laurentum. Chloris clung to me, while Myrrha rode behind Tacitus. Naevius took one of my servants behind him.

"There's a column of smoke," Tacitus said. "It's hard to see in the dark."

"There aren't no flames in it, my lord," Tranio said. "I think that's a good sign."

The column of smoke appeared grayish-white in the moonlight, like a fish washed up on the shore. But it brought back images of the column of smoke that had belched out of Vesuvius on the day of that catastrophe. I had been twenty miles away then, but had barely survived. My breathing grew shallower as we approached the edge of the village.

When we rode into the center of the village we found the main street blocked by a wagon. Scaevola and several of his servants stood between it and another wagon blocking the street at the other end of the block. Our horses pranced nervously.

"Stay back!" Scaevola ordered. "It's too dangerous for anyone to get closer. The building may collapse at any moment."

Through the shuttered windows I could see that the fire was on the second floor. It had not yet burned through the roof and the main floor seemed intact. "Why are you doing this?" I asked. "We should be trying to put the fire out."

"Once again, Gaius Pliny, you're trying to keep a magistrate from doing his duty," Scaevola said, stepping out from behind the wagon and crossing his arms over his chest. "I've got a crew coming to knock the building down before the fire spreads."

"But there are only two other buildings on this side of the street."

"My point exactly. If we don't get this under control, the whole town could be destroyed."

I was beginning to think that might not be such a great loss.

"Turn around," I ordered my people. "We won't interfere with the magistrate."

"But, sir ..." Chloris said over my shoulder.

I lowered my voice. "Hush. We're not leaving."

We cantered down the street to the bath, where I turned into a side street. "Everybody dismount," I said.

"What's the plan?" Tacitus asked.

"We've got to get some water on that fire. It's still small enough that I think we can put it out."

"But Scaevola's blocking the fountain across the street from the building."

"He's not blocking the aqueduct behind the building, though. Chloris and Myrrha, you stay with the horses. The rest of you, come with me."

"No, sir," Myrrha said. "You don't know what's back there. Naevius and I do. Have one of your servants stay with Chloris and the horses." She realized she was assuming too much. "If that's agreeable to you, sir."

I couldn't dispute her point. She should know the area behind the bath and Saturninus' building intimately.

This bath was the southernmost of the three in Laurentum. Its west side was overgrown with bushes and small trees. It might once have boasted an attractive garden, but now it was as decrepit as the rest of the town.

"Oh, no," Myrrha gasped as we came into the open space behind the bath. Ahead to our left we could see Saturninus' building. Smoke was coming under the door of the windowless rooms where

Myrrha and Chloris lived.

"It's odd how certain parts of the building are on fire," Tacitus said, "and others aren't."

"That's what I would expect if someone set the fire," I said.

"But why would somebody set fire to our place?" Myrrha moaned.

"Let's get the fire out and then ask that question."

Since this bath was at the end of the aqueduct, it was fed by a small spur of the larger aqueduct that supplied the town and the other two baths. The arches of the aqueduct were so low at the point where it ran into the bath that we had to stoop to get under them. The thing leaked so badly I felt like I was walking in the rain.

"This ground is like a marsh," Tacitus said as his foot sank in the muck. "How do they keep the bath filled when they're losing this much water?"

Someone—possibly the duovirs—had recognized the problem. Instead of fixing the leaks, though, they had cut a drainage ditch that led into the woods beyond the bath. It was too shallow for us to dip our buckets in.

"We need to get a couple of men up there," I said, pointing to the top of the aqueduct.

"What good will that do?" Tacitus asked.

"I hope to find some way to knock a hole in the channel and use the water to douse the fire."

"I don't think you can just punch a hole in an aqueduct with your fist," Tacitus said, "not even one as run-down as this one. An empusa might be able to."

"In that shed back there," Myrrha said, pointing to a small structure behind the building on the other side of Saturninus'. "There's an axe. Our neighbor picks up extra money splitting wood for the bath."

One of my servants ran to get the axe while I looked over the arches supporting the aqueduct. In its crumbling condition it provided a number of toe-holds and places to grab on for anyone trying to climb it.

"Are you seriously considering having one of your servants climb this thing?" Tacitus asked. "This stone might give way under too much pressure." He broke off a corner of a stone with his fingers.

"No, as the smallest man here, I'm going to climb it myself."

"Holding an axe in your third hand?"

In my haste I had not put on a belt, but one of my servants gave me his. I used it to strap the axe onto myself and, with a boost from Tacitus and a servant, grabbed the most secure spot I could find on the column supporting one of the arches. Stopping every few steps to try to clear my head of the dizziness, I worked my way to the top of the aqueduct and straddled it like a fat horse. Then I scooted forward until I was opposite Saturninus' building.

Now that I could see into the windows of the upper floor, I knew I had to hurry. Someone had piled clothing and blankets in the middle of the floor and set fire to them. With that start, the flames were spreading. Livilla's wooden bowls and utensils, tossed on the top of the pile, had started to burn. Fortunately the wooden floor was so thick it had so far only been charred in spots.

Straddling the aqueduct, I pulled the axe out of my belt and swung the hardest blow I could. The axe bounced off the stone. I had to duck to avoid being hit in the face. When I jerked to one side I shifted my balance so quickly that I felt myself starting to fall. Myrrha screamed. I barely managed to grab hold of the side of the aqueduct and pull myself back up.

Myrrha's scream brought men running from the street.

"What are you doing?" Scaevola yelled.

"I'm trying to put out a fire for one of my friends and save her property." I landed another blow on the aqueduct and saw a large crack appear in the aging stone.

"Get down from there!" Scaevola ordered.

"You'll have to come up and get me."

Scaevola apparently meant to do just that. He pushed some of his men toward the aqueduct. Tacitus led my servants as they gathered around the base of the arches to prevent anyone else from climbing them. The flickering, eerie light from the fire made the figures stand out against the dark. I heard shouts and groans as men came to blows.

One more solid blow opened a gap large enough for water to start to trickle through. A final blow knocked out a section of the side of the channel. Scaevola's men scattered as the stone crashed to the ground.

"Fill the buckets," Tacitus ordered.

I could see there wasn't enough water flowing out of the hole. I knocked loose another piece of stone and used it to block the stream of water and divert it out of the hole I had made. Now we had a small waterfall. A couple of my servants pushed Scaevola's men out of the way while the others filled buckets. I was glad to see all the men below on their feet. This wasn't worth killing anyone over.

Tacitus opened the door to Myrrha's quarters. The fire in that area had not gotten very large. Fire needs air, and the windowless rooms had quickly filled up with smoke. Oddly enough, the smoke produced by the fire helped smother the flames. A few buckets of water finished the job.

I worked my way down off the aqueduct while my men were dousing the fire. "How do we get upstairs?" I said. "The fire's got a good start there."

The man who had fetched the axe said, "I saw a ladder behind that shed, my lord."

The ladder proved to be about a cubit too short to get to the window. As soon as Naevius saw the problem he climbed the ladder, hooked his arms over the window sill and hoisted himself inside, ignoring the flames starting to show through the other window. "Get those buckets up here!" he called back down. "Be quick about it."

Forming a bucket brigade on a ladder was awkward, but we managed it. The gap from the top man on the ladder to Naevius reaching down from the window was the trickiest part. The Long of It lived up to his nickname, though. As fast as he threw the water on the fire, he tossed a bucket out the window to be refilled. One of my men caught it and held it under the stream of water I had diverted from the aqueduct, then passed it to the others on the ladder.

With six buckets on the move, we kept an almost steady stream of water on the flames. I hoped the ladder, which looked as run-down as everything else in Laurentum, would bear the weight of three men long enough.

Scaevola watched the whole process without lifting a finger to help but at least no longer trying to stop us. "If that dump collapses on you and your men," he said, "you can dig your own way out. And who's going to pay for repairing the aqueduct? I could bring charges against you, Gaius Pliny, for destroying public property."

"I'll have a crew here in the morning to repair it. They'll even fix some of the leaks back here—something the town's magistrates should have taken care of long ago."

"Will you be running for duovir this year?" Scaevola sneered.

"No, but I will pay much closer attention to the elections than I have in the past."

Naevius stuck his head out the window. "That'll do it. Fire's out."

Scaevola turned to leave. "You'd better have a crew here in the morning to repair that aqueduct, Gaius Pliny. By the second hour."

I ignored him and passed the axe up the ladder to Naevius. "Poke around a bit and make sure nothing's smoldering. We don't want the fire to break out again."

"Yes, sir. But I'm sure it's all right. What was mainly burnin' was some piles of clothes."

"We'll be up in a moment."

I sent one of my men up to the top of the aqueduct to remove the piece of stone with which I had blocked the channel. When it was set in place of the chunk I had knocked out of the wall, the waterfall was reduced to a trickle.

"Hardly any worse than any other leak back here," Tacitus said. "Do you actually have someone who can plug this thing up?"

"Yes. Several of the men on the estate worked on that addition I made a few years ago. They can handle this job and be home for lunch. Now let's go see what started this fire."

We first looked over the rooms where Myrrha and Chloris lived. Furniture had been upended, clothes pulled out of chests. Oil from the lamps had been poured out and set on fire.

"Somebody ransacked the place," Myrrha said in dismay. "Why would they do that? We've got nothin' worth stealin'."

"Somebody was looking for something," I said.

"But then why set a fire?" Tacitus asked.

"If they couldn't find what they were looking for, perhaps they didn't want anyone else to find it either."

"Maybe somebody was looking for Saturninus' will," Tacitus said.

I nodded. "That's a strong possibility. Let's go see what the upstairs looks like."

One of my men relieved Chloris from watching the horses and sent her to join us. When we got to the front of the building we saw that the door had been opened by cutting the leather hinges.

"We'll leave a couple of men here on guard tonight," I said, "and my crew will put stronger hinges on this door tomorrow."

"Thank you, sir," Myrrha said, hugging Chloris and drawing her close. I wondered how Chloris felt, going into the shop for the first time since she had learned who her grandparents were.

We lit a few lamps and surveyed the main floor of the building. It had escaped damage, except for the permeating smell of smoke.

"It looks like you'll still be able to do business," I said, "once you air the place out."

"I hope the smoke don't get into the cheese," Myrrha said. She opened the back room of the shop, where the cheese was stored. When she turned back around she looked hopeful. "I think we'll be all right, if we have our cheese-cutter back."

"Tomorrow morning," I promised. "Let's see what the upstairs looks like."

Chloris hesitated at the stairs. "I've never been up here. It seems so strange. All my life I've thought Saturninus hated me."

"It's all right, dear," Myrrha said. "Your grandparents loved you, even if they never could tell you so." She took her daughter's hand and they led us up the stairs.

The damage was not all that severe. As I had seen from the aqueduct, someone had piled up clothes and bedding and set fire to it. Like the women's rooms downstairs, this area had been ransacked before the fire was started.

"I think these old floors saved the place," Tacitus said. "They're just too thick to burn easily."

"But what was somebody lookin' for?" Myrrha asked.

"It must have been someone who didn't know that the strongbox had been removed," Tacitus said. "They wanted to know what was in it."

"Or maybe it was somebody who knew that it had been removed and knew exactly what was in it."

"But that would be just the people who were at your house when it was opened."

I nodded. "And we know where all of them were tonight, except for Licinius Strabo."

By the second hour the next morning my crew was at work repairing the aqueduct. Myrrha, Chloris, Tacitus, and I went to take a better look at the cheese shop in the daylight. We met Licinius Scaevola coming out of the broken front door.

"You have no right to be in there," I said.

"As a magistrate I was inspecting the damage from the fire last night."

"It was minimal. Myrrha and Chloris are going to clean up and will be open for business again in a day or two."

"What claim do they have on the place?"

"Saturninus left it to them in his will. They are his daughter and granddaughter, as I believe you know."

Scaevola pursed his lips. "As many of us in Laurentum have always known."

"How did everyone keep that secret?" Chloris asked. "Was I truly the only one who didn't know?"

"Not the only one, my dear. But those of us who wanted the secret kept did manage to keep it."

"They didn't want to admit it," Myrrha said bitterly, "so they could keep on whorin' with her, like you and your son."

Scaevola closed his eyes and nodded. "But that's all in the past, I gather. Have you seen this will, Gaius Pliny?"

"I have. Tacitus and I will vouch for its authenticity."

Scaevola turned to Myrrha. "I'm prepared to buy the shop." He named a price. Even given the poor condition of the building and the general decay of the town, it was still a very low offer.

Myrrha turned to me. "Sir, what should we do?"

"I don't think you should sell," I said. "This shop has an excellent reputation and a lot of loyal customers."

"And you ladies certainly have quite a reputation and a lot of loyal customers," Scaevola sneered.

"Including your son," Chloris said. "But those days are over."

"Speaking of Strabo," I said, "where is he?"

Scaevola seemed genuinely surprised. "I thought he was being held hostage at your house, locked up in your darkest cellar, I hoped."

"I haven't seen him since yesterday afternoon. He asked my permission to go home and I gave it." Apollodoros was also gone. I began to wonder if there was some connection.

"He never got there," Scaevola said. "I haven't seen him since our ... encounter on the road. But my worthless son isn't the issue here. I've made an offer for this shop. What do you say to it?"

I took Myrrha aside and asked her if she wanted me to act as her agent in this matter. She quickly agreed.

Coming back to Scaevola, I said, "We say that your offer is an insult. The shop is not for sale." Beside me, Myrrha nodded vigorously.

Scaevola threw his hands in the air. "If that's your decision, so be it. Just remember, there are three taverns in this town. The two that I own will no longer be buying cheese from you. I don't think my customers will care for that smoky flavor."

"Where will you get your cheese?" I asked.

"I'll start bringing it in from Ostia. It may be a bit more expensive, but there are some good shops there."

"Sir," Myrrha whispered, "what'll we do? If we can't sell no cheese, we'll have to go back to whorin'. It's too late for me, but I want Chloris to have a chance to get away from that, to have a decent life."

I put a hand on her arm. "I assure you that we will buy cheese for the house here and for my house in Rome from you. And I will encourage my neighbors to do the same. As my friends, you will have my full support." I turned to Scaevola. "We have nothing further to discuss."

"Just to give you fair warning," Scaevola said, "when you go out of business, my offer will be *much* lower."

"Let me give you an equally fair warning," I said. "These women are among my friends. They enjoy my protection. Anyone who tries to harm them or interfere with their business will find he's not dealing with just two helpless women."

"Gaius Pliny, if you think these women are helpless, you don't know your friends very well."

We went upstairs to the living quarters to see how bad the damage was and what could be salvaged. It appeared that some of the furniture would be usable. The arsonist had piled it up with the clothing and set fire to it, but the fire had not gotten hot enough to ignite much of the wood.

Myrrha pulled her mother's work table out of the charred heap. "I remember sittin' over there with Mama when I was just a little girl, learnin' how to make bowls."

"It's just one of the legs that is burned," I said. "I think it can be repaired."

"And the room itself wasn't badly damaged," Tacitus pointed out. "This spot in the floor looks like it needs to be repaired, but for the rest of it, it's just a matter of some cleaning."

Myrrha stirred a pile of partly burned clothing with a broom handle. "Maybe we should just sell and move somewhere else and start over. These people aren't never goin' to think of us as anything but whores."

"And that's how we'll think of ourselves," Chloris said, taking her mother by the shoulders and looking her in the face, "if we let Scaevola drive us out. It'll take some work, but there's nothing here that can't be fixed or cleaned up. We've got to stand up for ourselves."

"I'll have some of my women up here this afternoon," I said. "And a few of the men will repair this floor and help you move your belongings from downstairs up here. By the time you go to bed tonight, the place should be as good as it ever was."

Myrrha brushed tears from her face. "Thank you, sir. I can't believe you're bein' so kind to us, for whatever reason. Thank you."

"I would do the same for any of my friends." I leaned out the window and gave instructions to one of the servants working on the leaks in the aqueduct to go back to the house and bring the people I needed to get the living quarters repaired and cleaned up.

"Since we're up here," Tacitus said, "should we look for the clue to Macer's killer that Livilla mentioned in her letter?"

"Could that have been what someone was looking for when they did this?" Chloris asked.

"But why would they set the fire?" Myrrha asked.

"If they couldn't find it," I said, "they must have wanted to be certain no one else could. Or perhaps they did find it and it was something they couldn't remove, so they wanted to destroy the whole place and the clue along with it." I looked around as though the secret might be lying out in the open.

"Where could she have left a clue?" Chloris asked. "There aren't many hiding places up here."

"Saturninus made a good one under a floorboard for his strongbox. Let's see if the place holds any other secrets." I took Myrrha's broom and began tapping on the floor. Tacitus found a piece of wood that Livilla must have intended to work with and began testing the walls. Myrrha and Chloris looked under and behind anything that hadn't been ruined in the fire.

"Nothing," Tacitus finally said.

"Not in the floor either," I said, leaning the broom against the wall.

"Then I guess he found it," Chloris said, brushing her hair back and smearing soot on her forehead. Somehow she didn't look any less beautiful.

I looked over the room one more time. "I don't see what he or she—we have to keep an open mind—would gain by starting a fire if they found what they were looking for. It would mean staying in here longer and calling attention to what they'd done that much sooner. If they found it, why not just quietly slip away?"

"Then where is it?" Tacitus asked, sweeping his arm around the room.

"Hidden in plain sight," I said. "These people were good at keeping secrets, even when they were right in front of everybody."

Myrrha and Chloris exchanged a glance. "Are you meanin' us, sir?" The older woman hugged her daughter.

"Not in any derogatory sense," Tacitus said.

When her mother's brow furrowed, Chloris leaned over and said, "He didn't mean to insult us."

Since Livilla's work table had only three usable legs, I turned it on its side and leaned it against the wall, under the window where Livilla had worked on it. Kneeling next to the table, Chloris began wiping the soot off it.

"Mother, what was my grandmother like?" She spoke slowly, like someone using a language she wasn't entirely comfortable with. "Whenever I saw her looking out this window, she always looked sad."

"She was a quiet woman," Myrrha said. "I know she loved you and wanted to talk to you, but Papa was so angry at me, he wouldn't let any of us know one another."

Chloris stopped cleaning and peered intently at the bottom of the table. "Is there something written under here?"

I knelt beside her and looked where she was pointing.

"It looks like that Jewish writing," she said, "like the letters on the parchment in that little box of my grandfather's."

"It's probably some kind of magical incantation," Tacitus said from behind us. "Jews are supposed to write those on their doorposts—to keep evil spirits away, I think."

"I'll ask Naomi if she can read this script," I said. "I know she can read Greek, and it looked like she could read what was in that box."

"She might just have known what it was supposed to say," Tacitus said.

"True, but if she can read it, I'll send her up here. Maybe she can tell us what this means."

"She might not want to," Tacitus said. "The Jews I've known have always been reluctant to tell any of us Gentiles what their magical words mean."

"But their sacred writings have been translated into Greek. Naomi has gotten copies of some of their books for my mother. And there are a lot of Gentiles who go to their worship places—including my mother. I don't see why there should be anything so secret about this. It may be just some sort of blessing on the house or a prayer to their god."

"Or a curse on anyone who disturbs the place," Tacitus said, causing Myrrha's eyes to widen.

"But, if my grandmother wrote it," Chloris said, "doesn't that mean she was a Jew?"

By the time the sun was overhead my men had finished repairing the aqueduct. I also had them gather up enough pieces of stone to pave the alley leading from the street to the back of the building. The final step in refurbishing the place was to expunge the phallic symbol.

"No more whorin'!" Myrrha said as she and Chloris chiseled the image out of the wall.

We bought part of our lunch—some rather questionable fish—at the only tavern which Scaevola did not own and supplemented it with some of Saturninus' cheese.

"The smoke really didn't damage it," I said as I savored the first bite. "It looks like you'll be back in business by tomorrow."

"It's hard to believe, sir," Myrrha said. "Thank you again."

We were eating on the patio where Tacitus and I had first seen Myrrha and Chloris. "The sun is certainly bright out here," I said, holding up my hand to shield my eyes.

"This time of year, it can be," Chloris said.

Tacitus looked up at the wall of the building. "It shouldn't be too hard to construct a roof over at least part of this patio. Maybe you could even fix up these rooms enough to rent them out."

"Excellent idea," I said. "Some extra income. How would you ladies feel about having tenants?"

233

"As long as they're not whores," Myrrha said.

We heard noises from the front of the building, noises made by horses, vehicles, and a considerable number of people. "Hello! Anyone here?" a woman's voice called.

"That's my mother."

I hurried—dry-shod, for the first time—through the alley and saw my raeda disgorging its passengers: my mother, Naomi, Blandina, and several other servant women, all dressed in older gowns and with their hair done up, clearly ready for some heavy work. Some of my men were riding behind them in our largest cart, holding tools they would need to finish the repairs on Myrrha's and Chloris' building. They were already drawing a crowd from the taverns.

"There you are, Gaius," Mother said. "I thought we would come and see what needs to be done here."

"I just asked for some help in cleaning the place up."

"With my guidance these women can do more of that by dinner time than you could do in the rest of the month."

I took her arm and led her across the street. "Mother," I said quietly, "I thought you hated Myrrha and Chloris."

"Well, dear, Naomi told me a story of a harlot who helped to save the people of Israel. I guess these women were forced to do what they did. If we can help them get established here, perhaps they can make a new life for themselves."

She sounded like she was reciting lines she didn't really believe. "Or perhaps they can sell the property and go somewhere else? Is that what you have in mind?"

Mother blushed. "That might be the best thing for them. People in a small town like this can be so unforgiving. A fresh start in a new place would be wise—and if this business is fixed up and thriving, they can get more for it."

"And if they leave, some new whores will move in. In fact, some new ones will probably be in business by tomorrow."

"Yes, you men are like that, aren't you, even the best of you?"

I knew she was disappointed to have seen Chloris come out of my room the previous night. I wanted to say that Chloris came to me and that she intended to change her life, but it would be a pointless argument.

"We'll have to see what happens," Mother said with a pat on my cheek. "For now let's just do what we can for these women."

"You will eventually have to call them by name, you know. They are among our friends."

"I know, dear. Eventually. Let me take my time, please." She put her hand on my arm. "How are you feeling today?"

"Better, but still not entirely well."

"Are you still dizzy? You must have taken a harder blow on the head than we realized."

"I'm managing. My head is somewhat clearer than yesterday."

My servants were swarming over the cheese shop, the upstairs rooms, and the rooms in the back like ants, if I can indulge myself in a cliché. Work paused for a moment when my mother and I came up the stairs. She seemed to take a deep breath.

"Are you going to try to save any of this furniture?" she asked.

Myrrha shrugged. "Well, my lady, we don't have nothin' else."

"We'll send you a couple of beds, tables, a chest or two. You can throw that out." She pointed to Livilla's table.

Myrrha quickly stepped in front of the table. "That belonged to my mother. I'd like to keep it. Your son said he would have somebody repair the leg."

"All right, then. Aren't there rooms downstairs? Let's take a look at them and see what needs to be done. Naomi, I'll leave you in charge up here."

With glances of bewilderment at me, Myrrha and Chloris followed my mother down the stairs. I hoped the smoke had covered the frescos that had served to advertise the services the two women offered.

"You seem to have brought about a change of heart in my mother," I said to Naomi.

"She's a good soul, my lord. Seeing a mother and daughter discover one another brought her to tears."

Oh, yes, the lost daughter she would never find again. "And how did it affect you?"

"I was happy for them, my lord." Naomi turned away to give instructions to the other servant women and then motioned for me to come to Livilla's table.

"Did you notice these marks, my lord?"

"Yes. We thought they might be Jewish letters."

"They are, my lord."

"Can you read them?"

"Certainly, my lord. My husband taught me to read while he was teaching our son. They're not very well formed, but I can make them out." She looked at the letters for several moments, muttering to herself as her face grew more and more puzzled.

"Do you know what they say?"

"I believe so, my lord. The problem is that they make no sense."

"What do you mean?"

"Each line is a quotation from one of our sacred books, called the *Psalms*. It's a collection of poems and songs. But these lines are just snippets, taken at random from different poems."

"Try reading them aloud," Tacitus suggested. "Sometimes the ear will hear what the eye fails to see."

Naomi read the lines, haltingly the first time, then with more confidence. But when she finished she shook her head. "I'm sorry, my lord. They still mean nothing to me."

But they did to me.

"Can you translate them?" Tacitus asked.

Naomi turned the lines into Greek. "They're still nonsense, my lord, just random phrases."

"Read them once more in Hebrew," I told her, "pausing at the end of each line."

I closed my eyes and listened as she read, and I knew I was right.

# XVII

**C**LOUDS WERE GATHERING and threatened rain by the time we had Myrrha and Chloris settled into their new home upstairs. My servants even had time to give the large room a fresh coat of paint—just one color without any decoration, but it brightened the place considerably and covered the smoke stains. They also put a quick coat of paint over the erotic décor in the rooms where Myrrha and Chloris had plied their trade. My mother's cheeks were still red from her visit down there.

I decided to let Hylas practice on one of these walls before I turned him loose in my own house. Leaving two of my men to stand guard downstairs, the rest of us headed back to the house for a quick bath and a late supper.

"You might want to post guards there for a few days," Tacitus said as we rode along at the head of a little caravan, "just to convince Scaevola you mean to protect those women and their property."

"I could do that. Or I could tell him who killed his nephew."

Tacitus turned to look at me so quickly he almost lost his balance on his horse. "You know? How—?"

"Keep your voice down. I'll tell you when I can be sure we're alone. Someone in my house must be passing information to Scaevola."

"Why do you say that?"

"He could not have known we had found Aristeas unless someone told him."

"You had your servants out looking for the man after he disappeared, didn't you?"

"Yes."

"One of them could have run into someone from a neighboring

estate and told them what he was doing, with no intention of betraying you. In fact, he would have to tell them: 'I'm looking for a fellow about this tall, with a skinny beard'."

"I guess you're right."

"You don't need to be so mistrustful, Gaius Pliny. Cautious and aware, yes, but not so mistrustful. You'll be seeing an enemy behind every tree. And you've got lots of trees out here."

I knew Tacitus was right. I could worry myself sick.

But Tacitus hadn't read Aurora's note.


The rain started as we were finishing supper. Tacitus and I retired to my suite of rooms. The alcove which is my favorite part of the suite contains a couch and two chairs. During the day someone reclining on the couch has the sea at his feet, the villa behind him, and the woods at his head. Tonight, though, we each took a chair and had the windows closed against the weather. The lamps reflecting off the glass made the room glow. The distortions created by the waves in the glass made the world outside look like it was constantly shifting and changing, an impression heightened by the way my head still felt.

"Now, you must tell me," Tacitus said. "Who killed Scaevola's nephew and how do you know? How *can* you know, fifteen years after the fact?"

"You were the one who gave me the final piece of the puzzle," I said, just to torment him, and he was suitably tortured.

"How did I do that?"

"You said the ear hears what the eye often misses, and that's certainly true in this case."

"Does this have something to do with what Naomi read?"

"Most definitely."

"But she said it made no sense. The lines were random snippets from a collection of poems. Are you going to be like one of those fortune-tellers who picks lines from the *Aeneid* and predicts your future with them?"

"No, it's nothing so fanciful as that. The lines were, in fact, snippets, but they weren't picked randomly. They were chosen for the sound of their first letters."

"What?"

"The lines formed an acrostic. I heard it when Naomi read them aloud. I can't pronounce the words, but the first sound in each line, in Hebrew, was S, T, R, A, B, O."

"By the gods! Licinius Strabo killed Macer, his own cousin?"

"That's what Livilla was telling us."

Tacitus put a hand to his forehead and appeared deep in thought. When he looked up, he said, "But she didn't say she saw Strabo kill Macer. She said she saw him put the body in Myrrha's room, presumably in an effort to make her look guilty."

"How would he get Macer's body unless he killed him?"

"Granted." Tacitus still didn't sound entirely convinced. "But why would Strabo kill his cousin? And does it have anything to do with Aristeas' murder?"

I poured myself a little more wine. "Right now I can't answer either of those questions, but I intend to, within a day or two, I hope."

"Those aren't the only questions we need to answer, my friend."

"I'm not sure I want to hear any more." I rested my spinning head on my hands.

"You're convinced the two murders—Macer and Aristeas—were committed by the same person—Strabo. How could he move one dead body, let alone two, through the streets of Laurentum in daylight without drawing attention? Even if his family runs the place, a man lugging a corpse around would set tongues to wagging. And who did he get to help him take the women to somebody's house? And whose house?" Tacitus raised his cup. "It is a pretty complicated plot."

"And Strabo doesn't impress me as a strategic genius."

"His father doesn't think so, and who would know him better?"

I slapped the arm of my chair. "It had to be a simple plan. Both men must have been killed near Saturninus' building."

"The building behind Saturninus', on the other side of the aqueduct, would be a likely spot," Tacitus said. "Then he'd just have to haul the body a short distance."

"I wish Livilla had told us a little more. From what direction did Strabo bring Macer's body? Women make such poor witnesses. They're too emotional."

Tacitus nodded. "A dead eyewitness, male or female, is certainly inconvenient. To be honest with you, on the basis of her 'testimony'

239

and a few Jewish letters scribbled on the bottom of a table, I would never vote to convict Strabo."

"Nor would I." I rubbed my chin. "I wonder if we could get into that building and look around. It's deserted, isn't it?"

"It looked like it was a block of apartments, but I saw no sign of anyone in it while we were fighting the fire. No lights, no one hanging out a window to watch."

"When we go up there tomorrow morning to take some furniture, let's see if we can get in."

"What would we be looking for?"

"A place where a man could be strung up by his feet—a beam, a rafter."

"And you really think both of these murders are connected, with fifteen years between them?"

"This is a very small town. When two men both have their throats slashed and end up in the same woman's bed, I don't care how many years passed in between. There has to be a connection."

"Will we be having another pig roast to prove your point?"

The next morning the rain had stopped, but the sky looked like it could open up again at any moment. An acrid smell of burned and soaked wood hung heavily over the estate. Aristeas' pyre and the pile of wood on which we had roasted the pig were finally completely out. I gave orders for the two piles to be raked and spread out and, once we were certain there were no live embers left, for the ashes to be scattered in the woods.

Naomi was supervising the loading into a cart of pieces of furniture to be taken to Myrrha and Chloris. I remembered that I still had Saturninus' cheese-slicer in my room. In spite of the most minute examination I could give it, I had not been able to find traces of anything on it except cheese. When I returned from fetching it, Naomi was putting a cover over the furniture.

"Isn't my mother going?" I asked.

"She decided to stay home today, my lord."

Probably just as well, I thought. She had been civil, even generous, to the women yesterday; but it was clear she was forcing herself, and she made them nervous. I knew she wouldn't go in the downstairs rooms again until she was sure they'd been painted. Overall, it would be better to let the three women get used to one another in their new relationship gradually.

"Have you seen Tacitus this morning?"

"He left a note pinned to his door, my lord, saying he would prefer not to be disturbed. He will join you later."

"As gloomy as this day is, he has the right idea. Well, then, I guess we'd better get moving. Are you coming, Naomi?"

As soon as I said it, I knew I should have given her an order instead of asking a question. If I wasn't careful, she would soon be calling me Gaius.

"I would like to, my lord."

"Good. Things certainly went faster yesterday with your supervision." Watching her give orders to the other women, I had realized she was becoming a sort of female steward in my household.

"Thank you, my lord."

Our little caravan made up of the raeda, the cart, and several people on horseback must have been familiar to our neighbors by now. When we reached Laurentum I was pleased to see two women coming out of the cheese shop carrying bundles. If the women of the village would accept Myrrha and Chloris as the proprietors of the place, they stood a good chance of making a success of it. The men I'd left on guard overnight reported no signs of trouble.

We got the furniture unloaded and I returned the cheese slicer and the original copy of Saturninus' will. "I've added my testimony and my seal to this. Hylas made a copy, which we'll keep at my house, in case there's ever a need for it."

"Thank you, sir," Myrrha said, choking back emotion.

"It looks like things are going well," I said.

"Yes, sir." She wiped her apron over her face. "My father had a good supply of several cheeses laid up, so we've got some time to figure out what we're doin'. When I was a girl he showed me most of what I need to know, but that was a while back."

My mother had emptied a couple of our bedrooms and sent the furniture up to Myrrha and Chloris. They couldn't use the bedding from their old rooms because it smelled so strongly of smoke and held such memories of their lives down there, including the bodies of two dead men in Myrrha's bed. My servants moved in two beds with the bedding, several chests, and a small table. It wasn't our best stuff, but it was substantial and better than anything these women had before.

As we arranged the furniture I looked out the back windows, thinking about how Livilla sat here and watched her granddaughter play. Between the leaky aqueduct and the abandoned building beyond, it wasn't a cheerful place.

"Who owns that old building on the other side of the aqueduct?" I asked Myrrha.

"That belongs to the Licinius clan, sir. In fact, ours is the only buildin' in this block that don't belong to 'em. They pestered my father for years about buyin' it. I think they had some plan about buildin' a bigger bath, but the town's so run-down now I don't know why they'd bother."

"If they put pressure on you to sell—if they say anything that even feels like a threat toward you—let me know immediately."

"Thank you, sir. I will."

I sent my people home with a message to Tacitus not to bother coming. "I'll be home shortly," I assured Naomi.

When my servants were gone and Myrrha was downstairs, Chloris hugged and kissed me, with a different emphasis than her mother had. "Thank you again, sir. You've given us a chance to make a new life."

"I know you want to make things better for your mother and yourself. I hope you have the strength to do so."

"I take to heart what Aristotle said. If we act like good people, we can become good people."

I'm afraid my eyebrows rose too high and too quickly.

"Do you find it so remarkable that I've read Aristotle?" She stepped back from me. "Your uncle got me a very good tutor."

"Not at all. But I think you've just given me an important clue to understanding what's been happening around here the last few days."

I led my horse into the courtyard behind Saturninus'—no, Myrrha's and Chloris'—cheese shop and tied him up in the driest spot I could find. "I won't be long," I assured him.

The only entrance on the back of the old apartment building was firmly boarded up, as were the windows on the ground floor. I didn't know what the place had looked like fifteen years ago, but if

Strabo killed Aristeas a few days ago, he did not bring his body out this door. The top floor windows were shuttered, except where the shutters had broken in places.

An alley on one end let me get around to the front of the building. The woods marking the edge of the small town had grown right up to the walls, uprooting the sidewalk and the street. Branches from the trees brushed against the shutters. In a few more years the building would begin to crumble from the pressure of the roots.

The sky darkened as the clouds piled up. Even at mid-morning it felt like evening. The front of the building showed several boarded-up openings which had once been shops. On either end were sets of stairs leading up to the top floor. I intended to get in to all the entrances before I left, but the rain suddenly started pelting me and lightning flashed, so I picked the one that was easiest to pry open with my bare hands.

The stairway inside stretched all the way across the end of the building to the top floor. With the windows boarded up and no lamps or torches to provide light, the upper reaches disappeared into the gloom, but my eyes, with their preference for dim light, adjusted quickly and I started up the crumbling stairs. At some time the walls had been painted, to judge from the few flakes still clinging to the plaster. It looked like something in the geometric style that was popular before I was born.

The roof of the building leaked badly enough that the stairs had a slimy coating on them. Between my dizziness and the wet stone of the steps, I stumbled when I was halfway up and barely got my balance back before I fell down the stairs.

When I reached the top floor I saw two apartments opening off the landing. The door of one of them had been kicked down, splintered really. From the look of it, it had been a sturdy door. I stepped through the opening and found myself in the main room of an apartment. A door on the opposite wall led to what looked like a smaller room, which I assumed was a bedroom.

I saw no indication of a place where Aristeas could have been strung up and slaughtered—no hook or hooks in the ceiling, no beam over which a rope could be thrown. I decided to check the other room, although I expected it to be empty as well.

I paused in the doorway to study a large gray mass in the far corner. I took a step toward it but froze when a head raised out of the mass, and I realized I was looking at Daphne, huddled up as though cold or sick.

Her white face was truly ghastly as she snarled at me, "Gaius Pliny, go away while you still can."

"Are you ill?"

"I'm dying."

"Dying? Why do you think you're dying?"

"I need blood to drink."

"Aristeas' blood?"

She nodded. I instinctively moved toward her, but she held her hands up in front of her face.

"Don't come any closer."

"This can't be true."

"Why not? Because you don't want it to be?"

"No, because there is no such thing as an empusa."

She bared her teeth at me. "How can you say that when you're standing in front of one?"

"I'm standing in front of a young woman who has been told all her life that she was a monster because of her skin. You finally began to tell yourself that, and to believe it. Aristotle says we become good by acting like we're good, whether we are or not. You made yourself into a monster by telling yourself you were one, but you're not."

Daphne waved her arm at me, billowing her gray cloak. "But you saw the bat, the one that was wounded. And you saw the wound on my shoulder, in the same place as the bat."

The plaintive note in her voice told me I was close to the truth. I had been thinking about what Chloris said and how it might be true of Daphne in a perverse way. I hadn't expected to encounter her so soon, so I had to improvise what I wanted to say.

"I think you saw the bat injured and you injured yourself. If you can convince other people to believe in the myth of the empusa, you can convince yourself."

Her head sagged. Then she recovered and forced it back up. "Tell me why the bat was here, just when I got here. Explain that!"

I sighed, dreading the words that were about to come out of my mouth. "Coincidence. I think you've been playing on coincidences all your life. Or maybe opportunities is a better word. Something nefarious happens—an animal gets killed, perhaps a child dies in its sleep—and because you're there and people already suspect you of being some sort of monster, you take advantage of the opportunity to heighten their fear by claiming—or not denying—that you're responsible. It gives you power."

"It makes them leave me alone," she muttered. "That's all I've ever wanted."

I took a small step toward her and she did not protest. "Are you hurt? Is there anything I can do to help you?"

"The wound in my shoulder. It burns. And it's spreading. I can feel it. Tell me where Aristeas' blood is."

"I don't know. I thought it might be here."

"It's not. This is where he was killed—in one of the shops downstairs—there are blood stains on the floor. They took it all away." She ran her tongue over her dry, cracking lips. "I couldn't stand to look at the place, so I came up here."

"Do you know who killed him?"

"No, do you?"

"I think I do, but I don't know how to prove it."

"Why do you have to prove it?"

"Because that's how humans conduct their affairs in a just society."

She gave a chortle mixed with a growl. "Awful waste of time. If a man's guilty, then punish him."

"Is that how an empusa would do things?"

"What do you think happened to the man who tried to kill you that morning in the boat? He was sent here by someone named Regulus, by the way. He told me that much."

"Before you clawed his face off?"

"Of course, before. He didn't have much to say afterwards, just a sort of gurgling noise."

I knelt in front of her, as though I was talking to a child. "You didn't kill him, did you? You found him after some animal mauled him."

She slumped against the wall and turned her face away from me, powerless against my lack of fear. "It was a bear. I went up there to see if I could find out anything about who threw the rock, and I saw the bear leaving. It had blood on its mouth. The man had gotten too close to its cub."

"And so you threw him over the cliff."

"After he said something about Regulus. At least I think it was Regulus. There was so little of his face left, it was hard to understand him."

"Why did you care who threw the rock?"

"Because you've been kind to me. You're the only person who ever was, besides Aristeas."

Now we were ready to get to the heart of the story. "Who was Aristeas to you?"

"The dearest friend—the only friend—I've ever had. He lived on the street behind us. He was a simple man, hardly more than a child in many ways. He saw me one night when I was nine, but he wasn't afraid of me, nor I of him. I knew, even at that age, that he did not have his full mind, and I tried to take care of him. But I couldn't even get him to wear sandals. Of course, if I wore them, he might have."

"He wasn't your father?"

"No. I'm sorry I had to lie about that, but people never understood what we meant to one another. He might as well have been my father. My family did little more than feed me. His family barely cared anything for him. He had his music and they were content to let him come and go as he pleased. Sometimes he would stay out for days at a time.

"When I read about Aristeas in Herodotus, I told him and we pretended that he was Aristeas. He didn't really understand time anyway, so he began to talk as though he had lived for hundreds of years."

"What about the raven's head mark on his chest?"

"I cannot explain that, except as a coincidence. It was there when I met him. He showed it to me and showed me his raven-shaped plectron. When I read about the raven in Herodotus and about the laurel, the daphne, I think we both began to believe in one another. We even talked about going to Metapontum to see the statue Herodotus mentions."

"How did he learn to fall into that death-like sleep?"

She shook her head. "He could do it before I met him. The first time it happened, I thought he was dead. I cried and cried. But then he woke up. I learned that it might happen at any time, and it could last for any length of time. I just knew I had to stay with him when it did."

"You got him out of the stable, didn't you?"

Daphne nodded as lightning flashed outside.

I was relieved to see the gesture. "I knew Tacitus' explanation was too facile, especially the way it depended on the guard conveniently stepping away for a few moments at just the right time. What did happen to the guard?"

"He was so scared when I appeared that he actually passed out. As you know, I can approach people very quietly. In the dark I can be terrifying. I've made men soil themselves. I've learned how to make that high-pitched sound that bats make." She let out a note that made me cover my ears. "I climbed up on the paddock wall and dropped down in front of him."

"Like a bat."

"A very large bat." She chuckled. "I knew he would never tell anyone what he'd seen because no one would believe him. He didn't believe it himself. And he couldn't admit he passed out from sheer fright. It was easier to stick to his story that nothing happened."

"Where did you put the body? Why didn't you and Aristeas just disappear?"

She grabbed at her shoulder and winced. "I'd been following them for almost three years. That part of the story is true. I was tired of it. I knew Apollodoros was coming and I wanted to get him away from Aristeas once and for all. I thought you could help me do that, if I could expose Apollodoros for the fraud he is. I left Aristeas in my room in the inn at Laurentum."

"You carried him all that way?"

"My strength would surprise you, Gaius Pliny. Yes, I carried him, stopping to rest on the way, but I left him there alone. That was my mistake. I should have stayed with him, like I had always done before."

"Somebody moved him while he was unconscious?"

"They must have. But I don't know how they got him out of there with people around. I had to come in the back door in the middle of the night, carrying him upright like he was drunk, in case anybody saw us. Luckily, nobody did."

But, I thought, they didn't have to get him out right away. They could have just moved him to another room. "Did Aristeas ever say anything about … where he was during those times when he, let's say, wasn't in his body?" I couldn't find any other words to describe it.

"He just said he could never make me understand what he saw and felt."

"So you took care of one another, but you didn't drink his blood?"

"Why on earth would I do that? I tried to make people think I did, but—"

"That's why you dipped your finger in the pig's blood."

She nodded and smiled faintly. "And I almost vomited when I licked it off my finger. But it planted a thought in your mind, didn't it?"

"It certainly did. When did Apollodoros meet Aristeas?"

"Five years ago. And my world fell apart. They met in the bath. That was one place where I could not go with Aristeas. I worried every time he went in there that someone would take advantage of him. And Apollodoros did. He filled his head with stories about musical contests and prizes. I guess Aristeas told him about being the man from Herodotus, to impress him. I told him, over and over, not to tell that story to anybody else because they wouldn't understand the way I did. That was supposed to be *our* story, *our* little game. But he was too simple. He trusted everybody."

"So Apollodoros came up with the scheme to sell Aristeas' blood as an elixir for long life, if not immortality."

Daphne nodded. "The blood Apollodoros has been selling doesn't come from Aristeas, of course, but from animals they catch and kill."

"I guessed as much."

"Now, Gaius Pliny, I've told you all you want to know. Will you do the same for me?"

"What do you want to know?"

"Who killed Aristeas?" She grabbed my tunic and I was surprised—even a bit frightened—at the strength of her grip.

"Are you going to kill him?"

"I've never killed anybody. But I have a right to know who killed Aristeas."

"I'm sorry I wasn't able to protect him in the end."

"What protection is there against human greed? Now, for the last time, who killed Aristeas?"

"I believe it was Licinius Strabo. And I believe he killed Licinius Macer fifteen years ago, in the same manner."

"Strabo, eh? I should have finished him out there on the road." Her eyes widened and she began to gather herself.

"What are you talking about?"

"When I knocked him off his horse for you."

"But you're not—"

As a bolt of lightning cracked, she pushed me away, her eyes almost glowing with excitement. "And now you must leave, Gaius Pliny." Her voice took on a new strength.

I fell to the filthy floor. "You said you wouldn't kill him."

"I said I've never killed anybody. There's always a first time."

The pile of rags came to life as Daphne rose, opened her cloak, and spread her arms, like a bat. She stepped onto the window sill and pushed open the broken shutter.

"No! Wait!" I called, but she was gone. I ran out the door and started down the stairs. My feet slipped from under me on the second step.

# XVIII

**W**HEN **I** OPENED MY EYES I was lying on a bed. Myrrha and Chloris stood over me on one side and Tacitus on the other. I could guess I was in the rooms where the women used to live. I wondered why Tacitus was there.

"What are you doing here? I sent a message for you not to come."

"I'm glad to see you, too," he said. "When I heard you were staying up here by yourself, I figured you'd get in over your head—your badly bruised head, I should say."

I reached up and touched what now seemed to be several sore spots on my head.

"You took quite a tumble, sir," Chloris said. "Those stairs are really slippery." She took a cold cloth off my head, kissed me lightly, and replaced the cloth with another. It felt good. It all felt good. "Fortunately you won't need any more sewing up."

I tried to sit up, but Chloris held me down. "You need to be still, sir. You were babbling all sorts of things when we found you. You weren't making any sense at all."

"I need to talk to Tacitus. Will you ladies excuse us?"

Myrrha and Chloris looked at me dubiously. "Just be sure he don't try to get up, sir," Myrrha told Tacitus.

Getting up was the first thing I tried to do as soon as they were out of sight. Tacitus put a hand on my shoulder. "Take it easy. The women are right. You really have been injured. You're lucky you didn't break any bones in that fall."

I pushed his hand away and started to sit up. I got my feet over the edge of the bed, but dizziness forced me to stop at that point. I was also aware now of how many places in my body ached. There was a particularly sharp pain in my ribs. "We've got to warn Strabo."

"About what?"

"I'm trying to remember."

"Myrrha and Chloris said you were mumbling about Strabo and the empusa when they found you."

"Yes! That's it. Daphne—she thinks she really is an empusa. Or maybe she really is. I don't know right now. But she's going to kill Strabo because he killed Aristeas. We've got to stop her."

"Wait. Did you say Daphne is the empusa? There is no such thing as an empusa. That's what you've said all along. Why are you talking such nonsense now?"

"Because I saw her in that room upstairs. I talked to her."

"You couldn't have, Gaius Pliny. Daphne has been in your house all day."

"Has anybody actually seen her?"

"Well, I don't know. She didn't come down for lunch."

"Because she was in *that* room, upstairs!" I waved one arm in the direction of the old apartment building and cradled my head with the other. "Come on, I'll show you."

"You're not supposed to get up. Take it easy."

"I will not take it easy. I told her Strabo killed Aristeas and now she's going to kill Strabo."

"You don't know that Strabo killed Aristeas. Livilla's letter said he killed Macer."

"If he killed one, he killed both."

"But why?"

"Stop arguing with me and help me get to that room."

Leaning on Tacitus, I was able to cross the courtyard and show him how to get upstairs in the deserted apartment building. The stairs were so slippery by now that we practically had to crawl up.

"The steps going from my terrace down to the beach aren't this bad, even after a heavy rain," I said as we slid through the slime. I hated to put my hands on the walls to brace myself because they had a dark mold growing on them.

"This place will probably just fall down in a few more years," Tacitus said.

"It's there, where the door's been kicked in," I said when we got to the upper floor. "In the back room."

I hobbled into the back room where I had seen Daphne. There

was still very little light. Tacitus checked out the shutter, hanging now from one hinge, and walked over to a pile of dirty, discarded clothing in the corner.

"That knock on the head has you seeing things, my friend," Tacitus said, scattering the pile with his foot.

"But I saw her, I tell you! I talked to her. I really did."

"The way your head has been bounced around, can you be sure of anything?"

"That white face ... She changed into a bat, I think, and flew out that window ... or did she jump?"

"She could have reached that tree easily." Tacitus picked up a piece of white cloth and waved it at me. "In the gloom, with the lightning flashing, and your head so addled—I can see how you thought you saw her, even thought you talked to her. And I'd be surprised if she was the only bat in this place. Let's get you back to bed."

"No, you don't understand. She's going to kill Strabo. We've got to stop her."

"Why? If she is this monster you think she is, and if Strabo did kill Aristeas, why not let Daphne take care of it? It's really between her and Strabo. You have no reason to be involved and not enough evidence to convict Strabo. This way punishment will be quick and decisive."

"But if we let her take her vengeance outside the law, we're no better than barbarians."

"This from a man who—"

"I was defending myself. The law allows a man to defend himself when his life is in danger. It doesn't allow monsters—or people who think they're monsters—to go around dealing out 'justice' on their own terms."

"Scaevola hates you already. How do you think he's going to react when you accuse his son—his only son—of two murders?"

We found the boarded-up door on the ground floor which looked like it had been opened and then nailed shut again. As Daphne said, there were hooks in a beam in the ceiling and splotches of what could be blood on the floor.

"We had to pry open the door," I said. "How did Daphne get in?"

"Bats can squeeze through very small openings," Tacitus said without a smile.

"Let's go." I grimaced from the pain as I took a deep breath.

We walked up to Scaevola's house as quickly as I was able. His *janitor* admitted us to the atrium and pointed us to benches around the impluvium. Since the benches were wet and the rain was still coming in, we chose to sit in chairs against the wall. Scaevola made us wait. We could hear him, just out of sight, talking to someone. When he entered the atrium we stood. He bowed his head slightly to acknowledge us.

"Are you all right, Gaius Pliny?" he asked. "You look like you've been tossed around a bit."

"I'm fine." I started to tell him how I'd gotten the bumps and bruises, but then I remembered that the stairs I fell down were in a building he owned, a building I had broken into.

"Have you come to talk about selling Saturninus' building?"

"It's Myrrha's and Chloris' now," I said, "and you might as well get used to calling it that. They're not going to sell it."

"Then we have nothing to talk about." He started to turn away.

"What if I told you your son's life is in danger?"

Scaevola turned halfway around, smiled, and shook his head. "It's always in danger. I'm tempted to kill him almost every day."

"This is serious," I said, taking a step toward him. "Daphne wants revenge for the murder of … the man Aristeas."

"She must know her life will be forfeit if she lays a hand on Strabo."

"I'm not sure she cares. A wound of hers has gotten infected. She may die soon herself."

"Then I doubt my son has anything to fear from her. No one has any proof that Strabo had anything to do with that man's death."

"But I do have proof he killed your nephew, Macer."

Scaevola staggered back as though I had struck him and collapsed into a chair. "Strabo … killed Macer? How … What proof could you have after this long?"

"Saturninus' wife, Livilla, saw him carry Macer's body into the rooms where Myrrha and Chloris lived. She wrote Strabo's name on the bottom of her work table and, in a letter, identified him as the man who raped Chloris when she was ten. Strabo heard the letter when it was read at my house and, I believe, set fire to Saturninus' building when he couldn't find the clue Livilla spoke of."

Scaevola jumped up from his chair. "This is preposterous! You have no evidence, no witnesses. Just rumors and some letter supposedly written by a dead woman. You can't come in here accusing my sons—"

"Sons? Did you say 'sons'?"

"Macer was like a son to me. His mother died when he was born. My wife and I helped my brother raise the boy. My brother died when Macer was ten. After that he became my other son. I was going to adopt him."

More than most, I could appreciate the feelings of a man raising his nephew.

"We need to find Strabo," I said. "His life is in danger. Do you know where he is?"

Scaevola waved his hand in disgust. "He spends most of his time at one of our taverns. I'm just glad to have him out of my sight. He keeps several women here. His favorite is one called Nephele. Apparently she's quite … limber."

Tacitus' eyebrows arched. "So that was her name."

"Is that the tavern where the woman Daphne stayed when she came to town?" I asked.

"The only guest Strabo has mentioned in the last few days was a woman with some sort of ghastly make-up."

"That's her." And that was how Strabo knew Aristeas' body was in her room. It would have been quite easy for him to move it to another room and after dark, carry him to the deserted building. "On my oath, Licinius Scaevola, that woman is going to kill your son if we don't stop her."

The reality of the threat seemed to finally sink in. "Let's go," Scaevola said.

The three of us walked down to the tavern. Scaevola wore a leather cloak. Tacitus and I had to endure a further soaking.

The door of the tavern was closed against the weather, but Scaevola shoved it open like an officer of the Urban Cohort bursting in on a criminal. Four customers tensed, ready to bolt. Strabo sat at a table in the main room with Nephele on his knee. He wore a dinner gown, red with a gold border, even though it was much too early in the day for such a costume. She had on a gown that was practically transparent. Strabo jumped up, dumping the woman on the floor.

"Father? What are you doing here? I thought—"

Scaevola grabbed Strabo by the elbow, as though he were a child about to be scolded, and led him toward the stairs at the back of the room. "He keeps a room upstairs. We can talk there."

Tacitus and I followed the two men up the stairs and into a room that had been decorated much more lavishly than rooms in inns usually are, especially one as low-class as this one. The walls were painted with erotic scenes—better done and more graphic than the ones in Myrrha's and Chloris' rooms—and the furniture had been purchased from a more expensive shop than Laurentum had to offer. It came from Ostia at least, if not from Rome itself. Strabo had made this room his home away from home.

Scaevola shoved Strabo down onto the bed.

"Father, what's going on?" the younger man asked.

"A small matter. I'm sure we can sort it out. You see, *these* men"— he gestured at us lavishly, like Regulus at his best in court—"are accusing *you* of murder."

"Murder? That's ridiculous. Who do they—?"

Scaeavola's face was so close to his son's that either man could have bitten the other's nose off. "That man Aristeas, to begin with. And then ... Macer."

"You can't believe them. I didn't even know Aristeas. And Macer? Kill my own cousin? What sort of man do you think I am?"

"You're a fool." Scaevola spat the words into his son's face. "A cross-eyed fool. You always have been, not like Macer."

Strabo's face twisted up as though he might burst, like an overheated pot on a stove. "Macer, Macer, Macer! By the gods! That's all I ever heard. You'd think the man was a god."

"What did you do?" Scaevola grabbed Strabo's dinner gown and shook him.

I thought for a moment Strabo might stand up to his father, but his resolve had been broken years ago. He would have fallen if his father hadn't had a firm grip on his dinner gown.

"Nothing. I didn't do anything. I got sick of hearing you treat him like your favorite son, but I didn't do anything to him." He turned to me. "How dare you make these charges? What evidence could you possibly have?"

"Livilla, the wife of Saturninus, saw you carrying Macer's body into the rooms where Myrrha and Chloris lived," I said. "You heard her letter. You were at my house when we opened Saturninus' strongbox."

"She didn't name anybody."

"But she said she had left a clue in the room where she and Saturninus lived."

"So what?"

"After you heard that letter, you asked for permission to leave my house and return home. You went to Saturninus' shop and searched it. Since you couldn't find the clue, you set fire to the place in an effort to keep anyone else from finding it."

Scaevola cuffed Strabo across the face with the back of his hand. "You set that fire?"

"Why does it matter to you?" Strabo rubbed his cheek, which was already close to the color of his gown. "You've said for years you wanted to buy it so you could tear it down."

"You fool! You couldn't even do that right. The building is still standing." Scaevola yanked Strabo to his feet.

"And the clue is still there," I said.

Both men turned to stare at me, fear on the face of one, consternation on the face of the other.

"What clue? Where?" Strabo choked out.

"On the bottom of Livilla's work table, written in Hebrew letters."

Strabo gave a harsh laugh. "So that's what that scribbling said. You'll never prove anything in court with that kind of evidence."

"He won't have to," Scaevola said in the most frightening voice I had ever heard. It seemed to start somewhere down low in his chest and scramble and claw its way through his throat until it erupted from between his clenched teeth. "He won't have to."

Scaevola cuffed Strabo again, bloodying his nose this time. "Did you kill Macer?"

Strabo's calm surprised me. Some men, when they sense they're about to die, fight to the last breath. They make good soldiers. Others give in and accept the inevitable. I suppose they make good philosophers.

"You gave me every reason to, Father." He licked at the blood running over his lip. "You always favored Macer over me. We were raised together, but I felt like I was the one who didn't belong in the family."

"Did you kill Macer?" Scaevola threw his son against the wall. Strabo's head bounced off a fresco of Aphrodite on her knees before Adonis and he slid to the floor.

"Yes, I killed him. I had reason."

Scaevola turned to me. "May I kill him now, Gaius Pliny? As *paterfamilias* I have the right. Or do you want to hear his so-called reasons?"

"There are a lot of things I want to know," I said, "and I think you should let the law decide what happens to him." I hadn't come to save Strabo from Daphne's vengeance so I could turn him over to his father's, no matter how much he might deserve it.

"You talk to him, then. I can't stand the sight of him." Scaevola clenched his fists and held them in front of his face.

I stepped in front of Strabo as he stood up and rubbed the back of his head.

Blinking my eyes to clear my groggy head, I said, "You do admit, then, that you killed your cousin, Licinius Macer?"

"Yes."

"Why?"

"I knew my father had put Macer in his will, as though he was my own brother. I heard him tell our steward. I was afraid he might even adopt Macer and leave me nothing."

"I would never have done such a thing," Scaevola said.

"How could I know that? You favored him over me the whole time we were growing up. You never gave me that kind of love. When he died, you grieved over him like he was your son."

Scaevola opened his mouth, then obviously said something different from what he originally intended. "He was ... such a fine young man."

"And I'm not. I know. But Macer wasn't anything like what you thought he was,"

"What do you mean?" Scaevola asked.

"He raped Chloris when she was ten years old, not even nubile yet. He just held her down and forced himself on her."

"You can't prove that!" Scaevola yelled.

"He told me, and he told me how much he enjoyed doing it. He said I should have a go at her before she got any older. He showed me where he had rigged up a hook in the ceiling beam of that deserted building behind the cheese shop. He liked to tie Myrrha up there and whip her, like a slave, and then couple with her while she was still hanging. He said he'd like to string Chloris up and do the same to her."

Scaevola gasped and put his hand to his chest.

"Yes, Father, that's what your paragon of virtue was really like—a brute."

"But that didn't give you the right to kill him," Scaevola said. "You could have come to me and told me all this."

"And what would you have done? Admonished him? You never lifted a hand against him the whole time we were growing up. I was sick of him and afraid you were going to make him your heir, so I killed him. I thought I could make it look like Myrrha had done it. If anybody knew how he treated her, they'd find it easy to believe she might kill him."

"You must have been surprised when the body was found in the well and not in Myrrha's room, where you left it."

Strabo shook his head. "I couldn't say anything. Do you know what it's like to live with a secret like that for fifteen years? You're always afraid you'll slip and say something that will give you away."

I had lived, if only for less than a year, with a secret that could have landed me in exile, but I already knew what a burden it was. I couldn't imagine how heavy it was going to become as time went on.

"You had a motive—jealousy—to kill Macer. But why did you kill Aristeas?"

"It was Nephele's idea."

I pointed Tacitus toward the door. "Find her and bring her here."

Scaevola was back on his feet. "You let some whore talk you into killing a man? Is there no end to your stupidity?"

I stepped in front of Scaevola. "You said I could ask questions. We know what happened to Macer. Now I need to know what happened to Aristeas."

Strabo leaned against the wall and closed his eyes. "We found the body in that woman's room, next door."

"Daphne's room? What were you doing in there?"

"She looked so strange. Nephele wanted to know what kind of make-up she was using. We went in the room while Daphne was gone and there was this man lying on the bed. He wasn't breathing. We couldn't find any trace of life in him. I was sure he was dead, and I got the idea that I could use the body to make people think Myrrha had killed someone else."

"Why would that matter?"

"I knew my father still wanted to find out who had killed Macer. He wouldn't be satisfied until he had an answer. If I could leave another dead body in her room—somebody who was killed the same way Strabo was—Myrrha would be convicted of the murder and everybody would think she also killed Macer. But I would have to cut the man's throat in the same way Macer's throat had been cut."

From his corner of the room Scaevola groaned. "You said Macer was a monster—"

"I thought this man was already dead."

"But why did you drain the blood from his body?" I asked.

Before he could answer we heard a woman squealing outside the door. "Let me go!"

"Because of her," Strabo said.

Tacitus brought the woman in. From the scratches on his face it was obvious she had not come along with him willingly. He pushed her into the corner opposite Scaevola. "Sit down and shut up!"

"Was it your idea, Nephele, to kill the man you found in Daphne's room?"

"What? No! He was already dead." She glared at Strabo. "You're not going to blame that on me."

"You were the one who said we should drain his blood," Strabo said.

"Is that true?" I asked her.

She crossed her arms over her breasts. "All right. Yes. But he was already dead. We didn't kill him."

"How did you know he was dead?" Tacitus asked.

"We couldn't wake him up. He wasn't breathing. He was just lying there—dead."

"Why did you decide to drain his blood?" I asked.

Nephele tried in vain to cover some of the rest of herself. "A few days ago this man named Apollodoros came in here. He was looking for a fellow, a friend of his, he said. I was the only one here when he came in. There was … something about him."

"She coupled with him," Strabo said. "I hope you didn't eat on the table they used."

"All right, yes, I coupled with him. I didn't like it, though."

"Was he rough with you?"

"He was kind, but he took me … the way one man takes another."

"Did you pay you?" I still didn't understand what Apollodoros was doing with all the money he was supposedly making off of this scheme.

"He didn't have any money, he said, but he gave me this little vial of blood. He said it usually cost a hundred aurei."

"What would make it worth that much?"

"He said if I drank it, it would make me young for a long time, maybe forever, if I was careful. It came from the man he was looking for, a man with a raven's head mark on his chest. He was over seven hundred years old, he said."

"Did you drink it?"

"Of course. Wouldn't you?"

"So when you saw Aristeas on the bed in Daphne's room, you recognized the mark."

Nephele nodded. "We checked him over."

Strabo snorted. "She wanted to see how long his mentula was. That's why she lifted his tunic."

"You men are always bragging about that. When I saw the mark I thought we could take his blood and sell it."

"You fools!" Scaevola growled. "If the man was dead, how could his blood make you young forever?"

"The fella that gave me the blood told me I would have to be careful. It wasn't like I could jump off a cliff and not be killed. But, if I was careful, I would never grow old. Wouldn't that be wonderful?"

I turned to Strabo. "So you decided to take all of his blood."

He looked up at me, moving nothing but his eyes. The bad one almost kept pace with the good one. "I wanted to put his body where it would make Myrrha look like she had killed someone else. That meant I would have to slit his throat. As long as I was doing that, I thought we might as well drain the blood. We would both drink it and then sell vials of it, like Apollodoros was doing. I knew people who would pay dearly for it."

"Did Apollodoros tell you that you must never drink more than one vial?"

"Oh, yes," Nephele said. "Only one vial."

"If you drink a second one," Strabo added, "you'll die, right on the spot."

It was sad to see people deluding themselves like this. They were little different from Daphne and her delusions about being a monster.

"Did you drink the blood?" Scaevola asked his son. "And you believe it will let you live forever?"

"Of course I drank it. I want to be sure I live long enough to see you die, Father." Strabo spat out the last word. "And I'm going to become rich beyond your wildest dreams, or mine."

"Where is the blood?" I asked.

"I'll never tell you."

I didn't pursue the question. I would come back to it later. I've learned that, when I'm interrogating someone, I can get answers more readily if I circle around a question and pounce on it unexpectedly, rather than keep battering from the front. "You went to a lot of trouble to set up a scheme to get Myrrha and Chloris out of their rooms. How did you manage that?"

"I wanted them gone the whole day, so I would have plenty of time. I didn't know how long it would actually take to drain a man's blood. I arranged to have them taken to a villa not far from yours, Gaius Pliny."

Scaevola perked up. "A villa? On the shore? How could you get into one of those places? We can't afford one."

"No, but I know people who can. There's one on the south side of the bay that belongs to Marcus Aquilius Regulus."

That name thundered through my groggy head. "Regulus? He owns a villa here?" No one had ever told me that. Had my uncle even known it?

"He hasn't lived in it in years," Scaevola said. "He lived here, let's see, twenty-five years ago, perhaps. That was before your uncle bought his place. His father was in exile, but when Agrippina died and Nero began to rule in his own right, Regulus went to Rome and made a name for himself."

"A name for betraying people and seizing their fortunes." A *delator* was paid a quarter of anything the emperor took when someone was accused of treason or any other crime against the state. Regulus had begun his insidious career under Nero.

"Why doesn't he ever come back here?"

"He prefers his estates north of Rome," Scaevola said. "Or so I've been told. I think he had some problem with a woman around here. He rents this villa out or allows friends of his to use it. I don't know why he doesn't sell it."

Because, I thought, it gives him a spot from which to keep track of my family.

"How did you become acquainted with Regulus?" I asked Strabo.

"The steward of his house died about ten years ago. As duovir that year I kept an eye on the place until Regulus could appoint someone else. He appreciated it, and allows me to use the house whenever it's not being rented. I also knew a couple of men in Ostia who owed me money, so I told them they could settle the debt by helping me out for one day."

"Both women were at the same place?" Tacitus asked.

Strabo nodded.

I rubbed my chin, almost in admiration for Strabo's ability to organize a complicated plot on such short notice. He wasn't the fool his father took him for. "That meant you had men Myrrha and Chloris wouldn't recognize, and a place to take them for the day. Everything you needed."

"And that's why you were pushing me," Scaevola said, "to get the woman to Rome and into the arena before anyone could figure out she wasn't guilty."

"I knew, if you thought we had punished Macer's killer, you would be satisfied and I could quit worrying about the whole business."

Scaevola pushed me aside, grabbed Strabo's dinner gown, and pulled his son to his feet. "I won't be satisfied until the man who killed Macer is dead."

"But how can you kill me?" Strabo said with a smirk.

Scaevola threw Strabo back on the bed so hard the ropes holding the mattress sagged. We heard a crunch and then a red liquid began to seep out from under the bed.

Nephele screamed and fell to her knees. "No! No! Quick, get something to scoop it up. We've got to save as much as we can." Tacitus grabbed her and pulled her away from the bed.

Scaevola threw his son off the bed and tossed the whole thing up on end. There was the broken amphora with Aristeas' blood flowing out of the crack. There was still a pool of it on the bottom side of the amphora. Scaevola grabbed a silver cup off the table beside the bed and scooped up some of the blood.

"Father, no!" Strabo screamed. He realized what Scaevola intended to do before I did. He bolted out the door, knocking Nephele on her back. Scaevola ran after him.

"Gaius Pliny, aren't you going to do something?" Tacitus said.

"Why should I? Drinking somebody's blood can't kill a man, any more than it can make him live forever."

We followed the two men out the door while Nephele scrambled out the window, screaming all the while. I was sure Laurentum had seen the last of her.

As the handful of patrons ran out the door, Scaevola caught Strabo in the dining room and grabbed his son by the hair, bringing him to his knees. Yanking his head back, he held the cup of blood to his son's lips. Strabo couldn't scream any more without opening his mouth. All he could manage was a pitiful moaning as he turned his eyes toward me.

Scaevola finally managed to get the lip of the cup between Strabo's lips. Strabo tried to spit the liquid out, but his father kept jerking his head back and forcing more blood into his mouth. Tacitus and I watched from the head of the stairs as Strabo swallowed in spite of himself. His eyes widened and his breath came in short gasps. He started to shake and grabbed at his chest. His body gave a violent spasm, and he collapsed.

Dead.

## XIX

"**Y**OU CAN ARREST me for murder now," Scaevola said. He was sitting in a chair with Strabo's body across his lap. I wondered if he'd ever held his son like that when Strabo was a little boy. One of the few memories I have of my father is sitting in his lap and rubbing my hand over his chin on a day when he hadn't been shaved yet.

"I have no authority to arrest anyone," I replied, "and a father has the right to punish his own son for any crime he may commit. I am sorry for the death of your nephew."

"He wasn't my nephew."

"What do you mean?" To stop my head from spinning I sat down at the table next to Scaevola's and Tacitus pulled up a chair beside me.

"Macer was my son," Scaevola said, and a weight seemed to slide off his shoulders. It had to have been the first time he said those words to another human being. "My son by my brother's wife, Apulia. I was in love with her and wanted to marry her. I was never able to tell her how I felt. Our father arranged for my brother to marry her. There was nothing I could do about it. When, after three years of marriage, she and my brother proved unable to have children, she approached me and asked if I could father a child on her."

"That was a daring step for her to take."

"She was a bold woman. That was one thing I loved about her. My brother wanted a son and was talking about divorcing her and remarrying. She wasn't going to let that happen."

"Did she suspect that your brother was unable to father a child?"

Scaevola stroked Strabo's hair. "She thought that was possible. We always blame the woman when she can't have a child, but who's to say the man might not have something to do with it—not enough seed or the seed not strong enough. We see that when crops don't grow well. Apulia wanted to save her marriage. I think she actually loved my brother."

"Couldn't you have married her if your brother divorced her?"

"I was already married, to Apulia's younger sister, and my wife was pregnant. It would have been heartless to divorce her, especially to marry her sister. I, of course, was happy to oblige Apulia. We were together several times over the course of four months, the most wonderful four months of my life. Then, once she knew she was pregnant, she stopped seeing me."

"You never told her how you felt, even when you were coupling?"

Scaevola shook his head. "I knew she felt nothing for me. If I said anything, it would only complicate matters. Sometimes it's best just to remain silent. I thought a day might come when I could say something. Perhaps if she and I outlived our spouses. ... Then she died in childbirth. My brother grieved deeply. I did, too, of course, but he could show his grief, I couldn't. His son became almost a symbol of the loss of Apulia, for both of us. My brother couldn't bear the sight of Macer because he reminded him of her. I loved him because he was all I had of her. My wife took Macer as her own—he was her nephew, after all—and we practically raised him alongside Strabo. She nursed both boys herself."

"And you showed your favor for Macer."

"I couldn't help it, I guess. The child of the woman I loved on the one hand, the child of a wife I could barely tolerate on the other—"

"The resentment you felt toward your wife must have come out in your treatment of Strabo," I said.

Scaevola nodded slowly, pensively. "I guess you're right. It wasn't her fault that I didn't love her. She was a good wife."

"She's dead now?"

"Yes, eight years ago. Thank the gods. I mean because she didn't live to see this."

"I take it Strabo and Macer were about the same age?" Tacitus said.

"Yes. Strabo was four months older. It didn't help that I already felt like Macer's father before Strabo was born. And it didn't help that Macer was a beautiful boy—strong, intelligent, happy. From the first Strabo was difficult—slow in his schooling, always doing the opposite of what I wanted him to. And that damned eye."

"Did you give him his name because of the eye?" I asked.

"Yes. We noticed it when he just a baby. 'Strabo' isn't a cognomen my family uses, but I almost felt like I wanted to punish him."

"For not being Macer?"

Scaevola nodded. "Then my brother died when Macer was ten, and he did become my son in everything but name."

"Strabo was aware of how you felt about him."

"He couldn't help but be aware of it, even as obtuse as he was. I told him enough times." Scaevola bowed his head and began to weep. For himself? For Strabo? For Macer? For all of them?

As Scaevola regained control of himself, Tacitus asked, "Has it ever occurred to you that Macer might not have been your son?"

"What—?"

"Apulia must have been coupling with your brother during those months she was with you. She would have to, in order to convince him that any child she had was his."

"But they hadn't any children, and they'd been married for three years. My wife was pregnant within six months after we married."

"That often happens. It can take longer, though. My wife and I have been married for five years, but she didn't get pregnant until a few months ago."

The realization swept over Scaevola's face. "Macer looked ... so much like me."

"The sons of brothers can bear a family resemblance."

I knew Tacitus had just inflicted a worse punishment on Scaevola than any court could have.


"I've never seen a man as terrified as Strabo was," Tacitus said as we crossed the street back to the cheese shop. "Socrates couldn't have been that frightened when they gave him the hemlock."

"I think Socrates was ready to die. He knew the hemlock was a poison. The fact that it would kill him was inevitable. But drinking someone's blood can't really kill a man."

"Apparently it can if he believes it can."

I thought about that for a moment. "Can the mind actually have that much control over the body?"

"Something makes us want a partner for sex. And some men can't stop doing certain things, like gambling. Our bodies must not be the ultimate arbiters of our destiny."

I put a hand to my aching head. "Human beings are confusing enough. If what you say is true, I despair of ever understanding us."

The rain had let up, but the clouds still hung low. We had agreed we would let Scaevola announce that Strabo had died suddenly of an illness. Something he ate, I thought would be a good explanation, but I didn't suggest it. In a sense, that second dose of the blood of Aristeas had been what killed him. No one else had been in the tavern when Strabo died, and Tacitus and I weren't going to spread any stories. Nephele was probably halfway to Rome by now.

We left Scaevola cradling his son in his lap and mourning the wreckage of his life. He had lost the woman he loved, his brother, his wife, his son, and a nephew who might also have been his son. How many blows that hard could a man withstand? Just as the gate of a city being battered by a ram will eventually splinter and then crash, admitting an invading army, so a man's spirit could not hold out forever. The woes besetting him must finally take their toll.

What if a man could live for centuries? How many misfortunes would he have to endure? The sea, pounding even the hardest rock, wears it away over time. Death, while not something I look forward to, at least promises an end to the torments of life, just as sleep lets us escape from the worries of the day.

"You're very pensive," Tacitus said.

"Watching a man kill his own son leaves me that way."

Tacitus nodded. "Yes, it was unsettling, like watching a legion being decimated. But it answered a lot of questions."

"Not as many as it raised."

"What do you mean?"

"You heard Strabo. Regulus has a villa near here, practically next door to mine." I waved an arm in that direction. "He maintains an interest in what my family does down here."

"But now he's lost his informant."

We paused on the sidewalk outside the cheese shop.

"Only until he finds someone else. And years ago he had a problem with a woman in this area and hasn't been back here himself since then."

"That could mean just about anything."

"I'm willing to bet it means he got a woman pregnant and

wouldn't marry her."

"Wait a minute! Myrrha?"

"The timing is right. Regulus left here and went to Rome just after Agrippina's death. That's twenty-five years ago. And that's how old Chloris is. I have to ask her." I paused before giving voice to the most unsettling thought I'd ever had. "What if I … have been coupling with Regulus' daughter?"

"Is that a question you really want answered, Gaius Pliny?"

"If the answer is no, I certainly do."

"But how could ever be sure of the answer?"

"If Myrrha tells me Regulus was the father of her child and that he was the only man she had ever coupled with before she got pregnant, then I have my answer."

Tacitus put a hand on my shoulder. "Could you at least wait a day or two before you ask her? You've just found out about this possibility. Think it through first, like you always do. What could it mean to you—and to Regulus—to have this kind of connection?" He gave a short laugh. "By the gods! What if Chloris is Regulus' daughter and what if you fathered a child by her? She could be pregnant right now, for all you know. That would make you … the father of Regulus' grandchild, practically his son-in-law."

When the situation was explained that way, I had to ask myself if I really was that eager to know who Chloris' father was.

"Let's go home," I said. "My horse is under the aqueduct. Where's yours?"

We were halfway back to my house when I heard a high, piercing sound. Stopping my horse, I looked around, hoping to hear the sound again so I could locate where it came from.

"What was that?" Tacitus said.

"The sound of a bat."

"Why are you looking for a bat?"

"I said it was the sound of a bat, but it wasn't a bat that made it."

The sound—something between a screech and a whistle—rang out again.

"Over there." Tacitus pointed to our left.

I dismounted and tied my horse to a bush. "Come on."

Tacitus followed me as I tromped through the brush and low tree limbs away from the road.

"There she is," I finally said.

"She? Who?"

Without answering him I made my way to a pile of gray huddled under a bush, barely visible. Tacitus hung back.

"I'm here, Daphne," I said, kneeling beside her.

She looked up, her eyes red from fever, her body contorted with pain. Could the infection have spread so much farther than when I saw her earlier in the day? I held out my hand and she took it, squeezing it tightly.

"It'll be all right," I said. "I'll get you to my house—"

"No, sir," she gasped. "I can't fool myself any longer. I'm dying. And soon. Will you stay with me until … ?"

"Of course. Can I do anything to make you more comfortable?"

"No." She closed her eyes. "This is … all I need."

I waved Tacitus back toward the road and mouthed, "Get help."

"Thank you, Gaius Pliny, for everything you tried to do for me. You and Aristeas were the only people … who weren't afraid of me. I just wish we could have gotten to Metapontum. I would have loved to see that statue." She groaned. "Will you take care of …?"

"I'll see to everything. Would you like for your ashes to be taken to Metapontum?"

"Oh, that would be lovely … So lovely."

"The man who killed Aristeas is dead now. There was a woman who helped him, but I'm afraid she got away."

"No, she didn't."

"What—?"

"I was on the roof of the building next door. I heard all of it. When the woman came out the window, I was there to greet her. I killed her … but she had …"

Daphne raised her right arm and I saw a knife sticking out of her side.

"I still don't know how she hid it," Daphne gasped. "In that … flimsy dress."

She squeezed my hand, closed her eyes and did not say any more.

When we arrived at the house with Daphne's body in our cart, I kept everyone away. She never wanted to be gawked at. I told

Tranio to begin building another pyre and not to let anyone disturb Daphne's body.

"Do you want a guard posted, my lord?"

"There's no need for that."

"I didn't think so, my lord. Especially after what Volconius sent over this morning."

"What are you talking about?"

"Come see, my lord." He led us to the far side of the stable, out of sight of the animals. "Didn't want to scare 'em." he pointed to the wall of the stable.

Nailed to the wall, with its wings spread out, was the largest bat I've ever seen. It had a partially healed wound on its left shoulder and a white face.

"Volconius' men killed it this mornin', my lord," Tranio said. "Out in the woods between our place and his."

It wasn't just the blow to my head that was making me dizzy now. "Get that thing down! Right now!"

"But, my lord—"

"Get it down!" I raised my fist and would have hit the man if he hadn't jumped that instant to start pulling the nails out of the creature's wings.

"What should I do with it, my lord?"

"Put it in the stall with Daphne. And treat it kindly. We'll cremate them together."

At a quick trot, Tranio carried the bat around the corner of the building.

"Are you all right?" Tacitus asked.

"I don't know. I just don't know. Would you be up for a trip to Metapontum in the near future?"

Tacitus nodded. "Since Julia and her mother are off to Sicily in a few days, I have nothing pressing, except for some lunch."

"Agreed."

But Hylas was waiting for us in the atrium. He held a rolled-up piece of papyrus.

"May I show you something, my lord?"

"Certainly." I expected him to unroll the piece of papyrus right there, but he started back to the library. We had no choice but to follow him.

"My lord, I don't know what to make of this." He waved the piece of papyrus in his hand up and down. "I didn't want to leave it here and I didn't want to show it to you in the atrium. I simply don't know how to explain it."

"Explain what?"

"This." He unrolled the piece of papyrus and I saw the drawing he had made of Aristeas on the day we found him. "Do you notice anything odd, my lord?"

I saw it immediately, or rather I didn't see it. "The raven's head is gone."

"Yes, my lord."

Tacitus peered over my shoulder. "There was a raven's head on the drawing?"

"Yes, my lord. I drew exactly what I saw. The mark was here." Hylas put his finger on the drawing just above the man's left nipple.

"Do you remember the last time you saw it?" I asked.

"No, my lord. I hadn't looked at the drawing since I made those copies of the face for you. I locked it in the chest where we keep your most important documents. But as I was working this morning I needed to consult something in there. When I saw this picture I noticed at once that the mark was gone."

"And you're sure it was a raven's head?" Tacitus asked.

"Yes, my lord. Quite distinct, facing to the left."

I had to sit down. "Something very bizarre is going on. Domitian himself could not have gotten in here and removed the mark from this drawing without us knowing about it." I looked long and hard at Hylas. He was the only person who could have tampered with the drawing, but he met my gaze without flinching.

"Has it been erased?" Tacitus asked.

We inspected the papyrus closely, running a finger over it and holding it to the light at various angles to detect any sign of an erasure, but the sheet was as smooth as the day we bought it, just as smooth as Aristeas' own skin had been when we noticed the mark missing in Myrrha's bedroom.

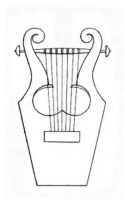

THREE DAYS LATER Tacitus had returned to Rome to help Julia and her mother get off on their trip to Sicily. I had ridden to Laurentum in the late morning, by myself, to ask Myrrha who Chloris' father was. She refused to tell me, saying it would not be good for Chloris or for me to know. The man had threatened to kill her, she reminded me, if word of his child ever got out. He would surely know she had told someone, because she was the only one who knew the secret.

"It's not Naevius?" I asked because she and Naevius were going to be married in a few days. The Long of It owned a small farm east of Laurentum and raised cattle. He'd been supplying Saturninus with cheese for some time.

"No, sir. It's not Naevius. That I can assure you. But please don't make me tell you any more. In spite of all you and your mother have done for me, it's something I just can't do. Even if it means you won't count me as your friend anymore."

There was nothing I could do but accept her decision and buy some cheese. Would I ever have an answer to that question? Did I really want an answer?

As I rode back home I tried to put the matter out of my mind. It was a beautiful day, I told myself. Tranquility had been restored in my life. My head finally felt normal again. The gold urn I had ordered for Daphne's ashes had been delivered the day before. Myrrha and Chloris were making a good start in their new business. In the last few days I had answered enough questions to satisfy even my itching curiosity. There was still the problem—at least as I saw it—of people employed by Regulus less than a mile from my house. And I still didn't know who in my house might be funneling information in that direction.

As I came to the turn-off to my house I noticed three riders approaching from the other direction. Being by myself, I started to urge my horse to get to the turn-off.

"Gaius Pliny, please wait," the front rider called out.

I recognized the voice and slowed my horse.

Apollodoros, with two handsome young men beside him, pulled his horse up in front of me. All three men were armed.

I dispensed with formalities or pleasantries. "I never expected to see you again."

"I'm sorry I was such an ungrateful guest and unreliable ally," Apollodoros said. "I hope I can make amends."

"Not until you've explained why you deserted us that night."

He lowered his head. "I am ashamed of that, deeply ashamed. When I volunteered to ride with you, I honestly thought I might be of some help to you. But when the moment came, I proved to be what the Spartans used to call a 'trembler'. Of no use to you or to anyone else."

"At least you sent the horse back. Why not the sword?"

"I felt I needed it a bit longer. But here it is." He motioned and one of his companions drew a sword and handed it to me, handle first.

"All right. That debt is paid. Where did you go and why are you back here now? My mother will not let you in the house, you know."

"Yes, I know. I'm not expecting to be invited in. I wanted to return the sword and to offer something to help with the expenses of Aristeas' funeral." From one of the bags tied over his horse behind him he drew out a small pouch which jingled. He urged his horse closer to me and handed me the pouch. I pushed his hand away.

"I don't want your blood money."

He gave a sigh of resignation. "All right, sir. That's how it'll be then. But I do want you to see this." He reached up and pulled down the edge of his tunic over his left shoulder.

On his chest, just where it had been on Aristeas', was a raven's head, facing left.

tected by glass windows and an overhanging eave. From the middle of the courtyard you go into an inner hall and then a triclinium, in which I take a lot of pride. It extends out toward the shore; when the southwest winds churn up the sea, the spray of the waves settles lightly on this room. All around the triclinium are folding doors, or windows that are as large as the doors, so that you have a view of the sea on three sides and, on the fourth side, a view that extends back through the inner hall, the courtyard with the porticos, to the atrium, all the way into the woods and hills beyond.

A bit farther back and on the left, not so close to the sea, is a large room, with another, smaller one next to it, with one window facing the morning sun and another admitting the light as the sun sets. This window also offers a view of the sea, but from a greater distance and without exposure to the waves. The angle formed by this room and the projection of the dining room captures and intensifies the sun's rays. This is where we spend most of our time in the winter and it is the location of the family's gymnasium. The only wind that can penetrate here is that which brings rain clouds, but the area can be used again soon after the rain departs. Around the corner is a room with one curved wall made up of windows so that the sun comes through all day. On another wall of this room are shelves with cases holding the books which I enjoy reading over and over. Next to this room is a bedroom, the floor of which is raised and fitted with pipes to circulate warm air and keep the room comfortable.

The rest of this side of the villa consists of rooms set aside for my servants, although most of the rooms are adequate for guests. On the other side of the dining room is a bedroom large enough to serve as another dining room. It gets sunlight, both directly and reflected from the sea. Behind that is an antechamber with a high ceiling that keeps it cool in summer and walls that protect it from the wind in colder weather. Another similar room and antechamber share a common wall with this room. Next to that is the cold room of the bath, with two swimming baths projecting from each side. They are more than large enough when you consider how close the sea is. Adjoining this is the anointing room, then the sweating room. Next is the furnace room and the hot room of the bath. There are also two latrines, quite elegantly, if simply, decorated. Beyond them is the heated swimming bath, which guests always admire. You have a view of the sea while you swim.

Close by is the ball court, which catches the sun's warmest rays in the afternoon. Next to the ball court is a two-story adjunct (turris), with two large rooms on the first floor and an equal number above, along with a dining room which offers a panoramic view of the sea and a number of the other houses along the shore. Another two-story structure has, on its upper floor, a bedroom which gets the morning and evening sun. Behind it is a large storeroom. On the lower floor is a triclinium, where you hear nothing of the sea but the sound of the waves breaking on the shore, and even that is muted. This dining room looks out on the garden and the promenade (gestatio), or exercise ground, which runs around it.

Around the promenade runs a border of boxwood, with rosemary where the boxwood doesn't thrive. Boxwood will grow well in the shelter of buildings, but it shrivels when it is fully exposed to the wind and spray from the sea, even if it is at some distance from the water. Along the inside of the promenade is a shady arbor of vines, where the soil is so soft you can walk bare-foot. The garden boasts a number of fig and mulberry trees. The soil here is especially good for those, though not as good for other varieties. The dining room on this side, although it sits away from the sea, has as lovely a view as the other dining room has of the sea. Two rooms run around the back of the dining room. From their windows one can see the entrance to the house and an excellent kitchen garden.

From that point extends a covered arcade (cryptoporticus), large enough to be suitable for a public building. It has windows on both sides, but more facing the sea. On the landward side the windows occupy every other bay. On nice days the windows can be left open. When the weather is less enjoyable, the windows on one side or the other can be closed, depending on the direction of the wind. In front of the arcade is a terrace, fragrant with violets. The arcade increases the sun's warmth by reflection and holds the heat on one side just as it breaks the force of the north wind. Thus it is as warm in front of the arcade as it is cool behind it. In the same way it breaks the force of the southwest wind, thus checking winds from opposite directions by one of its sides or the other. In the winter it is pleasant, but in the summer even more so because in the mornings its shade keeps the terrace cool and in the afternoon the garden and the promenade are kept cool as the sun rises to its height and then sinks, with the shadows falling longer or shorter on one side of the arcade or the other. In fact, the arcade receives the least sunshine when the sun is directly overhead, with its rays falling directly on the roof. With its windows open, the western breezes can flow freely, so the place doesn't get oppressive because of stuffy air remaining in it.

At the far end of the garden, the arcade and the terrace is my favorite part—truly my favorite part—of the house: a suite of rooms which I built myself. The suite consists of a sunny room which offers a view of the terrace on one side and the sea on the other. It gets sun on both sides. There is a bedroom with folding doors that open onto the arcade and a window looking out over the sea. Opposite the wall in the middle is an alcove which can be opened onto the main room or cut off from it by opening or folding back the glass doors and curtains. It is large enough for a couch and two chairs. When you lie on the couch you can see the ocean over your feet, the neighboring villas behind you, and the woods beyond. These views can be seen separately from each window or blended into one panorama. Next to this room is my bedroom. Unless the windows are open I don't hear any noise—not from my slaves talking, or the murmur of the sea, or the sound of a storm. During the day, not even sunlight penetrates. This profound peace and privacy are created by a passage which runs between the suite and the garden so that any noise is absorbed in the intervening empty space. A small furnace room has been built here, and a small outlet holds in or diffuses the hot air as comfort requires. There is an ante-room and another bedroom which catches the sun's rays as soon as it rises and holds them until midday, even though they strike it at an angle. When I settle in this sitting room I feel as though I am completely away from my house. I enjoy this sensation immensely, especially during the Saturnalia, when the rest of the house rings with the shouts and the freedom of the holiday. In my suite I do not interfere with their festivities, nor do they distract me from my work.

The house has one lack—running water, but we do have wells and springs which supply our needs. One curious characteristic of this area is that, wherever you dig you strike water near the surface and it is pure, not the least bit brackish, even though we're so close to the sea. The woods around us provide an abundance of fuel, and we get other necessities from Ostia. There is also a small village just up the road, which supplies our basic needs. It has three baths, most convenient if I'm making a short visit or if I arrive suddenly and don't want to heat the bath in the house.

The beauty of the shore is enhanced by villas either bunched together or scattered. When you look at them from the sea or another part of the shore, they give the appearance of a number of cities. The sand on the shore can be too soft to walk in if the weather is fine for a while, but it is usually hardened by the constant pounding of the waves. The sea doesn't provide fish of any value, but there are fine soles and prawns to be had. My house provides any produce we need, especially milk. Herds collect here when they come down seeking water or shade.

Have I made a good case for considering this retreat my favorite, a place where I love to be? You are a confirmed city-dweller, I know, but even you must want it. I hope you do and that you will come to see it. Your company would only make this house that much more enjoyable.

Farewell.

# GLOSSARY OF TERMS

**Actaeon:** in mythology a young man who, while out hunting, stumbled upon Artemis and her nymphs bathing. Even though the violation was entirely accidental, Artemis turned Actaeon into a deer and set his dogs on him.

**Clientela:** every wealthy Roman man had a number of people dependent on his generosity. 'Client' comes from a Latin word meaning to recline or lean on something. The upper-class man, the patron, was obligated to assist his clients if they were in financial difficulty. Clients were expected to appear at the patron's house each morning for the salutatio, the greeting. Formal dress—the toga—was required.

**Congius:** Roman unit of measure equal to 3.7 quarts.

**Diotima:** female philosopher credited, in Plato's *Symposium*, with being the one who taught Socrates.

**Empusa:** a shape-shifting monster from Greco-Roman mythology. Some accounts say she had one leg of brass and the other a donkey's leg, but she could take on the form of a beautiful woman in order to seduce men and drink their blood. She was related to a number of demons who seem to have originated in the Middle East. Ancient Babylonia had stories of the Lilitu, which gave rise to Lilith, Adam's first wife (according to extra-Biblical tradition), who was turned into a monster, and her daughters the Lilu. Lilitu was considered a demon and was often shown as living on the blood of babies. Such stories were probably an effort to explain Sudden Infant Deaths. The Jewish versions of the demons were said to gorge themselves on men and women, as well as on newborns. Eventually Empusa was used in a general way to describe witches and demons. Empusa was the daughter of Hecate, tri-form goddess of the underworld.

**Epona:** a Gallo-Roman goddess associated with horses, donkeys, and mules. Her cult had fertility overtones. She is shown in inscriptions riding a horse side-saddle, enthroned between two horses, or standing before a horse or horses. Her cult was spread over much of the Roman Empire by the auxiliary cavalry, especially those recruited from Gaul.

**Ergastulum:** a structure used to confine slaves who were being punished or were particularly troublesome. It was usually at least partly underground and windowless or had windows placed too high to be reached. It is sometimes, as in Juvenal's *Satire* 14.24, called a rustic prison (carcer rusticus). The emperor Hadrian (117-135) forbade their use.

**Exhedra:** an outdoor eating area in a Roman house, usually at the back of the house off the peristyle garden. Some of those in Pompeii have slanted concrete benches instead of couches in the familiar triclinium arrangement.

**Euxine Sea:** a common name in antiquity for the Black Sea. 'Euxine' means 'kind to travelers.' The Black Sea is anything but that. It has long been notorious for storms and tricky currents. Crediting something bad with an opposite quality was thought to be a way of averting the evil—apotropeia. Similarly, the goddesses known as the Furies were usually called the Eumenides, 'the Kindly Ones.'

**Garum:** a sauce made from scraps of fish and seafood. The material was allowed to ferment until a liquid developed. This was drained off and used to flavor foods. Amphorae found in Pompeii have raised the possibility that some garum may have been made only from fish with scales, so it would have been usable by Jews and other groups with dietary rules. Pliny the Elder makes a garbled reference to this (*Natural History* 31.44). He thinks that Jews eat only fish without scales, when the opposite is true.

**Marsyas:** a satyr who challenged Apollo to a musical contest, with the stipulation that the winner could treat the loser any way he chose. Accounts vary, but the general theme is that the Muses, acting as judges, proclaimed Apollo the victor. He had Marsyas skinned alive to make him pay for his hubris.

**Milesian tale:** a story with a convoluted, improbable plot, usually with bawdy overtones. Aristides of Miletus (2nd cent. BC) originated the form.

**Raeda:** a covered coach with four wheels which could carry as many as six people. The driver sat in an open seat in the front.

**Sinus:** when a man's toga was properly draped, a pocket was created on his left side. By moving his arm away from his body he had a place to carry whatever he needed. On the day he was murdered Julius Caesar was handed a message about the plot. He slipped it into his sinus to read later.

**Tali:** The Romans were almost compulsive gamblers. The emperor Claudius made people throw dice with him at dinner parties and, if they lost all their money, gave them more so they could continue to gamble. He also wrote a book on the subject (Suetonius, *Claudius* 33). Knuckle bones from an animal such as a pig were shaped into dice, called tali. Players threw four dice at a time, either by hand or from a small box. The Venus throw was the highest total possible. The Dog throw—also called the Vulture—occurred when the I came up on all four dice.

Praise for the first Pliny mystery:

# ALL ROADS LEAD TO MURDER

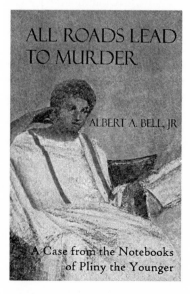

"Wonderful historical mystery set in the Roman Empire during the early Church and St. Luke's timeframes. . . helps the reader experience what it was like to live during Roman times. ... superb use of setting and characterizations. Historical figures come alive in his expert hands. – Bob Spear, *Heartland Reviews.* Rating: five hearts

"Superbly crafted, wonderfully written murder mystery ... thrilling detective story meticulously backgrounded with accurate historical detail. – *Midwest Book Review*

"The colorful characters, both fictional and historical, are well blended to reveal the sordid web of money, greed and ruthlessness hidden behind the facade of civilization. One hopes to see Albert Bell's Pliny again." – Suzanne Crane, *The Historical Novels Review*

"Superlative job of leading the reader into his Roman world. A winner all around!"– Margaret F. Baker, *Past Tense*

"Masterful blend of history and mystery. ... wonderful book. with splendid characters, vivid history and a fair and puzzling mystery. I heartily recommend it." – Barbara D'Amato, award-winning author of three mystery series, Past President of Mystery Writers Internationals and Sisters in Crime International

"Rich and rewarding read, in the tradition of Lindsay Davis' Marcus Didius Falco books or Steven Saylor's Gordianus the Finder ... succeeds both as an historical document and as a mystery. ... colorful tapestry depicting the sights and sounds, the smells and tastes that reproduce a lifelike portrait of the world of two millennia ago." – Jack Ewing, *Wicked Company*

"Bell promises us a series, and this reviewer for one looks eagerly forward to the next installment!" – Irene Hahn, Romahost, About.com

ALBERT BELL is a literary renaissance man. His previously published works include: nonfiction, historical fiction and mysteries. His articles and stories have appeared in magazines and newspapers from *Jack and Jill* and *True Experience* to the *Detroit Free Press* and *Christian Century.*

Dr. Bell has taught at Hope College in Holland, Michigan since 1978, first with an appointment shared between classics and history; and, since 1994, as Professor of History and chair of the department. He holds a PhD from UNC-Chapel Hill, as well as an MA from Duke and an MDiv from Southeastern Baptist Theological Seminary. He has been married for 40 years to Bettye Jo Barnes Bell, a psychologist; they have four children and a grandchild.

Bell discovered his love for writing in high school with his first publication in 1972. Although he considers himself a "shy person," he believes he is a storyteller more than a literary artist. He says, "When I read a book I'm more interested in one with a plot that keeps moving rather than long descriptive passages or philosophical reflection." He writes books he would enjoy reading himself.

Visit the author's website at:
www.albertbell.com

For more about

# Albert A. Bell, Jr

AND HIS BOOKS, VISIT HIS WEBSITE:

**www.albertbell.com**

For more about

FINE WORKS OF FICTION AND MEMOIR FROM

# INGALLS PUBLISHING GROUP, INC.

VISIT THE WEBSITE:

**www.ingallspublishinggroup.com**

CPSIA information can be obtained at www.ICGtesting.com
Printed in the USA
LVOW101553051211

257920LV00008B/30/P

# APPENDIX

Pliny's Letter about his Laurentine Villa
Ep. 2.17

**Author's note:** Although Pliny describes his house in great detail, he does not make it easy to reconstruct the floor plan. I have found six attempts at drawing a floor plan of the house based on this letter—all of them differing in significant details. I have put a few key Latin terms in parentheses. Pliny's writing style is typical of the so-called Silver Age of Latin literature, essentially the first century A. D. and the early second century. Like Tacitus, he writes in a clipped, choppy fashion. We often have to add a few words in translation to make his letters read more smoothly. This letter gives me a sense of being closer to Pliny because the first sentence in Latin reads, "Miraris cur me Laurentinum vel (si ita mavis) Laurens meum tanto opera delectet." Laurens meum—I was born in Laurens, South Carolina.

Gaius Pliny to his friend Gallus, greetings.

You may wonder why my Laurentine house (or Laurentian, if you prefer) gives me so much pleasure. You'll cease to wonder when you realize how attractive the house is, how ideally situated, and how broad an expanse of the shore it occupies. It's seventeen miles from Rome. Once the day's business is done, you can spend the night there without having cut anything short or rushed through it. The house can be reached by either the road to Laurentum or the one to Ostia. Leave the Laurentine road (via) at the fourteenth milestone and the Ostian road at the eleventh. Either way, the side road (iter) is sandy for a certain distance. In a carriage that makes for a somewhat slow journey, but on horseback it is a short, easy trip. On either side the scenery is varied. At places the road narrows when it runs through the woods and in other spots it widens when it passes through broad meadows, where flocks of sheep and herds of horses and cattle are brought down from the hills to graze in the pastures in the spring-like temperatures.

The house is comfortably large but not a burdensome luxury. You enter an atrium that is decent-sized and not at all undignified. Beyond that there are two porticos, rounded like a letter D. They enclose a small but charming courtyard, which is a nice place to shelter in a storm because it is pro-